Stay here with me. Spend the night.

Shocked by his thought, by his own needs and yearning for her, Cochrane muttered, "You still need rest, Ellen. Go home and get some."

Ellen nodded. "Goodnight." Before she could turn toward the door, his hand reached out and settled on her shoulder. Her eyes widened. Something new burned in his stormy gray gaze as he studied her. He wanted to kiss her! Panic tore through her. The grieving widow in her shied away. The woman emerging from grief wanted what he was offering.

"You have the darnedest effect on me, Ellen."

"Jim...I'm scared." The words were so soft that Ellen could barely hear them herself, but they had an impact on Jim. Instantly his hand slid off her shoulder and he took a step away from her. "I mean..." Ellen stepped forward and lifted her hand, sliding it along his strong, uncompromising jaw. To hell with it. She couldn't live her life always being scared. Standing on her tiptoes, she placed her lips softly against his cheek.

LINDSAY McKENNA

SILENT WITNESS

HQN™

ISBN 0-373-77071-5

SILENT WITNESS

www.HQNBooks.com

Printed in U.S.A.

Also available from Lindsay McKenna

Enemy Mine
Wild Woman
Sister of Fortune
Daughter of Destiny
Firstborn
Morgan's Honor
Morgan's Legacy
An Honorable Woman

TO: The Women of ROMvets.
All women who served in our military with pride and
who are now authors. I'm pleased to be a part of this
vital vet organization. Visit http://www.romvets.com.

Dear Reader,

Having been in the U.S. Navy, I'm familiar with the military. Most of the time, what I saw in the navy made me proud to be a member. At the same time, I was sexually harassed during my service, this trauma took away a lot of the energy that I might have had for my job. No woman should have to endure this kind of pressure or degrading message.

Someday I hope everyone will realize that when men stop harassing women and trying to make them second-class citizens, this world will be a much better place. Any time you put down a gender, you are losing fifty percent of the wonderful possibilities. Women have proved their capabilities in battle on the front as well as behind the lines. I think it's about time they were given equal respect, don't you?

Sincerely,

Lindsay McKenna

SILENT WITNESS

CHAPTER ONE

June 22

AGENT ELLEN TANNER HOPED she didn't throw up. A licensed psychotherapist, she realized yet again that she didn't always have neat, tidy emotions. This was disconcerting to her, but reality.

As she almost ran down the white-tiled hall, Ellen juggled her black briefcase and her bulky knapsack. She ignored the California palm trees outside the window. She was going to be late!

It was the first day on her new job—her new life. Commander Dornier, the commanding officer of JAG in the area, had kept her a little too long on the first floor of the building, regaling her with stories. She'd been assigned to the office of the Judge Advocate General at the San Diego Naval Station. She was to go to a second-floor office in Building 56 and introduce herself to her new JAG cohort, Lieutenant Jim Cochrane.

Ellen discovered the naval station sat on some of Southern California's most valuable real estate. Too bad Building 56 didn't afford a view of San Diego Bay, or the fourteen piers that housed every variety of modern naval ship, from Spruance class destroyers, Arleigh Burke guided missile destroyers, to state-of-the-art killing machines known as Aegis class cruisers. Aircraft carriers also used the busy facility, which employed forty-five thousand naval and civilian personnel. A two-star admiral was in command of this military beehive of perpetual activity. How would Lieutenant Cochrane react to her? Breathless, Ellen searched for office 204 and tried to control her frazzled emotions. At thirty-two, she realized she had to make the most of this unexpected opportunity. After a hellish and bleak two years, she couldn't stand the thought of *not* succeeding at this new job. Gulping, she skidded to a halt in front of room 204. Lifting her hand, her anxiety mingled with hope and dread, Ellen knocked.

At the polite knock at the door, Cochrane snarled across his shoulder, "I'm taking no prisoners today." Without looking up, he spread open the first file's contents. He leaned back in the protesting chair until it struck the reference table, wobbled slightly and then stabilized to bear his weight. He had no appointments until this afternoon, and with the mood he was in, maybe the person on the other side of his door would get the message to leave him the hell alone.

But then Cochrane heard the door open. Frowning, he let the chair thunk down. It creaked in protest as he turned to see who had come in without invitation. His eyes widened. A petite woman in her early thirties, with curly red hair framing her face, stared back at him. Her eyes were a willow-green color, reminding him of the soft spring leaves on the huge old willow near his family's homestead in Possum Holler. He felt a tug in his heart—a strange reaction to have to a stranger, he figured. He was two years into a nasty divorce that had left him raw and swearing he would *never* look at another woman again, or even begin to entertain the idea of a second marriage.

The woman was obviously a civilian, since everyone in his world wore a standard Navy-issue uniform. This woman's narrow denim skirt outlined her slender hips and extended to just above her thin ankles. Her Birkenstock sandals wouldn't qualify as proper foot gear in the U.S. Navy, much less the Chinese Navy.

His gaze ranged upward. She wore a loose white lacy blouse and long, beaded ear bobs, both of which underscored her femininity. Cochrane mentally corrected himself; his Missouri Ozarks upbringing was showing again. They were called earrings, not ear bobs. A very old, brown leather knapsack hung across her right shoulder. The words *rainbow child* and *hippie* crossed his mind.

"Yes?" he barked, knowing it wasn't very polite, but not caring.

"Lieutenant Jim Cochrane?" Ellen's heart banged away in her chest. The man did *not* look happy to see her. Despite his scowl, Ellen admitted he was very handsome. Probably in his thirties, if she was any judge.

"Reckon you've got him. What do you want?" Jim tried to ignore the warmth in her eyes—and the way his heart thudded once in reaction to her. Maybe he shouldn't sound so darn hard and crusty. She seemed like an innocent sheep wandering into a wolf's lair.

Ellen smiled nervously and placed her briefcase on his cluttered reference table. She shrugged out of the knapsack and set it down on the floor next to her. Fingers trembling, she began to rummage around in the briefcase. The officer's glare unnerved her. She hadn't expected this kind of a welcome.

"I'm Agent Ellen Tanner. I'm from Washington, D.C. I work for the Office of Inspector General, Department of Defense. I'll be your new partner." As she handed him her credentials, their fingers met accidentally. His were warm; she knew hers were icy with anxiety.

Cochrane had the urge to laugh hysterically, because someone had to be playing a joke on him. He bet this was the work of Lieutenant Eric Hillyer, another legal eagle in the JAG office. That little road apple was always rigging up some type of practical gag. Hillyer assumed Jim was lonely and pining for a woman and a relationship. This was probably his meddling, an effort to fix him up. *No way.*

Cochrane decided to play along, and took the identification case from her long, delicate fingers. He tried to ignore the way his fingertips brushed hers, and how he enjoyed the sensation a little too much. The photo

ID of Ellen Tanner repeated all the official information she'd just imparted. Looking up at her slightly flushed face, he handed it back to her. She seemed friendly and was obviously trying to put him at ease.

"Now, Miss OIG, what's this all about? You must be a joke. What could the DOD possibly want with the likes of poor ole me?"

"I've been accused of being a joker from time to time, Lieutenant, but not a joke. Certainly someone told you I was coming?" Ellen dropped the badge case back into her briefcase. What was *wrong* with this guy?

"Coming? No, they didn't," Jim answered tightly. Her briefcase slid to one side before she caught it and proceeded to snap it closed. He had to stop himself from reaching out and helping her. It was a natural reaction in him to help a woman, but the divorce had left him jaded and hard. Or so he'd thought—until now. With her. This hapless redhead. Jim was stymied by his powerful emotional response to Ellen Tanner. It left him feeling dazed. No woman had ever snagged his attention like this. What the hell was wrong with him?

Shifting the strap of the knapsack back onto her left shoulder, Ellen said, "I can show you my travel orders, Lieutenant." Maybe he was one of *them:* a bean counter, someone who dotted every last *i* and crossed every last *t*. Ellen didn't think that was a bad thing except if carried too far. She saw Cochrane give her a wary look, his intense gray gaze assessing her with a careful scrutiny he probably used in his courtroom trials. His hair was black, cut military short and emphasizing his pallor. Obviously, he didn't see much of the sun. A real indoor desk jockey, perhaps.

"That's not necessary, Ms. Tanner."

Casting a look around, Ellen said, "Didn't your C.O., Commander Dornier, notify you of my arrival? JAG caseloads need outside support due to the increased number of staff being assigned to Iraq and Afghanistan." Tilting her head, she gazed into his face. "I'm here to be of help to you, Lieutenant." She saw his eyes widen in shock. Wide-set, intelligent gray eyes that would just as soon turn her to stone. *Great...* Her heart sank. He was not pleased at all.

Jim sat rigidly in the chair, afraid to believe his ears. He couldn't speak. Frowning, he rubbed his chest where his heart thudded. Hard. And not from any joyous revelation. Well...maybe it was. What on earth was going on? He shouldn't be drawn to her.

Ellen nervously touched a few errant strands of her crinkly red hair. "Lieutenant? Did you hear me?"

"I heard you." He saw her face go soft with pity—for him. *Oh, balls of fire!* Every time she looked at him, his heart lurched as if he were a lovesick teenager. Jim felt as if someone had just slugged him and he was reeling from the blow.

"You've seen the newspapers," she reminded him. "There's been a lot of good reservist people leaving the service."

Grimly, he nodded. *No kidding,* he wanted to say. But he didn't trust himself to speak. In fact, he hadn't trusted anyone for the past two years. His career had gone from brilliant to shit, and he was still struggling to get out of the tub of the latter and back into the good graces of his superior.

"I think you've got me mixed up with someone else, Agent Tanner. I reckon I am plowed under, but…" He swept his hand toward his messy desk, piled high with the files of legal cases begging for his attention. "As you can see, I'm up to my rear end in jaw-snapping alligators right now. But it's nothing I can't handle on my own." *Liar, liar, pants on fire.* He tried to give her his best dour look to convey that he knew what the hell he was talking about. Did it work?

The nerve of this dude! Ellen bit down on her lower lip and counted to five before she spoke. "I see you've got a lot of work, Lieutenant Cochrane. My orders clearly state I'm to work with you. Perhaps you should talk to your immediate superior and get this confusion straightened out so we're both on the same page?"

Her voice was firm and pleasant, but it grated across his raw, exposed nerves. Unwinding his long, lean frame from the creaky chair, Jim muttered, "Stay put. I'll try to find out who you're to work with." Gulping hard, he stood there battling the shock over her arrival.

"Sure…" Ellen supposed she should take his attitude personally, but she refused to do that. Mr. Cochrane had problems and they weren't hers. He was going to try and get rid of her before she was even on board! Well, shoot! And here she'd thought a change of location would help her savaged emotional state.

Jim moved down the passageway—as far away as he could from this greenhorn who was supposed to be an OIG agent. She didn't look businesslike at all, much less capable. Now, if he'd met her at a bar or something, he'd be interested. But here? No way. As Cochrane strode along the highly polished tiled corridor, he passed the legal offices on his left. To his right were the yeomen and personnel clerks, all busy at their gray metal, standard-issue desks.

He tried to get a handle on his emotions. Was Tanner right? He was going to get civilian help? That would add insult to injury. He fervently hoped not. Commander Leo Dornier, his commanding officer, had a large, windowed office at the end of the second floor. Built like a bulldog, Dornier was in his early fifties. His face was a series of circles: apple dumpling cheeks that were always flushed a dull red, a round chin, and a mouth that turned downward toward the sides of his jaw.

In the three years that Cochrane had worked for Dornier, theirs had been a stormy relationship. But Cochrane didn't fault his C.O. completely. Jim's marriage breakup during the last two years had been messy—still was—and his work had suffered accordingly. As a result, Cochrane's Ozarks attitude—of letting things slide and not prioritizing them—had earned him dubious honors with Dornier.

He halted and rapped his knuckles lightly against the door bearing Dornier's name. Jim wondered if he was being punished for some as yet unknown sin he'd committed.

"Enter," Dornier boomed, looking up from his huge dark maple desk. He had just placed the phone back onto its cradle.

"Why was I expecting your visit, Mr. Cochrane? This just proves the grapevine works faster than official channels, as usual. Too bad we can't package it and sell it. That would lower the Pentagon budget, don't you think?" He waved his hand. "Don't answer that. Come on in."

Cochrane came to a parade rest in front of his superior's highly polished desk. The fact that Dornier's office looked painfully neat, with not a paper out of place, and Jim's office looked like a class 1 disaster area, once again emphasized the difference between them. "Sir, I just had an Agent Ellen Tanner from OIG come into my—"

"That's correct." Dornier reacted with a slight smile. "One wouldn't think a government steamroller could move so fast. But it has this time. I just talked to Agent Tanner for a bit and sent her down to introduce herself to you." He looked out the window as if to gather his thoughts.

"She says she's here to help me with my caseload," Jim rasped disbelievingly.

"Yes, that's right. She's your new partner, Mr. Cochrane."

"But—*why?*" Jim tried to keep the irritation out of his voice. He watched Dornier's small, piercing brown eyes zero in on him. Every time his C.O. gave him that mean-old-sow-protecting-her-young'uns look, he knew he was in for trouble.

"There's not a thing I can do about this assignment. I just got off the phone with Admiral Burger, who gave me the background on this new wrinkle out of the Pentagon." Dornier waved a thick, meaty hand in exasperation.

"Someone from the Pentagon thought it a brilliant idea to take bored OIG agents and integrate them into JAG, the Naval Criminal Investigative Service and the Criminal Investigative Service to help us with our investigation load. Admittedly, this war situation is slowly plowing us under, because we are severely understaffed due to our JAGs being assigned to the Middle East. People haven't quit committing crimes just because we're shorthanded. The Secretary of the Navy's request just went to the Deputy Inspector General, Department of Defense. Neither the admiral nor I expected things to move this fast. That's the reason you weren't informed of this new assignment." He squinted, then motioned him toward a chair. "Agent Tanner caught me by surprise, too. I'd heard of this plan, but hadn't expected it to get put into motion so quickly."

Dismayed, Jim reluctantly sat in the chair catty-corner to Dornier's magnificent desk. Dornier rarely invited anyone to sit in his office. This was a very bad sign.

Cochrane's hands were tense against his thighs. He felt pure, unadulterated rage. But he couldn't betray his feelings here. The havoc in his life from his divorce had already placed him on thin ice with his C.O. "Sir, with all due respect—"

"Can't do it, Lieutenant," Dornier growled, looking down at the sheaf of papers needing his signature. "Wake up and smell the coffee. This support idea is entirely beyond my control." He stood and placed both hands flat on his desk, then leaned forward. "Mr. Cochrane, you will work with Agent Tanner. This is a test in the U.S. Navy, to see if the whole plan flies or not. It's a one-year assignment, and could be extended, depending upon caseloads and personnel availability. It's a flux situation with no black-and-white answer for now."

Cochrane thought about rebutting, but decided against it. Rising out of the chair and coming to attention, he said, "Yes, sir."

"Oh, and tell Agent Tanner I'd like to see her once again after she gets settled in. According to her superiors, she's considered an irreplaceable asset to the OIG. Unfortunately, she has no investigative experience, so you'll have to train her. I hear she's smart and catches on fast. She's a Jungian trained analyst by trade. That won't hurt us. We're always needing a shrink's advice in our cases. Nice to have an 'expert' in-house, eh?"

"Yes, sir." But not in his office. And not working with him!

"One last thing, Mr. Cochrane." Dornier fixed him with his best you'd-better-not-screw-this-up look.

"Yes, sir?"

"Powers higher up than you and me have designated this little test as 'very important.' So, the partnership is equal. Agent Tanner is not here to fetch you coffee or deal with all the unpleasant little tasks on cases you don't like handling. She's not your secretary or assistant. It's up to you to make this a success. Is that clear, Lieutenant?"

"Yes, sir, very clear. I'll make it work." *How?*

Dornier smiled. "That's what I wanted to hear. Dismissed, Mr. Cochrane. In the next week, we'll find you a bigger office, so the two of you can fit into it."

Hell's bells! Jim left the room in shock. He didn't hear the normal workplace sounds, the low voices, or see the people looking in his direction as he stalked angrily back to his office. Tanner had no investigative experience! Of all things to saddle him with! Gone was his easy, rolling gait. He marched stiffly down the passageway, feeling like a boiler ready to implode. His pa's soft voice came back to him. *Son, don't bawl over spilt milk. Jest find yerself 'nother cow to milk, instead.*

Jim's gaze flew down the passageway. Ellen Tanner was in his office, leaning against his reference table, awaiting his return. She stood out like a sore thumb—completely out of place in his world of sharp, crisp uniforms. Her hair was wild, her face winsome, her green eyes gentle, not cocky. She was a damn shrink.

And what the hell was a "Jungian" analyst? He'd never heard of that type before. What had he done to deserve this curse? He was more frightened of her as a woman than as a cohort at this point. Some unknown power drew him helplessly to her on an emotional level. That scared the living bejesus out of him because of his split from Jodi.

His heart was pounding, jumping up and down and doing somersaults in his chest at the moment. He was feeling terribly vulnerable, completely off guard.

Slamming the door behind him, Jim glared at Tanner. "Okay, so we're partners," he snarled. *Ouch.* He saw the hurt leap into her eyes at his nasty growl. This wasn't the real him. He'd never snarled at a woman. Raking his hand through his hair, Cochrane railed at himself over his lack of manners. Ellen Tanner was a hapless pawn in this game, too. He shouldn't be firing salvos at her, but he was scared to death.

"Lieutenant, I think we need to talk about this situation, don't you? You're obviously unhappy." *Pissed off. Angry. Disappointed.* Ellen could add a litany of other adjectives that were clearly etched in his expression, voice and body language. She tried not to take it personally, but dammit, she was only human, after all—analyst or not. Worn out by the last gutting two years of her life, she felt wounded by his glare.

Jim turned. Those balmy green eyes had suddenly become focused—on him. Gone was the softness. He felt as if he was under the gaze of a red-tailed hawk intent on nailing her hapless prey. "Agent Tanner, the last thing I need right now is talk. I've just been informed that you're my partner. We'll get a larger office sometime in the next week. That's the only plus in this as far as I'm concerned." Panic struck him. Talk? *Not a chance!* She was a shrink. She was *trained* to talk. Cochrane did not want her inside his head, or have her expect him to spill his guts to her.

"You're acting like this is a death sentence, Lieutenant. I'm not your executioner." Although he wanted to be hers, no doubt.

"It is, and you are," Jim said, defiance in his growl. *Double ouch.* His fear was turning to anger to keep her at arm's length. Did she already know he was drawn to her? Hell, she was probably married. There was no wedding ring on her left hand, however, he noted. Cochrane struggled to tuck his real feelings down into a black hole. She was trained to see beyond the exterior of a person. Anxiety riffled through him. Taking a stack of files, he dropped them on the edge of his desk near the cabinet. "You civilians would never understand." He twisted to look up at her from his crouched position over the files.

"Try me," Ellen said, shifting into her therapist mode. "I think military people and civilian people possess the same brain and heart, if my memory serves me correctly. Or am I missing something in our dialogue?" She wouldn't take his jabs lying down. Coming from an Irish and German ancestry, Ellen was going to fight for herself in this situation, not wimp out.

"This ain't about anatomy and physiology, Agent Tanner." He was amazed that she seemed so unflappable. Those green eyes were so focused, so assessing as if she saw deep into his soul. His heart pounded with fear. With longing. "Being a civilian, you don't have the foggiest notion of how the military works." He saw her eyes narrow speculatively upon him.

"Colorful analogies, and you've got an interesting accent. Where are you from, Lieutenant?" Maybe if she turned this personal and stroked his ego a little, he'd settle down.

"Around here," he snarled in his best Ozarks drawl, "Ah'm knowed as Hillbilly Cochrane. You've heerd 'bout the Hatfields and McCoys? Li'l Abner? Wall Ah'm from them thar hills of Mazurey, Agent Tanner. Ah din't war shoes till high school. Ah got 'em off when Ah cud. I hate shoes."

As Jim stacked other files into some semblance of order, he continued. "Mah pa is a moonshiner by trade. He makes the best white mule in Mazurey. Mah ma is a witchin' woman anna herb doctor. Me ahn mah brothers were always in trubble."

Ellen stared blankly at him. Good God! What had he just babbled? And in what foreign language? She blinked a couple of times, trying to assimilate his words.

Cochrane could see her trying to understand his thick Missouri accent. Hill talk was a different language, although he'd been told that it was very close to

Old English as spoken in seventeenth century England.
Jim had learned years ago that his Missouri accent
could work for or against him. People tended to trust
him more easily on the one hand. On the other, during
a courtroom trial, he had to rein in most of his accent
or people assumed he was dumb and slow—which
worked against him and his client. When Jim entered
college, he'd been looked upon with prejudice due to
his roots. Most outsiders thought of him as an ignora-
mus.

Managing a slight, conciliatory smile, Ellen said,
"I'll give you points for being colorful and truthful,
Lieutenant." Maybe humor would ease the tension be-
tween them?

Jim stared up at her. Nope, she wasn't thrown off the
trail of bread crumbs he'd just scattered before her.
Damn. Smart and beautiful. As he unwound from his
position, he rubbed his palms against his tan slacks.
"That's my specialty," he answered. She looked faintly
amused, but not in a way that made fun of him. No, her
head was tilted like a bird checking out a worm—and
he was the worm.

"Lieutenant, I feel you're projecting a lot of mis-
placed anger toward me," Ellen began gently. "I didn't
ask to be assigned to you. I have a high regard for the
military and volunteered for this job. I had no idea
where I'd be assigned." That was the truth. The other
truth, which she didn't tell him, was that she was fighting to get away from her old life and to start anew.

"Really?" Jim was sardonic, and that wasn't like him, but frustration was boiling up through him and he was helpless to cap it. Glaring at her, he answered his own question. "You haven't a clue, Agent Tanner. Do you? I don't care *what* you do back at the OIG for DOD, it's still a civilian job. You can return to that job when this one-year trial balloon is over. It won't work. I have to train you on the job with time I don't really have. That sucks."

Running his fingers in frustration through his dark, cropped hair, he added caustically, "Not only do I get saddled with a woman for a partner, she's a civilian. What the hell have I done to deserve this?" He really didn't want an untrained partner, regardless of gender. But here she was: bright, pretty, gentle and very nurturing. All those things he so desperately craved and had lost. His heart kept going up and down like a roller coaster in his chest.

"Maybe it's not as bad as you think," Ellen protested in a stronger voice. "I'm a fast learner. I'll try not to be a pain in the butt to you." Realizing that Cochrane was not going to compromise, she erected strong, firm boundaries. Apparently the only thing he respected was fighting fire with fire. Ellen could do it, but she was so damn exhausted emotionally that it took a huge effort to assume that kind of warrior facade.

Laughing harshly, Cochrane cleared a chair for her. "I reckon you're in Hollywood la-la land when it comes to understanding the military way of doing things."

"La-la land is a delusional world, Lieutenant. I can assure you, I operate out of cold, hard reality." Ellen moved to the chair, and sat down. She placed the knapsack on the floor and folded her hands primly in her lap, her level gaze never leaving his. "My father was an FBI agent for thirty years. My mother still works as a policewoman in Minneapolis, where I was born. I think I have the blood and background to be a source of support for you, not the opposite." Ellen wasn't about to be scared off by this officer.

Sitting down in his chair, Cochrane thought her parents' backgrounds were a hopeful sign, but quickly nixed the idea. He said, "Someone is trying to hornswoggle you. Because of the training you'll need, my job will be twice as hard."

"Hornswoggle. Is that word from the Ozarks?" She didn't like that he was disempowering her by using a language she didn't understand.

"It's hill lingo. It means to pull the wool over your eyes."

"I won't slow your investigation efforts." Compressing her lips, Ellen gave him a narrowed-eyed look. "Aren't you being a bit paranoid about this?"

"Paranoid? You can be calm as you want, Agent Tanner, but I see the handwriting on the wall." Jim closed his fist and looked away. On the corner of his desk was a gold-framed photo of his six-year-old daughter, Merry. "This might be a trinket on your own career agenda, but it's like someone has just handed me a live grenade after they pulled the pin."

"I disagree," she insisted, her gaze on his. Despite his dislike of her, Ellen found herself drawn to the officer. That was crazy. And then she laughed silently to herself. Crazy wasn't a word she threw around lightly, but in this case, it sure fit.

"Well, you just go right ahead and disagree, Miss OIG." The phone rang. Jim yanked it off the cradle. He answered like a snarling dog protecting its bone. "Lieutenant Cochrane speaking."

"Mr. Cochrane?"

His brows shot up in surprise. Instantly, Jim wiped the derision from his tone. "Yes, sir, Captain Allison." Why was the head of the JAG office and the civilian-run Criminal Investigative Services at USNAS Giddings, the Top Gun facility just north of San Diego, calling him? Automatically, Jim picked up a pen and pulled over his ever-present yellow legal pad.

"I need your help, Jim."

Cochrane liked Captain Allison, and he'd worked with him on a number of investigations in the past. Although Giddings had its own civilian NCIS and JAG departments, Allison called him in on some investigations because Jim had always done an excellent job. It looked good for his career to have that continue. "What's going down, sir?"

"Lieutenant Susan Kane, one of our best Top Gun flight instructors, was found dead in her condo this morning over in La Mesa. That's not far from you. I just talked to your boss, Commander Dornier, and he's agreed to cut you loose so you can help us investigate this case. We think there's a possible homicide involving Lieutenant Kane. The La Mesa Police Department watch commander, Lieutenant Carl Erlewine, just gave us a call. It's his turf, and we're requesting a collateral investigation, under the circumstances. I can't use military law and procedures on civilian property."

"Yes, sir," Jim said.

"I need someone who's sharp and can deal with civilians. You're to talk to Detective Jerry Gardella, whose on scene already. Let me give you the address. I'd appreciate if you'd drop whatever you're doing and get over there right now, while the L.M.P.D is still conducting their evidence collection at the crime scene."

"I understand, Captain. Tell me what you've got so far, sir...."

CHAPTER TWO

JIM SAT UP, pen poised. His heart pumped hard with anticipation. This was the kind of case he was eager to take on, although he was never happy that someone was dead. "Have they taken the body away yet, sir?"

"No. The medical examiner from San Diego will be waiting for you to arrive, so you can check everything out before he removes the body to the coroner's office," Captain Allison said.

"How was the body discovered, sir?"

"Here's what I've got. An anonymous 911 call came into the L.M.P.D. this morning from a pay phone at a convenience store. A female caller said, 'There's a woman dying. Get an ambulance over to 1616 Horner Street right now.' Then she hung up. The dispatcher gave the info to the watch commander, who felt it was a legitimate call. He rolled two units on it, plus a paramedic team from the fire department. When the primary and backup officers got over there, they found the condo door unlocked, and went through standard entry procedures. They discovered the body. Lieutenant Erlewine called the M.E. and noti-

fied the investigations commander, who sent out two detectives."

"Was it a cold scene, sir?" Cochrane wondered if the
police units had caught anyone in or near the condo.
Without an apprehended suspect, it was tougher to as-
sess what went on. Evidence collection would become
even more important.

"Unfortunately, it was." Allison sighed.

"Reckon that's too bad, sir."

"Yes, it is. Look, Jim, politically, this is a media hot
potato. Susan Kane was the only woman instructor pilot over here at Top Gun, and a damn good aviator. I
don't want civilian media hyping this any sooner than
necessary. The Navy is just now getting out from under the cloud of the Tailhook scandal back in the early
nineties. We've made a lot of progress in gender equal-
ity, and this could hurt us and our ability to continue to
draw intelligent young women into Navy aviation."

Cochrane nodded. He knew Allison wasn't asking
him to suppress evidence, but would prefer him, as part
of the prosecutorial staff, to be at the crime scene. A hel-
lacious trial could come out of this. An attorney on
scene to help collect evidence and put in timely sugges-
tions to the detectives could be a real asset later on in
the courtroom.

"I'll do my best, sir," Cochrane promised.

"Good. I knew I could count on you, Jim."

Cochrane did not share the captain's confidence in
his ability to deal with civilians, but he wasn't going to

tell him that. His fingers tightened around the pen as he wrote down all the information. What a can of worms!

"Sir, how long ago did you speak to Commander Dornier about assigning me to the Kane case?"

"He and I just got off the phone. Will you get over there pronto so the newspapers don't get ahold of this too quickly?"

Mouth tightening, Cochrane rasped, "I'll work with Commander Dornier and get on it like fleas hopping on a dog. I'll be in touch ASAP, sir."

"Excellent."

Cochrane slowly placed the phone back onto the cradle. Captain Allison was a powerful military officer in the NCIS-JAG superstructure, and if he'd chosen Jim out of all the people at hand, this was a plum—of sorts. Maybe an answer to his prayer not to have his career sunk by being assigned this civilian trinket now sitting in his office. Rising, he tucked the legal pad under his left arm and told Tanner darkly, "Stay put. I'll be right back."

Heading down the passageway again, Jim spotted Dornier at the thirty-cup coffee urn, pouring himself another mug of the thick, black brew.

"Commander?"

Dornier nodded in his direction. "I thought you might be looking for me." He took a bite out of his Krispy Kreme doughnut and stared expectantly at Jim.

"Sir, Captain Allison just called me and—"

"I know."

"How can I handle the Kane case plus Agent Tanner?"

"Dovetail 'em, Mr. Cochrane." Dornier lumbered away from the coffee urn, doughnut in one hand, coffee in the other. He turned and added, "Lieutenant Kane is—was—a VIP in our Navy. The captain wanted a JAG investigation team that included a woman. That's why I suggested you two to him. He wants the media to report that we have a woman on this investigation, so we don't appear politically incorrect. Allison said it looked like possible homicide." Dornier shrugged his thick, rounded shoulders. "This case has priority over all the others on your desk. It's a favor to Captain Allison. Get on it ASAP."

"Yes, sir." Jim halted, his blunt-cut fingernails biting into the legal pad he held at his side. Well, so much for thinking Captain Allison wanted *him*. He wanted a man and woman on this investigation so it looked gender neutral.

Jim turned on his heel and went back to his office. Tanner glanced up at him as if he were a rabid dog foaming at the mouth. Wasn't he?

Tossing the legal pad on the desk, he felt his stomach twist into a knot. Rubbing the region unconsciously, he picked up his garrison hat. He settled it on his head, turned and went across the office to grab his battered, black cowhide briefcase. Maybe the briefcase mirrored him: beat up and worn with age and hard work. He'd been the only one in his family ever to attend college. His ma had asked her brother, his uncle Hiram, to make it for him as a going-away gift. The durable briefcase had seen lots of use when he'd attended the law program at Ohio State University, too.

Gripping the handle, he glared at Tanner. "You might as well come along and get your civilian feet wet on this investigation."

"What kind is it?" Ellen eagerly stood. If possible, Cochrane looked even more upset than before. What was that phone call all about? She felt off balance because she didn't know the story, and had to be careful not to assume anything with him. This relationship *had* to work, because she couldn't face going back to Washington, D.C. That part of her life was over....

"A possible homicide. Seems the female pilot who taught at Top Gun was found dead in her condo this morning. It's a potential media hot potato for the Navy." He grimaced. "I hate to think what spin reporters for television and newspapers will put on it. Let's saddle up."

Cochrane didn't wait for Ellen as he strode down the passageway. He was all legs, his rolling gait covering the ground. She finally caught up with him, slightly winded.

"You're having a bad day," Ellen murmured sympathetically. "First me, and now an unexpected case being thrown at you...us...."

"Reckon you're the mistress of understatement." Jim moved down the stairs two at a time.

Panting as she hurried down the stairs, Ellen caught up with him again. "Do you want to talk about it?"

He shot her an acidic look. Ellen Tanner was attractive. Her eyes were large and well-spaced in her triangular face. And all that hair… It was as if she'd put her finger in a light socket and got zapped good, Jim thought. "I know you're a shrink, but I'm not your patient. So put the therapy couch away, will you, Agent Tanner?" Oh, yeah, he wanted to talk to her! Well, maybe not talk, just be near her. What would it be like to reach out and touch her? Would she feel as warm and soft as he thought?

Where was his silly heart going? Jim didn't have time for this crazy reaction to her, and yet he couldn't seem to shake it.

Bridling internally, Ellen scowled. "Don't mistake genuine concern for therapy, Lieutenant. Obviously, you've never experienced therapy or you'd be able to tell the difference."

He held the door open as she walked past him, and answered at the same time. "Score one point for your side, Agent Tanner. Our relationship is professional, not personal," he said succinctly. "Got that?" He allowed the door to slam behind them and started down the concrete steps to the parking lot. And he wanted to be very personal with her. *Wrong time. Wrong place.* That was his luck.

Ellen caught up with him once more. "Oh, I've got it, Mr. Cochrane. Why don't we just put our guns away and start working as a team?"

He was startled by the gritty tone of her voice, and looked over at her. "Us? A team?" He saw the determination in her narrowed eyes. The breeze tossed her red curls slightly, and he felt a crazy itch to tunnel his fingers into that vibrant mass. Life without a woman for two years had been the worst kind of imprisonment as far as Jim was concerned. Ellen Tanner was reminding him of just how much he'd lost and how much he needed the warmth of a good woman in his life.

"This partnership we've been given can work either for us or against us, Lieutenant. I know you don't like me because I'm a civilian. And possibly, because I'm a woman."

"You won't hang gender discrimination on me, Agent Tanner. All civilians are fair game in my book, regardless of gender. I'm hill folk. We consider everyone to be outsiders. So it don't matter if you're man or woman."

"Oh yes, I forgot. You wear your hillbilly status not only with pride, but with obvious prejudice. I'm trying to communicate with you, Lieutenant! You're angry and upset, and you're using me as a convenient scapegoat for whatever series of crises you're experiencing. That's not right." Her soft voice had an underpinning of steel. "Do I look like a turkey? I didn't come out here to be a moving target for you to shoot at."

"I won't answer the first question you posed on the grounds it may incriminate me. Your second statement—well, I reckon there's a lot in life that isn't fair,

Agent Tanner. Maybe I'm having a bad day, but it just got worse. So do me a favor? Just stay out from underfoot. I know you don't have the first clue about a crime scene investigation. Hang back and be my shadow and watch." His conscience ate at him. Ellen really didn't deserve his tirade. She was blameless. But somehow he had to scare her off, because he was frightened by what he might do if she was even minutely interested in him. Doubtful, since he had done nothing in the least to make her like him.

What a galling day. Cochrane tossed his briefcase in the back seat of the gray Navy vehicle and slid in. The car engine sounded like he felt: ragged and unsteady. When was this emotional roller coaster going to end? It had started two years ago when Jodi had demanded a divorce after seven years of marriage. And now he had the worst possible choice in partner on this case.

Ordinarily, a criminal investigation was his favorite assignment. Jim knew he was good at it, like a bluetick hound on the scent of a coon. This was his bread and butter. Homicides were like hunting, and the good Lord knew he'd been raised to hunt, ever since he was old enough to walk at his pa's side with a 30.06 rifle in his hands. Trying to suppress all the emotional surprises of the day, Cochrane concentrated on driving. He couldn't help but be highly conscious of the red-haired woman sitting next to him. It wouldn't be so bad if she wore a wedding ring on her hand, but she didn't. And why couldn't she have been board ugly? On any other day, Jim would find her interesting, someone he'd want to get to know better. But not today...

"I DIDN'T REALIZE San Diego was so built up," Ellen said, trying to break the icy tension in the station wagon. Cochrane's intensity was consuming as far as she was concerned.

About her age—early thirties—he was conservative and all-business—a typical Navy officer. She wondered if he had a sense of humor under that blatant, ongoing sarcasm he called communication. But he was a lawyer, so what did she expect? They got paid for having smart mouths and steel-trap minds.

The JAG officer was pale-skinned, she noted again, not at all what she'd thought someone who lived in California would look like. His summer white uniform was pressed to perfection, his black patent leather corfams—shoes he'd said he hated wearing—were spotless and shiny. Presentation was something she'd noted a long time ago in military types. Some of that was good, and some of it wasn't.

Cochrane's light gray eyes kept drawing her attention. He was rangy and lean, and that Missouri drawl infused every word he spoke. Ellen noticed his large knuckles and long, strong-looking fingers. They had calluses on them. Why? She wanted to ask but didn't.

Pursing her lips, she gazed out the window of the car. Cochrane reminded her of a greyhound—very lean and in top physical condition. His face was long, his jaw narrow but pronounced. Maybe it was his mouth, which she could imagine stretching with an easy, almost lazy smile, that gave Ellen hope this tentative partnership could work. Not that Cochrane had smiled. He seemed to have a permanent frown branded on his broad forehead, his lips tight and drawn inward with unhappiness.

A part of Ellen felt bad about making his day worse. But she couldn't flail herself alive on that one. It wasn't her fault, and as an analyst, she clearly understood that she might be a catalyst in Cochrane's life, but wasn't the problem. Whatever Cochrane's projections were, they were his and she wasn't about to take them on or beat herself up because of them.

Lieutenant Cochrane was trying to make her think he was slow and backward—the usual prejudice outsiders had against hill people. But Ellen knew different. One look into those gray, deep-set eyes, and she could see what he was all about. He was clever as a fox, and very appealing to her as a man. Ellen decided to wave a white flag of surrender and start all over again. "In my business, I deal with the less visible, the unseen," she murmured.

Cochrane slid her a quizzical glance. "You practice psychobabble at OIG?"

"Actually," she said, relieved that his tone was less acidic and hard, "I worked for the FBI for four years before taking the job at the DOD about a year ago. My specialty as a Jungian analyst was to help them rework criminal profiles, mainly of bank robbers. When my husband, Mark, died unexpectedly of a heart attack at age forty, I quit the Bureau. We had met there, and I just couldn't deal with the memories. And to tell you the truth, I'd had it with criminal profiles."

"I see," Cochrane murmured. He glanced out of the corner of his eye at her.

Heartened by his mild expression of interest, Ellen dived in. "I had met June Catter, a senior investigator with the DOD. She was the one who suggested the analyst position with the OIG. It turned out to be a good fit. I had written my Ph.D. dissertation on the impact of job stress on military families. The service is a pretty terrorizing place for women and children. Especially those that have never been exposed to such a rigid way of living."

"Isn't that the truth?" His hands tightened on the steering wheel.

Ellen waited, but realized he wasn't going to add anything. Cochrane's generous mouth was thinned again, the corners pulled in as if he was experiencing some kind of secret pain. His voice had an undercurrent of emotion. She almost asked what he was feeling, as was her custom as a psychologist, but her intuition warned her against it. He would take her interest as intrusion into his space.

Plunging ahead, Ellen said, "After graduating with a masters in psychotherapy, and while working for the FBI, I've continued following about seventy military families and their lives for the last five years. I've done extensive, ongoing interviews with them. Right now, I'm in the process of writing a book. I hope to get a Jungian-oriented publisher to print my findings."

"What's 'Jungian,' anyway? I've heard of a lot of other breeds of shrinks, but not this particular variety of polecat."

Ellen rolled her eyes and laughed lightly. He was teasing her, and hope blossomed in her heart. Maybe he would soften a little. "Carl Jung was a Swiss psychiatric pioneer. He worked with Freud, but went on to see the world a lot differently. In our training, we put great stock in dreams, intuition, symbols, myths and archetypes." She paused for a moment. "I can tell you don't have much respect for therapists as a whole, Jungian or not."

He eyed her critically. "My experiences with shrinks leave me a little jaded, Agent Tanner. I've seen these professionals act as 'expert witnesses,' pumping out whatever the defense or prosecution wants a jury to hear. These so-called 'degreed' people who eagerly testify are nothing more than trained hound dogs, in my book." He shook his head. "I don't like psych types. I think they're in the business to straighten out their own screwed up heads and lives, if you ask me."

Ellen resisted feeling angry at his critical comments. Her brain told her to stay objective. Her heart, however, was pounding. She felt assaulted by his nasty view of her profession. She steeled herself. "I see. Does that same analogy apply to your world, too?"

"What do you mean?"

Ellen shrugged delicately. "Did you became a lawyer to understand right from wrong? To ensure justice to the limits of the law?"

"My view on shrinks is just that, Agent Tanner. I don't like them. They deal in fluff as far as I'm concerned. I deal with facts. It's that simple, so don't read anything more into it."

"You still haven't answered my question, Lieutenant." Ellen met his slitted gray gaze. She wasn't about to let this testy officer pigeonhole her with his concept of a psychologist.

"What? About becoming a legal eagle to learn about justice?" His derisive chuckle filled the car. "Where I come from, right and wrong are black-and-white. There are no gray areas, no maybes. If a score can't be settled with talking, then a shotgun settles it."

"I was merely taking your earlier generalization and applying it to lawyers. You've indicated that anyone entering my profession is basically crazy, that we've chosen a psychology career to learn how to become sane."

"Reckon you're smarter than I gave you credit for, Agent Tanner. Score two points for your side."

"I don't like being stereotyped, Lieutenant Cochrane. My work is very different from other forms of therapy within the psychiatric field." Damn but he was stubborn and opinionated!

"Well, we may get the chance to see whose stereotype is correct."

Ellen sat there, barely holding on to her rising temper. She realized again how Cochrane was projecting his anger and job stresses on her. "I know that we have different perspectives, Lieutenant, but with time I hope we can see the positive qualities we each bring to our team."

Cochrane slowed down and took the Spring Street off-ramp that would take them into downtown La Mesa, a sleepy community northwest of San Diego. "Different perspectives, Agent Tanner? Try different worlds. Different realities." He jabbed his finger toward the car window. "Right now I have a possible homicide on my hands. That's a reality, not a perspective. I'm not poking fun at you, your work or your degrees, but we have absolutely nothing in common. It's like trying to hitch a racehorse with a plow horse."

Ellen heard the rest of his diatribe: that whatever her experience or knowledge, she could not help him in this investigation. Grimly, she retorted, "I learn fast, Lieutenant. And I don't intend to be a millstone around your neck on this homicide."

"Possible homicide."

"Okay, possible." He wasn't going to give her an inch. Still, Ellen could swear she felt his interest in her, man to woman. It was a fleeting thing, but she'd sensed it a couple of times. There was a complex dance going on here and she felt swept up in it. She couldn't sort it out yet. Time with Cochrane would help. Ellen had to be patient, and remain open to him, even if he was constantly attacking her.

Cochrane braked the car and turned onto a quiet street off the main thoroughfare. "La Mesa is a small bedroom community. There are some wealthy people and a lot of middle class. There's also a Navy housing project for enlisted people within the city limits." He pointed ahead. "This condominium complex is where our possible homicide lived. See how new and upscale it is? Looks like our Lieutenant Susan Kane was very good at managing her money to afford these kinds of digs on a naval salary. Or maybe she has a rich pa."

Ellen glanced around at the Santa Fe–style architecture. The two-story stucco buildings were painted a pale pink and dressed up with red, Spanish tile roofs. "How can you say that? You don't know anything about her yet."

Cochrane pulled into the street in front of the condo. As he did so, he saw two La Mesa police cruisers. Farther down the street, there was an ambulance with San Diego Medical Examiner printed on its side. "I know what lieutenants make, and judging by this ritzy place, Kane was either into something illegal, or came by the place through her rich family connections."

Ellen stared at him. "How about she had a sugar daddy who kept her in the style she was accustomed to?"

Cochrane shut off the engine and released his seat belt. His mouth quirked. "Not bad, Agent Tanner. You surprise me. Maybe you aren't all fluff, after all. That's another possibility."

Frowning, Ellen shook her head. "Why don't you consider the possibility she saved her money so she could afford something like this?"

"I reckon there's a slim chance of that. Since we have to work together for God knows how long, you might as well learn how I go about investigating. It's obvious you know nothing about death scenes. So today starts your OJT—on the job training," he said, leaning over the seat to grab his briefcase.

"It's a step in the right direction." At least Cochrane wasn't going to cut her out altogether and ignore her. "This is a two-way street, Lieutenant. I may not know about homicides or investigative techniques, but I have a fair amount of expertise in how people behave."

"At a crime scene, that isn't going to be of much help," he said, opening the door and climbing out. "The dead aren't talking."

Ellen followed. The bright, warm June sunshine was blinding as they took the pale pink steps up to the front door. Breathlessly, she hitched her knapsack strap on her shoulder as they approached the police officer guarding the entrance. "Who has authority on this case?" she asked him.

"The L.M.P.D. I'm supposed to work with our civilian counterpart."

Ellen hesitated, her voice becoming suddenly taut. "Is—is the body still in there?" *Oh, God! A body? No...not again! Not another one!* She couldn't handle it. She just couldn't. In that moment, Ellen felt her whole world coming apart, leaving her cold and stricken.

"I reckon it is. You okay, Agent Tanner? You're looking kinda peaked to me."

CHAPTER THREE

June 22

DISTRACTED BY ELLEN'S sudden paleness, Cochrane showed his ID to the La Mesa cop, who went inside to tell Detective Jerry Gardella that they'd arrived. Ellen stood next to Jim, looking like the bleached bones of a dead seal he'd once seen on the beach—white and colorless. His hands itched to wrap around her shoulders and give her a squeeze of support. He wanted to tell her everything would be okay. But he knew it wouldn't be.

Somehow, he'd have to find a way to apologize for his boorish behavior earlier. A naval officer was a gentleman, not an angry boar running around hooking people with its deadly tusks.

A trim, tanned man, wearing stone-washed Levis and a red polo shirt, came out and shut the door to the condo behind him.

"Ah, the cavalry has arrived." The man extended his hand. "Detective Jerry Gardella, La Mesa P.D. You Navy types from Giddings?"

Cochrane shook the detective's hand. "No, sir. JAG

legal officer Lieutenant Jim Cochrane." He glanced to his right where Tanner stood, still white-faced. "This is my new partner, Agent Tanner, DOD, OIG." They both showed him their IDs.

They exchanged business cards and Jim made a quick assessment of the detective. Gardella was fifty-something, five feet eight inches tall, with that famous California tan and trim physique that seemed to go with the state's image. He had dark brown eyes to match the short brown hair with silver at the temples. His mouth was thin, like the rest of him, and his demeanor low-key yet commanding.

"We're performing a witness check right now," Gardella told him. "We'll give you anything we find."

Jim nodded. "I'm appreciative, Detective. We'll do the same if we stumble upon anything."

Gardella rubbed his hands together. "That's what I like—cooperation and teamwork. We're gonna get along just fine. Let's go in."

Cochrane pulled out two sets of latex gloves from his pocket and instructed Ellen to put on a pair before entering. He did the same.

As they moved into the condo, Gardella motioned toward the hall. "The body's in the bedroom down at the end, on the left. The tech boys have done their work. We did a generalized search of the bedroom, and the other detectives are in the kitchen right now. The bottle she took the pills from is still on the bedstand. There's also one capsule on the carpet next to her bed, which we left in place."

"We'll take some photos, measure a couple of things and keep out of your way. Did you find out anything else about that anonymous call that tipped you off to Kane's death?" Cochrane asked.

"The L.M.P.D. dispatcher received the 911 call at 3:10 a.m. The caller gave Susan Kane's name and address, said to get an ambulance over here in a hurry, and then hung up. I just sent the backup unit to that convenience store where the call originated. I'll talk to the person on duty to see if they saw anyone at their pay phone at that time." Stifling a yawn, he continued, "I got here just after 6:00 a.m."

"I see." Cochrane slowly looked around the living room of the condo. The walls were painted a nondescript beige. The furniture was antique, obviously old and well cared for. The drapes at the front window were lacy—the only indication that a woman lived here and not a man. Jim glanced down at Ellen and observed her gazing around the room, her eyes wide with anxiety. Her hands were clasped and she seemed nervous. Again, he wanted to put his arm around her and give her solace. Maybe he should tell her to leave? But she had to learn the procedures.

"You any good with photography, Ellen?" he asked, still torn over what to do. Maybe putting her to work would get her mind off the fact she was going to see a dead body for the first time in her life.

Ellen jumped at the sound of his voice. "Me? No. I'm not very good with a camera. Why?" She could feel

snakes thrashing around in her gut. This was the *last*
place she wanted to be. Her instinct was to run—as far
away as she could. There was a dead body in the bedroom. How would she ever handle it? When she saw
Jim giving her an odd look as he pulled out a compact
camera, she knew she had to explain. Her voice came
out raspy and tense. "I can't do it. At least…not today.
Maybe on another case?"

"Sure, no problem. Let's check out the body of Lieutenant Kane." Moving down the passageway toward
the bedroom, Cochrane eyed all the impressive diplomas and awards hanging on one bulkhead.

"Well, she was neat and clean," he noted, glancing
back at Ellen. The Queen Anne cherry desk was not
only highly polished and dust free, but not a scrap of
paper cluttered it. At the end of the passageway, he discovered the master bedroom. He knew Ellen was
watching him for a reaction when they entered, but he
donned his usual expressionless mask.

The medical examiner, a man in his late fifties with
graying hair and wire-rim glasses, stood in the corner
of the room writing notes on a clipboard. A police officer was on his hands and knees on the opposite side
of the bed, obviously still looking for evidence. By law,
there had to be an officer in the room with the body until it was removed to the morgue on the M.E.'s order.

Jim introduced themselves to both officials. The
M.E., John Williams, grunted his name and gave a per-
functory smile, then continued with his notes. The po-

lice officer gave them permission to examine the crime scene.

Lieutenant Susan Kane lay on a flowery print comforter on a canopy bed, on her right side. She was in her dress white uniform. Her dark brown hair was regulation short. What struck Cochrane the most was that Kane looked like a perfect wax museum replica of a human being—not a dead body. Her uniform was spotless and pressed to perfection. She wore white heels, her slender, nylon-clad legs drawn up toward her body in a semifetal position. As his gaze ranged upward, he shook his head. In her arms was a large brown teddy bear. Of all things.

Something didn't jibe in Jim's mind. Here was a hotshot Navy pilot and instructor at Top Gun, the cream of the naval fighter community, dead, with a teddy bear tightly pressed to her breast, her arms wrapped around it as if she had been clinging to the bear for dear life.

Susan Kane was prettier than most. She was tall and slender, her face oval with a slightly stubborn chin, full lips now parted in death, and thick brown lashes that fanned out across her cheeks. The M.E. had placed tape across her eyelids. People died with their eyes open, not shut, Jim knew.

He heard Ellen give a strangled croak, and glanced over at her. "You okay?"

She touched her throat with her fingertips and stared at the dead officer. She opened her mouth, but when no sound issued forth she shut it again. Obviously wanting to cry, she turned away and tried to take several deep, steadying breaths. It was obvious to Jim that his new partner was not going to get through this today.

Lifting the D-70 Nikon, Cochrane took several shots from different angles, careful where he stepped in the bedroom. "You get used to it after a while," he growled softly, taking the barb out of his tone. The bedroom reminded him of some fantasy land of long ago. Certainly not the bedroom of a modern-day jet jock.

Rubbing her moist brow, Ellen muttered, "I'll never get used to this. It's awful…." She pressed her hand to her stomach, unable to watch what Jim was doing. She heard a number of clicks of the camera as he continued to take photos. How could he be so calm?

Bothered by Ellen's frozen-deer-in-the-headlights response, Jim took a photo of the Queen Anne table that served as a bedstand. He noted a white handkerchief edged with delicate lace in Kane's right hand. Had she used it while crying? He was sure she had, and anguish tugged in the region of his heart.

Susan Kane looked peaceful in repose, and Cochrane thought what a shame it was to waste such a young life. The tragedy shook him. It shouldn't have, but it did. Was it her ethereal look, even in death? The fact that she was holding that ridiculous teddy bear? The bedroom's decor, too, hinted at a bygone era, and perhaps a romantic side she probably hid from the prying eyes of the military.

He heard Ellen gulp noisily and make another attempt to speak. Bothered that she was upset, he tightened his lips to hold back emotions of his own he hadn't expected to feel. It simply wasn't a professional reaction.

Keeping his voice gentle, he turned to her. "Why don't you join Detective Gardella out in the living room?"

"Thank you. I will…." Ellen said, then quickly left.

Cochrane moved to the bed. He knelt down and took a close-up photo of Susan Kane, from the waist up, then several more of her face and neck. Something was badly out of kilter with this scenario. *Was* it a suicide? A homicide made to look like a suicide? Why the hell was she clutching a very old, obviously very worn, much-loved teddy bear in her arms?

His daughter, Merry, had a teddy bear that was her "blanky," a source of security. She went nowhere without her beloved Pooh Bear, which he'd brought to the hospital two days after she was born. Merry had grown up with that now-ragged bear. Had this old stuffed animal that Susan Kane held meant the same thing to her? What was the story behind the bear? Was there a story at all?

Sometime later, he heard footsteps enter the bedroom.

"Uhh…" Ellen stood unsteadily, her hands gripping the door frame. "Sorry to bother you…."

Cochrane turned to find she was now a pale green. "Yes?"

"Detective Gardella said the search in the kitchen turned up nothing." Ellen gulped loudly again and pressed one hand across her mouth.

"Okay. Do yourself a favor, Ellen—go heave your guts out and then come back in here and help me?" He wanted to tell her to just leave and not come back at all, but she was supposed to learn procedures, not be missing in action. Internally, Jim hurt for her, and it nagged him he couldn't give her the solace she needed.

Ellen blanched even more, turned on her heel and disappeared. Nearly running down the hall, she barely made it to the bathroom in time.

Cochrane felt a twinge of conscience. Why was he so het up, so angry? It wasn't Ellen's fault that she'd been sent out here from D.C. She'd lost her husband. Maybe she'd found him dead? And maybe that's why she was so upset having to see a body today? Jim didn't know. Muttering a curse, he finished taking necessary photos.

The M.E. closed his notebook and came around the bed. The pathetically gaunt man introduced himself and pointed to the body. "You done?"

"Yes, sir."

With another grunt, the M.E. walked closer to the bed. Gently, he grasped one of the teddy bear's ears and eased the toy from Kane's arms. He would place the bear in a brown paper evidence bag for Gardella, although Cochrane was sure it was an extraneous piece of evidence that would just gather dust in the L.M.P.D.

holding locker. The M.E. left the room, and Jim followed. As he passed a closed door, he heard Ellen retching, and felt like hell for her. He wanted to do something to help her.

The past two years since the divorce had been grim ones, with him acting like a polecat more times than he wanted to admit. He wasn't the fun person he once was in the JAG office. The country boy from Missouri, who used to always have an easy smile to cheer up the gloomiest comrade-at-arms, had been missing in action. He'd gone from a joker to a joke. Most of the people in his office avoided him now, and Jim didn't blame them. The divorce had been hell. His love for Jodi had died like a vine cut off at its root. Not seeing Merry every day broke his heart. He could hardly stand being away from his daughter.

To hell with it. He walked quickly back to the bathroom. After knocking on the door, Jim eased it open. Ellen Tanner was on her knees, hugging the commode, her face pale, the coppery freckles across her cheeks standing out in sharp relief.

"Hold on," he murmured, touching her shoulder gently as he moved past her. He grabbed a washcloth, wet it in the sink and squeezed it out. "Here, wipe your mouth." His fingers tingled as her shaking, clammy hand met his. Jim found a glass and filled it with tepid water.

Ellen sat there, sniffing and coughing. Huge tears rolled down her face. Setting the glass aside, Jim took the cloth from her and rinsed it beneath a stream of warm water. After wringing it out again, he pressed it against her dark, anguished eyes, then gently wiped her face. Just that little contact sent a frisson of yearning across his heart. It had been a long time since he'd touched a woman, and it sent an ache through him, one so acute he didn't know how to react.

"Th-thanks…" Ellen murmured. Oh! How she needed this kind of care and attention right now. She was starved for a little humanity from Cochrane. And he wasn't disappointing her.

"Dress you up, can't take you anywhere, gal," Jim teased huskily. *Damn! Where had that endearment come from? To him, "gal" was a term for one's sweetheart.* Flustered, he muttered, "Stay where you are."

He handed her the glass and she took it in a shaky hand. Tears continued to spill from her eyes. She took a gulp of the water and rinsed out her mouth. Jim leaned down and patted her shoulder awkwardly.

"It's gonna be okay," he soothed. "Sorry I've been acting like a bear with a toothache toward you. Just take your time coming out. First time you see a body, you see a lot of the bathroom, too." *So much for hearts and flowers, Cochrane. That sounded real understanding.*

"O-okay, thanks." Ellen's heart twisted violently in her chest. The past was overlaying the present. Clinically, she knew her reaction was caused by PTSD, posttraumatic stress disorder. When a person witnessed something horrible, it would come back to haunt him.

The body and brain remembered such shocks for a long, long time. Cochrane's kindness was exactly what she needed. She watched as he turned and left the bathroom.

Ellen finally forced herself to her feet and filled the sink. The water refreshed her as she splashed it repeatedly against her face. More than anything, she'd desperately craved another human's tenderness and care.

Somehow, Jim had known what she needed, and it gave her a bit of solace as she continued to tremble. Him calling her "gal" had soothed her anxious state. Had he used the endearment on purpose? Or had the word just slipped out unbidden? Reeling, Ellen knew she couldn't afford to think about him and his offhanded remark for too long. She had to find a way to keep the past from tarnishing the present.

Jim felt out of place standing in the living room with its Victorian furniture. Lieutenant Kane's condo was tastefully decorated, nothing like the cluttered apartment he now called home. The deceased's worn teddy bear was a stark contrast to her surroundings—another point that aroused his suspicion. Looking into the paper bag, Cochrane thought the stuffed animal seemed even more lonely since it had been separated from its owner.

A painful wave of recognition passed through him. How many nights had he arrived home late from the office and silently stolen into Merry's bedroom to watch her sleep the sleep of the innocent? She would be holding Pooh Bear tightly against her tiny body. All the hogwash of the workplace would roll off his tense shoulders and neck. No matter how badly his day had gone, just standing in Merry's room and absorbing her vulnerable features as she slept was enough to heal him, enough to help him handle whatever the world threw at him.

In death, Susan Kane reminded him of his six-year-old daughter. Shaking his head, Cochrane rationalized that the pressure of the divorce and the drastic change in his lifestyle were the real reason for his strong response to the teddy bear. He turned away.

"She new?" Detective Gardella asked as he ambled into the living room and gestured toward the bathroom.

Glad for the distraction, Cochrane roused himself from his reverie, his heart aching because he missed his daughter. "Oh, Agent Tanner?"

"Yeah."

"Afraid so. This is her first day and first case."

"Thought so. She was looking a little green around the gills. I think I saw some saltine crackers in a cupboard above the kitchen stove earlier when I was doing the evidence search."

"I'll give her a couple. Thanks." By the time he'd located them and opened the box, Ellen had reappeared. From across the kitchen, he saw how pale she looked, but at least the green tinge was gone from her waxen features. Her hair looked even more frizzy as she blotted her lips with a damp cloth. "Here," he said, holding out a couple of crackers, "eat these. They'll help settle your stomach."

Ellen reached for them. "Thanks." Again, Cochrane was surprising her with his sensitivity.

He placed the cracker box on the tile counter and turned to her. Right now, Ellen looked frail, just like Susan Kane did. Like Merry did. He figured he knew what had spooked the agent. It wasn't every day a person saw a dead body. But what had made Susan Kane take her life? Had someone killed her?

"I've got more questions than answers on this case," he said, looking around, hoping to snag her interest. Ellen's green eyes lightened a little, possibly because of his far more civil tone.

Ellen nibbled the cracker cautiously. "Oh?" Her stomach was settling down now, though her heart was still overwhelmed by memories. Somehow, Jim's soft, Southern accent was a healing balm washing old wounds, making her feel better. Like a starving beggar, she absorbed the tender look of concern in his gray eyes.

"Yeah. There's lots of crazy inconsistencies here."

"What do you mean?"

With a shrug, Cochrane gestured around the kitchen. "Stepping into Kane's condo is like stepping back in time."

"The Victorian furniture?"

"Right." He glanced at her. Ellen was getting a little color in her wan cheeks and her eyes didn't look quite as glazed as before. "What I know about jet jocks is that they're ultramodern, not into old furniture and history. Not into the past like this. They're on the cutting edge of technology, not holed up with antiques."

"Maybe," Ellen ventured, her voice still wobbly, "she lived two different lives, a professional one and a personal one."

"Reckon so," Cochrane said, then shook his head. "Something bothers me about this case and I can't put my finger on it. Consarnit, I hate when this happens. I was hoping this would be cut-and-dried, but there are too many loose ends."

"Was it murder?"

"It's possible. If it wasn't, I'd like to understand what made her commit suicide. So far this case doesn't have rhyme nor reason." He gazed around the kitchen. "I think we'll check this out again, even though they've already gone over the scene. How are you feeling now?"

"Better. The crackers helped. Thanks for caring." Ellen looked up into his narrowed gray eyes, his pupils huge and black. There was such intelligence there. Such warmth and concern. Jim Cochrane wasn't the nasty bastard he'd like her to believe he was. No, he'd showed a lot of tenderness toward her in the bathroom. For that, Ellen was grateful.

Cochrane frowned. "We need to go back into her bedroom. You up to it?"

"I'll try to be." Ellen didn't want to go, but she had to learn the elements of a good investigation.

"If you can't handle it, it's okay," Jim said gently as

he moved down the hallway. "We'll work around it this time."

Nodding, Ellen whispered, "I feel like an interloper here. Susan's still so beautiful, as if she's not really dead, just sleeping. I keep thinking she's going to wake up and ask us what we're doing in her home."

"It takes some getting used to," Jim agreed, his voice soft.

Ellen turned and saw Cochrane studying her. "Death is, well, so terribly personal and private." She opened her hands in a helpless gesture.

"Yeah, it is."

"I just wonder how many tears Susan cried into that handkerchief before she died?"

Shaking his head, he growled, "Don't even go there, Ellen. You have to protect yourself from all of this. Now, let's go to work."

She stood off to one side and watched as Cochrane searched the room with slow deliberation, missing no detail. Despite how she felt emotionally, she committed his movements and lessons to memory.

"Nothing," he said flatly as he finished. "Not a piddling thing to give us a clue as to why she took those pills. *If* she took pills. We don't know that yet. The autopsy will tell us what she died of and what time she expired, but no answer as to why."

"You're saying that someone might have forced her into taking them?"

"It could be a professional hit."

Ellen's eyes rounded. "Who on earth would put a contract out on Susan?" The thought was so foreign to her. Murder wasn't something she would ever comprehend.

Shrugging, Cochrane muttered, "Could be she knew something? Maybe someone bought the services of a professional to shut her up? Or maybe it was someone in her personal life? All good questions, but no answers."

"But, there's no sign of violence," Ellen protested. "Didn't you say in order for it to be a homicide, there had to be signs of a struggle?"

"Usually there is." Jim pointed toward Kane's head. "Professional hit men have a lot of ways of killing that don't seem obvious. That's why I was looking real close around her mouth to see if I could detect any signs of bruising."

"I was wondering why you were studying at her so closely." Ellen shivered and avoided looking at Susan Kane's body. She simply couldn't handle all the emotions that were surging up within her. It took every ounce of strength she had right now just to look and sound professional.

"I was searching for even the slightest marks on her neck, jaw or mouth. Professionals know just where to put pressure on nerve points to make a person open their mouth out of pain. Once they got their mouth open, it's real easy to dump a bottle of tranks down them."

"What a horrible way to die."

"The coroner will tell us more. They're trained to look for such things." Cochrane studied Kane's mouth. "They also have a means of detecting fingerprints on the victim's flesh."

Ellen shook her head. "I never realized that."

"It's not exactly public knowledge. Gardella was telling me that the tech people will look in case it's a professional hit." He rubbed his chin as he stared down at Susan Kane. "What a crying shame. Did you see her certificate out in the passageway?"

"Which one? There are so many."

He laughed a little. "Yeah, she was hell on wheels when it came to her career, wasn't she? Kane's a ring knocker from the Naval Academy, and she graduated at the top of her flight class from Pensacola, which is no small feat, believe me. She was an F-18 Super Hornet Top Gun flight instructor. Those are pretty darn impressive credentials for a woman *or* a man. Talk about having smarts. And somewhere, in her spare time, she was able to get a Ph.D. in aeronautics from MIT. Lieutenant Kane was obviously a go-getter, a real Type A personality. No grass grew under her feet, as my ma would say. Pride of the Navy, for sure."

Ellen kept her hand pressed to her stomach. "She's so beautiful. I have this crazy desire to go over and touch her shoulder, lean over and tell her, 'Wake up.'"

"Yeah, I know what you mean." Cochrane shook his head. "Nothing fits. I mean, why was she clutching a teddy bear, of all things? And look at this bedroom. It reminds me of something Walt Disney would decorate for *Beauty and the Beast* or *Cinderella*. Yet every other part of her condo is filled with antique furniture. There are some pictures on the television set and her accomplishments are displayed on the bulkhead. Normal things. You come in here, and it's like Hollywood la-la-land."

"Maybe there *were* two very different sides to her," Ellen said. Then she grimaced. "I'm sorry, but I have to leave this room. My stomach—"

"That's fine. Meet me out in the living room," Cochrane said, feeling for her. Seeing the relief on Ellen's face, he added, "I'll be out in a few minutes. There's just a couple of details I want to check out. I can talk to you about them later."

Ellen closed her eyes and clutched her stomach. "Okay. This is so upsetting to me. I just, well, I've had a couple of rough years with death."

Jim sized her up and saw devastation clearly marked on her pale features. He wanted to ask what she meant, but that was too personal. And right now was not the time. "I'll be out in a little bit," he stated. "Go eat a few more crackers."

Nodding, Ellen quickly left.

Cochrane shook his head and went about cataloging the scene by shooting photos of even smaller items. Ten minutes later he sauntered into the living room, where Ellen was studying a set of framed pictures.

"Did you look at these photos?" she asked. She

wanted desperately to show him she could contribute to this investigation.

He ambled over to the television set. "Yes. What about them?"

"Look at them, Lieutenant Cochrane. This one shows Susan with two men about her own age. They're all smiling and happy. Family?"

"Significant others?"

Ellen gave him a dirty look. "Why is it a man's mind always runs in that direction first?"

"You must be feeling better, Agent Tanner." Cochrane grinned lopsidedly. "I'm not thinking in that particular direction. Doesn't it strike you that Susan Kane doesn't have a photo of her pa or ma here? Was she an orphan? Adopted? This other photo is of a woman, and they're smiling and happy. And they have their arms around one another."

Ellen looked up at him. "Maybe her sister?"

"Maybe she was a lesbian, and that's her lover."

Ellen stared over at him. "You think?"

"Anything is possible. There are gays and lesbians in the service no matter how much the military wants to deny it." He bent over to look at the photos. "I'm going to ask the police to take these along as evidence. Maybe they'll help us crack this case."

"Do you think it was murder?"

"I reckon I don't know," Jim answered slowly. "That autopsy report will help supply the answer."

Ellen looked around the condo. "Susan did such a

beautiful job of decorating. Everything is so clean, so neat." She laughed shortly. "If you could see my old apartment back in Washington, D.C....! It looks like a hurricane zone in comparison to this one."

"Mine's worse. A hog looking for a new waller would probably take one look at my place and gleefully move in." Jim made an expansive gesture. "What you fail to understand is that military people are taught to keep things neat, clean and organized. I'm sure four years at Annapolis instilled those values in her." He gazed around the living room. "But this is too clean. It's as if Kane were waiting to get an E rating."

"E rating?" Ellen questioned.

"Every operation in the U.S. Navy has a periodic Inspector General's inspection. That's when the boys from D.C. and the Pentagon descend like a flock of buzzards on a ship or station wearing white gloves, and examine every last thing there is to inspect. They look not only at appearances but at performance and record keeping. Station commanders quake in their boots over an I.G. They refer to it as an E rating. A bad rating and their career is torpedoed. And the unlucky officer that heads up the section with the poor results can kiss his career goodbye, too." Cochrane snapped his fingers to emphasize the point. "Just like that."

"And Susan's condo is ready for inspection?"

"Yep. Nothing, and I mean *nothing,* is out of place. It's as if she planned the whole thing. Even the window-sills and other ledges you'd normally find some dust on are clean. An I.G. team would be hard-pressed to find anything out of order. She doesn't even have an Irish pennant on her uniform."

"Irish pennant?"

"A Navy word for a thread hanging off your uniform."

"Oh."

"Did you look closely at Kane's uniform?"

"Uhh, no."

"Well, I did. No Irish pennants. Each brass buttons on her jacket is polished to perfection. All of her medals are straight and perfectly aligned to the left breast pocket. There's no lint on her black-and-gold shoulder boards. I looked at the white heels she wore, and there aren't even any smudges on the backs of them. Everything is too tidied up."

"Too perfect?"

He gazed around and frowned. "Yes. I've got law briefs scattered from my kitchen table to my coffee table in the living room. I've got socks lying on the deck of the head."

"In other words, your apartment has a lived-in look?"

He gave her a sour smile. "In my place someone could die and not be located for a week. This place seems to be too clean for even death to visit."

"I can smell a faint odor of Pine-Sol," Ellen confirmed. "So maybe she washed the walls?" Her stomach was settling. Jim's warm, engaging teaching style was helping her deal with her memories.

"Reckon she got everything spotless, as if ready for one final inspection. Was she expecting someone to come over? Did they? If so, who? Did this other person or persons push Kane into taking those pills? Was it the 911 caller? If so, was this a lover's spat? What the heck were Kane's actions telling us?"

Ellen followed him back to the couch and sat down, her voice low with emotion. "I don't see how anyone wouldn't be touched by seeing Susan clutching that teddy bear to her breast. I had this feeling she was more a little girl rather than a grown, mature pilot with a multitude of impressive degrees."

"There's such a split here. Kane was obviously on the fast track in the Navy, yet she's got this doggone teddy bear." Cochrane scratched his head. "In some ways, she reminds me of my daughter, Merry."

"What a pretty name. How old is she?" Ellen saw the tension in his face melt instantly, and his gray eyes grow warm. Clearly, there was love for his daughter shining in them. How she ached to see such a look for her on a man's face. But Ellen had realized that a great love came only once in one's life, if ever. And she'd had hers. Still, she absorbed that look on Cochrane's face, feeling like a thief.

"Six years old." Jim smiled and rocked back on his heels. "I've loved that kid from the day I laid eyes on her. I couldn't be with Jodi, my ex-wife, when Merry was born—I was on temporary assignment to Washington. I arrived home two days later." He pursed his mouth and revisited the pain of missing his daughter's birth.

Ellen said quietly, "I've found from my study that being a military wife is at times an awful burden. The man of the house is away more than he's at home. It builds a lot of tension, and a lot of anger by the wife toward the husband." She could see the devastation in Cochrane's eyes. To miss your child's arrival, one of life's most precious moments, would be awful. She saw the angst in the set of his mouth, the tension returning to his features.

Rubbing his palms on his slacks, Cochrane nodded. "No need to tell me, Ellen." He shoved his hands into his pockets. "Jodi pulled the plug on our marriage two years ago. We split the blanket. I can only see my daughter on visits. She doesn't live with me and it sucks."

Ellen sat very still. "Divorce is like going through a death." Shrugging, she whispered haltingly, "My husband…Mark…died of a heart attack two years ago. I was at work at the time. I came home and he…" Ellen shut her eyes and whispered, "He was lying dead in the living room floor. At first, I thought he was playing a game with me. He was always such a tease. I bent down to shake his shoulder and… It was such a shock."

Jim scratched his head and shifted uneasily. "I didn't know that." Placing his hands on his hips, he looked beyond her. "Sorry." And he was. When her lower lip trembled, he again found himself wanting to reach out and touch her, to try and soothe the pain he saw in her face. The ache in his own heart was very real. Whether he wanted to or not, he felt deeply for Ellen. Far more than he should, and he didn't understand why.

Ellen wiped her eyes self-consciously and mustered a slight smile she didn't feel. "How could you know, Lieutenant? I didn't tell you."

He nodded, and said apologetically, "I reckon we're both struggling, then. Your husband died and so did my marriage. We're a fine pair, aren't we? Only I'm not so sure that divorce isn't a continuing kind of dying process that has no finish, no end. It's an ongoing emotional torture."

Ellen took a deep, ragged breath. "I can't argue with you. Since Mark died, I've had a huge hole right here." She pointed to her heart. "I was glad to get this assignment, if you want the truth. It got me away from everyone who knew us back in D.C." She held his sudden, intense gaze. "In a divorce, there's no walking away, especially if children are involved. It's a painful situation for everyone."

Cochrane grimaced. "Life isn't pretty, is it? Never mind, don't answer that." He forced himself to get back to work. Talking with Ellen Tanner was easy. Too easy. Speaking more to himself, he muttered, "This place is too meticulously clean. Kane's too neatly dressed."

"It's suspicious to me, too," Ellen admitted. "Suicidal people usually don't care about their appearance when they're in that frame of mind."

"You're very observant. Suicide types usually have sloppy homes. They're depressed. They don't care what they or their place look like. This officer's home is too spit-and-polish perfect. Had she worn the uniform somewhere at an official function and then come home?"

Ellen brightened. "Did anyone find a letter from her? An explanation why she took her life? If she did?"

"I understand there was no suicide note found," Jim stated, perplexed. "I've never seen a suicide yet where the person didn't leave a note."

"So," Ellen said, "you think this was a murder?"

"It's angling that way. As I said, we'll know more after the M.E. performs the autopsy," Jim said. "Let's go. We're done here."

Never had Ellen wanted to hear those words as much as now. She nearly tripped on Cochrane's heels getting out of the condo. Lifting her face to the sunshine, she gratefully took several deep breaths to steady her unsettled stomach, then hurried to catch up with Jim as he strode along.

"Where are we going now?" she asked.

"We've done everything we can do here. I need to get back to the JAG office and drop this film off to Chief Hazzard at our crime lab. I want you to take the rest of the day off while I run a lot of errands. I have to get my case files squared away so we both can make sense of them in the coming week. I'll drop you off at your hotel. You can come in at 0800 tomorrow morning. We'll start working together then."

Jim realized Ellen needed time to deal with being

around a dead body. He understood that seeing Susan Kane had resurrected her husband's death for her—big-time. He kicked himself, knowing he should have been more sensitive to begin with, asked more questions. Instead, he'd been so tied up with his own reaction to having an untrained partner that he'd let her fall through the hole all by herself. A good partner didn't do that. He swore silently he'd make it up to her in some way.

"Good, because I don't even have my bags unpacked yet." Ellen gave him the address of the hotel where she was staying.

Cochrane started up the car and put it in Drive. "I have so many consarned things ahead of a dead body to deal with."

"Family obligations?" Ellen guessed, softening her tone. Her heart was settling down now, most of the pain dissolved. Part of it was due to Jim's care of her. Despite his growly initial response, she realized he was a man who cared. Hope burned bright in her and she relaxed for the first time since they'd met.

Cochrane's mouth flattened as he drove the car out of the condo area and back onto a main street. "Hill folk are taught to take care of their families." He slanted her a quick glance. "A family for us is knit tighter than a pair of crochet needles. This splitting of the blanket is the worst thing that's ever happened to me. My folks are still het up about the divorce. They love Merry, too. We visited them every year, so they got to see her growing up. Now—" his mouth turned down "—now it's going to be next to impossible to take Merry back to see them, what with the judgment handed down by the local court."

She nodded. "I imagine, coming from hill folk, you're one of the few in your family who's gone on to a professional career?"

Cochrane laughed bitterly. "Yeah, I reckon in one way I'm the apple of my family's eye, becoming an attorney. I'm the only one of my generation to leave the hills and go 'outside,' try for a brass ring other than becoming a wood carver making walnut bowls for the tourists, a farmer or coal miner."

"It's nice to see a man close to his family," Ellen said, folding her hands in her lap.

"I think what split my wife and I up was my long hours. Sometimes I wouldn't get home until midnight or later. Jodi got crossed-patched about spending evenings alone, and I tried to tell her that with my caseload, I couldn't just drop work and run home to her and Merry."

"You strike me as someone who cares deeply about his cases. You aren't about to do a sham job on one."

"That's right," he said grimly. "Jodi just wouldn't bend. I told her that when I made lieutenant commander rank, my load would ease and we'd have more time together."

"When do you get that rank?"

"I should be up for early consideration in about a

year, but I've been out of sorts and it's reduced my chances. In fact, going through this divorce could about put the last nail in my coffin—for good."

"You're not as hard or tough as you'd like people to think you are."

He glanced at her, a slight smile lurking at the corners of his mouth. "Keep it a secret, will you?"

Ellen smiled in return. "I will."

"You're still looking a little peaked. How's the stomach doing?"

"Still a bit upset. I keep thinking about Susan, about the awful shock it will be to her family."

"You had a right to feel that way," Cochrane said, pulling up to the Embassy Suites. He stopped the car at the entrance.

Ellen managed a weak smile and climbed out. "Thanks for the lift. I've got a rental car coming tomorrow morning and I'll have my own wheels."

"See you at 0800 hours."

She threw him a mock salute. "Yes, sir." What she wanted to do was throw her arms around him and thank him for his compassion. Seeing the smile in his eyes, that glint of humor, Ellen suddenly longed for Jim to stay. She'd like to spend time just talking and getting to know him better. After all, he'd salved her wounds at the condo. Maybe she could be a good friend to him in return.

CHAPTER FOUR

"MR. COCHRANE, come in for a minute," Commander Dornier called, waving from his office doorway.

Jim scowled inwardly but kept his expression neutral. It was 0750. The official start to his day was 0800. Things were on a fast track, it appeared. He changed his trajectory and headed to where his boss waited for him.

"This will only take a moment," Dornier said briskly, standing aside to allow him into the spacious office.

"Yes, sir?"

"This Lieutenant Kane investigation?"

"Yes, sir?"

"She's a media disaster just waiting to bite the Navy's ass, Mr. Cochrane, and that's worse than being a hot potato."

"Yes, sir."

"Do you know she was up for early lieutenant commander and rotation to the Pentagon for a cushy assignment? It's obvious she had a sponsor shadowing her career. Admiral Caruthers, Chief of Naval Operations, is *very* upset over her death. He wants answers now."

Didn't everyone? Cochrane nodded but didn't say that. "I'm on it, Commander."

If an officer was lucky enough to gain a sponsor—someone of higher rank who followed the junior officer's career and helped get plum assignments—it was like having an unofficial guardian angel. Not all officers had sponsors. And the junior officer never knew who his or her sponsor was. The benefits went only to promising officers who had a hell of a lot on the ball and the moxie and intelligence not to screw up when handed a rare opportunity to show their stuff. These officers got rewarded lavishly as a result, gaining early promotion or working with the powers that be—the admirals.

"Good. This could get nasty, Mr. Cochrane. You may dig up some shit that no one wants the sun to shine on. Be sure to interview the Top Gun people about Kane. They won't like it, but that's tough. I know you have other, less important cases to handle, but you're going to have to juggle them, regardless. How are you and Agent Tanner getting along?"

Jim paid strict attention, and if he didn't know better, he'd swear he saw curiosity in Commander Dornier's eyes. "Fine, sir. No problems at all."

"That's what I wanted to hear. Dismissed, Mr. Cochrane."

Cochrane left the office and headed past the large secretarial pool. He saw Ellen Tanner waiting for him in the passageway that lead to their office. It was exactly 0800. His heart pounded to underscore her presence in his life.

Her hair was wild as usual and she wore her characteristic bright clothing. Her loud crimson skirt, white short-sleeved blouse and red vest had him wincing internally. There was nothing remotely conservative about Ellen. Not to mention the dangly gold-and-red earrings made her look more like a gypsy fortune teller than an agent from OIG. However, her face was more set than usual, her eyes serious. Despite all of her contrasts something good and cleaned flowed through him. Cochrane nodded in Tanner's direction and murmured, "Good morning."

Ellen's heart sped up. "Good morning." Last night she'd realized she was attracted to this officer. There was a nice connection between them, even though their beginning yesterday had been awkward. Her reaction to him stymied her, and she was still too tired to examine it too closely. She followed Jim into the office.

"You get a good night's sleep?" he asked, motioning for her to sit down across from his desk.

"I did. But now you have dark circles under your eyes."

"Comes with the territory, Ms. Tanner," he told her teasingly. Lifting a file, he said, "I've been warned things could get real rough on our investigation of Kane. The possibility of an officer or officers from Top Gun being involved in this investigation is on the table. The aviation fraternity will close up tighter than a drum if they think they're being investigated. It's possible I'll make a lot of enemies of officers above me, and trust me, they won't forget. I'll be so dirty even the hogs won't associate with me. What a land-mine situation we're in."

Ellen folded her hands in her lap and said, "Do all officers have this level of paranoia about their careers or is this investigation unique?"

His mouth curved. "You'd better believe it. We live from one Fitness Report heaven or hell to the next, Ellen. Unlike you civilians, we survive in a cloistered environment where everyone knows everyone else. Fitreps are put out twice a year, and they can make or break your career. You're either in or you're out. Several bad fitness reports in a row and your dreams and goals are shattered. The handwriting's on the wall—you won't make the next rank, so resign your commission and get out. I like my job too much not to take this Kane situation seriously."

"I came across this same anxiety when I was doing my Project Demonstrating Excellence or P.D.E. on the Fortress," Ellen said. "The families in the service lived in as much fear as the father or mother did. Usually, the military member was the man. So I can relate to a degree with your concerns."

"It's not a very comforting situation," Cochrane agreed unhappily. Still, he felt good. Hell, if he had to choose a word to describe how he felt around Ellen, it was *happy.* An emotion he hadn't savored in two solid years.

"So what made you join the Navy, with such stress built into it?"

Cochrane sat up and placed his hands on his desk. Ellen's smile was kind and sincere, and he absorbed it hungrily. "I have a lot of pride in the Navy. It means something to me, in spite of its warts."

"What's to stop you from practicing law as a civilian?"

Shrugging, Jim said, "Nothing, I suppose. A company outside the military has all the problems that we do, but in the Navy it's... Hell's bells, I don't have all the answers." That soft smile was a trap, he realized. "See how easily you shrinks slip into your analyzing mode? Don't try and make a patient out of me." So what *did* he want her to be to him? Jim shifted uncomfortably, refusing to answer that question. At least, right now.

"I don't view you as my patient." Ellen opened her hands. "The way I see it, you're highly regarded around here, Jim."

He angled a glance at her. "Well, like the old Missouri saying goes, when you're lower than a snake's belly in a wheel rut, there ain't no place to go but up. This Kane case puts me dead in the gun sights of a certain group of jet jocks who could one day be over me in rank. And if I piss them off, they can get even at that time."

She laughed. "At least you've got a sense of humor. That's healthy."

He nodded. That sunny smile of hers went straight to his heart, wrapped around it, and his pulse took off like a freight train going downhill. "What about you? What's this gig going to earn for you when it's all over?" Ellen's smile slipped and he saw darkness come to her eyes. "Is this a year in hell for you? Or heaven personified?" Jim tried to keep his voice light and teasing, though his heart felt a twinge. Damn. He saw pain in her eyes.

Ellen tried to keep her voice even. "I really don't know yet. I looked forward to this change."

"What do you want out of it?" Jim pressed. There was confusion in Ellen's readable face. And she was blushing. He'd known a lot of weasels in his time, but she was artless. Having her around made him feel cleaner about the whole mess that had been piled on him, and he had no idea why.

"I want to know I did a good job." That was the truth, Ellen decided. There were lots of other responses she could give, but she didn't know if she could trust Jim with such personal details yet.

Cochrane shook his head. "You've got an innocent face just like Susan Kane did. What is it about some women that they look too vulnerable to make the grade?"

Ellen grinned. "I might look that way, but life goes on. All humans are vulnerable, not just certain women. I choose to remain open and not closed up. It's a choice."

With a groan, Cochrane stood up. "I reckon I'm not in a philosophical frame of mind." He gave her a quick smile. "Come on, we've got work to do. Best to leave unexploded land mines alone, I always say." There was still a lingering darkness in Ellen's glorious green eyes, and he wanted to discover why. His sixth sense told him getting too personal was a dangerous thing right now.

Feeling an unexpected warmth in her chest, Ellen decided that being with this JAG officer lifted her spirits. His soft Southern accent, those gray eyes that could turn from a warm look of concern to that of an eagle ready to swoop on a quarry, amazed her. "You mean, work on Susan's case?"

"Yes. Now there's an enigma. What do you think about Susan Kane?" he asked.

"You want my professional opinion?" Ellen rose and picked up her knapsack and briefcase.

"Yeah. I'm bugged by the fact she chose to die in her dress white uniform. If she committed suicide, I think it's some kind of symbolic last gesture, but darned if I know what it means."

Ellen followed him out the door. "White is seen as a sign of purity and innocence," she suggested, lengthening her stride to keep up with him.

"When the fleet sails into San Diego, I'll just bet the city fathers don't view all those horny sailors, dressed in their white liberty uniforms, as symbols of purity and innocence," Jim drawled, stopping at the desk to pick up the keys for their assigned car.

Laughing, Ellen said, "There are many ways to look at the color white, Mr. Cochrane. Susan could have chosen any set of clothes to die in, if it was suicide. Why dress whites, then? Why not her nightgown, or her favorite pair of sweats?"

"Come on, let's mosey over to our office pool car. We've got places to go."

As Cochrane put the car into gear and headed out into traffic, he glanced over at Ellen. "What else have you got up your therapist's sleeve about Kane?"

"I'm ignoring your sailor analogy, Mr. Cochrane," Ellen said, chuckling.

"I thought it was a pretty good remark."

She grinned. "So did I." Taking a deep breath, she got serious. "Maybe Susan really loved the Navy and put on her dress whites as a way to honor her career?"

"If her death was a suicide, usually it's done over a career screwup or some personal emotional disappointment," Cochrane conjectured. "I can't see her wearing her dress whites if that was the case. She'd be deeply shamed."

Ellen considered the possibilities. "Where are we going, anyway?"

"Back to Kane's condo."

"Ugh." She automatically pressed her hand against her abdomen.

"You're going pale on me," he warned.

"My stomach's rolling."

"The body's gone," he reassured her in a low voice.

"All we're going to do is snoop, see if anything else catches our interest. The police crime scene team is done with their work. I want to get in before the moving van arrives to cart off her things."

Ellen gulped unsteadily. "I'm glad Susan won't be there. I've been so upset by seeing her in that bed. I had awful dreams last night." Ellen touched the skin beneath her eyes. "I know I have circles here."

Driving in bright California sunshine made Cochrane squint. He pulled on a pair of aviator sunglasses. "I'm not surprised. The first time I saw a dead body at a scene, I ran for the bathroom and heaved my guts out, just like you. It's a pretty common response. No college class can prepare you for a corpse." Jim gave her an apologetic look. "And walking in and finding your husband dead, well, I felt real bad about that. If I'd known earlier, I wouldn't have put you in that position. Next time, speak up?"

"I didn't want you to think I was weak," Ellen said.

His mouth curved at one corner. "That's not bein' weak in my book."

"Thanks for letting me know."

"I also had a crazy dream about Kane last night."

Ellen raised her brows. "Really? Tell me about it."

Laughing, he said, "Spoken like a true shrink."

She realized he was teasing her. Maybe Cochrane was trying to make up for yesterday, and how tough it had been on her emotionally. "I'm curious, that's all. I know why I had those terrible, fragmented nightmares last night. I was traumatized by seeing another dead person."

"It must be rough," Cochrane agreed, glancing over at her. He lowered his voice. "You said it happened two years ago?"

Ellen avoided his glance and looked down at her tightly clasped hands. Her voice grew strained. "Yes. I'm still processing a lot of grief. I miss Mark. I miss our talks, the way he saw the world. He was a wonderful person. One of the best."

"You were lucky to have a marriage like that."

Ellen whispered, "I was." She glanced out the window and watched the palm trees and houses flash by. "The sunlight is comforting. I feel like Persephone from the Greek myths, pining away for spring on Earth. I've been feeling so cold inside."

And then she saw Jim lift his long, large-knuckled hand and place it on hers. His touch was butterfly light, his gesture completely unexpected.

"Real love's hard to find. Harder to keep. I'm sorry." Lifting his hand away, he quickly replaced it on the wheel. Jim knew he shouldn't have done that, but there was something so touching about Ellen in that moment he'd done it without thinking.

Biting her lower lip, Ellen gave a soft sigh. Jim's gesture had been exactly what she needed. How had he known? She found herself wanting him to touch her in just such a way again. "You remind me of a knight on a white horse, a crusader. Maybe a throwback to an earlier time."

"Don't go putting me on pedestals, Ms. Tanner. I fall off real easy. Deep down, I see myself as a knight tilting at the windmills of injustice and trying to right wrongs when I can."

"Don't pay any attention to me. I'm an emotional puddle right now."

"I've been there once or twice myself," he assured her in a husky tone. "We all get splattered with mud. Thanks for the compliment about the knight and all. I read all of King Arthur's books growing up, so chivalry is important to me. It's nice to be thought of in such glowing terms."

"You're pretty readable, Mr. Cochrane. Now, are you going to tell me your dream about Susan Kane?"

"Nothing much to tell," he said. "She came up to me in a dream and asked me for my help. After she left, I woke up."

"How did you feel during the dream?"

He grinned. "I can feel you stalking me like a coonhound on a scent trail, Ellen."

She smiled slightly. "Dreams are very important. More important than most people realize."

"I see. Well, I felt real emotional when I saw Susan. She was still in her uniform. I was standing in the middle of nowhere and she came out of the mist and light. She had blue eyes."

"And?" Ellen heard Cochrane's voice go softer, and the line of his mouth was no longer as tight.

"She had tears in them. That shook me for some

reason, but then, I can't stand to see a child or woman cry, anyway. Susan held out her hand toward me and seemed to speak, but no sound came out of her mouth. I asked her what she wanted and she handed me her teddy bear." He made a wry face. "There was something unnerving about that bear. Then I realized the bear had no eyes. The one taken for evidence from her condo had large, shiny black button eyes. But the one in my dream didn't."

He turned off on the Spring Street ramp and slowed the vehicle. "What do you think?"

"I feel it's very significant she gave you her teddy bear and it had no eyes. The bear obviously means a lot to Susan, and for her to give it to you meant she was trusting you to help her. The fact that you took the bear meant you would help her. The bear having no eyes fascinates me." Excitedly, she turned to him. "Eyes are to see with. She gave you a bear with no eyes. What aren't you seeing about her death? Did we overlook something? What didn't we see clearly? Or not at all?"

Cochrane shrugged. "Beats me." He sighed. "What would a blind teddy bear mean?"

"Maybe we need to delve more deeply into her childhood. A bear also symbolizes healing. The Native Americans put great stock in bear medicine as being the most powerful healer of all. By Susan giving you her bear, she was asking you to heal her, or perhaps, her situation."

"I think you're drawing entirely too many fanciful

conclusions out of my dream. It was probably caused by the anchovies I had on my pizza last night." He turned onto the street that would lead them to the condominiums.

Ellen laughed huskily. "I feel there's a special tie between you and Susan. You didn't seem at all affected by anything yesterday," she observed, watching his expression closely.

"I was feeling a lot, I just didn't show it."

"Oh? Like what?"

Cochrane guided the gray Ford Taurus into the parking lot of Susan's condominium and shut off the engine. "For some stupid reason, Kane's case has grabbed me by the throat. I don't know why." He reached into the rear seat for his briefcase, pulled it forward and settled it on his lap. He dropped the car keys into it and took out a door key for the condo. "Maybe because Susan reminds me of my daughter. I don't know."

Ellen climbed out and caught up with Cochrane on the sidewalk, near some large, shiny-leafed hibiscus bushes with red, pink and white blossoms. She realized Cochrane trusted her with that highly personal tidbit of information. "Your daughter has a teddy bear, too?"

He smiled fondly. "Yeah, a cute little Winnie the Pooh bear I bought her. I couldn't be there for her birth. As soon as I put the bear in Merry's tiny little hands, she grabbed onto it." His voice lowered with feeling. "I just stood there and cried because she was so perfect. So beautiful. And that bear's been Merry's security blanky ever since."

Ellen gave him a soft look. "How special. That bear's a real bond between you and her."

"My ex-wife used to tell me that when I had to leave, Merry would clutch that bear like it was her life. And when I would come off TDY, temporary duty assignment, and return home, she'd put the bear back on her bed and sleep with it at night, like she usually does when I'm around."

"Mmm," Ellen murmured. "Bear and Daddy are one in the same, then. She equates the bear with you and feeling safe." They mounted the stairs to the condo.

He arched one eyebrow as he fished for the condo keys in his pocket. "More psychobabble from the shrink?"

She grinned. The glint in his eyes conveyed kindness, not nastiness. "It's excellent information, Mr. Cochrane."

"Merry doesn't like it when I'm not at home, but now, well, I reckon she's used to it since the split-up."

Ellen heard his voice sink at the last admission. Gently, she steered the conversation to something less painful. "Do you have any feel for a bear without eyes and what it means?"

"I'm plumb in the dark about it," he said, shoving the door open. "How about you? What would a shrink say?"

"A bear could also symbolize one's primal survival, too. Perhaps no eyes meant she couldn't see any way to continue to survive."

Cochrane walked into the condo and stepped aside to allow Ellen to enter. "Interesting theories."

She followed him into the quiet, cool condominium. "If Susan couldn't survive something, she may have taken her life."

Cochrane shut the door and placed his briefcase next to the couch. Straightening, he slowly looked around the living room. "I don't know. The autopsy may or may not tell us if it was a murder, as we've said. The police called me early this morning and verified Kane's prints on the prescription bottle. Let's nose around, shall we?"

"What are we looking for this time?" Ellen was glad Cochrane had finally said "we." It meant he was accepting her as his partner. That made her feel relief. And hope.

"Anything. Everything. I guess I'm trying to look for clues that would tell us what brought her to this point in her life." He handed Ellen a pair of latex gloves.

She nodded. "I can work on the living room if you want to take another room?"

"No, we'll do this together. We can use it as a good training opportunity."

Ellen nodded in approval. They started with the side table, which contained two drawers. Jim leaned down and opened them. One contained several files.

"Here, you take care of these," he said.

She had put on her latex gloves and now carefully pulled out the folders. "They look like seminar or conference files to me. They're all dated this year. This last one is from the Ares Conference in May. It was a defense seminar. Should we take them?" she asked.

"Yes. We might be interested in Kane's comings and goings these last couple of months. And who went with her." He unfolded an evidence collection bag and handed it to her. "Put them in there and mark what it is on the label. We'll take them back to the office and, when we get time, check them out."

Ellen tucked the files into the paper bag and set them aside. The bookcase along the wall was next.

"Look at these titles," she said, gesturing. "All leather-bound books."

"Leather is a rarity today," Cochrane agreed. "And they're all classic literature. Not to mention valuable."

Ellen pulled out *Don Quixote,* a dark burgundy, leather-bound book with gold lettering. She cradled it in her left hand and gently flipped through the pages. "She's underlined some of the passages."

"A technique from her academic days. You know how we had to underline stuff in school," Cochrane said.

Ellen put the book aside and opened another. "My books are highlighted in blue, yellow and pink." She smiled. Opening about a dozen books in turn, she carefully went through them. "There's no underlining in these. Nothing," she reported, looking over at Cochrane, who was going through the other bookcase book by book.

"None?"

"None."

He frowned and picked up *Don Quixote* again. "What do you make of that?"

"Maybe she felt like Don Quixote? All he did was tilt at windmills and generally make a fool of himself. Everyone laughed at him and called him crazy."

"Sounds like how I feel sometimes," Cochrane said wryly, sitting down on an overstuffed chair and thumbing through the book. Frowning, he looked up at her and said, "He had a companion."

"Sancho Panza."

"Exactly." Jim held Ellen's gaze. "Did Susan have a buddy? A good friend, I wonder? The 911 caller? Was it a relationship gone bad?"

"A lover?"

"Possibly. Reckon I'd give my right arm to know who the caller was on that 911 tape. Detective Gardella said no one who lived in that area saw a woman at the phone booth outside the store. Tomorrow we have to go over to personnel, get Kane's records and set up squadron interviews regarding her death. Maybe that will turn up a clue."

Ellen sat down near Cochrane. "Isn't it interesting that this is the only book so far to have passages underlined? Who were her windmills? Her enemies?"

"What little I remember of the story," Jim said, "is that Don Quixote was an idealist who romanticized his world. He never saw people or situations exactly as they were."

"He was out of touch with reality," Ellen agreed. "I wonder if Susan felt she was out of touch with reality. And who was making fun of or shaming her?"

"Whatever her reality was. Reckon we don't even know that at this point."

"True," Ellen said, rising and going back to the bookshelf to continue the search. "Do you think Susan's personnel record will tell us more?"

"Not likely, but we can hope. We'll have to start interviewing people who knew her. That way, we can begin to get a fix on who and what she was."

"I think we should hold *Don Quixote* as evidence, Jim. If you want, I'll go over each of those passages she underlined this afternoon. Maybe there's a clue there."

"Good thinking. Who knows? Maybe you're going to make a better investigator than I originally thought."

She had called him by his first name for the first time. It was a huge step toward intimacy. Ellen watched his expression for a reaction. His gray eyes had grown warm when she'd spoken his name. Her heart responded by melting, and heat spread throughout her chest. Ellen felt good about taking another barrier down between them. Hope flared within her, sweet and full of promise.

CHAPTER FIVE

June 24

"ANOTHER BEAUTIFUL DAY in paradise," Ellen sighed as she got out of the government car. It was already Thursday, and the week was flying by. Every day she looked forward to working with Jim. Her world of gray was now shimmering with color. Ellen felt the shift in her heart and soul. Hope was burning steady and strong, and it caught her completely by surprise.

"You're an idealist, Ellen." Cochrane gave her a jaded look.

"To a fault," she admitted wryly. "I don't like the alternative." As they walked toward a group of buildings situated on USNAS Giddings, Ellen heard and recognized two Super Hornet combat aircraft in the distance, preparing for takeoff. She had boned up on all things Navy when she was told of the coming assignment. The howl of thunder rolled across the station. She turned and stared toward the flight line. The entire Navy station seem to rumble and vibrate from the earsplitting growls as the jets hurtled down the runway and leaped into the air.

Jim couldn't help but smile. He wanted to make Ellen feel a part of the investigation. "Today we're the Jim and Ellen team. Red hair. You know, red-haired women have always been hellions of the first order." Giving her a sideward glance, he added, "And with your red hair being curly as all get-out, I think you're right about needing to work in a loose social structure. The military isn't your cup of tea."

Laughter bubbled up in Ellen as she noted his gleeful expression. Absorbing his unabashed smile and the teasing glint in his eyes, she felt the darkness continue to dissolve. "Thank you for having pity on us red-haired hellions, Jim. I'm deeply grateful." And she was. Any lessening of tension between them was another step in the right direction, as far as she was concerned.

Cochrane cradled her elbow and guided her into the building. "Don't tell me you're going to get hornswoggled by that display of raw naval aviation power and become a jet jock groupie?" Reluctantly, he released her as they entered the Top Gun facility. Much to his consternation, Jim discovered that touching Ellen was a need in him. He was fighting an attraction to her, pure and simple.

"Give me a break, will you?" She walked at his side through the door toward administration. Her skin tingled where he'd cupped her elbow. How she looked forward to these unexpected moments of contact. "They're human beings like us—no more and no less. They aren't little tin gods in my book of life."

Just inside the polished passageway, Cochrane halted. "Good to hear that. Listen, you mosey down to personnel, identify yourself and ask for Lieutenant Kane's file. Oh, and arrange to pick up files on these Top Gun personnel, as well." He handed her a list that contained twelve names. "Susan Kane went to the Ares Conference with two other women—Lieutenants Jillson and Hawkins. They work here at Ops. You can get those files now. We'll pick the others tomorrow morning. With Captain Allison wanting the ball rolling on this case, we have to move a lot faster than usual."

Ellen nodded. "Okay. Where are you going?"

Cochrane opened the door. "I'm gonna amble over and make an appointment with Captain Warren Oliver. He's the C.O. of Top Gun. I reckon I'd better clear the forthcoming interviews with his staff through him. I'll be back." He glanced at his watch. "Should take about ten or fifteen minutes, and we'll meet at the car. Late tomorrow morning we'll come back over to Ops and start the interviews."

"Ops?"

"Slang for Operations. Can you stand being without me that long?"

Ellen tilted her head. "Uh-oh. Let down some of the social structure and you're a big tease, Lieutenant." She saw him smile broadly. He was incredibly handsome in a devil-may-care way when he smiled. Being teased felt good, too. It meant that Jim was accepting their relationship. And if Ellen wasn't wrong, she saw a hint of something else in his gray eyes, though she wasn't sure what. "You'll meet me at the car?"

"It's a date." Cochrane turned and headed down the hall, his beat-up briefcase in his left hand.

A date? Stunned by his choice of words, Ellen stared at his back as he walked confidently away from her. Jim was a lawyer and used to finessing people with the right words. "Date" was not an accident, Ellen decided as she turned on her heel and walked in the opposite direction.

She found her way to a large office that had Personnel above the door frame. She was eager to get this case started.

June 25

THE OPERATIONS COMPLEX housed the meteorology division, air control operations and Top Gun facility classrooms. Cochrane and Tanner entered through the main double doors. The floors—or "decks," Jim told her— were laid with light green tiles, which glowed from a daily waxing job by some enlisted person low on the totem pole. The stairs leading to the air control tower rose to the left.

Ellen followed as Cochrane sauntered down a busy passageway where Navy pilots dressed in dark olive-green or bright orange flight suits jostled past. Class must have just let out. They gave the "foreigners" the once-over as if they were aliens from another planet. Ellen felt their disdain, arrogance and curiosity.

"In here," Cochrane said, motioning to an empty of-

fice. "I got permission from Captain Warren yesterday
to use this room." Once Ellen entered, he quietly closed
the door. "We can interview the captain at 1100. It's a
mere formality, but it has to be done. When you are going to interview an entire group beneath its C.O., he or
she goes through the same process even if not a suspect.
Until the captain arrives, let's start going over their personnel files, getting specifics typed into our laptop
spreadsheet."

Ellen took a seat at a long table and removed the files
from her briefcase. "Last night I was looking over the
possible list of people we should interview based on the
files we collected as evidence from Susan's condo." She
glanced across the table at Cochrane, who sat down and
took off his garrison cap. "At first I didn't think those
files in her drawer would be important. Goes to show
you what I don't know." She grinned. "We got some
names out of them right away."

"Good going. You're not a talking head after all,"
Cochrane said. "You're doing just fine, Ellen." He set
a copy of Kane's file before him. And yet he had trouble focusing on the case. Ellen looked so beautiful—
wild, colorful and so out of place in his uniformed world
of order and discipline. His heart pounded in response
to the soft smile she gave him. After two years of utter
darkness in his life, she was a beam of light to him, a
way out of the pit he'd lived in for so long. She was
something special, and he tussled inwardly with that
knowledge.

"I can help you schedule them." Ellen brightened beneath the look of pride he gave her. It felt damn good to be appreciated by a man once more.

"That's fine. Jillson and Hawkins are first on our interview list. The commanding officer of station operations also gave me permission to schedule interviews directly with the individuals concerned. He just asked us to respect their duty requirements."

"That's good news, too."

"Reckon it is. Why don't you go out to the Ops desk and try and set up interviews with Hawkins and Jillson? This afternoon, if possible."

She got up. "Do you think I'm going to be given a hard time again, as I was over at personnel?" The officer in charge there hadn't been enthusiastic about giving her all the files, but in the end he had.

Cochrane looked up and grinned. "Wearing those rainbow-child clothes isn't going to help you."

She scowled. "Just because I don't look official doesn't mean anything, Mr. Cochrane."

His smile widened and he went back to perusing Kane's file. "Maybe if you wore a conservative suit, you might not get such stray voltage from us rigid, disciplined military types...."

"Not a chance. They either take me as I am or tough noogies."

Her eyes sparkled. She truly was a wild child, Jim mused. And alluring in her own unique way. Why, he'd even woken up this morning looking forward to going to work—because he knew Ellen would be there. He chuckled. "I was wondering where your temper would show up."

About to exit, with her hand around the brass door-knob, Ellen turned and gave him a quick wink.

When she left, the room fell quiet and Cochrane continued to chuckle. So the red-haired mouse wasn't passive or sedate, after all. Of course, those colorful clothes were an indicator that Ellen was a headstrong individual. He liked discovering her different qualities. She had fire, spirit, plus she wasn't afraid to meet him toe-to-toe.

And he liked what he saw a lot more than he should.

ELLEN CAME BACK twenty minutes later, flushed and triumphant. Cochrane set Kane's record aside as she sat down with a notebook in her hands.

"We're in luck! Lieutenant Hawkins is a meteorologist and she's on duty at the weather desk right now. Lieutenant Jillson is an air controller and she's due to come off duty at 1500. I've set up interviews with both."

"Good work." It took an effort to tear his gaze from her as she ran her fingers through those red curls.

"What did you find out about Susan?" Ellen pointed to the personnel record in his hands. The heated look Jim gave her made her melt inwardly, but she didn't have time to sort it out. They were under such pressure to get this case solved.

"Pretty much what I expected. She's got 4.0s on her

Fitreps, all glowing reports on leadership skills and abilities. She's had all kinds of recommendations, from Annapolis up to and including her present duty station." He tapped the file thoughtfully.

"Is that important?"

"To get early anything is indicative that she had a sponsor—someone of much higher rank who was watching her career very carefully. Whoever it was might have orchestrated her career to a degree, giving her the opportunity to climb the ladder of success sooner rather than later, as we discussed before. In fact, Commander Dornier indicated that the CNO himself was inquiring about Susan's death. To sum it up, Ellen, Lieutenant Kane was bright, aggressive and had the world by the tail. And a whole passel of people are shore interested in the outcome of our investigation. No doubt about it. That spells SPONSOR in capital letters."

Clasping her hands, Ellen said, "Let's say the autopsy declares her death a suicide. I don't think it's out of line to suggest a monumental failure might have driven a perfectionist like Susan to such a drastic act."

"Since I'm not a perfectionist or obsessive, I reckon I wouldn't kill myself just because I failed a test or didn't make early rank," Cochrane retorted dryly.

"But you're not Susan."

"The hole in your theory is that Kane never failed." He handed her the file. "Take a look. She had a straight 4.0 at Annapolis, at Pensacola—at anything she did. This woman didn't know *how* to fail."

"My point exactly, Mr. Cochrane," Ellen said primly as she opened the file. "Once they get in the rut of success, people like Susan don't know how to fail. Certainly not gracefully."

"Your shrink theories are just that." Jim said it teasingly, though her green eyes narrowed on him, her lips pursed. He wondered what it would be like to kiss those lips.

"You're really opinionated. You know that, Mr. Cochrane?" She met his grin and was amused by the fact that her partner was blushing. Yes, there was something terribly vulnerable and appealing about him.

"Like a Missouri mule. Thank you, Ellen." Feeling the heat in his face, he avoided her dancing green gaze.

"You're not welcome, Jim."

He glanced at his watch and then up at her. Ellen was doing her best to suppress her smile, which compelled him to get back to business. "I reckon it's time to interview the C.O. Let's saddle up."

ELLEN WAITED UNTIL THEY were headed toward the parking lot before she spoke about the interview with the commanding officer. They were going to catch a late lunch over at the Officers' Club, then come back to interview Hawkins and Jillson. "I would hope that all our interviews with the Top Gun people aren't like this last one. What a bust!"

Cochrane laughed. "Get used to it, Ellen. Why should Oliver open up to us? For all we know, everyone may have hated Susan Kane, but the captain isn't going to tell us that. If he did, it would reflect poorly on his leadership abilities. Did you see him almost come out of his chair when you suggested sexual harassment?"

"Boy, did I. Everyone is post-Tailhook PC, aren't they?"

"You'd better believe it. And now the Air Force Academy is handling its own rape scandal among the cadets. No sirree Bob, sexual harassment toward women in the military is not a dead issue at all."

"The 2003 Air Force rape scandal is a grim reminder that women in the military are still threatened," Ellen said in a pained voice. "Still, it was obvious the captain sincerely believed in Susan and her extraordinary abilities." She climbed into the car. "I hope Hawkins and Jillson are a little more forthcoming."

Cochrane drove out of the parking lot. "Captain Oliver was being politically correct—say nothing bad about anyone. That's the big windy, you know? Shit happens all the time on this station, but you'll never hear of it or see it in the newspaper. The Navy, like any other service or corporation, has airtight compartments on disasters. They know how to keep everyone in line. If people speak out, their career is finished. That's a pretty heavy threat, Ellen, and it works very well in most cases."

"This is like a Dark Ages code of silence. I mean, Captain Oliver didn't give us anything at all."

"The Captain gave us information that couldn't hurt him or his career. My bet is that all the pilots we interview are going to pull the 'hear no evil, see no evil, speak no evil' response."

"If Captain Oliver is typical, we're in trouble before we even start."

"Reckon I've heard that before," Cochrane drawled as he pulled into the parking lot of the Officers' Club. "And yet, I like figuring out puzzles, Ellen. Come on, let's go eat. I'm a starving cow brute."

"Cow brute?"

He grinned as they walked toward the entrance of the O Club. "Ozarks lingo for a bull."

LIEUTENANT ANN HAWKINS, one of Susan Kane's companions on the last night she was alive, wiped her palms on her uniform skirt as she stepped inside the office.

"Come on in," Cochrane invited with a friendly drawl.

The woman nodded. "I'm Lieutenant Hawkins."

"Lieutenant Cochrane," he said, standing and shaking her hand. "This is my partner, Agent Ellen Tanner from OIG. Have a seat and we'll get started."

Shutting the door, Ann sat down in front of the desk, while they sat opposite. "This is about Susan Kane's death, isn't it?"

"That's right," Cochrane said.

"How did Susan die? Did someone hurt her? Was it murder?"

Jim saw the raw grief, the shock in Hawkins's reddened eyes. "We don't know yet, Lieutenant. That's what we're trying to find out right now."

"We heard about it from Captain Oliver the day it happened. I just can't believe it."

"Lieutenant, I have to run through some legal matters with you in regards to this investigation of Lieutenant Kane's death."

Ann wiped tears from her eyes. "I—I'm sorry," she murmured, digging for a tissue from her pocket.

"That's okay, Lieutenant. Take your time. Had you any contact with Lieutenant Kane on the day preceding her death, June 21st?"

"No, I was off duty and away from home the entire day."

"No contact of any type on the day in question or in the early morning hours of the following day, June 22nd?" Jim repeated.

"None."

"What can you tell us about Susan, Lieutenant Hawkins?"

Sniffing, Ann whispered, "She was my best friend. My very best friend."

"How long had you known her?"

"We met back at Pensacola years ago."

"Tell us about your relationship," Ellen Tanner urged gently. She glanced at Jim as if to get his silent approval to ask questions. He nodded in response. Heartened by his support, she returned her attention to Hawkins.

Ann sniffed and blotted her eyes again. "Susan wasn't the kind to complain. She didn't confide in many people, but she trusted me for some reason. I don't know why. You see, Susan always knew she was being watched."

"Watched?" Ellen asked. In a way, this felt like a therapy session between her and a patient. Interviewing wasn't so different or difficult. She felt a swell of quiet confidence over that realization.

"Yes, the male pilots watched her because she was a woman. Susan knew she had to do everything better than a man in order to be accepted and get passing grades. She was so smart. Susan always achieved 4.0s in whatever she undertook. She was a role model for all women who tried to follow in her footsteps."

"Did she date or socialize with any officer here on the station?"

"Not that I know of. She used what little spare time she had to volunteer. If a group of school kids came to tour our facility, Susan was always the first to volunteer and talk to them, to take time out of her schedule to accommodate them. She also volunteered at the San Diego Zoo."

"I see. What can you tell us about Susan Kane's lifestyle?" In her gut, Ellen felt this information was important, but her partner looked bored. As a psychologist, she knew that family dynamics set a person up for life. This was her bread and butter. If she was going to become a good investigator, she had to use the tools and skills she had at her disposal.

"You mean her family?" Ann's mouth pulled downward. "Her father, Robert Kane, is a retired Navy captain. He put in twenty-four years and was a fighter pilot. Since he retired, Susan told me, he's made a fortune in the stock market. She has two brothers. Brad Kane is a lieutenant commander and Tommy Kane is a lieutenant. They're both Super Hornet pilots serving aboard different carriers."

"So it's a Navy family," Ellen said. "The father was a pilot and all three children followed in his footsteps. What about Susan's mother? Do you know much about her?"

"It's sad, to tell you the truth. Her real mother, Rachel Kane, died giving birth to Susan. Her father remarried six months later."

"Six months?" Ellen blurted.

Ann nodded. "I think it was a marriage of convenience. As a Navy pilot, Robert Kane was out at sea six to sixteen months at a stretch. He either had to marry the first woman who came along to take care of his three children, farm them out to relatives, or give up his career and raise the kids by himself."

"Isn't that a pretty harsh judgment of him?" Cochrane inquired, hearing the anger and tightness in Hawkins's voice.

"Susan told me many times that her father was the ultimate Navy pilot. He was an ace in the closing days of the Vietnam War and made his one hundred missions. At the time of her mother's death, he wasn't there, which can be typical for pilots who are deployed on a carrier in the middle of some ocean. From the Navy's perspective, Kane's mission was far more important than the mere birth of a child."

"How awful for Susan," Ellen murmured.

"It was," Ann whispered, wiping her eyes. "Her stepmother, Georgia Huntington, was a Southern socialite. Susan grew up learning politics from her stepmother. Georgia caught on to Navy politics real fast. And she was the consummate Navy wife to Robert."

"How did Georgia get along with his children?" Ellen wondered.

"She got along well with the boys. She was indifferent to Susan. All three children grew up in Robert Kane's shadow. Frankly, I don't think either Georgia or Robert particularly liked having children."

"Did Georgia see Susan as competition?" Ellen asked.

With a sigh, Ann said, "Let me put it this way—Robert Kane hated his daughter."

"Why?" Cochrane asked. "It's not uncommon for a Navy father to be away on deployments. Being removed from the family wouldn't mean he hated his children."

Ann turned to him. "It's pretty simple, really. Susan killed his wife, the woman he loved. He never forgave her for that."

"I'm confused," Ellen interrupted. "How did Susan kill her mother?"

"Rachel Kane was thirty-two years old when she got pregnant with Susan." Ann wiped her eyes. "She was young and healthy and yet she died during her daughter's delivery. Robert held Susan responsible."

"He shouldn't have blamed her for something she couldn't control," Ellen responded.

"Worse yet, one of Susan's brothers accepted his father's logic."

"How do you know that?" Cochrane asked pointedly.

"Because Susan told me. After many years of friendship, she let out a little bit here and there about her family. I remember one day I finally got her to go over to La Jolla for a break. The beach became her favorite place, you know. She loved the ocean. That day, Susan was really depressed, and I couldn't get out of her what was wrong. We picked up some fast food from a restaurant and took a blanket and a bottle of wine along. As the sun set on the ocean, Susan began to talk about her life, her family."

Ann took a shaky breath. "When we returned from the beach, the subject was closed and never brought up again, no matter how I tried to approach her." She gazed at them, no longer trying to stop the tears from falling. "Susan was a pariah, an outcast, in her own family. The only one who stayed in touch with her was Tommy, the younger brother."

"How awful for Susan," Ellen murmured.

"Yes," Ann said, her voice off-key. "It was unfair. Susan had done nothing to earn her father and older brother's anger and hatred. But I'll tell you something—Susan paid for her mother's death in so many ways that it made me sick. I—I don't know if I'll be able to restrain myself from decking both Robert and Brad Kane at Susan's funeral." She grimaced. "They may not show up. It wouldn't surprise me if they didn't. I'm sure Tommy will be there, and I know Susan's other friends will come to tell her goodbye."

"What about Susan's stepmother, Georgia?" Ellen asked.

"Georgia died some time ago," Ann said bitterly. "Susan was at Pensacola. She got a call from her father telling her she didn't have to come home for the funeral."

Ellen gasped. "How terrible!"

Ann studied the investigator for a moment. "Maybe, but Susan went anyway—out of duty. She had a very strict and high code of honor and ethics. She did the right thing, regardless of how some family members felt. Susan was the most courageous person I've ever met. But a person can only take so much hurt, for so long."

"Susan served as the family scapegoat," Ellen suggested. She saw Ann's eyes flash with anger. *Bingo!* Excited, Ellen felt she had a much better understanding of Susan. And Jim's nod of approval made her heart soar.

"You hit the nail on the head. Susan paid for every transgression that ever went down in that family."

"Did Susan's father verbalize those things to her?" Ellen inquired as she rubbed her forehead.

"Many times. Susan was continually reminded of it when her dad was rotated back to a station from carrier duty. When it was her real mother's birthday, her father always got drunk, and when Robert Kane was drunk, he got mean."

"It sounds as though Robert continued to love Rachel very much," Ellen ventured.

"I'm sure he did," Ann said, bitterness tingeing her voice. "For eighteen years Susan endured her dead mother's birthday and the drunken rages of her father."

Ellen said sympathetically, "How unfair."

"Other than Tommy, her grandmother Inez was the only close family member who didn't hold her responsible for her mother's death. She felt the tragedy was an act of God and that no rational person could ever blame a child. When her grandmother died four years ago, she left Susan the bulk of her estate—probably close to a million dollars."

"That's why she could afford that expensive condo," Ellen said, giving Cochrane a telling look.

Jim raised his eyebrows in acknowledgment.

"She didn't need the Navy for financial reasons. Susan was out to prove she was the best." Ann shrugged. "A lesser person would have buckled under, given that kind of family pressure, but she didn't." Lieutenant Hawkins stared defiantly at Cochrane. "Susan was a very strong woman. A good person who did right by others regardless of how they dealt with her. Susan didn't have enemies, only people who were jealous, envious or competitive toward her."

Cochrane nodded. "I see. Reckon you've given us some good background information, Lieutenant Hawkins." He handed her his business card. "If you think of anything else that might help in solving this case, give me a call?"

Ann glanced at the card. "Yes, I will." She took a deep breath. "Susan's funeral is set for Monday afternoon. From what the station chaplain said, she's going to be buried over at La Jolla. Susan would like that. Are you going to be there?"

Cochrane nodded and rose. "You can probably count on her funeral going down at that time. The M.E. is just about done with his findings. And yes, we'll be at her funeral."

Grimly, Ann stood up and smoothed her skirt, slipping the business card in her pocket. "Do me a favor, then?"

"What?"

"Check out Robert and Brad Kane if they show up. They're a real set of bookends. I've never met them personally, but it'll be interesting to see if they mourn her death. I doubt they will." She gave the investigators a stony look and exited.

CHAPTER SIX

ELLEN'S HEART TUGGED at the sight of the coffin. She stood with Cochrane, removed from the group somberly gathered at the sun-washed grave site. Susan Kane's funeral was over and approximately forty people, including the three Kane men, were dispersing.

"Who's first to be interviewed, Jim?" she added, sidling a glance at her partner.

"Lieutenant Commander Brad Kane. Come on, let's mosey."

On the way over to the Marriott Hotel Cochrane glanced at her. "For a hound hunting for a scent, you're awfully quiet," he observed. He'd seen the stress at the corners of her soft, full mouth.

"Funerals don't do a whole lot for me," she answered in a low voice.

"I understand." He frowned and gave her an apologetic look. Ellen was obviously struggling with emotions. "You okay?" Without thinking, he reached over and squeezed her shoulder. He tried to tell himself he'd done it out of sympathy. It was that—and more. Being around Ellen was rapidly dismantling every wall he'd erected after the divorce. He released her shoulder.

"As okay as I can be." Her skin radiated heat where he'd made contact with her. "What's this, Mr. Cochrane? A little care? A little humanity?"

"Didn't think I had any in these nasty bones of mine, did you?" He said it in jest to lift her sagging spirits. Jim found himself wanting to make Ellen smile.

She folded her hands on her light blue cotton skirt. "You've got a lot of hard edges, Jim, but I know you mean well."

"I've earned every one of 'em. They're bought and paid for."

She studied his profile briefly. "You have a gruff facade, but underneath are feelings and a conscience. You just hide them well." Looking at the grassy lawns and pastel stucco homes they passed, Ellen said, "I feel like I knew Susan Kane. I cried for her. She was a nice person and her death seems like such a waste."

"Dying's always a waste."

"Were you touched by the service?"

"Funerals are for the living, not the dead."

"Always the cynic, Mr. Cochrane." Ellen shook her head.

"On some things, I am. Let's focus on these interviews, shall we? That could turn up some answers on why Susan is dead."

COCHRANE KNOCKED ON THE hotel room door, and in a few moments, Lieutenant Commander Brad Kane greeted him.

"Yes?" The man demanded in a deep, impatient voice. He possessed the same square jaw as the elder Kane, his black brows straight and thick across pale blue eyes. There was an aloof quality to Brad, but then, a lot of carrier pilots thought they were special.

Cochrane held his credentials in front of the officer. "I'm Lieutenant Cochrane and this is Agent Tanner. May we come in?"

Kane stepped aside only after he'd raked them with a glare. "You're coming in whether I want you to or not."

"We could do this at another time, if this isn't convenient," Cochrane offered.

"No. Let's get this the hell over with."

Cochrane heard the tension and bitterness in Brad's voice as he checked out the hotel room. A small duffel bag sat on the neatly made bed. An acrid odor permeated the room, and he saw a smoking cigar balanced across a drinking glass on the table. Brad Kane didn't seem to care that this was a nonsmoking room.

Kane stood stiffly by the door after he closed it, surveying them as if they were enemies. Cochrane supposed they were, in one sense. The officer was about six feet tall, physically fit, and Cochrane guessed that most women would find him heart-stoppingly handsome, with those frosty blue eyes, strong nose and imperious mouth—the picture-poster image of the Naval aviator ideal.

"Let's make this short, Lieutenant. I've got a hop to catch."

"I know," Cochrane said, pulling out a set of papers. He'd seen Kane's fingers tremble briefly on the cigar, but that wasn't unusual. Landing a multimillion dollar machine on a carrier deck made a lot of pilots' hands shake.

Jim sat down at the table and spread the papers out before him. When he put the small tape recorder between them and glanced up, he saw Kane's icy look change to a laserlike glare.

"Is that necessary?" Kane demanded.

"I'm afraid it is, Commander. We don't pretend to rely on our memories."

"Let's just get this over with then."

Cochrane remained unruffled as the aviator spun around and stalked toward the door. For a man who had just lost his sister, Brad wasn't exactly the epitome of grief-stricken. Ellen sat down to take notes and observe his questioning technique of Kane.

"When was the last time you were in contact with your sister, Commander?"

"Telephone, letter or in person?"

"Doesn't matter. Any or all of the above." Cochrane held the officer's pointed, angry look.

With an exasperated sound, Brad jammed the cigar into the corner of his mouth and settled his hands tensely on his hips. "It was a long time ago, Lieutenant Cochrane. I don't remember exactly when."

Cochrane held on to his anger. The aviator was purposefully being vague, but Jim had experienced this tactic during many investigations. "Commander, can you be more specific as to what type of contact you had most recently with Susan?"

Puffing strongly on the cigar, so more clouds of smoke drifted around his head, Kane snarled, "A letter from her, I guess. Maybe six months ago."

"Do you still have the letter?" Cochrane inquired smoothly.

"Hell no! I live out on a carrier, mister. Even you shore huggers know there's no room on board for many personal effects."

Cochrane remained impervious to the man's agitation. "Do you remember the contents of the letter?"

"Of course not! Six months is a damn long time in my business."

Ellen coughed, stood up and went to stand next to the window. With her fingers against her throat, she said, "Commander, do you remember the tone of Susan's letter?"

His thin lips clamped the cigar. "No. Just what the hell does this have to do with her dying?"

"We're trying to find out the circumstances of your sister's death," Ellen said more firmly, then coughed again. "And we're not sure it's suicide yet."

Kane sucked heavily on the cigar and turned on his heel. "Susan and I weren't in touch with each other very much at all. I saw her in person two years ago, but that's the last time."

"Commander," Ellen said gently, breaking the tension, "do you know if Susan had a significant other?"

"If she did, I wasn't privy to that information."

"Was she a lesbian?" Cochrane asked.

"Just what the hell kind of question is that?" Kane's face went black with fury.

Cochrane held the officer's angry stare. "Just answer the question, sir."

"I don't know." The words came out like ice shattering.

"Aren't you interested in how your sister died?" Cochrane asked.

Brad jammed the cigar back into his mouth and bit down on it, his teeth barred. "Not particularly. The Red Cross contacted me and said she'd died. It wasn't until I arrived stateside that I heard it could have been a suicide or a murder."

Cochrane reached into his pocket and pulled out a photo. He stood and walked over to the pilot. "Here, take a look." He thrust out the color picture of Susan dead, on her bed, holding the teddy bear.

Kane blanched visibly as he stared at it. He refused to take it, even though Cochrane continued to hold it out to him. His eyes widened momentarily, flaring with surprise. "Jesus H. Christ!" he snarled, and turned away. "That's enough, Lieutenant!"

Jim heard the strain in the aviator's baritone voice. So, Kane was affected.

Jim placed the photo back in his shirt pocket. "What does the teddy bear mean?"

His face taut, Kane swung around as if stung. "Get out of here," he rasped. "Get the hell out."

Cochrane held his ground. "Not until you tell us what that stuffed bear means, Commander."

Kane looked over at Tanner, and then back at Cochrane. He took the cigar out of his mouth, and his broad, proud shoulders slumped. "The bear was a gift from our birth mother to Susan. She bought the damn thing before Susan was born. She said every child should have a stuffed toy, a friend, something to be close to. When things went wrong, Susan would always hold the bear and cry."

"I find it odd she'd die with the bear in her arms, don't you?" Cochrane asked.

Small beads of sweat covered Kane's furrowed brow, and he was breathing erratically. His blue eyes were stormy and filled with an emotion Cochrane couldn't fathom. He waited patiently as Kane wrestled with what were obviously violent feelings.

"Susan dragged that damn thing around with her everywhere." With a muffled curse, Kane moved around him and went over to the bed where his travel bag sat. "I'm concluding this interview, Lieutenant Cochrane." Glancing at his watch, he snapped, "And I've got a plane to catch." He doused the cigar in the water glass and threw the strap of his bag across his left shoulder. "First," he said frostily, "I'm going to say goodbye to my father. If you have anything else to ask, you can contact me on the carrier. Is that clear?"

Cochrane walked to the table and put his pen down on the papers. "Perfectly, Commander. Thank you for your time. Tell your father we'll be up shortly to interview him." Jim shut off the tape recorder.

Kane walked to the door, jerked it open and left.

After the officer departed, Ellen ventured, "Wow! One hell of a interview! I never expected that kind of reaction. Did you?"

"No, I didn't. But Ann Hawkins warned us, you know."

"Yes, she did." Frowning, Ellen said, "Don't you find it odd that Brad hadn't been in touch with Susan recently? Doesn't it make sense that if she was suicidal, she'd automatically reach out to her family?"

"Normally, I'd say yes. But if the family didn't love her, as Hawkins claimed..."

Ellen snorted.

"Most families aren't fairy-tale perfect, you know," he added.

"I find it impossible to believe that one of these three men didn't know what was happening with Susan. Don't you?"

Cochrane looked at his watch. "I don't know yet. I'm going to give Robert Kane another ten minutes before we walk up to the fifth floor. It's my guess that retired Captain Kane doesn't like meeting people earlier than scheduled." Jim studied Ellen. "Judging from what Hawkins told us about the Kane family yesterday, I don't think we should automatically assume Susan contacted them."

With a fierce shake of her head, Ellen muttered, "I find it impossible to believe she didn't contact at least one of them."

Rising, Cochrane said, "Well, let's find out, shall we?"

They found Robert Kane's room on the fifth floor, and Jim knocked. When the door finally opened, he saw a man in his early sixties, his steel-gray hair military short. He had a long, narrow face, with a pronounced scar on the left side of his brow. Like his son, he was about six feet tall, his expensive suit made him look taller. Lines of age—from the crow's-feet at the corners of his eyes to the slash marks that bracketed his mouth—suggested that this man had weathered a lot of life. Kane's flesh had a decided pallor and his nose was slightly red. Cochrane wondered if he'd been drinking before the funeral, though he smelled nothing on his breath.

"Yes?" The man's voice was low and brittle.

"I'm Lieutenant Cochrane and this is Agent Tanner. We're here to interview you about your daughter's death. May we come in?"

Kane stepped aside. "Why not?" he said with a note of sarcasm. As they entered the room, Kane walked over to the window and looked out toward the bright California sun. "This is a disaster. A disaster." He watched Cochrane turn on the tape recorder.

"In what way, Mr. Kane?" Ellen asked in a gentle, searching tone. She was gun-shy after Brad's interview.

Was his father just like him? In any case, she figured a soft approach might be better.

He glanced across his shoulder briefly. "My daughter has shamed our good family name. My two sons, now serving, may suffer from her failure."

Cochrane looked at Ellen, whose mouth had dropped open. She quickly snapped it shut, disbelief etched in her expression. "We're sorry that it happened, Mr. Kane," he said. "From all appearances, your daughter was an exemplary naval officer."

"Yes," Ellen added, through gritted teeth, "she accomplished more than most men."

Kane's steel-gray brows knit and he turned toward them, his hands clasped in front of him. "Susan could never do anything right. Ever. This is just another example of her botched performance."

Jim held the pen steady in his hand. A swell of anger rose, but he quickly tamped it down. "Did she have any enemies?"

"Not to my knowledge."

"How long since you've been in contact with her?" Ellen asked.

"Years. Susan was an interloper to our Navy family. When my second wife, Georgia, died five years ago, Susan made it clear she wanted nothing to do with any of us after her funeral." He glared at them. "I acknowledged her wish to divorce herself from our family. I haven't seen her, spoken to her or received any kind of communication from her since that embarrassing day. Now she's committed suicide. A coward's path."

"What I meant to say, sir…" Jim hesitated in an effort to control his mounting rage. "We're trying to determine what might have driven Susan to take her life. Or if she had an enemy who wanted her murdered."

"Susan killed my first wife. That was the worst sin she committed—the worst of many. I don't care how many diplomas she had, or her standing in the Navy, Lieutenant. In our family, she caused all of us nothing but pain." His mouth flattened. "Now, she's not only created more pain, but embarrassment, as well. If she'd been a man, she wouldn't have committed suicide. She couldn't even die with honor."

"Perhaps that's the point," Ellen whispered tightly. "That you wished Susan were a son instead of a daughter?"

Kane stared at her through slitted eyes. "Susan was always a problem. As a child, she was underfoot. She was always sick. She caused my second wife more problems than my two sons combined." Kane looked at his watch and then headed to the phone. "Susan always did what *she* thought was right. She was headstrong and independent. Too damn independent, if you ask me, but that's a moot point now, isn't it?" He picked up the phone. "This trip back through family history has nothing to do with the Navy's investigation of her death. So unless you have anything more pertinent to ask, this interview is concluded."

"I'm afraid we have a few more questions before you make your calls, sir." Frustration surged through Jim, overshadowing his better judgment. He couldn't believe Kane's callous attitude. Rising to his feet, Jim took the photo from his breast pocket and thrust it forward. "Is this how you expected your daughter to die?"

Kane took the photo and gazed at it, his eyes narrowed speculatively. His mouth worked momentarily, as if to bite back something. "How dare you," he barked, throwing the photo on the carpet. The man's breath seemed to come in gulps, as if someone had hit him with a two-by-four.

"How dare I?" Cochrane rasped, standing within inches of the taller, older man. "Something isn't right here, sir. I know enough about your daughter at this point to realize she was a damn fine woman—and a superior Navy officer. You don't get better evaluations than Susan Kane earned and we both know it. So why all this coldness? First, your son Brad acted like he couldn't care less if Susan was alive or dead. Now you. What the hell is going on here?"

Cochrane couldn't steady his breathing or get a handle on his emotions. But he didn't care. Susan Kane deserved better than this. She deserved understanding from her family, not this bitter, cold treatment. Were all the Kane men heartless?

Red-faced, Robert Kane took a step backward. "I shall report this unprofessional conduct to your commanding officer. You disgrace the uniform you represent."

"Jim!" Ellen made a grab for his arm before he could lunge at Kane. Her fingers sank into tense flesh.

Cochrane blinked. He felt Ellen's cool, firm fingers wrap tightly around his arm. She guided him away from Kane. Breathing hard, he steadied himself and felt Ellen's grip loosen. Turning, he picked up the photo that Kane had thrown down. "This, isn't right," he growled. "You treat your daughter like she was an alien from another planet, or some maggot you can squash under your foot, Captain Kane."

"You're way out of line, mister," Kane snarled. "Now get the hell out of my suite! I don't have to put up with little shits like you throwing your weight around. This case is closed! Susan is dead. Leave, dammit."

"Jim?" Ellen tugged on his arm. "Come on, please?"

"You're right." Cochrane was trembling with rage. After placing the photo, tape recorder, and papers into his briefcase, he snapped it shut with authority. Time to leave, drive over to the other hotel and talk to Tommy Kane.

AS THEY WALKED TOWARD the next hotel entrance. Jim watched how the wind lifted strands of Ellen's curly hair around her slim shoulders. How he wanted to pull her into his arms. Instead he put his hand briefly on her shoulder. "Thank you for being there."

Surprised, Ellen looked up at him. "No problem. I'm glad I could help." Her skin tingled beneath his firm touch. They had stopped walking and stood face-to-face. Unconsciously, she leaned forward enough to see the look in his eyes slowly change. Did he want to kiss her? No. Impossible. Ellen was startled by what she thought she saw in his gaze. His fingers briefly tightened on her skin.

"I'm glad you pulled me off Robert Kane. I came so close to hitting him. My good sense just about went out the window."

She gave him an understanding look. Ellen bemoaned the loss as he lifted his hand. It had been two years since a man had touched her. She never thought she'd want the caress of another man since Mark's death, but she ached for Jim to do exactly that: make sweet contact with her again. Instead, they turned and walked toward the entrance.

Jim opened the glass door for her. "Don't start giving me that starry-eyed look, Ellen. You just happened to hit on one of my sore spots. It burns my craw that her family would think so little of her, of who she was."

"Well," Ellen said gently, "in my heart, I think you're right. I'm glad to see your human side, Jim." She wanted him to touch her again...and kiss her. Her whole world had turned upside down in those seconds when he'd reached out for her. Now, a keening ache was beginning deep in her body. Ellen felt she was awakening from the long sleep of grief.

They walked up to the brass elevator doors. "Oh, I'm human as hell."

"There's a real person under that Navy uniform?" Ellen kidded. She saw the tender regard in his gaze, and smiled at him.

"Maybe I'm just getting used to being around you, and I'm letting my hair down."

She stepped into the elevator with him. "It's okay." She realized he trusted her. Heady stuff on top of her attraction to him.

Cochrane watched as the doors slid shut. "For whatever reason, I'm glad you understood my moodiness. I want you to conduct the interview with Tommy. I'm not in a good space. Are you up to it?" The elevator doors opened and they walked down the wine-colored carpet.

"Of course I will," Ellen said, surprised and pleased.

"Good, because I don't think I can handle three cold bastards in a row."

CHAPTER SEVEN

TAKING A DEEP BREATH, Ellen halted at room 301 and knocked. She quelled the butterflies in her stomach, gearing up for the unexpected opportunity Jim just gave her. There was no answer. She glanced at Cochrane, who stood behind her. Again she knocked, this time more authoritatively. With her ear to the door, Ellen could hear a TV blaring inside the room. She was beginning to suspect that Tommy Kane wasn't going to answer. Maybe Brad or Robert had phoned ahead to warn him.

Before she could decide her next move, the door opened. Ellen wasn't prepared for what she saw. Dressed in gray military sweats, Lieutenant Tommy Kane, stood before them, a nearly empty shot glass in his hand. The Kane family resemblance was striking, especially the pale blue eyes. And yet Tommy Kane's eyes were red-rimmed from crying. His light brown hair was uncombed, as if neglected for days. Ellen's heart lurched in sympathy.

"You must be the investigators?" Tommy croaked.

"Yes," she said gently, and introduced herself and Jim.

He grimaced and stepped aside. "Come on in."

The man's hotel room was a far cry from the others. Ellen could smell the distinct, nose-wrinkling odor of whiskey even before she spotted an open bottle on a small, round table in the corner. Kane's cloth suitcase was open, the uniform he'd worn to the funeral, thrown haphazardly across the bed. Tissues littered the floor around the wastebasket.

Kane passed her on the way to the noisy television set, gave her an apologetic look and turned it off. He set the shot glass on the table and pulled up chairs so they all could sit down. As if realizing his disheveled condition, he pushed his long fingers through his short hair to tame it into place.

Ellen thanked him for pulling out her chair. There was none of the family coldness in Tommy Kane. She was struck by how much he looked like Susan, and wondered if they both took after their mother. Brad Kane certainly favored their father in looks, manners and attitude.

"Sorry for the mess," Tommy muttered, going over to the bed to jam his dress whites into the suitcase and then drop the lid.

Ellen saw the uncertainty in his eyes and felt the barrage of emotions he barely held in check. His face was flushed and his eyes remained suspiciously bright. What a contrast between family members. According to his personnel record, he was due to get his lieutenant commander's leaves next month.

"I'm sorry we have to conduct this interview so soon after Susan's funeral," she began softly, holding his gaze. "We'll try to make it as painless as possible, Lieutenant Kane." She asked Jim to turn on the tape recorder.

Clearing his throat, he said, "Call me Tommy. Everybody else does." He waved his hand in a helpless gesture. "And I'm glad you came. Do you know how Susan died?" He hesitated. "My father, the captain, says it was suicide, but I don't know whether I believe that or not. I got word on my carrier, *The Nimitz,* that she was found dead in her condo. No cause was given. I just couldn't believe it." He searched their faces earnestly for answers.

Ellen swallowed hard. "She died of an overdose of sleeping pills, Tommy. We don't know if her death was the result of suicide or a homicide. We're interviewing people who were close to her to try and find out more, but so far, we have very little to go on."

He gave them a stricken look. "I just don't understand. God, I don't...." He stared at them. "If Susan was in trouble, why didn't she try to get ahold of me? Or someone?" He clasped his hands together. "You don't have any leads?"

Cochrane shook his head. "No, that's why we're checking with the family first. There's no indication, thus far, of anything gone wrong in Susan's life. But something must have."

"Susan was doing great! She had everything she wanted." Tommy shook his head and stood, shoving the chair away from the table. He moved jerkily to his well-worn suitcase, threw the lid open again and rummaged around for a full minute before he found what he was looking for. "Here," he said urgently, dropping a couple sheets of paper on the table. "It's her last letter to me. She sent along forty-eight photos from the Ares Defense Contractor's Conference she'd attended in May. Susan always sent me photos and info from the seminars she goes to because I can't make a lot of them, being on sea duty."

Cochrane reached for the packet of photos. "Mind if we take them for evidence?"

"No, not at all. She always sends—I mean, sent me photos. I don't know what good they'll be to you, though."

"We'd like to look at them in any case," Cochrane said. He wrote "ARES" on the outside of the envelope and placed the photos in his briefcase. Then he opened the letter and began to read, handing the sheets he finished to Ellen, one at a time.

Ellen read the handwritten letter.

Hi, Tommy,
I'm sure looking forward to seeing you when you come off sea duty! Are we still on?

Work is going okay for me, but I'm having some trouble with three of the instructors at Top Gun. You know the old saying, a few bad apples will spoil the barrel? They've got it in for me, always playing nasty practical jokes that really aren't meant to be jokes at all. It's their way of telling me I'm not welcome in the Men's House. Tough. I get so mad sometimes, but I tell myself that if I lose my cool, I'll be as bad as them. I'm not going to sink to that level. Without the flying, and the other instructors, who are wonderful, this Top Gun School assignment would be the pits.

The Ares Conference pictures are included. I have more to send you later, and they are inflammatory. This conference made my gut clench. There's a real need for change in the Navy Air community. Someone's got to get these guys— post-Tailhook idiots who didn't get the message when it happened in '92—out of these conferences. You're lucky you weren't there. I'm still collecting photos from other people who attended, because I didn't take many shots myself. You won't believe it, but I can share them with you and they won't go anywhere. If all conferences were like this one, I'd stop going, but it's the exception, not the rule.

Listen, I gotta run. Got a ton of paperwork to prepare for my next class. Call the ball on that Super Hornet of yours and get back here safe and sound, huh? I love you, bro. See you soon!

Susan

Ellen looked up at Tommy and then over at Jim. "This letter wasn't written by someone wanting to commit suicide."

"No," Tommy whispered, a catch in his voice, "it wasn't."

"We'd like to keep the letter for a while." She handed the pages back across the table to Jim. "Tommy, did Susan ever mention the names of those three aviators who were giving her problems?"

He shook his head. "One thing you don't do in this man's Navy is name names, Agent Tanner. Never say anything you wouldn't put in writing, and never put anything in writing. We both know that little caveat." He pointed to the letter. "That's why she didn't name them there. If anyone other than me had read the letter, the grapevine could get the word back to them. The air community is small and everyone knows everyone else's business. If you have a problem, you solve it in-house."

"Do you suspect who the three were, Lieutenant?"

"No, I don't." He sighed and looked down at his hands. "Ever since Tailhook happened in the early nineties, the aviation community has really tried to make amends and get things on an equal footing for women pilots. There are pockets of resistance, though, even now." He pointed to the pack of photos. "And there's some pretty incriminating evidence of what went on at the Ares Conference. I can see why my sister was upset. Plus, she said there were more photos to come, but I never got them."

"Are you aware of any incident involving her outside of what's mentioned in her letter? Did she e-mail you later, perhaps? Phone you about it?" Ellen asked.

He shrugged helplessly. "No, nothing. Like I said, some of those photos are pretty provocative. No names, just the actions taking place. But if she was collecting other raunchy photos, I don't have them."

"I'm going to cross my fingers they're in that file in the office." Ellen frowned. "You could help us in a roundabout way by telling us a little about your family life, and your growing-up years. You're not obligated to do so, just if you'd like to share. It would help us understand Susan a little better. Were you close to her?"

Tommy smiled and relaxed. "Yeah, we still are—I mean—were close."

"Was Susan close to Brad?"

"No, he was the oldest and saddled with the two of us underlings." With a shake of his head, Tommy said, "The captain hated Susan. My God, to this very day I'll never understand his reaching such a warped conclusion about her. She wanted so much to have Dad love her."

"How did that affect Susan growing up?" Ellen murmured.

Tommy lifted his face to the ceiling, sniffing and fighting back fresh tears. "Susan was a good person and she tried so hard to do everything right—even perfect. That way, she stayed out of trouble. The captain had weekly inspections when he was home, and he made it clear it was up to Susan to make sure all our bedrooms were white glove clean."

"Where was Georgia in all this?" Ellen demanded.

"Georgia…" His mouth pulled into a twisted line. "I shouldn't speak ill of her now because she's dead, but she was a piece of work, let me tell you. A real shark of a Southern belle with a nose for rank. She married the captain when she was twenty years old." Tommy sobered a little. "I'll give Susan this—as much as she was picked on by our parents, she never broke. She was tough and had a backbone of steel. And God knows, Susan was the scapegoat for everything. In the end, I think it just made her stronger, more determined to reach her goals."

"Did Susan ever have a significant other?" Cochrane asked.

Tommy nodded and sat back down. "Susan was pretty. She was the class president four years running, at two different high schools. She was smart, popular, and everyone liked her. Tons of guys wanted to date her, but the captain wouldn't allow it."

"That's terrible," Ellen said with disgust.

"Yeah, tell me about it. We boys were allowed to have girlfriends. I don't know how many times Susan lay on her bed on Friday nights and cried because the captain forbade her to go to school dances. She was glad to get out of the house when she was eighteen."

Ellen compressed her lips when she saw Cochrane draw out the photo of Susan from his shirt pocket. He handed it to her and she swallowed hard. "Tommy, what can you tell us about Susan's teddy bear?"

The man's face crumpled and tears filled his eyes.

"We have a photo of Susan the day she died, and she's holding the bear. Try and prepare yourself to look at this photo, if you want. You don't have to," she said, handing the photo to Tommy.

He inhaled sharply, his gaze pinned to the picture. "Oh, God…" He pushed the print back toward Ellen. Pressing his hands against his eyes, he turned away. "Oh, God…"

Ellen went over to him, slid her hand across his back and felt him trembling. "I'm sorry," she soothed, patting him gently. "So sorry…"

Cochrane went over to the minibar and returned with the same bottle of whiskey that Kane had been drinking out of. After sloshing the contents into the water glass, he thrust it into the aviator's hand. "Reckon you might want a drink of this."

Tommy nodded, pressed the tumbler to his lips and gulped down the liquid. He handed the tumbler back to Cochrane and nodded in thanks.

Ellen felt Tommy's sorrow as though it were her own. It brought back the clear, cutting pain from the untimely death of her husband. Fighting her own tears, she walked back to the table and sat down to wait until Tommy could get hold of his emotions.

At last, wiping his flushed cheeks, Tommy said, "I'm a mess. I'm never like this, never. I'm sorry. It's just that I loved Susan so much and I can't believe she's dead. I just can't believe it…." He covered his face with his hands.

To Ellen's complete surprise, Jim came over to stand by her. He placed his hand on her shoulder for just a moment, as if to communicate that he saw her pain and wanted to comfort her. Stunned by his unexpected gesture, she twisted to look up at him, and saw raw anguish in his eyes. Maybe he had never experienced a loved one's death, but in her mind, divorce was akin to it. In his own way he understood, or at least by his gesture, he was trying to reach out to her. Tears jammed into Ellen's eyes and she had to look away. All she wanted to do was throw herself in his arms and feel his protective embrace.

The silence was no longer strained, just pregnant with feeling. Ellen was glad that Jim remained near her, a silent gesture of support. It was enough. Tommy Kane had touched them both, as had the story of Susan's traumatic upbringing. Susan had been a good person caught in a bad situation. But what had tipped that precarious balance Susan had always maintained? What?

Tommy cleared his throat and when he spoke, his voice was rough. "That teddy bear was a gift from our mother to Susan. We moved every two years to a new station, so we lost a lot of school friends, and I think it was hardest on Susan. Even as a baby, she knew that teddy bear was from Mama. I swear she did, because if Georgia put the bear in the crib with her, she'd stop crying immediately. Every time. When Susan was old enough to walk, that bear went everywhere with her. The captain tried to shame her out of carrying it around, but she wouldn't give it up.

Susan would jut out that little chin of hers and stare up at him defiantly, holding on to that little fella even more tightly."

Wiping his eyes, Tommy sat up straight and gave them a wobbly smile.

"I see," Ellen murmured.

"Where is her bear?" Tommy suddenly asked.

"The police are keeping it as evidence, for now," Cochrane answered.

He nodded. "When they're done with it, could you send it to me?" His voice cracked. "Please?"

"Normally, most effects go to the parents," Cochrane said.

"The captain will throw it away." He rubbed his hands slowly up and down his thighs. "I'll keep it. Maybe, someday, when I have a family of my own, I can give it to my daughter." He looked searchingly at them. "That bear means a lot to me."

"We'll make sure you get it," Cochrane promised.

"Susan stayed in close touch with me. Always. I— I just can't figure this out. Anytime she had problems, she'd write or e-mail me if I was on carrier duty, or call me if I was based at a station."

"What kind of problems?" Ellen inquired.

"Three years ago Susan fell in love with a naval aviator who was married. Lieutenant Commander Todd Weston. The dude was on temporary duty, assigned to her squadron for four months. During the romance she didn't know he was married, and when she found out, she broke off the relationship. She was devastated and embarrassed. This guy was a real manipulative bastard. He talked about Susan to some of the other fighter jocks, and it became a real mess. Susan almost resigned her commission because some of the squadron lowlifes plagued her about the affair. It hurt her career and her name. She put in a request for a transfer, and that's how she got the Top Gun assignment. Someone looked out for her interests and she was transferred here. I don't think she ever got over the humiliation of being suckered in. It really burned her bad."

"What happened to the lieutenant commander?" Ellen asked.

"He returned to his original squadron, acting like a happily married man. Of course, you know it's always the woman's fault," Tommy said.

"So, she did have one serious relationship," Cochrane interjected, changing the direction of the conversation.

"Susan wasn't very adept at male-female relationships," Tommy told them. "She never got any 'training,' if you will, during her growing-up years, mostly because the captain wouldn't allow her to date. I think he was afraid of her getting pregnant out of wedlock, and the effect it would have on his career. She just didn't understand the personal side of guys. How could she?"

"Did she have someone special here at Giddings?" Cochrane asked.

"Not that I know of. After that debacle at the other

station, Susan was staying away from the aviation jocks like poison. Weston got even—he had some photos of her in a bathing suit that he'd taken at the beach. He had copies made and passed them around to every jock that wanted one. Plus he put them on the Internet for a time, until Susan hired an attorney and the guy took them off his Web site."

With a sigh, Ellen looked up at Jim. "I think we've got what we need."

Tommy said, "My sister was a good person, Agent Tanner. Please, find out what happened. Why did she die? Why?"

"We'll find out," Cochrane told him, determination in his tone.

CHAPTER EIGHT

June 28

ONCE THEY ARRIVED AT the Embassy Suites, Jim braked the car and looked over at Ellen. The day had been pure hell and he needed her. He placed his hand on her shoulder and gave it a small squeeze. "You did a good job today. Those weren't easy interviews." Touching her helped him. He saw tenderness shining in her eyes, and it made him feel better about their rotten day.

Ellen's heart galloped. Jim's eyes were soft and dusky and full of promise. His fingers lingered and then began caressing her shoulder. Ellen absorbed his caress as if she was starving. She wanted him to stay here with her. She wanted to turn and face Jim—and then what? Anxiety riffled through her. No. She had to get away from him in order to think clearly. Of course, he wasn't trying to confuse her, but he didn't realize how vulnerable she was, especially with this case they were investigating. With shaking hands, she gathered up her notes and briefcase. "I'm glad I could help."

Reluctantly, Cochrane lifted his hand away. His heart

sank when he noted the anxious look in her eyes. Perhaps he'd overstepped his bounds with her. But somehow, Ellen's presence opened him up, and he was acting in a way he never had before. Clearing his throat by way of apology, he rasped, "You did a hell of a good job of interviewing Tommy. I'm impressed."

"Thanks, Jim. That means a lot to me."

He didn't want her to leave just yet. "Tell me about yourself? We've got a few minutes." Seeing the surprise in her eyes, he added, "Were you a wild redhead growing up?"

Sitting back, Ellen laughed. "My parents were in law enforcement, so I was a good little kid, contrary to what you might think about red hair." She drowned in his hungry gaze and her spirits lifted. "I lived in Minneapolis, Minnesota. I come from German and Irish stock, and according to my mother, who's still a police officer, I'm stubborn as all get-out."

"Stubbornness can be good," Jim said. "Especially on an investigation where you can't give up. You have to finish it." He smiled over at her. "How did you become an analyst?"

"I love people. I have forever been curious as to why they act and react the way they do. Even as a teenager, I was fascinated with people and how they dealt with life."

"Did you have patients back in Washington?"

Shaking her head, Ellen said wryly, "You aren't going to believe this, Jim, but it's too painful for me to be a therapist. That's why I went to work on the mind-set of bank robbers, to create a profile on them for the FBI. I guess I'm incapable of staying at arm's length with people's feelings. Mom calls me empathetic—I feel another person's pain. I'm not apologizing for it either. I'd rather be in touch with my emotions than suppress them. And that's what I'd have to do in order to be a psychotherapist with patients."

"You used all your skills today. I saw how you worked with Tommy."

"My education does come in handy every once in a while." Ellen flashed him a hopeful smile. "I'm glad you see me as a positive now, and not a negative."

"You weren't the problem," he said apologetically. "It was me, Ellen. Having a partner isn't so bad, after all."

"I think you were so used to working by yourself that when I crashed into your life out of the blue, it threw you off balance." She laughed. Her anxiety over his unexpected caress melted into raw need. Ellen wanted to sit here and just talk with him—about so many things. To explore Jim on all levels. When he touched her shoulder once more, she sighed in response.

"You always seem to know when I need that," she murmured. His hand was butterfly light, and she ached for more contact.

The desire to lean over and kiss her nearly overwhelmed Cochrane. Shocked by his need, he cleared his throat. "Get going, Ellen. I know you're trying to line up an apartment. You've got plenty on your plate even after work. I'm going to drop over to see my daughter. I'll be home after that, trying to catch up on our other cases. Let me know if you need anything."

Ellen felt relief, then sharp disappointment. She had seen the look in Cochrane's eyes: he'd wanted to kiss her. Even more shocking, she'd wanted him, too. "Okay. I hope you enjoy your time with Merry. You're right, I've got a list of apartments to call about and then check out." She raised her eyebrows. "Then I'm going to unexpectedly drop in for a visit with Ann Hawkins." She lifted her hand. "See you later, Jim."

As she scooted out of the car, Ellen felt deeply for him. Even mentioning his little girl's name made his eyes lighten with love. As she closed the door and turned toward the hotel, she found herself wanting him to look at her the same way.

ANN HAWKINS'S FACE mirrored surprise and then shock when she opened the door to Ellen.

"Hi, Lieutenant Hawkins. May I come in? I've got a few more questions that need to be answered." Ellen saw the redness around the woman's eyes and knew that she had been crying.

"Well, I guess." Ann hesitated. "Come on in."

"I know this is an awkward time," Ellen said as she entered the foyer of the apartment. "I appreciate your letting me in."

After shutting the door, Ann ushered her into a small,

cozy living room filled with Japanese black lacquered bamboo furniture. "I thought the investigation was over," she said, gesturing for Ellen to sit on the beige-and-green couch.

Ellen eased onto the sofa. "We're still collecting evidence." She opened her briefcase and took out her notepad and tape recorder. "You went with Susan to the Ares Conference, didn't you?"

Ann became more guarded. "Yes. Why?"

"Well, aside from dealing with some of the squadron boys, the Ares Conference is another logical place to investigate." Ellen wouldn't mention the photos or the file they'd gotten from Susan's condo. At least, not yet.

Ann stood, folded her arms across her chest and paced the length of the room. "I don't know anything," she said in a clipped tone.

Ellen sensed the woman's mounting nervousness and decided to pull back a little in her questioning. "Can you go over the last phone conversation you had with Susan before she died?"

Whirling around, Ann snapped, "I don't want to talk about anything, Agent Tanner. It's too much. I—I'm too upset!"

Ellen set aside her notes and shut off the tape recorder. She stood, her gaze locked with Ann Hawkins's tear-filled eyes. "Something happened, didn't it, Ann?" Ellen softened her voice. "Susan was a very unique woman. You were her best friend, her confidante. What aren't you telling us? You know her father is blaming Susan and calling her a coward for taking her own life. I think you can help us. Please?"

Tears streamed down Ann's taut face as she pulled her arms tighter around herself. "I just can't," she cried. "If I do, I'm the one who will suffer."

"How's that?" Ellen whispered.

"My career! I lied to you in that interview. I panicked because I was afraid of getting in trouble."

"Ann, if you love Susan, and I know you do, I think you'll take the high ground on this investigation. Would Susan have lied to us about you to protect herself?"

Shaken, Ann looked away and her shoulders drooped.

The tension was palpable between the two women. Ann seemed to struggle against a barrage of emotions. Ellen waited, allowing the silence and pressure to build.

"Would you turn off that thing?" Ann gestured angrily toward the tape recorder.

"I already have." Ellen showed her the machine.

"Thank you," she whispered, her anger seeming to dissolve. "Susan called me the night she died." Wiping tears away with trembling fingers, she continued, "Only, I wasn't home. Oh, God, I wish I'd been here for her. I'm sure I could have stopped her." Ann covered her face with her hands and sobbed.

Ellen put her arm around the woman's waist and led her to the couch. "Come on, sit down," she coaxed. Once she located a box of tissues nearby, she handed several to her.

"Th-thanks." Blotting her red eyes, Ann whispered in a choked tone, "Susan's message was on my phone recorder when I got home at 0300." Blowing her nose, she added, "When I heard her voice, I went into shock." She squeezed her eyes shut. "I'm so ashamed of myself—of what I did."

Ellen's fingers tightened on the woman's shoulder. "What did you do?"

"I was a real coward." Ann's lower lip trembled. "I was afraid for my career, so I drove to the nearby convenience store and stopped at a pay phone. I didn't want the call to be traced to my apartment, in case something happened."

"I see."

Raising her head, Ann said in a raw voice, "I made that 911 call to the La Mesa Police Department. Then I drove over to Susan's. The police were already there. I didn't stay long because I knew the worst had happened. I don't know how I got home, I was crying so hard. I was so worried, so ashamed of myself, my cowardice."

"You did what you felt was right," Ellen said consolingly.

"It was too late, too late."

"Do you still have that tape?" Ellen asked, holding her breath in anticipation.

Ann dabbed at her eyes. "Yes, I have the tape. I—I should have told you before." She gazed miserably at Ellen. "I'm not the friend Susan thought I was. But it really doesn't matter, does it? I lied to an investigator and I'll pay the price. I didn't help Susan when she needed me the most."

THE DOORBELL KEPT RINGING. With notes and legal papers strewn across his belly, Cochrane had fallen asleep on his couch. The doorbell jerked him awake, and when he sat up, the notes fluttered all over the polished white pine deck. He rubbed his face and looked at his watch: 2330. Who the hell was at his door at this time of night? Disgruntled, he got to his feet.

"Hold your horses! I'm coming, I'm coming," he yelled down the passageway. Pushing strands of hair off his forehead, he jerked the door open. Ellen Tanner stood there, her face flushed, her eyes bright with anticipation.

"Do you know what time it is?" he asked thickly, though he was glad to see her.

"Yes," she said excitedly, "I do." She brushed past Cochrane. "You've got to hear this, Jim!" She dug into her briefcase and produced a small cassette tape. "I went over to Ann Hawkins's place and we hit pay dirt."

Frowning, Jim took the tape and rubbed his eyes. "What are you rattling on about?" Her cheeks were tinged with pink and her eyes were dancing. She was the last person he'd expected to see, but the one he most wanted to. He'd been feeling damn lonely tonight. Ellen filled his heart and made him hope again.

"Susan called Ann the night she died. She left a message on this tape. You've got to hear it, Jim! Right now! It's going to help us," Ellen said breathlessly.

He turned and led her to his bedroom. The place was a mess, the bed unmade. He went to his dresser, where he pulled out a cassette tape player. "Let's mosey to the kitchen. This had better be good, Ellen. I was asleep," he growled.

"I think you'll forgive me after you hear the tape." In her eyes he looked like a disheveled, vulnerable little boy. Jim's eyes were puffy, his movements slow, his speech even more thickly accented than normal. Her heart opened widely, and all she wanted to do was throw her arms around him and hold him. What was it about Jim Cochrane?

"Don't count on it." They sat down at the kitchen table, the only family heirloom Jim had begged from his parents. It was an old hand-hewn, maple table that he'd eaten all his meals on while growing up. Still groggy, he had trouble placing the tape into the recorder. Ellen shifted from foot to foot, obviously unable to contain her excitement.

Clicking the machine on, Jim turned up the volume.

"Ann? This is Susan. By the time you get this message, it will be all over. You're my best friend. I'm sorry, so sorry, but I can't go on like this. Jesus, I don't want to die, but I don't see any other way out of this. S-something horrible happened at Ares, you were right. Something was wrong with me, but I couldn't tell you. Not even you. I can't let it be found out. P-please forgive me.

We've been through so much together. Goodbye. Tell my brothers…tell them I love them. I'm such a coward at heart. A failure. I hope you can forgive me for what I've done. I hope all women can forgive me. Goodbye, dear friend…"

Jim's fatigue vanished. He sat there, stunned by the anguished last words of Susan Kane. Barely aware that Ellen had sat down at his elbow, he rewound the tape and played it again. This time, he took his pad and pencil and wrote down some of the phrases. After the second time, he shut off the machine and looked at Ellen. "Ann Hawkins had this tape all along?"

"Yes, and she was afraid to tell us about it."

He sat there for a long minute, pondering the notes he'd written. "This is a nice piece of work, Ellen."

She smiled. "Even if I roused you out of a dead sleep?"

"You did the right thing." He tapped the pencil against the pad. "'Something horrible happened at Ares. I can't let it be found out.'" He glanced at Ellen. "Mighty interesting statements, aren't they?"

Heaving a sigh of relief, Ellen said, "Yes. I was so excited by this information that I had a hard time driving over here. I must have gotten lost five times before I found your place."

Chuckling, Cochrane got up and poured himself a glass of water and drank. When he put the glass on the counter, he said, "Well, all the evidence was pointing to a suicide. What we were missing was a suicide note."

He tapped the cassette tape. "This clears up that missing link. Now I reckon we should aim our investigation at what Susan was hiding regarding the Ares Conference. And that makes the file we found at her condo very valuable."

"Something terrible must have happened. What else could make Susan take her own life?"

"Good question," Jim said as he sat back down. He fingered the tape recorder. "She sounded desperate, felt as if she was a failure."

"I know."

"I found out off-the-record from my JAG friend Hillyer that a hell of a lot went on at Ares. Hillyer spends a lot of time with the Top Guns over at the O Club at Giddings. He's a good resource for me." Jim shook his head. "But I can't believe a leg shaving, butt pinching or being groped in a passageway would make Susan Kane want to die. That doesn't make a pile of sense."

"Jim, don't jump to that conclusion. One person's depth of shame might not be someone else's. Susan was walking a tightrope, especially here at the station. Even Ann said that Susan's most important duty was to serve as a perfect role model for other women. What meant more to Susan than anything—her image?"

Jim heaved a sigh. "There's a list of possibilities. Could Susan have gotten drunk? Slept with another aviator? Was the aviator a male or female? And was she being pressured by that partner? The scenarios and motives are endless. One thing I've learned in my years as

an investigator is not to guess. We need facts." Cochrane rubbed his unshaved jaw and continued to think
out loud. "No, it might not be so obvious. Maybe something else…"

Eagerly, Ellen stood up and brought her briefcase
into the kitchen. She set it on the table and opened
it. "When I left Hawkins's place, I dug through Susan's Ares file, and look what else I found." She
pulled out another packet of photos. "These are the
other pictures Susan was referring to in her letter to
Tommy. The ones she'd been collecting and hadn't
sent him yet. Cameras supposedly weren't allowed at
the conference. It's obvious that Susan had collected
the pictures from many sources. And they are incriminating, from what I can see. But you'd be a better
judge."

Jim scowled. Silence settled in the kitchen as he
studied each photo carefully. His mouth tightened and
he glanced up at Ellen. "Yeah, you're right on all accounts. These are damning photos."

"If my memory serves, didn't the Tailhook scandal
happen because aviators and others came forward with
photos to identify the guilty parties?" She pulled out a
chair and sat down next to him.

"Yes, ma'am. There's a central computer back in the
Pentagon at BUPERS, the Bureau of Naval Personnel,
that has pictures of every person in the military. They
scanned the photos, sent them to BUPERS. When they got
a match, they had a name to put with a face. Then these

individuals were questioned as to what they saw and so on."

"Why couldn't we use that computer system now?" Ellen asked.

Jim rubbed his eyes, then spread out the photos. "I'm sure we'd be able to, and it's a good idea. Since Tailhook, there's been a genuine effort to make the Navy gender neutral. Judging by some of these photos, sexism isn't dead, after all."

Turning several over, Ellen said, "I already checked the backs of these photos, and there are no names on any of them. No source or date, either. I haven't really studied the pictures too closely. I was hoping Susan might be in one of them." Her heart picked up in beat as they sat side by side. Jim was so close, so agonizingly close. Perhaps she was too tired, or maybe too excited about her coup, but all Ellen wanted to do was turn and throw her arms around his shoulders, squeeze the hell out of him and celebrate their victory. How long had it been that she wanted to share anything, good or bad, with a man?

"You don't know my luck, Ellen. That would be too good to be true," Cochrane drawled as he sifted through the photos. "That'd be as unlikely as a fifth ace showing up in a poker game."

"I'd say having these photos is a fifth ace that just came our way. We can examine the ones that Tommy gave us, too." Ellen slowly sorted through them. "You're right. From the looks of some of these shots, not everyone was on their best behavior, were they?"

"Wait! That's another tie!" Cochrane said, straightening. A lopsided grin spread across his features. "The good-conduct medal was missing from Susan's uniform! I'll be damned! Something *did* happen at Ares! Something that made her take off that medal before she died. In her own way, she was clueing us in. I was just too darn stupid to note that it was missing."

Ellen's eyes widened considerably. She placed her hands on her hips and stretched her back as she straightened. "Okay, but what happened? Who was involved?"

"We probably won't find out until we begin interviewing the jocks over at Top Gun. Most all of them were at that conference, according to my info." Cochrane looked with disgust at some of the photos. "Wednesday is the earliest we'll be able to interview them. I'll make a call to BUPERS and get us hooked into the main computer for identification purposes tomorrow morning. We'll scan these photos and send them by e-mail to the Pentagon. As soon as we get names, we can compile a list for interviewing."

"What if some of the people are on a carrier? Or at an overseas station?"

"No problem." Cochrane shrugged. "We make a phone call via satellite hookup to their ship or station. We've got an Iridium sat phone at JAG."

"That sounds like a plan, Jim." Ellen saw the glint in his eyes, like a dog on a scent. There was no question he loved this detective work, and she did, too. Even more, she liked being in his company. Feeling happy, yet unsettled, Ellen realized that she was now ready to move on. She could keep Mark in her heart but she had to focus on her present and future. And with one heated look, Jim awakened her dormant sexuality and longing. She wanted a special man in her life. Her emotions felt out of control just then, so she tucked them away for later, in the quiet of her hotel room.

"I'll start making calls tomorrow, Ellen. In the meantime, you can leave the two packets with me. I want to look at our information a little more closely." Jim gathered the photos and pushed them to the side of the table.

"No problem. I'll see you at 0800 tomorrow?" A part of her didn't want to leave. She was alone here with Jim. Her heart clamored for closeness with him. What should she do? Jim would not initiate any serious intimacy. He was an officer and a gentleman. Yet he seemed to feel the same attraction. Had she read the intent in his eyes correctly? Ellen gulped, feeling unsure of herself.

"Zero eight hundred is fine." Then he added, with a note both of teasing and sarcasm, "I didn't think you civilians started before 0900."

"Just try and keep me away from the office, Mr. Cochrane." Ellen gave him a dazzling smile when she saw the burning look in his eyes—toward her.

"Well, I reckon I just discovered my first-ever dedicated government employee. A civilian at that. My tax dollars are finally being well spent."

"Jim, you can be a real pain in the butt. You know that?" Ellen returned his silly grin.

"You hurt my feelings," he drawled. Putting his hand dramatically over his heart, he said, "Me? A pain in the posterior?"

"I'm not going to feel sorry for you, if that's what you're trying to weasel out of me," Ellen said. "And no apologies either for my opinion."

He brightened considerably. "My ma always said I was meaner than a copperhead snake throwed into a hot skillet."

"I think that picture fits you perfectly on your bad days."

He sighed and tried to get serious. "I probably had that coming."

"Wow, I'm too excited to go to sleep," Ellen stated. "Getting the tape and photos from Ann Hawkins was a real high."

Cochrane scowled. The words damn near flew out of his mouth: *Stay here with me. Spend the night.* Shocked by his thoughts, by his yearning, he muttered, "You still need rest, Ellen. Go home and get some." He stared at the packets. "We'll start going over these pieces of evidence later. Tomorrow is soon enough."

Ellen nodded. "Good night." Before she could head toward the door, she saw his hand reach out. It settled on her shoulder and brought her to a halt. Her eyes widened. Something new burned in his stormy gray gaze as he studied her.

Automatically, her lips parted. His fingers tightened slightly on her shoulder. He wanted to kiss her! Panic tore through Ellen. The grieving widow in her shied away, but the woman emerging from darkness wanted what he was offering. Torn, she saw him move closer, until his body was scant inches from hers.

"You have the darnedest effect on me, Ellen Tanner."

Her breathing ragged, she saw a teasing light in his eyes, along with desire. Her skin tingled beneath his masculine touch, and her heart seemed like a freight train chugging so loudly he had to hear it. Ellen lifted her lashes and met his burning look.

"Jim, I'm scared."

The words were so softly spoken Ellen could barely hear them herself. Yet they had an impact on Jim. Instantly, his fingers slid from her shoulder, and he took a step back. He shoved his hands into the pockets of his Levi's, a contrite, little-boy expression on his face. At that moment, he looked completely vulnerable.

"I mean..." Ellen stepped forward and lifted her hand. Following her instincts, she slid her palm up to his strong, uncompromising jaw. She felt the beard stubble beneath her fingertips, that dark shadow that made him seem so dangerous and mesmerizing. To hell with it. She couldn't live her life always being scared. Standing up on her tiptoes, she placed her lips softly against his other cheek. "Good night, Jim. I'll see you tomorrow morning."

June 30, Sunday

AFTER DROPPING OFF MERRY at Sunday school, Cochrane arrived at work fifteen minutes early. Jodi would pick her up afterward.

He stifled a yawn as he trudged up the stairs to his office. Ellen and he had worked until midnight the night before. They had gotten everything done, including the Pentagon hookup to the computer. Normally, no one worked the weekends, but the pressure to solve Susan Kane's case made it an exception.

He shortened his stride when he noticed his office door was already open. When he spotted Ellen working hard at her desk, he immediately relaxed. His heart raced as he remembered her soft hand sliding across his jaw, that tender kiss on his cheek. Hell, he couldn't stop thinking about it.

Rubbing his recently shaved chin, he slowed his pace, giddy teenage feelings roiling in his chest. He'd wanted to kiss Ellen that night. Looking back, he wondered if he wasn't tetched in the head or something. After swearing never to fall for another woman, Jim found himself in a helluva dilemma. Ellen's wild red hair, that soft mass of curls framing her face, those guileless green eyes, had all conspired against him that night. He'd seen the uncertainty mixed with yearning in her eyes. Well, he'd felt similarly. It was a stalemate of sorts, and he'd backed off. They'd worked like the good team they were becoming, both very careful not to touch one another.

Why had Ellen kissed his cheek? Was it out of platonic affection or something more? Or was she simply celebrating finding Susan's tape? Women did crazy things, and he couldn't begin to understand their behavior.

As he stepped through the open door, he realized she was wearing the same clothes as yesterday. When she looked up, he saw telltale dark circles under her eyes.

"I thought you were going to head for home right after I left," he muttered, placing his briefcase beside the desk. The sudden thought entered his mind that she could have come to his apartment, to his bed. She was like the mythical mermaids along the coast of Scandinavia, singing her siren song and leading him to uncharted territory. All Ellen had to do was look at him, and Cochrane felt himself melting like ice cream on a blistering hot summer day. His lower body felt especially scalded and needy. Did she realize how much she affected him?

Pushing her curly hair away from her face, Ellen sat up and rubbed her neck. "I was going to go home, but I was too excited about sending the photos to the Pentagon. I wanted to see if we'd get any identification." She yawned. "It was worth it, Jim. Come and look at what the computer found."

He walked over to her desk as Ellen spread several items in front of him. With all the paper cups strewn about the desk, he figured she'd fought to stay awake all night by drinking a hell of a lot of machine coffee.

"You must have a cast-iron gut, Ellen."

"Hmm? Oh, the coffee. Yes, well, it keeps me going."

She smiled warmly over her shoulder and crooked her finger. "This is going to blow your mind."

Cochrane leaned across her shoulder and said, "Fire away, you're on a roll." His nostrils flared, detecting the a slight spicy fragrance of her perfume. How easy it would be to slide his hands around her small shoulders, turn her around and... No, he couldn't go there. Ellen Tanner was his work partner, and he'd sworn off women. That jerked him back to reality as nothing else could.

"Okay, here goes. Last night I fed into the Pentagon computer the names of Susan's Top Gun colleagues who attended the Ares Conference. That info was run against the scanned photos. People from Top Gun came up as hits with these photos Susan had in her Ares file. Equally noteworthy is that only three—Hodges, Michelson and Bassett—are missing from Tommy's photo packet." She hesitated, letting her comment sink in, and then continued. "That could signal the possibility that they're either involved in something with Susan or not at all. For me, it was an interesting anomaly. I've collated the two categories." She pointed to a stack of faxes and photos clipped together. "All three pilots were in photos of what I'm terming 'problem areas' at certain rowdy-looking defense contractor suites. Furthermore, four different photos show them at the Leopard Radar Corporation suite, where some of the worst action seemed to have taken place."

Ellen straightened and rubbed the muscles across her

lower back. "I had to ask myself why Susan didn't send any photos of these three to Tommy. You want one more surprise?"

"I reckon I could handle it," Cochrane said, rummaging through the neat stacks of her handwritten reports and various photos.

Ellen raised an eyebrow. "How about the fact that Brad Kane was at the Ares seminar?"

Stunned, Jim stopped flipping through the reports and stared at her. "What?"

"Yup." She grinned mischievously. "I checked the official attendance list and he's on it."

"I'll be damned," Cochrane rasped. "That good ol' boy told us a big windy. He must have seen Susan there." Putting the report aside, Jim said, "You've come up with a lot. Nice work, Ellen." In the worst way, he wanted to trail his fingers along her flushed cheek, but checked himself. His voice deepened with concern. "You're plumb tuckered out. My pa, who's a fiddle player, would say you look as worn out as one of his fiddle strings."

"Gosh," Ellen said, wrinkling her nose and smiling, "that sounds pretty tired to me."

"Why don't you go back to the hotel and take the rest of the day off?" What he wanted to say was: *Hey, let's go to the beach and make a day of it. We can sit and get to know each other....* But kept the thought to himself.

"That's an idea whose time has come." Ellen walked over to the corner and lifted her knapsack off a wall hook. Turning, she pointed to another note on Cochrane's desk. "NCIS just e-mailed us that they sent a team over and searched Susan's office at Top Gun on Tuesday."

"Damn! I was hoping we could get over to her office before they tracked all over everything. It's not likely we'll find anything there once they get done."

"According to their e-mail, they've packed everything up. The office was sealed on the day she died, which made it off-limits to everyone until it could fully be checked out. I'd really like to go over there with you if you're going to search. Maybe I can learn a thing or two more about investigating?"

Jim nodded. "Let's try to squeeze it in first thing Monday. I'm going to schedule Lieutenant Hawkins in for another interview on July 1, and clean up this 911 call thread that's hanging loose. You should go hit the rack, Ellen."

She grinned tiredly. "What are you going to do?"

"After work today I'm going to meet Jodi and Merry and have dinner at the zoo. My little girl loves animals."

Smiling softly, Ellen said, "Isn't that interesting? We're both going to be doing something that Susan Kane loved to do. After taking a nap, I'm going to the beach to unwind, and you're taking your family to the zoo."

He gave her a dark look, a grin lurking at the corners of his mouth. "Come on, Ellen. You gonna start that psychobabble synchronicity stuff with me again?"

Laughing, she shook her head. "Not with you, Mr. Cochrane. I'll see you Monday morning. Have a great evening with your family."

Jim sat down after Ellen left. It took minutes before his heart would settle. He found himself wishing that he could introduce Merry to Ellen. Somehow, he knew his little girl would get along famously with her. Again, it was not to be, so he tucked that tender desire deep into his heart. He rummaged through her findings and shook his head in disbelief. So Brad Kane had been at Ares. What did he know? Something, that was for sure.

Muttering under his breath, Cochrane got busy reading the information spreadsheet Ellen had put together, relieved and happy they'd finally been given a break in the investigation.

"We're going to find out what happened to you, Susan," he said, looking critically at each photo. "One way or another. And by default, you just might have given us the biggest clue we need to break your case."

CHAPTER NINE

"AT LEAST YOU DON'T LOOK like death warmed over this Monday morning," Cochrane said to Ellen as they approached his car. Her answering smile warmed his heart. Now, Jim wished he'd kissed Ellen, but it couldn't have happened. Not in a Navy office. Still, he wondered if her full mouth was as soft as he suspected.

"Thanks for the compliment, I think," Ellen chuckled as she slid into the passenger side and buckled up. "And thanks for picking me up this morning." She had a rental car, but she liked riding with Jim. This way they got a few precious moments alone together.

"A pleasure, believe me." And it was. More than Ellen realized.

He was getting used to her colorful fashion choices, and today was no different. She wore a dark blue jumper with a bright pink blouse. A purple scarf in her hair pulled back most of the frizzy red mane from her face. Jim noticed that her nose and cheeks were red, obviously from her being out on the beach too long.

She flashed him a shy smile and hefted her briefcase into the back seat. "I may not look like death warmed over, but I'm burned. I love the ocean, but I forgot to take a hat along to protect my face." Touching her nose, she said, "You can call me Rudolph if you want."

Grinning, Jim pulled the car out into traffic. "Red becomes you, Ellen. So, you had a good day off?"

"Yes. And you?"

"Couldn't have been better."

"I can see that."

He gave her a questioning look.

"You aren't as thundercloud dark as usual," she said. "Normally, you wear a scowl and your mouth is turned down. Sort of like a high school librarian giving threatening looks to everyone to be quiet or else...."

Cochrane was unable to keep the smile from spreading across his face, even though he wasn't sure he liked the comparison to a librarian. "You make me sound like an ogre." In a way, that hurt, but Jim knew he could be cantankerous as hell. Jodi had often pointed this out, and he was grappling daily to change his demeanor. After glancing at the broad expanse of bright blue sky dotted with tall, slender palm trees, he returned his attention to driving.

"You have your days, Lieutenant," Ellen replied lightly as Cochrane merged onto the highway and headed toward the Naval air station.

Cochrane enjoyed her teasing. He was beginning to respect Ellen's insights and abilities, despite her less than practical appearance. Her mind was sharp and perceptive, and that was something he could admire. Not to mention she was arrestingly beautiful in her own sparkling way. Sort of like the only red flower in a patch of white ones. She touched his heart without trying. Since meeting her, Jim woke up every morning looking forward to the day, which was highly unusual. Today, for example, he'd actually hummed his favorite hill tune as he shaved. Her influence was deep and cleansing to him. Ellen was the nicest surprise he'd had drop into his life for a long, long time. Was it real? A figment of his imagination, conjured up by his loneliness? Was she interested in a relationship? A serious one? Jim wouldn't entertain the thought of any other type.

"Before I picked you up, I dropped over to Susan Kane's condo one last time before the packing boys moved in to take everything away."

"Oh?" Ellen asked.

Cochrane took a piece of paper from his pocket and held it out for her inspection. "I got a list of phone calls made by Susan before she died. Her phone has a function that records the last five numbers dialed. Not only that, I wrote down all the numbers and names she had on her speed dial. I'm sure Detective Gardella has 'em, but I wanted them, too."

Ellen studied the list with interest. "Did you find anything?"

"With the speed dial information I identified four of the last calls Susan made."

"We already know Susan she phoned Ann Hawkins on the night of her death. Was that one of them?"

"Call number four was to Hawkins. Call number one was placed to her friend Becky Jillson two days earlier. Numbers two and three were to Operations at Giddings. It's the last call, number five, I wasn't able to identify. Susan phoned someone after she called Hawkins."

Ellen's brows shot up with surprise. "That would've been right before she died. Can we get the telephone company to identify the number?"

"I called the last number and got a busy signal. And yes, Ms. Watson, I've already dogged the phone company. It'll take them less than twenty-four hours to tell us."

She smiled. "Lieutenant Sherlock Homes, thank you for bringing me up-to-date."

"By requesting a second interview with Lieutenant Hawkins," he told her, "we'll set the official record straight."

COCHRANE SAVORED his morning coffee. Outside Giddings's Ops building he could hear several jets winding up to take off. Ellen was busy unpacking her briefcase for the coming interview. The more time he spent with her, the more he felt just how special she was becoming to him.

What to do about it? He wasn't sure. His body definitely had ideas, but he wasn't built for a one-night stand. And Ellen deserved better than his knee-jerk desire to throw her on a bed, make love to her and then walk away. No, somehow he had to keep working through what she meant to him. Clearly, she liked him. But having been burned by experience, he was a crazy ole dog, to even think of having another long-term relationship. And yet that's what Jim was wanting—logical or not.

Rousing himself, he said, "Reckon I almost forgot to tell you I dropped off the original tape from Hawkins's phone to Detective Gardella of La Mesa Police Department. They made us a copy, which we'll keep over at the JAG lab."

Ellen sat down, pushed some errant curls out of her eyes and looked up at him. "Does Detective Gardella concur that it was suicide, then?"

"He does now. Gardella is closing the case. There are some loose ends he has to clean up, but technically, Kane's case is closed with the L.M.P.D. The M.E. is calling her death a suicide."

"Isn't Detective Gardella interested in why Susan killed herself?"

With a shrug, Cochrane said, "With his caseload, he's more interested in what happened and who's responsible. Details like why don't matter unless it impacts on the first two."

"I'm glad we care, then."

"Eventually, these baffling pieces of information will fall into place. But we can't keep the case open forever. The Navy is going to push hard for a very speedy resolution, which is why we're doing double time right now to see it gets done," he said.

"Sort of like a big jigsaw puzzle?"

"Reckon it is. The tough kind, you know? The one with thousands of itty-bitty pieces. That's our job, Ellen, to figure out where to put these pieces, and later, to see the bigger picture of what's taken place."

"I never realized an investigator had to see not only the microcosm, but the macrocosm, as well."

Jim gloated. "Yeah, we're just all-around cosmic folks, aren't we?"

"Gimme a break, will you?" she laughed.

Cochrane saw Ann Hawkins come through the partially opened door. He stood, gestured for her to come over to the chair and sit down. Hawkins was pale and nervous, her hands shaking as she sat in front of them. Ellen greeted the woman, then closed the door.

For Jim, it was going to be a long day. He yearned for the quiet privacy of his office and having Ellen there with him.

ANN HAWKINS CONCLUDED her testimony. She moistened her lips and added, "Something changed Susan forever at the Ares Conference. I was her best friend. In all the years I've known her, she'd never had a migraine headache. Yet she had a horrible migraine there the morning before we left."

Ellen frowned. "Could Susan have been faking it for some reason?"

"No, I don't think so. She vomited in the bathroom, and you can't fake stuff like that." Ann shrugged. "Susan carried a lot of secrets. If she was feeling bad, I might find out about it after the fact or by the way she looked. She always suffered in silence."

Cochrane turned off the tape recorder. "You've been more than forthcoming, Lieutenant Hawkins. We appreciate your continued help and your detailed information."

With a slight, wan smile, Ann nodded. "I'll help in any way I can."

Ellen waited until the door closed before she turned to Jim. "I feel the behavior of these men at the convention was downright criminal."

"Reckon we need further proof and actual evidence before we can charge anyone with a crime at the convention," Jim replied. He knew that Ann's story accusing the three Top Gun officers from the school—Hodges, Michelson and Bassett—would not be enough. It would be her word against theirs, which wouldn't hold up in this man's Navy, let alone in a court-martial proceeding. More hard evidence, provided by other witnesses, was needed.

"Don't you feel that something terribly traumatic happened there?"

With a shrug, Cochrane looked at the list of interviews lined up on Monday. "I'm not ready to draw such a conclusion."

"You heard Ann tell how these three were drunk and abusive to women. Could there be something from this abuse associated with Susan's suicide?"

He glanced up at her. "All this information is preliminary and way too early to form legal conclusions, Ellen."

Frustration laced her voice. "I see a connection. And look at some of those photos. They certainly prove Ann Hawkins was telling the truth about party animal antics at that conference."

He smiled briefly. "You don't pin an investigation on just one person's testimony if you can help it. We're looking for corroborating evidence as well, gal."

Ellen's heart did a flip-flop over the intimate endearment. His warm gray eyes widened and held hers.

"Do you think Ann was lying?" she asked.

"No, I don't." He placed the papers back down on the desk. "I think what we should do is a little strat and tact, though." Jim was bewitched by the tender look in Ellen's green eyes.

"What's that?"

"Strategy and tactics. My pa always said you don't catch a fox without a chicken hanging around." He drummed the desk with his fingers, thinking out loud. "We need to arrange the order in which we interview these three guys. They'll be shocked at being called in by JAG in the first place. That will throw them off balance. We should interview Michelson first and then Bassett. We'll leave Hodges until much later. I'm going to make Hodges sweat like a hog in the middle of summer. This will make him think his two friends ratted on him."

"I see."

Cochrane's smile deepened. "It's called 'baiting the hook,' Ellen. I have no doubt these three were involved in some of the shenanigans at the seminar. By putting pressure on Hodges, we might get more than the standard aviation line of bull." When he locked onto her wide green eyes, he felt his heart open. For the rest of the day she was going to be with him working on other cases. That lifted his spirits. Filled him with hope. Real hope. "Come on, we got work to do, gal."

July 6, Tuesday

COCHRANE HAD JUST SET UP everything for their morning interview at their temporary office in the Giddings Ops building on Tuesday, when Ellen swept in, out of breath.

Though he pretended to be busy, Cochrane looked up at her. "Mornin', gal." He saw her cheeks flush over his pet name.

"Hi, Jim," she said breathlessly. "I had to stop and put down a deposit on my new apartment."

"Take yore time," he suggested. "You look like you just ran a marathon."

Laughing a little, Ellen said, "I was late to begin with. My hotel didn't ring me. That serves me right— I have to buy an alarm clock."

"You're not late, so relax." Things were going better than expected with the spreadsheet. With the help of the central computer in the Pentagon, they'd cobbled together identification of the people in the photos taken at Ares. He'd also contacted security at the Barstow Hotel, where the conference had been held. The next step was contacting the Reno Nevada police for any official complaints registered at the time. All of this was added to the spreadsheet.

The rest of yesterday had been spent on the Iridium phone. They had interviewed some conference participants not stationed in the San Diego area. Ellen had been no small help in that regard. She was not only much more of a computer geek than he was, she was an excellent interviewer and had a real touch in pulling information out of unwilling participants.

"Jim, you aren't going to believe what I found out from the phone company yesterday night after I left our office," she said, setting her laptop down on the desk. Her heart lifted with joy as he held her gaze. Ellen saw longing in Jim's eyes—for her. No longer did she fight or question his interest in her. It scared her and at the same time thrilled her in some forbidden yet tantalizing way.

"Reckon I have to wave a white flag, Ellen. What stunning surprise did you find? They were supposed to get us the fifth caller identification. Did they?"

She grinned and leaned down to place her briefcase at her feet. "I received the e-mail." She dug furiously into one of the pockets of her skirt. "I know it's in here somewhere."

Cochrane sat and watched. He couldn't help but smile. "You're pawing around like a skunk digging through a patch of sweet potatoes, on the hunt for worms and grubs. What are you looking for? Your crystal ball?" His gaze fell on her lips. Ellen never wore makeup, but she didn't need it. He liked the crazy quilt of freckles across her pale skin. It reminded him of the Milky Way spilling across a night sky—just as beautiful. Ellen was comfortable with how she looked, unlike Jodi, who always wanted to dress up and smack on a layer of foundation to hide her natural beauty. Jim never understood why women did that. He guessed he never would.

Ellen laughed breathily. "Crystal ball? Really, Mr. Cochrane, you surprise me. Today I don't look like a rainbow child, and all I get from you is grief, anyway."

"No," he said dryly, "you certainly don't look like a hippie today. More like Zelda the Gypsy, who can't find her trustworthy fortune-telling tools."

Compressing her lips, Ellen dug into the other pocket. "The only crystal ball I have in my possession is my gut intuition, for your information. Oh, good! Here it is!" After unfolding the paper with exaggerated ceremony, she triumphantly handed it to him. "You were right about Susan's call going to Ann Hawkins's phone."

He studied the numbers and names of the callers. "So the last call went to the Red Cross?" He scowled. "Of all places…"

"Yep." Ellen opened the lid on her laptop computer and plugged it in.

"Hmm, mighty interesting." Jim studied the telephone company printout, his brows dipping. "Both calls occurred in the last half hour before her time of death."

Ellen sat down. "Why the Red Cross, Jim? Did she have a friend there? Someone we don't know about yet?"

Shrugging, he tucked the printout into the left breast pocket of his tan uniform. "Good question, gal. I don't know." Frowning, he put his official papers and the police reports in order. "We'll be done with interviews by 1500 today. After that, we're going to drive down to the Red Cross and see what we can find out." When he saw Ellen blushing again at his endearment, Jim found himself wanting to reach out and caress that soft cheek. He forced himself to keep his hand on the table.

"Susan volunteered at the zoo. Did she volunteer at the Red Cross?"

"Got me." He grinned widely. "Do I look like I have a crystal ball tucked away somewhere on me?" He began to pat his shirt and then his pants pockets, pretending to look.

"Oh, stop! Now you're making fun of me! I find this case just gets more fascinating all the time. Who knew that Susan's compiled photos would help us maybe understand why she died?"

"Me? Would I ever make fun of you, gal?" Jim held up his hand. "Don't answer that on the grounds it may incriminate me."

Laughing softly, Ellen typed her password into her laptop. "You're so full of it, Mr. Cochrane. You got more names and colorful adjectives for me than I can throw a stick at. And the latest one—gal. Now, what am

I supposed to think of that? Is it a compliment? An insult? Or something in between?" How Ellen wanted it to be a special name for her alone.

His brows rose. "Why, that's a pet name." He saw her eyes grow merry with humor.

"As in a name for a pet rock, maybe?"

Groaning, Jim shook his head. "Everyone knows 'gal' is a compliment." He snorted softly. "Pet rock. Gimme a break, will you?"

"For all I know," Ellen said, grinning, "it could be a name for your pet bullfrog!"

He was unable to stop from laughing out loud or watching her every move. Ellen was more than desirable, but when her green eyes became dappled with gold sunlight and her mouth curved wickedly, teasingly, Jim found himself hungry for her in every possible way.

Jodi had always accused him of buttoning up like a proverbial bank vault, unwilling to communicate with her. As a result, Cochrane tried daily to change some of his old habits. Lifting his hands now, he earnestly met Ellen's dancing gaze. "Gal is a special name. Not a pet rock or a frog's name. I—well—it just slipped out." But then Ellen's smile vanished and her eyes became serious. Unsure if that boded good or bad, he asked almost defensively, "Did I make you uncomfortable or angry when I used it?"

"I thought it was a compliment," Ellen said in a low voice. "But I wanted to make sure. You know how assuming something can get you in trouble."

"Oh, yeah," Jim said, relieved.

"So 'gal' is a nickname for a *friend?*" Ellen wondered. In her heart she hoped it was a more intimate term. She'd had a few days to get over the shock of being attracted to Jim. Her fear was receding and in its place was a raw longing she was unable to ignore.

"It's a name you'd call someone you feel comfortable around."

His gaze narrowed on Ellen. In a nervous gesture, she ran her fingers through her unruly hair. Heart thumping with fear, he added, "Hey, I didn't mean comfortable like an old couch. It meant someone you care about. If you don't like the term, I won't use it again. I can see you're unsettled about it."

"Oh, Jim. No, I *love* the endearment!" Ellen reached forward, her fingers brushing his hand. "I—well, gosh. I mean, I kissed you on the cheek the other day. I think it's nice." She lifted her hand away. "I like it." More than he would ever know.

"You do?" The question spilled out of him like that of a gawky teenager asking the girl he had a crush on to go out with him for the first time. Seeing her eyes go tender with warmth, Jim melted inwardly. His skin tingled where she'd unexpectedly brushed his hand. This woman had the most maddening way of turning his mind to mush and his heart into a free-flying kite.

Sighing, Ellen looked toward the door. "I think we deserve to set some time aside to have a serious talk about how we feel toward one another. Not here, for sure, but when we can squeeze out an hour or so... Jim, you look like I just shot you."

One corner of his mouth hitched upward. "I'm just surprised, is all. But yes, we need to carve out some time outside Navy demands to sit and chat." That would be something he'd look forward to with trepidation. He knew he wasn't on solid footing with Ellen—yet. The spontaneous part of him wanted to be. His head, the rational part, called him an idiot for even thinking about love after being burned so badly by the divorce.

"I'd like that." Fear and joy stirred inside her. She had healed enough to realize her life was moving forward. Here and now, with this Navy officer who had such a soft Missouri accent. Quickly running her fingers through her hair, Ellen refocused herself on work and opened up her file for the coming interview.

Cochrane lost his smile and became much more serious. "Well, whether we like it or not, we gotta stick to the business at hand. Our first interview is with Lieutenant Neil Michelson. If my hound dog nose is twitching right, he's going to show up with an attorney. I think everyone here is running scared since we issued the order for Ares participants to drop by for an official interview. They know the winds of change are blowing strong and hard. It ought to get a little stiff and formal in here real quick. And since Michelson has been identified in some of those undignified photos, he'll want to protect his butt."

Ellen rubbed her hands together, giving him a grin. "Well, let's find out, shall we, pardner?"

CHAPTER TEN

NO SOONER HAD ELLEN opened her laptop for the forth-coming interview than the office door opened abruptly, almost as if leaping to attention. Cochrane recognized Michelson and his civilian attorney, Douglas Baden, frowning at his side.

Neil Michelson's broad shoulders were squared, his prominent jaw thrust forward, as if daring them to give him a hard time. He had the swaggering gait of a third generation Navy man. His grandfather had retired as a three-star admiral. His father, Rear Admiral Hugh Michelson, worked in the hallowed halls of the Pentagon. A glint of absolute, unshakable confidence burned in Neil's eyes as he approached.

Watching him carefully, Cochrane realized the man had a lot more to lose than most other naval officers because his pa was a powerful admiral. If the son's wrong-doings were aired, the entire family's honor would be stained. Not only would the young Michelson go down in flames, but the father's illustrious and prestigious reputation would be tarnished by association.

Cochrane saw the black snake tattoo that Michelson

had on his left, inside wrist—no doubt because of his call sign, "Cobra." Studying him, Jim decided he had "snake eyes," a term hill folk used for someone not to be trusted.

Jim noticed Ellen staring at the charismatic Michelson. She seemed in awe. And why wouldn't she be? Aviators had the right stuff, and Jim had yet to see a woman immune to their iconic standing as the ultimate air warriors.

"My client thinks this is a tremendous waste of his valuable time, Lieutenant Cochrane," Douglas Baden said smoothly.

"So do I," Cochrane said, smiling like a shark, his gaze pinned on Michelson. "But, I'm just a worker bee on the Susan Kane investigation, so I reckon we'll just have to persevere through this together, won't we, Mr. Baden?"

Baden grimaced and glanced at Ellen, then back at Jim.

Cochrane switched on his laptop and double clicked on a particular file. "You see, Mr. Baden, this interview is going to explore what went on at the Ares Conference Lieutenant Michelson attended on May 15th through the 18th."

"The Ares Conference?" Michelson growled. "It was just one of many conferences I've attended this year. This is a waste of my time. I'm an instructor here at Top Gun and I have a mandated flight in two hours."

"We'll get you out of here in plenty of time," Cochrane said dryly, studying the screen on his laptop. "My pa always said if you were up to your boot straps in cow manure, you'd want to be anywhere but in the barn, too."

"Just what the hell is that Ozarks hillbilly crap supposed to mean?" Michelson demanded tightly.

Cochrane looked over his computer screen at the aviator and then at the attorney. Michelson was a ring knocker—he didn't like little people like Jim scampering around his spit-shined flight boots. "Let me explain something to you, gentlemen." He patted his laptop affectionately. "We've got forty-eight color photographs that were taken at the Ares Conference. The photos show civilian and military people in what I'd term pre-Tailhook shenanigans, all caught on camera. We're also working closely with the Reno Police Department, who just got done calling in the temporary employees hired for Ares, and taking statements from them. The R.P.D has copies of these photos. The employees were shown them two days ago for positive identification.

"We're still in the middle of compiling this information. That's why we want to interview military personnel who attended. Those being asked to come and talk to us were either on the Ares Conference list or were identified in a photograph or by a Barstow Hotel employee who recalled the aviator in question."

Michelson gasped, his eyes bulging. He seemed to catch himself, then cut a look to Baden and jerked his attention back to Cochrane.

"You see," Ellen interjected sweetly, deliberately breaking the building tension in the room, "those photos were given to Susan Kane. We discovered them in her condo. We know that the photos were not hers, but gathered from many sources. Maybe the photos were sent by a spouse of an officer who attended the conference, by any number of young women from Reno who were there, or by one of the 'professional' help hired to entertain at this particular defense contractors' convention." She hesitated, then added in a serious tone, "Or perhaps Navy officers in attendance, properly incensed by what went on, took the photos."

"But...but...cameras weren't allowed at Ares," Michelson croaked.

"Gosh and by golly," Cochrane drawled, "I guess some folks didn't follow the rules, did they? But then a lot of rules weren't followed at Ares, were they, Mr. Michelson? Taking pictures is the least of the offenses, from what we can discern."

Michelson glared at him. "I wouldn't know, Mr. Cochrane."

"Oh, I reckon you do know," Cochrane murmured. He saw beads of sweat popping on Michelson's furrowed brow. The aviator sat so rigidly in the chair it seemed he might snap from the strain. Let him. Michelson had done a fair amount of abuse to Ann Hawkins at Ares, according to her interview. It was a matter of getting solid evidence to nail him.

Michelson had a lot to sweat about. It was one thing

to screw up your own career. It was another to soil your father's and grandfather's exemplary careers. That was an unforgivable sin to commit in a military dynasty family.

"Look," Michelson pleaded, lifting his hands and opening them. "Boys will be boys, Mr. Cochrane."

"Really?" Ellen goaded, holding the man's startled gaze. "Boys aren't boys when they start assaulting women, or violate their oath of professional conduct, *Lieutenant*. This is the post-Tailhook Navy, in case you had forgotten." Her words were biting but she didn't care. Michelson pushed her buttons!

"Well, this was a private affair, not a military function, er... I mean, we're military men," Michelson mumbled. "We risk our lives every day, Agent Tanner. Landing on a carrier is like flying a death wish."

Ellen frowned. "Your bravado is lost on me, Lieutenant. You chose this line of work." Damn his arrogance and belittling of women. Ellen would have none of it. She glanced over at Jim, who was trying to suppress a smile.

Michelson gave his lawyer a panicked look. He gulped and sat back, his hands clenched on the arms of the chair.

Cochrane knew he had to get Ellen off the aviator's back for the moment. "Are you telling me you were never in the Leopard Radar Corporation suite any time during the Ares Conference?" Cochrane allowed a good bit of sarcasm to enter his voice. He knew Michelson had a hot temper and an equally short trigger on any-thing that needled him. He was one of the more arro-gant jocks at Giddings, and Cochrane had to take advantage of that fact to squeeze an ounce of truth out of this lying bastard.

Nostrils flaring, Michelson rapped out, "No, I was never at that goddamn suite! Okay?" Sweat trickled down the sides of his face.

"Reckon it's not okay." Cochrane pointed to the lap-top. "According to one photo, plus an eyewitness ac-count, you were seen with Lieutenant Bassett going into the Leopard Radar suite on—" he looked more closely at the screen "—1700 on Friday, May 15th." Looking up, he said, "Is that incorrect?"

"Whoever told you that is lying!" Michelson snarled.

"Really?" Jim slowly rubbed his jaw. "I don't know, Lieutenant. This person was an eyewitness and was real close to the situation."

Michelson's jaw clenched. His eyes became slitted. "I was never at that suite."

"My client is faithful to his recollection," Baden said silkily. "What he's saying is that he does not recall vis-iting the suite in question. These activities took place two and half months ago and at a very busy, crowded conference."

Michelson eagerly nodded in agreement.

"That's kinda interesting," Cochrane drawled. "This witness says Lieutenants Michelson and Bassett were present when a female Naval officer was forced down on her knees to drink from the dildo penis drink dispenser in front of a Leopard mural. What about that incident, Mr. Michelson? Anything to add?"

His face flushed, Michelson sat there for a long moment. "I do not recall."

"Is that your answer? That you do not recall the incident in the Leopard Radar Corporation suite or that you do not recall ever being in the suite at the time in question?"

"I do not recall visiting the suite in question."

"Was Lieutenant Bassett with you at any of the seminars at Ares?"

"Hell, yes! We attended every seminar together."

"How about after the sat-com talk?" Jim saw Michelson's face go a darker red.

"I went to my room."

"You were seen leaving the seminar with Lieutenant Bassett and you went to the third-floor patio, and later to the Leopard Radar Corporation suite."

Clenching his teeth, Michelson said softly, "I went to my room. I wasn't feeling good."

"Really?" Cochrane let the silence build as he held Michelson's outraged glare. If the pilot could have leaped across the table, grabbed him by his collar and punched him out, he'd have done so. However, since this was an official interview, he knew that course of action was foolhardy.

"What was your room number, Lieutenant?"

"I was in room 1562."

"I again ask you, Lieutenant, where did you go after the sat-com talk?"

"Excuse me," Baden interjected. "May I have a private consultation with my client?"

Cochrane hesitated but knew he couldn't deny any client-attorney interface. "Reckon you can step outside into the passageway if you'd like," he invited with equal smoothness.

Both men went out and shut the door behind them. Jim glanced at Ellen, whose outrage was evident. Fortunately, the door and bulkheads weren't very thick, and he could hear every word spoken by Baden. Somehow, this made them feel a lot better.

"Goddammit, Lieutenant. Either tell the truth or say you don't recall. You're not good enough to make these things up on the spot. That legal beagle in there will burn your ass for false testimony if you get confused. Got that?"

"Yeah," Michelson snarled, "I got it."

Ellen put her hand over her mouth and Jim could see laughter dancing in her eyes. He would have gladly shared in her amusement, but they weren't done yet. He carefully arranged his face when the door opened and the two men returned. He tried to seem occupied with the laptop while they took their seats again, then he looked up.

Cochrane tapped his pencil slowly once, twice, three times on the table. All the while, he stared unblinking at Michelson. When he spoke, his voice was hard and uncompromising. "We have a witness who says Lieutenants Michelson and Bassett literally dragged the witness into the Leopard Radar Corporation suite from the third-floor patio area immediately following the sat-com talk."

Michelson's eyes bulged and he held himself taut, almost at attention.

Cochrane could tell the man realized that Ann Hawkins had fingered him. The officer went from a plum color to a pasty white, and then back to an angry red. Michelson struggled, his sharpened gaze dropping to his hands, which were clenched tightly in his lap. A rivulet of sweat ran down his jaw.

"If you're referring to Lieutenant Hawkins, I'd forgotten all about that." Michelson scowled, looked to the right and then to the left as he seemed to ponder how much to tell. "We were met by Lieutenant Hawkins. She grabbed us by the arms and asked us to go with her to some of the defense contractor suites. Even though she was insistent, we declined. I went to my room and left her at the doorway of one of the squadron suites. I don't remember which one."

Cochrane controlled his disgust. "So, you are able to place Lieutenant Hawkins and Lieutenant Bassett, arm in arm, at the doorway of one of the suites. It may or may not have been the Leopard Radar suite, at approximately 1900 on May 15th?"

Michelson's eyes grew wide with fear, as if he was realizing the gravity of his admission. He'd just placed his best friend at the Leopard Radar suite with Lieutenant Hawkins. Michelson made a croaking sound of terror and turned swiftly to his attorney. The last thing the man wanted to do was identify a fellow aviator.

Baden glared at Michelson and then looked over at Cochrane. "My client stated he didn't recall the name of the suite in question. He then left the parties and went to his hotel room."

"I told you, I went to my room," Michelson repeated, wiping sweat off his brow.

Jim didn't speak for a good long minute. He fingered Michelson's personnel file and studied it intently. "You're married, with two children." He looked up at the tight-jawed aviator. "Third wife? Right?"

"Yes."

"It's tough being a Navy aviator," Cochrane said with a sympathetic sigh. "You're gone a lot, the family suffers, the wife gets lonely and has to handle everything by herself."

"What's this leading up to?" Baden demanded tightly.

With a shrug, Cochrane smiled. "Three wives in eight years makes Lieutenant Michelson look a little rocky in the responsibility department, don't you think?"

"What the hell!" Michelson exclaimed. "My personal life is my own, not part of this damn investigation!"

"It becomes part of the investigation when a photo

shows you and a prostitute, Penny Anderson, going to your room on Saturday evening, Lieutenant."

Michelson gurgled and choked.

"My client's private life is not up for examination," Baden warned darkly.

"It's not his private life we're discussing," Jim retorted. "We're attempting to take the lieutenant's statement on his activities at the Ares Conference. With identification of the people in these photos or eyewitness accounts, Mr. Baden, all I have to do is type in Lieutenant Michelson's name and any report that concerns him comes up at my fingertips. Which is what I'm going to do right now." He lifted his hands and rested his fingertips on the keyboard, taking his time to type in the officer's name.

"While he's doing that," Ellen said softly, "I'd like to ask Lieutenant Michelson if he ever saw Lieutenant Susan Kane at the conference."

Michelson wiped his brow, dividing his attention between Cochrane's printer and Ellen. "I—don't know. I don't remember."

Ellen smiled gently. "She was at the same seminar at the end of the day as you were, Lieutenant."

"It was a crowded room, Agent Tanner. I don't remember seeing her."

"Oh?" Ellen rolled the pen between her thumb and forefinger, studying it for a long moment, letting Michelson squirm. "That's odd, because an eyewitness placed you with her shortly after the seminar broke up for the day. She was also on the list of people to attend that sat-com talk."

"I don't recall."

"I see…." Ellen glanced at Cochrane, who was still busy punching in information. Michelson was sweating heavily, and she could see dark splotches appearing beneath each arm of his flight suit. "What did you think of Susan Kane?"

Michelson gave her a startled look. "Pardon?"

"What was your personal opinion of Lieutenant Kane?"

"She was an excellent instructor here at the station and a good pilot."

"Is that all?"

He scowled. "What else is there to say?"

"Well, how did you feel about her personally?"

"I don't have a personal opinion of her."

Ellen could see the man was lying so decided to probe further. "Why not?"

"I just don't."

"Did you get along with her here at Top Gun?"

"She did her job and I did mine."

"Did she ever go over to the O Club with you after work?"

"No."

"Why not?"

Michelson struggled. "Kane wasn't one of us, Agent Tanner."

"What does that mean?"

"I'd think it was obvious what it means," he retorted.

"Humor me, Lieutenant. I'm a civilian. Can you be more precise?"

"Kane was a woman. She wasn't one of us."

"Oh? She was an aviator and an instructor just like you."

"You don't get it. It isn't politically correct to say in today's environment, but no woman will *ever* be a part of a fighter squadron." His voice lowered to a snarl. "I don't care if she wears gold wings or not."

Ellen raised her brows slightly. "How do you feel about women in general being Naval aviators, Lieutenant?" She felt her temper rising. Gripping the pen in her fingers, she barely kept the anger out of her tone.

"Again, I know this isn't PC, and this is my personal opinion. I don't believe women should be taking a combat billet. To be perfectly frank, I'd rather see them in my bed than taking my jet away from me. You can get killed flying a combat aircraft. Only men should die in a war, not women."

Ellen nodded and tapped the pen deliberately on the notepad. "According to this fourth report, you were in the Leopard Radar Corporation suite on Saturday, May 16th, around 2200 when they had a stripper come in and dance for the boys. She accuses you of groping and pinching her while she tried to dance. Then you allegedly hauled her down on the deck and forced her on her back with at least a hundred other civilians and a few aviators yelling and screaming at you to screw her in front of everyone."

"I want to know who the hell is accusing me of those kinds of things!"

Jim interceded. "I reckon the names will stay with us until we decide whether or not there are reasonable grounds for a court-martial, Lieutenant. At that point, your attorney will be sent the names because we'd call them to testify."

Wiping his mouth with the back of his hand, Michelson gave his lawyer a pleading look.

Baden stirred. "Really, Lieutenant Cochrane, this is all hearsay. As for these prostitutes, well, who's going to take their word over that of a fine young Naval officer? As I stated earlier, they are not very credible witnesses and I think you know that."

"The security guard is credible," Cochrane snapped, pointing to the reports. "And his record of Mr. Michelson escorting Ms. Penny Anderson from the hotel are facts."

Baden smiled sourly. "My client stated he went to his room. If he was propositioned by a prostitute on the way to his room, he did not accept her offer, nor does he recall anything later in the evening in question. Does the security officer mention my client by name or merely the lady in question?"

Cochrane smiled slightly, all the while holding Michelson's wild-eyed gaze. The pilot was in a full sweat. He squirmed in the chair, barely able to maintain eye contact. "They're lies," he charged angrily.

"Would you like to change your story about either

Friday or Saturday evening, Lieutenant Michelson?"
Cochrane asked.

"I have nothing to say."

Baden leaned forward, his expression intense. "Lieutenant Cochrane, if you have evidence…"

Jim shifted his gaze to the sweating officer. "Lieutenant, we have eyewitness accounts and photos to back up everything we've asked you about in this interview. I hope you understand the Navy term 'deep shit.'"

The interview was terminated after Michelson continued not to recall anything. That was fine, because Jim had the photo proof that said otherwise. And for once, he felt confident he could eventually help Susan Kane rest in peace.

"WELL?" Ellen said wearily as they wrapped up their interviews. "What's our score so far?" They'd questioned three pilots that morning, and though it was barely noon she was ready to call it a day.

Cochrane put the laptop back in its black nylon case. "Pilots zip, us zip. No one threw himself on his sword and confessed."

"With all the information we had on Michelson I thought he was going to break."

"I was hoping he would, but he didn't. He's like a tough old boar—hard to kill even with a shot directly to the head."

Ellen stood and made sure they left nothing of consequence behind. "Michelson's more like a cat, if you ask me. He used up eight of his nine lives today, and he's still going. Even with an eyewitness, he has the gall to lie. He's supposed to be a Navy officer."

"Michelson is not going to hurt his father, who is an admiral. He'll lie to protect his family tree and the military dynasty he sprang from. What's truth got to do with it?" Cochrane hefted the computer by the strap and placed it over his shoulder, then picked up his bulging briefcase. "Just because you're a Navy officer doesn't mean you're an officer and a gentleman," he told her as they walked down the passageway.

Ellen gazed longingly at the afternoon sunlight slanting through the open windows. In the distance, she heard jets taking off. "Fraternity?"

"Yeah, it's called the Brotherhood. They don't rat on one another, regardless of what their rank is."

"Even if they've done something wrong?" she asked, glad to leave Ops behind and feel the warmth of the sun. A breeze lifted several strands of her hair.

"Sure, it's believed 'the system' can fix itself from within."

"Obviously that isn't true. What kind of role models do they think they are if they'll lie, cheat or stonewall to protect one of their members who's guilty of something?"

"Reckon that's part of their lesson. Officers aren't gods, nor are they automatically good role models. There might have been twenty or so military men involved in the extreme behavior at Ares. Most of the attendees were unidentified civilians. Those twenty bad apples are hardly representative of Navy officers in general." Cochrane stopped at the car and unlocked it.

"Doesn't it sadden you?" Ellen asked, sliding into the passenger seat.

Cochrane got in and buckled up. "The men in my family were all in the Navy, and I was taught to be proud of that fact." He put the key into the ignition. "Hell of a lapse between idealism and reality, isn't it?"

As they drove away, Ellen shook her head. "Michelson was lying through his teeth. It was so obvious. And Baden sat there like his client wasn't guilty at all."

"That's his job—to defend his client against all accusations. I'm sure Michelson hasn't told Baden everything," Jim said.

"You think so?"

"Yeah."

Ellen gazed at the tall, stately palms lining the avenue. Giddings was a large, sprawling station very close to the freeway. "I thought you were supposed to tell your attorney everything."

Chuckling, Cochrane said, "Well, in a naval aviator's world and realm, blood is thicker than water. Baden may be his attorney, but he's not part of the air community. In fact, Baden may not want to know all the details, so he can't be responsible if Michelson is lying."

"This whole legal system is sick," she muttered as she looked out the window.

Cochrane turned onto the freeway, "It reads 'innocent until proven guilty in a court of law.' Let's find that Red Cross office and see what Susan Kane's phone call was all about, shall we?"

Ellen shrugged. "I hope the Red Cross is more forthcoming than Michelson was."

"I reckon they'll do everything they can to help us. They can't have as many things to hide as Michelson does. That poor bumpkin was like an amateur magician with all his cards falling out of his sleeves."

CHAPTER ELEVEN

"MAY I HELP YOU?" A white-haired woman in her sixties with gold-framed glasses sat expectantly at the reception desk of the Red Cross.

Cochrane removed his hat and tucked it beneath his left arm. "Yes, ma'am," and went on to explain why they needed to talk to a supervisor.

"Of course," the woman said, picking up the phone. "I'll tell Ms. Ebsen, Lieutenant."

Within five minutes, they were ushered into Madeline Ebsen's office, a small, pale pink room filled with healthy green plants. After taking a seat, Cochrane pulled out the information given to them by the phone company. Ms. Ebsen, a trim and elegant woman in her midfifties, took the piece of paper he handed her and read it quickly.

"You're in luck, Lieutenant Cochrane. Linda Farmer, who took the message, is still on duty. If you'll wait here, I'll go see if she remembers anything about that call. In the meantime, I'll have my assistant locate those records and bring them to my office."

The wait was short. Linda Farmer entered the office and reviewed the phone records brought by the assistant.

"Oh…" Linda said with a sad smile, "I remember this call, Maddy." She glanced at Cochrane. "The woman said her name was Lieutenant Susan Kane, and she seemed intoxicated."

"Intoxicated?" Cochrane said.

"Yes. I remembered the call because she slurred her words so badly and took forever to put a sentence together. When I sat down at my computer, she hung up."

"Why?" Cochrane demanded.

Ms. Ebsen went over to the computer and sat down. "Wait a moment. Let me retrieve that file." She quickly typed in the name Kane, and all the information popped up on the monitor.

Cochrane and Ellen got up and leaned over her shoulders. "Yes, this is her. She was slurring her words."

"Who was the message to?" he asked.

"Umm, wait. Ah, here it is—Tommy."

Ellen looked up, shock bolting through her. "Tommy…"

Cochrane knelt down beside the Red Cross volunteer to get a better look at the monitor. "What was the message?"

Linda Farmer sighed. "That's just it, Lieutenant. There was none. I must have spent ten minutes on the phone with her and she became increasingly incoherent. I couldn't understand her, so I made her spell out the words, and even then I couldn't grasp all she was saying. I couldn't find out who Tommy was or where he was located."

"Why did she hang up?" Ellen asked.

"I think it was too much for the poor dear," Linda Farmer said. "She struggled so hard to get the first part of what I needed for the message that I think she just gave up. Her voice was getting weaker."

"What did she say?" Jim asked.

"That she wanted to contact her brother."

Ellen pursed her lips. "Did you say anything about the emergency?"

"No, she didn't. I was just getting to the body of the message when she suddenly hung up. She'd refused to give me her phone number, so I couldn't recontact her. Caller ID was blocked."

"Dadgum," Cochrane muttered, standing up. He glanced at Ellen, who also looked defeated. "Can you give us a copy of your report?"

"Of course." Ms. Ebsen hit the print button. In moments, the record appeared. She tore it off and handed it to him.

"You don't remember anything else she said?" Cochrane asked.

"No, not really," Linda Farmer said. "Fortunately, everything that is said is written down and kept in the computer. I do hope this situation wasn't too serious."

"Susan Kane is dead," Cochrane told them. "That's why I'd like you to try and remember anything else you can recall."

"Oh, dear," Linda Farmer murmured apologetically, "I didn't know. I'm very sorry. She seemed like such a confused young woman. It was so hard to talk to her." Linda tapped her chin in thought. "I do recall that she said she loved Tommy very much, and he was the only one who could help her."

"With what?"

Linda shook her head. "I don't know, Lieutenant."

"If you think of anything else, ma'am, give me a call at the office?" He handed her his business card.

"Of course I will. This is all so sad...."

ELLEN CAUGHT UP WITH Cochrane out in the parking lot. "So close and yet so far away, huh?" Their hands brushed as they walked. To her surprise, Jim quickly wrapped his fingers around hers and gave them a quick squeeze. Then he released her hand.

"Okay with that?" he asked, smiling down at her. This investigation on Susan Kane was eating a hole in him, but Ellen's presence helped salve it. He hadn't planned to touch her—it just happened. When he saw her eyes go wide with surprise, he had to make sure it was okay. Holding his breath, he waited for her answer.

"I'm okay with it, Jim," Ellen answered softly. And she was. Seeing the look in his gray eyes, that banked warmth directed at her, she felt herself lighten up from the heaviness of the investigation. "You pick me up just when I need it. This business with death gets to me a lot more than I'd like to admit."

"I didn't want to overstep any bounds with you," he said huskily. "You need to keep telling me what is or is not appropriate toward you, Ellen."

She brushed some curls off her face. "I can do that. But it works both ways, Jim."

Nodding, he said, "I know." He took a deep breath. "The truth is, gal, you shed sunshine in the darkness of my life. The last two years have been a special hell for me. When you dropped into my world, I thought it was bad news, but now I can see I was wrong."

"Well," Ellen whispered, giving him an encouraging smile, "that's a wonderful revelation. I thought I was still a pain in your ass."

"Far from that," Jim said. He held out his hand to her as they walked. "Peace between us, pardner?"

She slipped her fingers into his strong ones. "Peace." *And happiness. You make me happy, Jim.* Ellen bit back the words. "Whether you realize it or not, Jim, you make my days a joy. Before this, things were pretty dreary, gray and depressing. I didn't have anything to look forward to."

He grinned and felt heat rising from his neck into his face. Good grief! He was blushing! Him! Unable to hold her earnest green gaze, Cochrane said, "That's good news, gal. I never thought I'd hear that from a woman again."

"Hey, Mr. JAG officer. I look forward to waking up in the morning now. Before this assignment, I didn't. Even on your grouchy-old-bear days, it's still a pleasure to work with you." She met his startled gaze and smiled into his eyes.

"Gosh and by golly. Does that mean there's hope for us, gal?" His heart took off in flight as he saw her soft lips curve.

"I'm in it for the long haul, Jim. I'm not an overnighter, if you know what I mean."

"Of course I do. And we're more alike than we probably realize. I don't do one-night stands, either. I do long term."

"That's good to know," Ellen breathed. She wanted to do more than hold his hand now. She wanted to kiss him until their mouths melted together as one. Somehow, Ellen knew Jim would be an incredible lover. He was sensitive, observant, and truly liked to please her. She had never imagined falling for someone so swiftly. She'd known Mark for over a year before she realized she was in love with him. Had his death changed her? Had she grown up and matured since then or was her attraction to Jim Cochrane that of a widow coming out of two years of grieving? Ellen wasn't sure. She didn't have all the answers, but she knew one thing: Jim appealed to her on every level. Giddy, Ellen felt her fears receding.

"I want you to know I won't allow our personal life to interfere in our work," she told him.

"I know that," Jim said, slowing his pace. "We just haven't had time to pursue anything personal. And Susan's case isn't going to free us up anytime soon."

"This is a complex case," Ellen agreed. "And I can wait until we have quality time, Jim. I'm okay with it."

"Good." He wasn't. He was positively itching to get his hands on Ellen, explore her and feel her come alive beneath his caresses.

"Right now, I'm trying to understand Susan's modus operandi," Ellen said, getting back on a more professional topic. She wanted their personal conversation, the exploration, to continue, but realized it wasn't the right time.

"That's what most investigations are like," Jim said. "Never any straight-to-the-heart clues, just ragged edges of puzzle pieces. Sort of like a hound following the tracks of a clever coon who's crisscrossing back and forth to make him lose the scent."

"A crazy quilt being pieced together." As she climbed into the car, Ellen said, "Based on the evidence, I think Susan only trusted Tommy in her family."

Cochrane put on his seat belt and started the car. "Reckon so, but what was she trying to tell him before she died?"

"I wonder if Tommy realizes Susan tried to contact him?"

"Probably not, because the Red Cross didn't send the message. And Tommy said nothing to us. I think he's the only one of the three who was dirt honest in our interviews."

"What was Susan going to tell Tommy? Or Ann?"

As he pulled out of the large asphalt parking lot, he

put on his aviator glasses to shield his eyes from the sinking sun. "Talk about liars, we have those interviews with the Top Guns coming up."

"They're an interesting bunch, no doubt about it. And not all of them are liars. Just a few bad apples in there from what I can see so far."

"Gordon Bassett is in the frying pan next. I'm curious to see what he says or recalls about Susan Kane."

Ellen's nostrils flared. "I hope he's not like Lieutenant Michelson."

"We'll see." Jim chuckled. "Michelson didn't waste any positive feelings, did he?"

Ellen frowned. "No. It took everything in me to just sit there and not get angry over his Neanderthal philosophy about women being homemakers while boys make war."

"I saw the anger in your eyes."

"I hope it wasn't too obvious?"

"Like a fox licking her chops when she's got a hen in her den." He grinned. "Michelson saw it, too. He had problems when you asked the questions."

"Why?"

"Because you're a woman and a civilian. Michelson tried that 'boys will be boys' stuff with you and it didn't work. He didn't know how to respond to you. And I think you got more out of him than I would have." Cochrane slanted her a glance after he'd turned onto the freeway. "Come the morrow, I want you to interview Bassett."

"With pleasure," she assured him.

July 7

LIEUTENANT GORDON BASSETT, known as Gordie the Glacier by his squadron mates, had the appearance of a young college athlete. To Ellen he didn't look more than twenty-two—a freckle-faced, square-jawed kid with high color in his ruddy cheeks. She saw the errant strand of chestnut-colored hair dipping rebelliously across his broad, smooth brow. His mouth was full and impish, his brows thick and slightly arched across his large, penetrating brown eyes. In Ellen's opinion, he was the archetype poster boy for a college jock.

Bassett gave her a ten-thousand-megawatt smile as he entered their office.

Ellen kept a cool head though she was tempted to scowl. She wasn't fresh bait, and that was the gist of his flirting look, as if she were a painted doll in this drama. She saw Bassett give Cochrane a steadier look, no smile, his brows dipping to express his obvious dislike of the legal officer.

Bassett's lawyer was short and a little overweight, with a potbelly not disguised by his rumpled, dark blue, double-breasted suit. Ellen didn't like the lawyer's attitude or how his small hazel gaze flickered between her and Cochrane like a coyote checking out its enemies.

After asking the men to sit down, she introduced herself and Cochrane.

Bassett grinned at her. "Haven't I seen you around the O Club before?"

Ellen's scowl deepened. "Put a choke chain on it, Lieutenant."

The man's smile slipped considerably. He nervously cleared his throat and glanced at his lawyer. "This is Harvey Goldman, my attorney."

Cochrane shook Goldman's hand and so did Ellen.

"Okay, let me get through the prelims and then Agent Tanner will question you, Lieutenant Bassett," Cochrane said.

Bassett's gaze snapped to Ellen briefly, sizing her up before he gave his full, undivided attention to the JAG.

Ellen couldn't keep feeling nervous. The way Bassett kept cutting his gaze in her direction was intimidating. The playful, flirtatious quality she'd seen before had been replaced with the studied coldness of a killer. She had to remind herself that all aviators were just that—paid to put their lives on the line, to kill or be killed.

Bassett seemed at odds with the killer image, though. He had the face of an innocent, yet his eyes were old and intense. He'd flown in the Iraq war and had shot down one enemy aircraft before being assigned to Giddings a year ago, Ellen knew. She'd been up until one in the morning preparing her questions, based upon information they'd collected.

Cochrane gestured at last. "He's all yours, Agent Tanner."

"Thank you, Lieutenant." She kept her voice low and firm. Bassett was staring at her, trying to psyche her out.

Fat chance, Dude. You picked on the wrong woman this time. This was why Cochrane was treating her more formally. Bassett was the kind of person who would use any weakness to his advantage—at least, that's what her intuition told her. Ellen lifted her chin and stared back at him, unblinking.

"We'd like you to tell us what you did, where you were and what activities you took part in at the Ares Conference in May, Lieutenant Bassett."

"Sure," he said, giving her a flirty smile, "no problemo."

As he launched into his account, Ellen kept her original notes on hand, making small checks where his testimony contradicted what they had compiled from their various sources. She glanced over and saw that Cochrane realized something was amiss, also.

"Your story is very different from info we have here," she said, pointing to the files next to her laptop.

With an easy shrug of his broad shoulders, Bassett smiled again and said, "You know how it is, Ellen. With time, you forget some things."

"It's Agent Tanner to you, Lieutenant."

"Sure, whatever you want." Bassett's mouth thinned.

Ellen almost heard the nonverbal *honey.* Anger nipped at her and she allowed him to see it in her eyes. Unlike Michelson, Bassett was cool like that glacier handle of his, obviously at ease in tense situations. She went over several points and he answered them in a drone. Ellen decided to jolt him out of his complacency.

"Did Lieutenant Michelson discuss his interview with you?"

Bassett's brown eyes hardened. "Why, no, ma'am."

"You're under oath, Lieutenant," Ellen said.

His lips pulled away, exposing his teeth. "Are you calling me a liar, Agent Tanner?"

Ellen's stomach clenched as the aviator leaned forward, his attention fixed on her. "Lieutenant Michelson signed papers swearing he wouldn't discuss this investigation with anyone. I find it unusual you would mention the lieutenant's headache."

"Some details stand out in my memory. Others don't. This particular one did. He's not prone to headaches, usually."

Though she didn't like his arrogance or confidence, Ellen continued, "We have a witness who places you just outside the Leopard Radar suite that Friday evening."

Bassett sat back, propping his fingertips together. "If you're referring to the alleged activities that may have taken place in the third-floor corridor, my answer is no. Like many others, I passed through that area from time to time during the conference. It was always crowded and sometimes I bumped into people."

"Were you in the Leopard Radar Corporation suite at any time?"

"Sure, everyone moseyed through there at some point in the conference." Bassett gave her a very smug look. "It's likely your witness had been drinking and her powers of observation were impaired."

"Very well. Lieutenant, I want to ask you about Susan Kane, an instructor in your squadron here at Top Gun. Did you see her at the conference?"

"Sure. She was drinking like everyone else. I also saw her later, after I returned from the movie." He raised his finger in emphasis, "I walked through the patio to see if there was anyone around I knew. When I didn't find anyone, I went straight to my room like a good little boy."

"Who was with her?"

"I saw a couple of guys assist her off the patio—strangers to me. I assume they took her to her room. Or at least they were heading toward the elevators. That's all I remember."

Ellen looked down at her notes. She decided to rattle him, if possible. "It says here that you're married?"

"Yes, a second marriage with children." Wiping his mouth, he glared at her.

"Tell me about your kids, Lieutenant."

Bassett's eyes narrowed speculatively, and he shifted in his seat. "I have two sons."

"Do you hope they'll follow in your footsteps? Carrying on in Navy tradition?"

He shrugged lazily and tried to look relaxed. "One might, but the other one won't."

"Why is that?"

"He's..." Bassett gave her a pained look, then

looked up at the ceiling when he muttered, "Jake has a severe learning disability."

"I see." Ellen saw the pilot express real emotion for the first time. Anguish flared momentarily in his eyes and the macho aviator facade dropped away. Bassett didn't seem to want to discuss it, but she persisted.

"Is Jake the oldest?"

"Yes."

"Is he in school?"

"Sort of." Bassett squirmed.

"What does that mean, Lieutenant?" Ellen noticed the anger and pain in his eyes.

"It means that on my Navy paycheck, I can't afford the special schooling Jake needs. I'm hoping to get my early lieutenant commander leaves, which will put me into a pay bracket where I can afford better schooling for him."

Ellen gave him a sympathetic look. "These financial constraints must be awfully hard on you and your wife."

Bassett looked away and in a barely audible voice said, "Things are a little tight right now."

Cochrane intervened. "When asked about being seen with Lieutenant Hawkins in front of the Leopard Radar Corporation suite, you stated that—" he searched his papers to find the exact quote "—'it's likely your witness had been drinking and her powers of observation were impaired.'"

"So?" Bassett sneered.

"I don't recall Agent Tanner saying the witness was female," Cochrane said in a soft tone.

Bassett flinched and went a little pale. "Uh…"

Cochrane continued more strongly, "Our witness, a male naval aviator, places you and Lieutenant Hawkins standing at the doorway to the Leopard Radar Corporation suite at 1900 on May 15th."

Bassett shifted in the chair, his knuckles white as he gripped the arms. "The witness is mistaken, whether it be male or female," he croaked.

Cochrane gave the pilot a big grin, as if to say, "I got you, you son of a bitch."

From then on, Gordie the Glacier repeated, "I don't recall," like a litany to any question Ellen asked him. She decided to conclude the interview. They'd gotten what they'd wanted.

CHAPTER TWELVE

ELLEN LOOKED AT HER WATCH. Fourteen hundred hours. They'd just finished their third interview of the day with Giddings pilots, and Cochrane had gone to get them coffee. Their luck had changed after Bassett's interview. Lieutenant Commander Douglas, an instructor at Top Gun, brought in photos his wife had taken at the Ares Conference. He'd been a strong supporter of Susan Kane and female pilots in general. The man was devastated by her untimely death and had wanted to help find out why she had died. He'd gladly handed them his wife's pictures, and they had helped the investigation immensely.

Ellen scanned in the photos and sent them directly to the Pentagon computer for use in their ever-widening search for military personnel who had attended Ares. She hoped the new photos would produce matches.

She spread her notes out to the right of her laptop. After typing in Susan Kane's name, she waited to see if it would pop up back at the main terminal. Nothing happened. She typed "woman, tall, short brown hair, blue eyes." Nothing. Persisting, she typed in "woman in uniform." The monitor lit up with several titles of interview reports. She highlighted the photos one at a time and sent them to the printer.

Waiting impatiently, she saw Jim amble in with their coffee.

"Get something going?" he asked, handing her a cup.

"I'm working at it. Thanks." Their fingertips brushed. Ellen absorbed the contact like a starving thief. But now wasn't the time to wonder about their future. On Sunday evening, a captain who worked directly with the CNO at the Pentagon had called Jim at home. He'd strongly advised that Lieutenant Kane's reason for suicide be found as quickly as possible. More pressure from above, and Ellen knew what that meant: working long hours, 24/7.

Right now, she enjoyed Jim's company and loved working with him. He was an excellent teacher: patient and gently teasing her when she made mistakes. It was easy to learn from him. Pointing to the printer, she said, "Look at this!" There were three photos, with dates and names of the source written below.

Grinning, Cochrane studied the images. "Bingo. There's Susan and she's in uniform."

Ellen studied one photo intently. "She's at a portable bar, just like Bassett said."

"Yes, and the date and time fit, too. I'm surprised he gave up that kind of information. Michelson didn't."

"Michelson was supposedly not there, remember?"

The other photos were of different female officers and didn't lead to any information regarding the Kane investigation. Ellen studied the monitor again. She looked at the second photo on the screen. A Navy aviator was identified as Morgan, A., Lieutenant, *USS Abraham Lincoln*. The printer cranked up again after several minutes, and Morgan's name appeared. Ellen stood there, reading the Super Hornet pilot's report to a Pentagon advisor.

"I think I made a connection, Jim!" She excitedly turned to Cochrane, who lifted his head.

"Well, what did the computer whiz find now?"

Ellen punched the paper and smiled triumphantly. "According to this interview, Lieutenant Al Morgan from the *USS Abraham Lincoln* stated that he saw, and I quote, 'A very drunk, tall, pretty woman in a Navy uniform at the elevators on the third floor, just off the patio. She was stinking drunk and the man who was with her was in civilian clothes, holding her up so she wouldn't fall. She was semiconscious, leaning heavily on that man.' Maybe this is Susan." Reading rapidly, Ellen added, "Morgan got off on the ninth floor, but he saw the man punch the button for fifteen."

Cochrane raised his brows. "Kane had a room on the tenth floor, though."

"Where did Bassett, Hodges and Michelson have their rooms?"

"We know Michelson was on the fifteenth floor.

Let's see where Bassett and Hodges were…." Cochrane went to the computer terminal and found the information. He grinned a little. "Sooooey! They all had rooms on the fifteenth floor."

"'Sooey'?"

He laughed. "That's a hog call, Ellen. We use it to call them in at night. It's kinda like 'wow' to you people who live outside the Ozarks."

Ellen smiled. "You never cease to amaze me with your dazzling array of language skills, Lieutenant Cochrane."

He bowed slightly. "Thank you, ma'am. I'll take that as a compliment."

"You would." She became serious. "I wonder if it was Susan that Morgan saw?"

"No way of telling. We'll have to contact him on his ship by Iridium phone hookup and ask him. We'll supply him with an e-mail picture of Susan, so he can verify if it was her or not."

"I want to make that call right now."

"Okay." Jim looked at his watch. "It will be 1000 tomorrow in Japan, if I remember my time zone changes correctly."

Ellen was barely able to contain her excitement, and he eased back in his chair, stretched his arms over his head and grinned. "You look like a bloodhound on a scent."

Laughing softly, Ellen nodded. "I'm really excited. I mean, we're finally getting some essential info on

Susan." She waited impatiently while the phone made the hookup.

"Lieutenant Morgan speaking."

Her heart accelerated momentarily, and she quickly introduced herself. "We've got your report and I wanted to ask you some additional questions."

"Like what?"

"Could you identify either the man or the woman in the elevator you were on?"

"No."

"Please, this is important."

"So is my career, Agent Tanner."

"I understand, Lieutenant Morgan. Do you think you could identify the man?"

"I didn't know who he was, if that's what you're asking."

"Do you recall anything about him?"

"No, not really. I was a little tipsy myself, and to be honest, I didn't pay much attention to him or the woman officer."

"What time did you see them in the elevator?"

"Around 2300 on May 15th."

"What was he wearing?"

"I remember a bright-colored Hawaiian shirt. I think he was wearing tan chinos and maybe some white tennis shoes, but I can't be sure. I do remember the shirt, though."

"What colors?"

"Uhh, I think it had a white background with bright red flowers or some other print on it."

"What do you remember about the woman?"

"She wore a set of gold aviator wings on her uniform."

"She had a name tag over her left breast pocket. Do you recall seeing that?"

"No, not really. She was almost unconscious, and the guy was holding her up."

"Color of hair?"

"I don't remember."

"And you remember the male pressing the fifteenth-floor button?"

"Yes, I do, because I was standing right next to the panel and he lunged by me to hit it just as the doors slid shut."

"Did he say anything?"

"Just that his girlfriend was drunker than hell, I think."

Ellen sighed and held the phone a little tighter. "Did the woman speak?"

"No, she just moaned from time to time. Actually, she was leaning heavily against the guy, her head over his shoulder, and he was holding her around the waist so she wouldn't fall."

"Do you recall smelling alcohol on them?"

Morgan laughed a little nervously. "Listen, I was drunk, and I'm sure I smelled of beer, too."

"So, you smelled beer on them?"

"I'm not sure. The odor of beer was in the elevator after the door shut. It could have been any one of us or all of us. I just don't know."

"You've been a big help, Lieutenant Morgan. I'm going to e-mail you some photos for identification purposes. You should get them shortly. If you do recognize anyone in them, e-mail me back right away?"

"Okay, but I'm not sure I'll know any of them."

"Just do your best. Thanks for your time, and I'll send you an e-mail transcript of this phone call for your records. Goodbye."

Ellen hung up and looked over at Jim. "I'm beginning to like this work."

"Yeah." He chuckled and stood up, ambling around the desk to study the notes she'd put on her laptop. "I can tell. But don't think this high tech stuff is normal investigating. Shoe leather is the common methodology."

"I understand. Still, I feel I'm doing a credible job."

"The only measure of this job is credible proof. But, hey, don't let my pessimistic nature get you down. You're doing swell."

"Good grief! Praise!"

Grinning, he saw her place her hand dramatically over her heart.

"Come on, Ellen."

"Seriously, you always tease me and let me know what I didn't do right."

"You're turning into a 4.0 investigator. Okay? I liked the way you questioned Morgan. You scored some good points. That's the sign of a detective in the making," he said.

She sat there, a warmth stealing through her. Jim stood next to her and she savored his closeness. Looking back down at her laptop, Ellen forced herself to focus on the job. "I like searching through the computer. It's a faster way to solve this puzzle."

Cochrane placed his hand on her shoulder. "If you're trying to impress me, Ellen, you're succeeding." God knew, he had been wanting to touch her more and more lately. He'd resisted. Barely. But today, Jim was helplessly ensnared by her natural ebullience. He squeezed her shoulder gently.

"Enough to take me to dinner tonight?" Oh no, did she say that out loud? Ellen sat there, stunned at herself. This just wasn't like her. But then, nothing about this quasi relationship was normal. Her eyes widened and she cast an anxious look up at Jim. He seemed a bit shocked, too.

"Sure. Why not?" His heart sped up. She'd invited *him* on a date! The idea permeated through him like hot butter melting in a skillet.

"Why did you hesitate?" she asked.

"You caught me off guard. That's all." Jim was beginning to enjoy her spontaneity. It was helping to free him from his frigid fortress.

"I surprised myself, believe me." Ellen managed a wry smile. Her pulse picked up as she considered her bravado.

Cochrane set his pen aside and trained his attention on her. "I thought you'd gotten enough of my company on this high-pressured case."

Ellen nodded. "You were an unknown quantity to me at the start of this investigation, but I'm not tired of you or it. I would love some time just to sit and talk with you."

"I like the idea," Jim agreed. He'd been aching to carve out personal time with her.

Ellen grinned. "Now that that's settled, I'd sure like pizza tonight." She saw Jim's gray eyes go wide with pleasure, and her heart swelled. Just the idea of being alone with him, out of the office, sent her into a tizzy of joy, laced with just a bit of anxiety. What did he think of her invitation? Apparently, he liked it.

Cochrane brightened. "Good, I know just the place! There's a guy who has this huge old pipe organ and plays it while old silent movies run above him on a screen. It's a real family restaurant—lots of kids and parents. I take Merry there as often as I can. She loves the place."

"I like kids."

"I kind of thought you might. Okay, pizza it is." Jim turned and went back to work, then looked up at her again. "What kind of pizza do you like?"

"Vegetarian style."

He groaned.

"What does that moan mean, Mr. Cochrane?"

Laughing, he said, "It means we get two pizzas. One all-man pizza with everything but the kitchen sink, and a second wimpy pizza for my vegetarian pardner."

As far as Ellen was concerned, Monty's Pizza Palace was like a miniature Disneyland. At 6:00 p.m., the large, bustling establishment was packed with families. The noise level was high, but when Monty, a short and plump man in his fifties, came out to play the immense pipe organ, patrons magically quieted down.

Ellen thought Jim looked so different tonight, besides the change into more casual clothing. He wasn't like the intense legal officer she'd come to know. Even his hair, slightly mussed, gave him a younger air, of someone carrying fewer responsibilities. He sat across from her, a huge piece of pizza cradled in his hands, eating with unabashed relish. The pipe organ began to play loudly and dramatically as a silent movie flickered across the huge screen above. Ellen glanced at the old western, munching contentedly on her vegetarian pizza. They agreed to talk once the movie and music ended.

After dinner, as they strolled toward the parking lot, Jim placed his hand against his belly. "I feel like an old boar who discovered the local garbage dump and ate too much."

Ellen laughed. "For someone who made fun of my vegetarian pizza, you sure ate a lot of it."

"Well, I had a little room left after I finished off mine. You know, us starving hill boys can't be choosy."

At the glint in his eyes, Ellen felt her face turn hot. How she wished she'd stop blushing. That teenage reaction had stopped when she graduated from high school. Why was it starting again? She noticed shadows playing across his boyish face. Jim had a disarming quality. She liked the way his mouth stretched into a lazy, almost contented smile.

"I feel like I'm with a different person tonight," Ellen murmured. "Don't you?" Glancing up at him, she saw his gaze was tender and assessing. How badly she wanted to kiss him. The urge was so real Ellen had to force her hands to remain at her sides as they slowly walked along together. Sometimes their hands brushed as they wove through the crowded parking lot.

"A hog can't change its spots. I'm the same person, different uniform, gal."

"Nice try, Jim. You act differently, so it's more than just the clothes you're wearing. I'm glad I got spontaneous and asked you out."

"Look at you," Cochrane said, pointing to the body-fitting jeans she wore. "You're out of your hippie clothes. Right now you look more like a college student." She was shapely and didn't look like a skinny fashion model. Jim liked women with flesh on their bones. Ellen was filled out in all the right places as far as he was concerned.

"Oh, please," she protested, touching her flaming cheek. She saw the sparkle of mischief in his eyes.

"Reckon us thirtysomethings can look twentysomething at times."

"You sure do," she said. "I'd never have thought you'd wear a pair of ratty—I mean—"

Chuckling, Jim opened the car door for her. "Ratty's

the operative word, Ms. Tanner. Us hill folk don't dress fancy for anyone. Growing up, I was usually in a pair of ragged Levi's that needed the knees patched, and a holey ole T-shirt and no shoes. Ma could never understand me preferring my old clothes instead of others that were in better shape. I used to exasperate the daylights out of her with my choices."

As he stood holding the car door open, Ellen heard the pride in his voice and saw it in his face. "I think your hill upbringing gave you some solid values, no matter what you wore."

"What do you know? A woman who can see the man and not his clothes."

Grinning, Ellen settled into the seat. "Are you stereotyping me again?"

"I wouldn't dream of it, Ms. Tanner. No, you defy description yourself," he said conspiratorially as he shut the door.

Ellen wasn't about to let him get away with that statement. "Don't you think it's about time men and women started treating one another as individuals and not as stereotypes?" she asked as he settled in his seat.

Starting the car, Jim gave her a lazy smile. "It would help. When you came down from changing clothes at your new apartment, you surprised me. I thought you were going to be wearing some hippie outfit, but instead you looked like a young'un, jeans and all. This West Coast sunshine must be rubbing off on you."

"So that's why you gave me that odd look. I couldn't

figure out whether you liked what I was wearing or not."

"You sort of reminded me of my past, my growing-up years."

Ellen remained silent, digesting his words. She had thrown on a pair of comfortable jeans and a pink tank top, and tamed her hair back into a ponytail. She stole a look at Jim now as they drove through El Cajon. His face was expressionless again. His voice, however, was anything but devoid of feeling.

Ellen nervously knit her fingers in her lap, unsure how to take his compliment. If it *was* a compliment. For the first time since her husband had died, Ellen felt an exhilarating emotion enter her heart—a giddy, spiraling sensation that left her a little breathless. Absently, she touched the center of her chest, feeling wonder that, of all people, Jim had stirred her so, made her want to start living again.

Ellen slanted him a quick glance. Jim seemed unaware of her thoughts and feelings. Why wouldn't he be? She wasn't communicating and he wasn't a mind reader.

"Tell me about yourself, Ellen. About your growing-up years," Cochrane urged. "How about your parents? Any brothers or sisters?"

Pleased that he was interested, she said, "I'm the oldest daughter of three. Both my sisters are policewomen. They followed in Mom's footsteps, while I followed in Dad's. He used to tell us nonclassified things about his job with the FBI. I fell in love with detective work, then." She smiled wistfully. "Growing up, I was the quiet little girl in the back of the room. Really shy at the time." She touched her red hair. "I know you think I'm a brazen woman, but I'm not."

"Only around me," Cochrane chuckled.

"Yes, I guess you bring out that side of me," Ellen said with a grin.

"What got you into psychology?"

"My parents. My mother had to take courses for her police training and I used to pore over her books at home. My dad was a natural at human psychology. I used to sit with them and ask them both questions." She shrugged. "I guess people and their behavior have always fascinated me."

"Sounds like you got the therapist genes from your parents, for sure."

"Even now, I call them about once a week. There have been many times when I've asked their opinion on something that stumped me. Of course, I'd never mention the case or names, but they were always helpful, giving me information based upon their decades of experience."

"It sounds like you're close with your family, too."

"Oh, yes. My dad loves to fish. In Minnesota we have over ten thousand lakes, and my parents built a cabin up on Rock Lake, about three hours north of Minneapolis. I went up there on weekends. I loved the quiet of the lake, of nature, and the loons that lived there. Their call is so haunting."

"Nature girl," Jim said. "That's what I had you pegged as. Not a city slicker, even though you came from D.C."

She absorbed his pleasure. "Give me a choice, I'll take the country, Mr. Cochrane."

"I'm with you on that, gal. I found it healing to jog the rocky hills around San Diego County," Jim confided. "When Jodi split the blanket with me, I did a lot of hiking out there, trying to figure out where I'd gone wrong." He gave her a sad look. "The hardest thing was no longer having someone to share things with or hold in my arms at night. You get used to that stuff."

Touched, Ellen studied his profile. "I missed that the most after Mark died." Opening her hands, she whispered, "I guess we're both walking wounded of a sort. At least, that's how I see myself. These last two years have been a special kind of hell for me. I took for granted what we had, never dreaming I'd lose Mark or our happiness so soon."

"Has coming here to San Diego helped or hurt?"

"It's helped."

"How?"

"I threw myself into this project. Getting out of Washington was a godsend." Ellen gave him a searching look. "You're a tough taskmaster at times. I knew from the moment we met that you didn't want me around. I felt you couldn't trust me to do a good enough job, so I worked harder and put in longer hours to make up for my investigative deficiencies."

Cochrane pulled onto the freeway leading back to the heart of San Diego. The sulfur lights along the highway made huge amber splotches on the black asphalt—light against darkness. "I didn't mean to be hard on you, Ellen. You probably don't believe me, but that's the truth."

"I do believe you," she said.

"I think you're a softy at heart." Cochrane exited off the freeway at B Street. "Being a softy isn't all bad," he told her. "When I was fourteen, I fell in love with a little red-haired, freckle-faced girl name Pansy. She was like you—all feelings. She used to cry at the drop of a hat over some poor bug getting smashed, or some animal being hurt. She used to cry for me…."

Ellen didn't want the car ride to end, but her apartment was coming up. Jim was revealing himself and she wanted to continue exploring him. "Why did she cry for you?"

"Pansy was my first true love. I fell head over heels for that little freckled face of hers. I followed her around like a lovesick puppy. My grades slipped because when I wasn't with her, I was up in my tree house, daydreaming about her. I didn't do my homework, and my pa reminded me I got what I earned."

Jim braked the car and pulled into the pink stucco apartment complex surrounded by stately palm trees. At the entrance he parked the vehicle. Shifting, he turned toward Ellen, resting his arm across the back of the seat. "Pansy was the first to realize that I'd gotten a whipping for my failing grades after I took my report card home. She cried for me and it did something to me. Something...good and warm."

"That's because she loved you," Ellen whispered, looking up into his darkened gray eyes, so alive with feelings. She stifled an urge to touch those errant strands across his forehead.

"I'd never had anyone cry over me before," Cochrane said, his voice oddly off-key. He shrugged. "I saw the same look in your eyes a couple of times when I told you about my divorce problems with Jodi, or when I talked about Merry." He reached out, his fingertips lightly touching her ponytail. "And you remind me a little of Pansy. Maybe that's why I call you 'gal' when I can get away with it."

His stroke was electric on her unruly hair. Scalp tingling wildly, she swallowed, caught in the burning intensity of his searching gaze. Unconsciously, Ellen parted her lips, and saw longing in Jim's eyes—the kind that made her feel desirable. Shocked by the revelation, she panicked and reached for the door handle. She had to escape the sudden emotional intensity swirling between them.

"She had your kind of hair. Did I tell you that? Wild, frizzy curls like a red halo around her face." Cochrane saw Ellen's anxiety and lifted his hand away. "Pansy used to keep it in pigtails so the other kids wouldn't tease her so much about her funny-looking hair."

"Naturally curly hair like ours is hard to deal with," Ellen admitted in a small voice. Would Jim caress her again? Did she want to be touched? Her feelings were seesawing violently, and she disliked herself for being such an emotional coward. Jim didn't deserve this.

Swallowing hard, she asked in a low tone, "Do you think we have any kind of a future, Jim?" There, it was out. The words had been wanting to come out all night. It was so hard to be courageous in a relationship. Given their backgrounds, their jobs, could they ever make it work?

"I'm not sure," Jim admitted quietly. "As you know, I really didn't want you as a partner, but as the days went by, I found myself eager to see you, to know you'd be there in the office." His mouth pressed into a sad line as he held her gaze. "Ellen, I'm mixed up. I have this ongoing battle with Jodi over visitation rights to see Merry. I'm trying my darnedest to be there for my daughter when she needs me, but my workload these last two years has been brutal." He lifted his hand and gently touched her hair. "And then there's you and me. I don't know what you think and I'm still finding out what all these unexpected discoveries mean to me and my heart. One thing's for sure—I'm glad you've come into my life."

Ellen smiled tenderly. "Me, too. Like you, Jim, I feel like I'm betwixt and between right now. I'm leaving my grief behind. Like you, I wake up in the morning looking forward to coming to work. Part of it is because you're there. It's great to discover I'm not dead inside." She touched her heart and held his hooded gaze. "I'm scared spitless, if you want the truth—and I always want to be honest with you. The fact is I feel good. The depression I had is almost gone. It's an amazing thing. Frankly, I didn't expect to meet another man who would ever interest me like Mark had. And yet—" she sent Jim a lopsided smile "—here you are."

Running his palm tenderly along the top of her shoulder, Cochrane said in a low tone, "I'm glad to know you feel good about me being in your life. It's mutual." Sighing, he added, "This is complicated, Ellen."

"I know it is. More for you than me. Death has a finality to it. Divorce doesn't, especially if a child is involved. I understand why you're so torn, Jim."

Nodding, he frowned. "I wish things were easy and straightforward here, but they're not."

"More than anything, I want you to always see your daughter and be with her whenever you can. That's your first priority." She saw relief in his eyes. His fingers stroked her shoulder gently, and her flesh tingled. His caress was wonderful. Her whole body cried out to be stroked like that.

"Thanks, gal. I really needed to hear that." Studying her in the dusky light, Cochrane said, "In the Navy we have red light for stop, orange for caution and green for go, as a way to communicate between a man and woman. Between us, which is it?"

Shrugging, Ellen said, "A combination of orange and green?"

He laughed softly, "Only you would combine them, gal."

"What about you? How do you see us, Jim?"

His hand stilled on her shoulder. "A combination of orange and green."

Chuckling, she shook her head. "The pot calling the kettle black."

"Guilty as charged." Jim absorbed her tender gaze. "Orange because I have so much to balance, what with work, Jodi and my daughter. Green because I've never been drawn to a woman like I have to you."

Heart fluttering, Ellen closed her eyes. "I go through such a dazzling array of emotions in any given day with you, Jim. I feel panic. Anxiety. Happiness. I feel like jumping up and down for joy. The orange is all of that. As we said before, I'm a long-term person. I like to take things slow. I want to make sure the man I'm interested in is first of all my best friend. After that, everything else can fall into a natural order between us."

"I'm a long-hauler, too." Cochrane looked around as dusk began to darken to night. Returning his attention to Ellen, he added, "And I like the idea of learning to be your best friend. Maybe what we both need is time and no pressure."

"Yes. Definitely no pressure." She could tell Jim wanted to kiss her. Her mouth went dry. Her heart started pounding. She felt his hand move as if to draw her against him.

"May I kiss you, Ellen Tanner? I don't want to pressure you or assume anything with you, gal." Jim felt a stab of fear. What if she said no? Never had he wanted any woman to say yes more than her.

"And if I say no, Jim?"

He felt a pang of disappointment. "I won't hold it against you. I'm a big boy and I'll get over it." He frowned, knowing that it was a outright lie. "More than anything, Ellen, I want you to be comfortable around me. I'm trying to learn from my past mistakes, and God knows I made a ton of 'em. I don't want to make them with you if I can help it." That was the truth. The words came out low and filled with emotion.

"It makes all the sense in the world, Jim. Thanks for sharing all of this. It helps me sort things out in myself when you level with me like this."

"Thank Jodi for this 'new me,'" he said sadly.

For a man who was so deeply wounded, showing his vulnerability was the greatest gift he could give her. Ellen slid toward him and put her hand against his whiskery jaw. "Kiss me?"

"Gal, you are one surprise after another…." he whispered, lowering his head toward hers.

Closing her eyes, Ellen felt Jim's mouth ease tentatively against hers. His breath was warm against her skin, his hands coming up to frame her face. His long fingers were gentle as he captured her head and raised her chin slightly so he could fit his mouth fully against her parting lips. Whispering his name like a prayer, Ellen sank against his tall, lean body. She could feel his heart thundering against her breasts.

His fingertips brushed her temples, and the heat of his mouth created a conflagration within her body. Her breasts tightening against his chest, Ellen moaned softly. When one of his hands trailed down her jawline in a featherlight caress, she felt tears well in her closed eyes. Everything about Jim Cochrane was gentle and worshipping. In that moment, Ellen felt herself hungry with desire. His mouth was strong, cajoling, and yet allowing her to respond freely. She inhaled the fragrance of the lime aftershave on his skin, felt the prickle of stubble against her cheek and reveled in his heated breath against her flesh.

Ellen had no idea how long Cochrane kissed her, but she wanted it to go on forever. Reluctantly, she felt him ease her away from him. There was an anguished look on his face. She sat up and touched her throbbing lips, and realized her own pain was about desire—for him. It hit her and then dissolved like beads of dappled sunlight into her hungry body. "Wow," she whispered. "What a kiss."

Reaching out, Cochrane tunneled his fingers through her curly red hair. "I can say the same, gal. You knocked me into another universe with that kiss of yours." He smiled shyly.

Jim's reverent touch made Ellen feel as if she were the most precious woman on earth. Closing her eyes, she absorbed his lingering caress. "You are…wonderful."

"So are you, gal. And we have time."

She opened her eyes and nodded. "Yes, we have

time. Thank you, Jim, for everything. You make me want to live again." Ellen saw his expression lighten, saw joy sparkle in his stormy eyes. There was no question that he would take her to bed if she asked. The thought was frightening. Heady. Alluring. But Ellen wasn't ready for that yet.

"Listen, you'd better get going. We've got a long day ahead of us come the morrow. It's not going to be an easy one."

Ellen nodded and opened the car door. Happiness vaulted through her as she turned and caught his look. Cochrane's face was alive with tenderness aimed directly at her. Tonight, they'd turned a corner with one another—and it was mutual. That was as scary as it was exhilarating. "I know it won't be. Thanks for the pizza, Jim. It was fun."

"Yeah, it was, wasn't it? We'll do it again sometime soon, gal. Good night."

Climbing out of the car on suddenly weak legs, Ellen replied, "Good night." She almost turned and invited him into her apartment. Overheated and restless, her body clamored for union. Ellen knew he'd be a wonderful, caring lover. Exactly what she desired. Swallowing, she lifted her hand and stepped away from the car. It wasn't the right time. Not yet.

CHAPTER THIRTEEN

ON TUESDAY MORNING, Ellen arrived right on time at the office. She was surprised to see Commander Dornier there, wanting an update from Jim on the Kane investigation. Ellen said good morning to both men and then settled down to business. She obviously couldn't mention the beautiful, tender kiss they'd shared last evening. If Jim only knew how she'd tossed and turned all night.

As she gathered items for their forthcoming interviews at Giddings, the fatigue hit her hard. Before falling into an exhausted sleep at 3:00 a.m., Ellen had come to the conclusion that she'd have to have blind faith in the future where Jim was concerned. And if his quick, welcoming glance today was any indication, he'd gotten the same amount of sleep as she had.

Commander Dornier didn't leave until Jim stood up, peered at his watch and told him they had to get to Giddings. After asking her to drive, Jim got on the radio with NCIS people regarding other investigations under their wing. No personal talk today. Ellen resigned herself and mentally prepared for another grueling day of interviews.

ELLEN EASED HER SANDALS off her feet after Becky Jillson had left. The office was quiet except for Cochrane's hen-pecking on the computer keys. It was nearly noon, and she was famished. She placed her hand on her stomach to try and muffle the growling.

Cochrane looked up and gave her an elfin grin. "Is the big bad mama bear starving for lunch?" How badly he'd wanted to discuss the kiss they'd shared last night. There hadn't been time, and he found himself frustrated by the continuous string of interviews they had to conduct.

Laughing, Ellen slowly stood up and slid her fingers down her spine to ease the tension from sitting so long. "Yes, I guess I'm hungry." She ached to lean over and caress his hand. Under the circumstances, it was impossible. If they were ever seen during work hours "consorting" in a personal way, Ellen knew they'd be split up and she'd be sent back to Washington. That was enough to make her squelch her longing. She was going to have to be patient.

"You just can't keep a secret," he chuckled, typing up some final notes from their last interview. Lieutenant Becky Jillson had given them a lot of info.

"No, certainly not compared to Susan Kane. Now, there's a real secret-keeper." Ellen watched him highlight certain parts of Jillson's report. "What do you make of Becky's statement? She thinks Susan was implicated in something at Ares. And how about the fact that Becky saw those red marks on Susan's wrist when she visited her in the hotel room? Now that's something new."

"Reckon it could be inflammatory as hell. Although it offers nothing concrete on Michelson, Bassett or Hodges." Jim could smell the faint scent of the gardenia perfume Ellen wore. He inhaled it hungrily.

"Ann Hawkins fingered them."

"But she's not willing to flush her career down the commode to have them charged but not found guilty, either." Cochrane shook his head. "We'll need better evidence to prosecute any of those bastards. Someone else will have to break the code."

"Becky didn't seem too worried about reprisals. She gave us full testimony about what went on at Ares." Ellen kept her hands at her sides. She wanted to rest them on Jim's broad, proud shoulders.

With a snort, he muttered, "If she's lucky, she'll put in her twenty and get the rank of commander. Jillson has no great career opportunities like the men, so in effect, she has nothing to lose by telling us. Her husband is another story, though."

"I didn't realize how rough it got in that hallway outside the Leopard suite. According to her, women were running a gauntlet between drunken civilians and some pilots. Just like the Tailhook scandal. I thought that was done and over with."

"Yep, Tailhook, or a mini version of it, was alive and well at Ares. If that's so, some of these Top Gun aviators are in a lot of trouble. Like riding on the back of a wild razorback boar naked, my pa would say. And that's rough." Jim shut down the program and closed the laptop. "I found Susan's wrist injury to be interesting, too, didn't you?"

With a shrug, Ellen went back to her chair and slid her sandals on. "I think so. She was in a melee the night before in that same hallway outside the Leopard suite. I think it's quite possible she got hurt then, don't you?"

Standing, Cochrane picked up his cap and settled it on his head. "I don't know. For me a red flag went up over the wrist."

"Come on, Cochrane, I'm going to start gnawing on your arm if you don't take me over to O'Learys. My gut is waving a red flag, too. It's hungry and so am I."

At O'LEARY'S RESTAURANT, on base, Jim sat across from Ellen. He'd ordered his favorite—corned beef on rye—and she had a chicken breast salad. Today, she wore a short-sleeved white blouse and a long, purple cotton skirt. And those ever-present Birkenstock sandals. He tried to keep the smile off his face as he watched her pick through her greens.

"What is it about women and salads?" he wondered, biting into his thick, sauerkraut filled sandwich. Thousand Island dressing dripped between his fingers.

"What is it about men and their corned beef sandwiches?"

Wiping his mouth with a paper napkin, he noted the

challenging gleam in her eyes. "I thought you were going to say you were watching your weight."

Ellen arched an eyebrow. "Give me a break, Jim. I don't go for this 'thin is in' stuff. Women shouldn't be starving themselves into being paper dolls, with an eighteen-inch waist. I'm curvy and I'm staying that way."

"I knew you'd say something like that," he said, picking up his large glass of cola. After a sip, he set his drink aside. "I like your curves." And he wanted to explore them. Seeing her green eyes go soft, he whispered, "That was a compliment."

Cutting into the salad, she smiled at him. "Thank you. I took it as one." Ellen fantasized that his hands would linger here and there over her needy body. Never had she been so sexually hungry. Two years of celibacy was letting her know how much she missed good loving and sex with the right man.

"That one kiss sure brought my world to a halt." Jim saw her cheeks turn a bright red. Knowing he was in uniform and there were eyes everywhere, he did not reach out to touch her hand, but satisfied himself with holding her gaze. "Are you sorry it happened, gal?"

Ellen put down her fork. "No," she admitted in a low voice. Other patrons were sitting around them and she didn't want them to overhear.

"You're hesitant." Jim motioned with his hand. "You have dark circles under your eyes. What happened? Did you lie awake all night incriminating yourself over kissing me?" He grinned wolfishly at her. Ellen touched her hair, which he was learning was a sign of nervousness. He hoped their mutual kiss was a good thing, but she appeared unsettled by it.

After pushing the salad aside, Ellen folded her hands and leaned forward. "I *didn't* sleep much last night," she confessed.

"Uh-oh."

"Oh, don't go there! Can you put yourself in my place?"

Nodding, he lowered his voice even more. "Yeah, I can. You lost the man you loved two years ago, and here you've just kissed a frog that didn't turn into a prince. That is a bummer."

Shaking her head, Ellen laughed. "You are such a master of misstatement, Cochrane!"

Jim set his sandwich aside. This conversation was a helluva lot more important than eating. Wiping his hands on the napkin again, he said, "Maybe I did get a little dramatic on that one. I know there are folks who view me as a warty ole frog, but you're not one of them." He saw Ellen relax, some of the tension dissolving from around her lovely mouth. A mouth he wanted to claim again— and again. "I didn't get to sleep for a long time either, gal."

"I didn't think you would," Ellen said sympathetically. "Probably rehashing the divorce and swearing not to get involved with anyone after that. Right?"

"Say, you're good."

"I'm an analyst. My life is about understanding people's motives and problems. Even my own."

"So, are you sorry you kissed me?" Cochrane's heart skipped a beat as fear snaked through him. What if she said yes? He couldn't stand the thought of that, now that he'd tasted her, felt the softness of her hungry mouth against his.

"No. Just wrestling with a lot of stuff, Jim. For the life of me, I never entertained the possibility of running into another man that I'd be interested in." Ellen gave him a glittering smile and touched her hair. "After all, I'm a red-haired throwback to Irish warrior. There aren't many men willing to take me on."

"They can't appreciate you. But I like what I see. I like what you do in the investigation. You gain people's trust immediately and they give you good intel."

"I guess," Ellen said, folding her arms on the table, "I'm learning to trust *you*, Jim. I was awake until 3:00 a.m. thinking and feeling through that kiss we shared. I wanted you to kiss me. I wanted a lot more than that from you, but I'm afraid to go there. At least so far."

"I felt the same way."

"Thanks for not rushing it."

"I'm trying to learn to read signals," he told her wryly. "Men aren't very good at things like that. I'm trying to clean up my Neanderthal act."

Ellen laughed and gave him a broad smile. Those gold flecks were dancing in the depths of her green eyes, he noted. Jim wanted to drown in her gaze like a lovesick puppy, but knew he couldn't.

"You've never been a Neanderthal."

"Phew! That's a relief."

Ellen smiled gently. "I'm not sorry, Jim."

He picked up his Reuben sandwich and gave her a twisted grin. Cochrane was going to enjoy this moment alone with her. There was an interview that afternoon, and another scheduled tomorrow afternoon with Lieutenant Chuck Daily, a Top Gun instructor. Would this investigation never end? He wanted desperately to figure out why Susan had killed herself. And then he wanted time alone with Ellen to explore this whole new world that had suddenly opened up for them.

July 11

"WHAT DO TEDDY BEARS MEAN?" Cochrane asked Ellen as they waited for their next interviewee, Lieutenant Chuck Daily.

"In a symbolic sense?"

"Yeah, I guess so."

"What's this? The pragmatic attorney is actually going to look at something outside his own lens of reality?" She glowed inwardly over his asking her such a question. This was her bread and butter.

"Come on, Ellen, be kind to this poor ole country bumpkin, will you?" For a second night Cochrane hadn't slept—this time due to torrid dreams of making long, slow, delicious love to Ellen. He woke up more than once, finally took a cold shower at 3:00 a.m. and then finally fell asleep.

With a laugh, Ellen said, "Bears can represent many things. From a Jungian standpoint, it's important to ask what it meant to the person."

"Oh."

"Every archetypal symbol has a general meaning, Jim, but it may have some unusual or unique meaning to the individual. For instance, you love pizza."

His smile broadened. "No secret there."

"Really. Pizza means something to you."

"A full stomach."

"What else does it mean?"

He sat back in the chair and laced his fingers across his belly. "Okay, I'll get serious. It's food. It's salty and it tastes good. I love the cheese."

"And what if I handed a creature from outer space that same pizza? What do you think his reaction would be?" Ellen asked.

"He might think it wasn't food, perhaps."

"Exactly. That maybe it was a sacred object, or a pretty symbol that certainly shouldn't be eaten. Or a god or goddess that had suddenly appeared in front of him. If it was a pepperoni pizza, he might think the little round pieces of meat were eyes."

"I see your point. And here I thought this was going to be easy."

"Nice try, Mr. Cochrane. Therapy and psychology aren't simple. And Susan Kane was complex, although on the surface she seems to present a consistent pattern of behavior."

"Reckon you're right," Cochrane said grimly, sitting up and tinkering with the pens and pencils near his laptop. "Miss Perfect Role Model. Miss Perfect."

"Why the sudden interest in teddy bear symbology?" Ellen prodded.

His brow furrowed. "I woke up dreaming about Susan again yesterday morning. After our kiss, I wasn't sleeping too well. I got up, took a cold shower and went to bed. It was then that I had this dream." He wasn't going to tell her about the other dreams he'd had. Not a chance.

"A second dream about Susan?" Ellen turned in her chair, alert.

"I knew you'd jump on this like a duck jumps on a june bug. Certain word combinations are triggers for a therapist. 'I had a dream' is like manna from heaven for you." He held up his hand and laughed.

She grinned. "Guilty as charged. Spill it, Jim. In your first dream, she came to you and asked for help without being able to speak."

"That's why I didn't tell you about it in the first place," he said, his tone grumpy. "In this second dream, I saw Susan appear out of a light mist or fog. She was wearing chains around her shoulders and upper arms. They were wrapped around her neck, too. She wore a flowing lavender gown. The chains were so tight around her throat I reckon she couldn't speak. All I could hear was her rasping and trying to say something. Then she raised her hands in front of her so I could look at them. I saw red marks on her right wrist, the same ones that

Jillson told us about yesterday morning." He raised his brows and held Ellen's gaze. "That was it. I woke up."

"Wow! That's synchronicity! You dreamed of those red marks before Jillson told us about them! That is really interesting."

He held up one hand. "Calm down, gal, will you? I knew you'd be over the moon about this."

"Those red marks on her wrist really do mean something, then. Oh, don't go giving me that look of yours. I know you think I'm not being rational."

"Oh, you're rational," he said, suppressing a smile. "But what does it mean? The dream didn't give me any answers. Just more questions."

"Chains around her throat and upper body. What would that mean to you?"

"She's tied up or trapped in some situation?"

"And they were wrapped around her throat to stop her from talking."

"Yeah, real tight."

"Did the chains look old or new?"

"I didn't really notice." Jim sat back and closed his eyes. After a few seconds, he opened them and said, "I think they were old and rusty. Maybe even antique looking."

"Hmm, it could mean the chains were from some event earlier in her life. Rust could equate with the past. If the chains had a shiny metallic look that would suggest they were from the present, possibly, not from her childhood."

"I'm more interested in that red mark I saw on her wrist. To hell with how old the chains were."

Ignoring his sarcasm, Ellen said, "What was Susan's expression when she appeared in your dream?"

"Desperate. Her mouth was contorted—in fact, her whole face was. Sort of like *The Scream* by that painter in Norway? Everything about her seemed misshapen and pulled out of proportion."

With a shake of her head, Ellen said, "Let me feel my way through this dream in a symbolic sense. Maybe something will jump out at me later."

"All I got out of it was a bad night's sleep."

CHAPTER FOURTEEN

July 11

ELLEN LOOKED OVER AT JIM. They had just finished interviewing Lieutenant Daily. It seemed to her that Giddings was in fast-forward today. More jets landed and took off than usual, causing the building to shake and growl continuously. She dusted off her hands and closed her laptop. "How about I take some time to go through Susan's effects in her office before they're taken down to storage?"

Cochrane looked up. "That stuff is going to be shipped to Robert Kane in a day or two. NCIS has been through her office and personal items. They didn't find spit. We looked yesterday between interview appointments and didn't find anything. What do you think you'll find today?"

"We got to half of the twelve boxes. I want to look through the last six. Besides, I reread the underlined passages in Susan's book *Don Quixote*, last night. I'm drawn to her as a person. She had so many facets," Ellen said, picking up her knapsack. "I just feel we're missing something, that's all. I want to do one last check."

"Go for it. But I doubt you'll find anything, gal." He frowned and typed the last of his notes on his laptop.

Grinning as she slung the pack across her right shoulder, Ellen said, "With my background in psychology, I'm fascinated by how each person involved sees Susan a little differently."

"And somewhere among all their statements lies the truth?"

"Perhaps." She stopped at the door, her fingers resting on the polished brass doorknob. "I'm intrigued by what Daily said about her just now."

"Which part?" Cochrane closed the lid on his computer.

"About Susan's reaction to his children when she babysat for them. Daily saw her military mask slip at those times."

"If you think her office is going to reflect the personal part of her, you're barking up the wrong tree. If anything, her office here at Giddings was the model of military expectation."

"You're probably right. But those boxes contain her personal effects and I want to check them out more closely."

Jim nodded. He dug in his pocket, producing a key to open the NCIS padlock, and gave it to Ellen. Glancing at his watch, he added, "I've got to pick Merry up from ballet class at 1730. I'll finish up here and call the office for messages. Can you be ready to leave in about fifteen minutes?"

"You bet." Ellen waved as she stepped through the doorway and hurried down the hall.

It was five minutes before the last class of the day ended at Giddings. Susan Kane's office was closed, with an official-looking sign posted at the door, which was secured with a large, sturdy lock. After quickly opening it, Ellen stepped inside. Twelve cardboard boxes sat in one corner of the room. In the center was a dark gray metal desk, once Susan's work center. Ellen placed the knapsack on the desk and sat down in the chair, which squealed loudly in protest. The American military industry could build some of the most technologically advanced fighter planes in the world, but they couldn't produce a chair that didn't squeak.

Her lips pulling into a smile, Ellen leaned forward and lifted the cardboard box marked seven of twelve. She opened the lid and peered inside. There was a small gray clock, plus a pen and pencil set with a marble base. Numerous items from the officer's desk drawers included stacks of colored index cards, a stapler and staples, plus a small gold bear on a key chain. Was this all that remained of a person's life? Who *was* the real Susan Kane? Ellen quickly riffled through the contents, asking herself that question over and over again. Susan was a woman who bought teddy bears for Becky Jillson's children. She volunteered her few free hours at the San Diego Zoo. And she doted on Daily's children, as well.

Taking the bear key ring out of the box, Ellen studied it. Had Susan used this key chain? Had someone given it to her as a gift, someone who knew she loved bears? After touching the electroplated figure with her fingertips, Ellen gently placed the key ring back in the box. She closed the lid and returned the carton to the floor.

In the eighth box, Ellen found a variety of certificates of accomplishment, duplicates of the originals Susan had hanging on the walls of her condo. Why had she killed herself? A woman like Susan could have made it much more easily out in the civilian world. Ellen found another copy of *Don Quixote* and quickly paged through the book. Some different passages were underlined, and that caught her immediate interest.

The first passage said: "She be honored and esteemed by all the good men of the world; for she shows in it, that it is only she alone that lives therein with honest intention." The words rang strongly in Ellen's heart. Tears jammed into her eyes and she grimaced. "Thou art a bad Christian...for thou never forgettest the injuries that are once done to thee: know that it is the duty of noble and generous minds not to make any account...." Did Susan see herself as a "bad Christian" here at Top Gun? Had something happened to make her feel that way about herself?

The final highlighted portion of text said, "...and I begin to suspect, by your words, that all that which you have said to me of chivalry, and of gaining kingdoms and empires, of bestowing islands and other gifts and great things, as knights-errant are wont; are all matters of air and lies...."

Wiping away her tears, Ellen knew in her gut something awful had happened, either of Susan's, or of someone else's making. Something unspeakable. She quickly went through the other boxes, until only one was left: box twelve.

It contained some writing paper and, apart from *Don Quixote,* the only personal, nontechnical books Susan had kept at the office. Ellen ran her hand tentatively across the spines, then hefted one of the tomes to read the title. Settling into the box again, she noticed a tiny gray book barely visible between two others. The title, *The Little Red Bear,* was a child's book from all appearances.

"Oww!" The nail on her index finger snapped and broke, a piece of it flying onto the green-and-white-tile floor. "Darn," Ellen muttered, looking at the ragged nail. She'd broken it down to the flesh and a small drop of blood oozed out. Sucking on the injured finger, Ellen reached with her other hand to try and ease the gray book from the box.

"Come on," she muttered, struggling to get a firm hold. Whoever had packed this box had crammed it too tightly. NCIS personnel certainly wouldn't make good movers. *There!* Ellen held the gray book in the palm of her left hand. A smile touched her mouth.

"The Little Red Bear..." Oddly, the book had been

recovered in a plain gray paper jacket. Ellen set the book in her lap to leaf through its pages. As she opened the front cover she saw printed in huge, shaky letters "SUSIE." The last name was covered by the gray paper, so Ellen eased the book out of the cover to get a full view of the name. SUSIE KANE. The book was very old, obviously much read and loved.

The pages were dog-eared from age as well as use. Susan had probably pulled this book from the shelf and read it to Daily's children when they had visited Top Gun. Commander Daily told her that groups of school children would come to Top Gun and it was always Susan who took the awed students through the facility. Ellen's eyes teared up again as she realized that the remnants of Susan's life would be shipped to her father. Ellen could only guess what he would do with these boxes. He'd destroy them immediately, not wanting to be reminded of his badly behaved daughter who had brought only shame to the family's good name. Out of sight, out of mind.

As Ellen turned to pick up the book's gray covering, something caught her eye. She wondered why she hadn't seen it before, but she'd been entranced with discovering one of Susan's own books. The gray covering was much too large for such a small book, so it had been neatly reshaped, leaving a two-inch double fold on the inside front and back. The object that had caught Ellen's attention was tucked into the back.

It was a digital photo. Ellen put the book aside and

reached for the cover. The picture was taped to the jacket so it wouldn't accidentally fall out.

Devoting her attention to getting it loose, Ellen eased the tape from first one edge, then another. When all the adhesive was removed, she turned the photo over.

"Oh, my God!" Her heart slammed into her rib cage and fluttered wildly in her breast. Her fingers tightened on the print as she stared down at it in horror.

Ellen leaped out of the chair, tore around the desk and jerked the door open. Luckily, classes had let out for the day and very few aviators seemed to be left in the facility. She quickly locked the door, even though her knapsack was still inside. Ellen ran, winded, clutching the photo.

"Jim!" Her voice carried down the passageway as she turned the corner. "Jim! Wait!" He was just leaving the room where they'd done the interviewing.

He halted, a puzzled look on his face as she came racing up to him.

"What's wrong?"

Ellen gulped for breath. "Come back inside the office! You have to see this, Jim! You have to…"

"Ellen, I'll be late picking Merry up."

"This can't wait!" Ellen grabbed him by the arm and dragged him back into the interviewing room. She shut the door firmly, resting her back against it. "Here, look at what I just found." Breathing raggedly, she tried to catch her breath as she thrust the digital photo toward him. "You aren't going to believe this. I'm not sure I do."

Scowling, Cochrane set his heavy briefcase on the floor and took the photo. As he straightened, his eyes narrowed.

"Jesus H. Christ," he exclaimed.

"It *is* her, isn't it?" Ellen whispered off-key. She saw Cochrane's brows draw down, his eyes become slits. "I thought I was seeing things, Jim. The picture was taped inside a book jacket—a book from her childhood. I—I didn't see the photo until I was going to put the cover back on the book." With trembling fingers she pushed her hair from her brow.

She cautiously edged around Cochrane's shoulder and looked at the photo again. It was of Susan Kane, naked from the waist up, sprawled out on a king-size bed. A bedcover was pulled up to her hips.

"Oh, my God," Ellen whispered, pressing her hand to her heart. "This is awful. Awful!"

Cochrane cursed and dropped the photo on the desk. "Dammit, we may have just destroyed any possible prints on this photo, Ellen." Putting his hands on his hips, he leaned closer and inspected it. "But it's pretty shocking, isn't it?"

Ellen swallowed hard. "I don't want to believe it, Jim. I really don't. Yet there she is."

"I'd give anything to know where this was taken." With a shake of his head, he said, "Just goes to show you, you don't really know anyone, do you?"

Trying to steady her pounding heart, Ellen shook her head. "I find this unbelievable, totally unlike the Susan Kane we know."

"We can't be naive. This type of stuff goes on all the time."

She colored fiercely. "It's just that Susan didn't *seem* like the exhibitionist type."

"Yeah. Miss Perfect. Goody Two-shoes."

"Jim!"

He straightened and looked over at Ellen. "This photo is pretty damn graphic, wouldn't you say?"

"Yes—it is, but—" she stabbed her finger at it "—look at Susan's face."

"Her eyes are barely open. She knows what she's doing."

"Are you *sure?*"

Jim smiled a little. "Reckon you're awfully indignant about this, Ellen."

"There *are* explanations other than the *obvious* one you seem to be endorsing."

"Such as?"

Ellen felt heat crawling into her face. "I'm not pretending to be an investigator like you, Jim, but my question would be was Susan a willing or forced participant in this?"

"She looks dazed," Jim admitted, studying the photo closer. "Probably been drinking too much."

"According to everything we know about her, Susan didn't drink."

"Maybe she's high on drugs."

"Jim, you're a pain in the ass sometimes!"

"So humor me. Who took this photo, then?"

"I don't know."

"And why did they take it?" Jim scratched his head. "And how long ago? And why was it taped inside a book jacket?"

Ellen sat down, resting her arms near the photo and studying it. "Wait, look at this."

Jim leaned forward. "What?"

"The bedspread! Don't you recognize the pattern of it?"

"No," he said, "of course I don't."

Ellen made an exasperated sound. "That's the bedspread design at the Barstow Hotel in Reno, where the Ares Conference took place. The brochure we have from the hotel shows a color photo of one of their rooms, and *this* is the bedspread on the bed."

"Consarnit, I'm going to be late picking up Merry. Hold on while I make a phone call. Don't *touch* that photo anymore. Maybe we can still get a partial print from it."

Ellen straightened. "Darn, I forgot to put on my latex gloves. I'm so sorry. You taught me to always put them on before touching evidence." She withdrew her hands, feeling guilty over her mistake.

Cochrane dashed out of the room, leaving the door ajar.

Ellen got up and shut the door to keep out prying

eyes. When Cochrane returned ten minutes later, he looked thoroughly agitated.

"What's wrong?"

"Jodi wasn't too happy about adjusting plans. I tried to explain to her—oh, hell, never mind." He closed the door and hurriedly moved to his side of the desk, the photo between them. "I've been thinking. Look at what's holding her wrists to that bed. White web belts. Military gear."

"Yes, I saw that, too. But look closely at her right wrist."

Leaning over the photo, Jim squinted. "It's pretty red and raw looking."

"Precisely. Just like Jillson told us earlier today. When she visited Susan in her hotel room, she saw these marks. This was no 'flu' episode. Maybe Jillson accepted Susan's explanation, but I sure don't know. My hunch is that this photo was taken sometime on May 16th, at the Ares Conference."

Sitting down, Cochrane nodded. "But were the red marks on her wrist from struggling to get free or just part of the normal bondage lovemaking she took part in?"

"That's a disgusting suggestion."

"Ellen, from a professional standpoint this photo neither confirms or denies Susan Kane's participation in this. For all we know, she did this kind of thing on a regular basis."

"Or Susan was coerced," Ellen said flatly, anger in her tone.

"But how do we know?"

She stared at him. "We probably know more about Susan than anyone, and you can sit there and say that she'd willingly do that kind of thing?" Ellen just couldn't believe it of the dead aviator.

Holding up his hands, Cochrane said, "Whoa, Ellen. From an investigative point of view we *can't* deduce one way or another, because we don't have any corroborating evidence. If there is a fingerprint on this photo that hasn't been destroyed by us, it might give us a lead."

"I just *can't* believe Susan would do this kind of stuff."

"Kinky sex. How about that?" Jim shook his head. "That would sure as hell blow her role model image right out of the water if it were made known."

Frowning, Ellen muttered, "That crossed my mind, too. What if Susan got drunk and did do it? Did someone take this photo to embarrass her maybe?"

"Blackmail would be more like it."

Ellen wrinkled her nose. "Ugh, what dirty little secrets are held by the Navy if that's so, huh?"

Grimly, Cochrane said, "The military is comprised of human beings who, just like the civilian population, are capable of things I reckon I'd never even think of. Or could be a civilian episode and have nothing to do with the military. We just don't know yet."

"I can see why your work would be such a downer. I'm feeling horrible about this photo, what it will do to Susan's wonderful career, her reputation."

"First things first," Cochrane cautioned. "I reckon we're going to have to thoroughly search Kane's office again. NCIS dropped the ball. They should have found this during their search. We'll take everything we find down to the JAG lab for fingerprint analysis."

"Maybe NCIS thought that since Susan's death took place off the naval station, they didn't have to do a thorough job?"

"I'd hope not. All of us were sloppy, pure and simple." He retrieved a latex glove from his briefcase and slipped it on his right hand. "When the JAG lab does a complete analysis of this photo, I'd sure as hell like to find a set of prints of someone other than ours or Susan's on it."

"We needed a break on this investigation, but I'm not sure I like this one," Ellen agreed wearily.

Jim reached out and squeezed her hand. He saw the stress in her green eyes. Knowing she was on Susan's side, he said, "Take it easy, gal. This is your first investigation and you're getting too personally involved." Releasing her hand, he added, "So am I, but I'm trying to stay impartial."

"Thanks for telling me that," she whispered, feeling deflated. Pushing her hair off her forehead again, she gave Jim a hopeful look. "Do you think JAG forensics will find fingerprints on the photo other than mine?"

"I don't know. On the way to the office tomorrow morning, I'll drop this off at the lab. After that, it's hurry up and wait."

CHAPTER FIFTEEN

July 12

ELLEN WAS RUNNING LATE on Thursday morning. She arrived at the office at 0915, a frothy mocha latte in one hand and a large paper evidence bag containing Susan Kane's bear in the other. She set the bag on top of the file cabinet and turned to Jim. His eyes were bloodshot. Fatigue shadowed his features. And yet he'd taken the time to shave, since he still had a small piece of tissue lodged against a cut.

"You look like something the cat dragged in," she said as she sat next to him and placed the latte aside. "Sorry I'm late." Ellen wondered if he was still tossing and turning because of their kiss. Last night she'd slept deeply, then dreamed of making love with Jim. That had awakened her too early, her body aching for him. Her heart, as well.

"Hmm? Reckon I do."

"Matter of fact," Ellen said, putting her knapsack on the desk, "you still have some evidence of your shaving left behind."

Cochrane lifted his head. "What?"

"Hold still for a moment." She gently pulled the paper away. "There." She got up and dropped the tissue in the wastebasket.

Rubbing his throat, Cochrane said, "Thanks." Ellen's contact electrified him. Made him want her so badly his body was twisted into a knot. The woman had a caress that magically awakened him. Lately, he was thinking more about her than the case.

"I can't take you anywhere, Mr. Cochrane," Ellen teased. She sat back down and rearranged her dark green cotton skirt. "What did you do? Work at the JAG office last night, after I left?"

He glanced down at his uniform. "Does it show?" He grinned tiredly.

"I'm afraid it does."

"Consarnit." He gathered up a bunch of papers next to the printer. "That photo really broke loose a lot of questions in my mind. I decided to take it over to the JAG lab after you left. Everyone was gone except for the skeleton night crew. After that, I drove over and apologized to Jodi for not picking up Merry when it was my turn. Then I went home. I'd no sooner stepped into my apartment than I got another call from that captain who works with the CNO. He told me in no uncertain terms they're watching Kane's case very carefully." Cochrane picked up his coffee and took a sip. "I got the message to stick on this case like glue. I'm sure now that Susan Kane had a sponsor. Probably the CNO himself, if I'm not mistaken. The captain never would have said so, and I wouldn't ask, either. It was implied." He frowned. "It shows how important this case is to the Navy. So I thought I'd spend more time on it here in the office." He grimaced. "At about 0500, I went back to the apartment, took a shower, shaved and came back over."

Ellen gave him a sympathetic look. "It's tough balancing a job like this against a family's needs."

"I'm trying to be a better father to Merry. See her more often, not less." Jim brightened a little. "At least Jodi didn't light into me this time. She forgave me, and that's good."

"A juggling act, for sure, Jim," Ellen murmured understandingly. She saw how he fiercely loved his daughter. And maybe that was why the Kane case was so important to him. "What's your take on Susan Kane now that you've had a chance to think about it overnight?" Ellen herself felt protective of the female aviator.

"Just because Kane was having kinky sex with someone at the Barstow Hotel during the convention doesn't mean we enter the details into the computer and have it open conversation throughout the Navy. And I made no mention of it to that CNO assistant captain, either."

"For Susan's sake, I'm glad." Ellen breathed a sigh of relief. "Can we keep that photo out of the investigation?"

"We're the caretakers of that picture and only we will decide who gets to see it. There's not a snowball's chance in hell I'll enter it into any records unless, of course, it has something to do directly with the investigation. Chief Hazzard called me before you arrived, by the way. Besides our prints, he found only a partial print of Susan Kane and another one that's too smeared to identify. And don't worry, the chief can be trusted to keep quiet. He's from the hills, like me, and we have an honor code we don't break."

"That's sad about the fingerprints. Darn it," Ellen muttered.

"On a more positive note, I called Lieutenant Morgan again by satellite phone last night. He has informally identified Susan Kane as the woman in the elevator with our unknown man."

"That's great!"

"Informally identified." Jim smiled a little. "Baby steps. There are still some puzzle pieces missing."

"Right now, I'll settle for *any* step forward." Ellen saw him give her a wink. Oh, how she wanted to reach out and touch his hand. Hug him, maybe. Decorum was the order of the day, however, so she stifled her wild urges once again.

Cochrane scratched his head. "That opens up a lot of questions or possibilities to us now."

"Such as what?"

Picking up a pencil, Cochrane twirled it absently. "Such as where did Susan go when she left Jillson and

Hawkins at approximately 1930? She was next seen at 2230 on the patio, then at 2300 on the elevator, by Morgan. Bassett places her drunk on that patio at 2200, and he's probably lying. Susan was seen by her two friends in her hotel room at 0900 the next morning. Somewhere in between, the photo incident took place."

"And if this was a forced act, why didn't Susan go to the authorities or the police? Where else could she have gone to lodge her protest?"

He snapped his fingers and sat up in the chair. "Gem of a question, Ellen. That may be the clue we're poking around for."

She felt heat climb into her face and noticed the dancing light in his eyes. There was a clear intensity in his gaze and she enjoyed seeing it. "Okay, out with it. What clue did I just uncover?"

"Chain of command. That's where Susan went."

"Captain Warren Oliver! The C.O. of Giddings?"

"No, no." Cochrane shook his head. "Who was the senior officer of the three conspirators? Her boss—Lieutenant Commander Hodges."

Ellen sat there, considering the information. "So if she was coerced, Susan might have gone to Hodges instead of reporting it to the hotel police?"

"Why not? It's the military mind-set. What do you do when there's trouble? You go to the next person in COC."

"And we haven't interviewed Hodges yet," Ellen said thoughtfully.

"He was scheduled for today, until I canceled the interviews because of my brainstorming here at the office. Right now I'm too whipped mentally to do much of anything."

"Don't you feel Susan Kane is innocent? That she got caught up in something at Ares?"

"Not yet," Jim said softly, holding Ellen's fiery gaze. "I'm being an attorney looking at this like a court of law would view the photo. You aren't. You have personal buttons being pushed. I know you want to think Susan Kane was an honorable woman caught in a nasty little scenario, but we're still piecing things together." Cochrane took a quick peek out the door. When he saw no one in the passageway, he squeezed her hand as if to soothe her flustered state. Ellen's eyes were filled with frustration. Instantly, he saw the tumultuous feelings ebb as he ran his fingertips across the back of her hand. How he wanted to hold her! He didn't like to see her this upset; it triggered something deep and protective within him.

She turned her hand over and quickly squeezed his fingers in return. "Don't you think Susan was honorable?"

"Personally? Yes. But professionally, I get paid to look at *all* the angles. If I don't, I guarantee it will bite me in the ass in the courtroom. And secondly, I don't want the photo to become the center ring in a three-ring-circus act."

"I see…." Ellen nodded.

"I wonder why Susan was seen on the arms of three different men within one hour of each sighting. Kane was allegedly drunk, so drunk her knees were buckling beneath her. How do you explain that? Everyone from her skipper on down says she never touched alcohol. And if she was drinking heavily, isn't it conceivable she may have had sex with whomever? She wouldn't be the first inebriated female to fall prey to a guy in that context."

Ellen rolled her eyes. "Yes, it appears she was drunk. And yes, everyone has said she was a teetotaler. But darn it, Jim, it just doesn't *fit* Susan's psychological profile as we know her. It doesn't."

"And yet it happened. We have to try and find out why."

"What also bothers me," Ellen said irritably, "is the fact that the photo was taped to the inside of that book jacket, facedown, so no one could see it."

"Obviously, Susan was hiding it," Jim said. "It's not something you put in the family photo album, is it? Especially with her family."

"I *wish* I hadn't smudged that print!"

"Let it go. I've got Chief Hazzard from the lab working on the photo some more to see if he can divide the fingerprint layers. We should know sometime tomorrow if he can or not."

Ellen said, "That would sure simplify our task, wouldn't it?" There was nothing she wanted more right now than to identify that other fingerprint.

"Yes, but cases don't normally break clean like that. They open up because of basic hard work and not over-looking any details."

"My gut hunch is that her commander, Hodges, is involved in this somehow."

Jim gave her a proud look. "You're getting good, El-len. We'll make an investigator out of you yet." He eyed the mysterious paper sack sitting in the corner. "Did you catch any other new fish this morning? You were late. That's not like you."

"I had a couple of stops to make," she answered. "I drove over to Giddings and showed Ann Hawkins and Becky Jillson a document copy of the photo of Susan on the bed. They promised to keep it a secret, and I be-lieve they will. They were her best friends," Ellen said. "Both held the same belief—that Susan would never willingly do anything like what the photo suggested. Ann still wouldn't name any of the people at Top Gun who may have been pressuring Susan."

Cochrane nodded and pushed himself out of his squeaky chair. "I'm not surprised. Dead-end leads. We'll interview Hodges tomorrow. Let's get to work."

Ellen glanced up at him as he took a few files from the cabinet and handed them to her. "Jim, do you miss being married?"

He raised a brow. "The fighting? No."

"I meant..." She shrugged. "Having a home, I guess."

"Oh, that. Reckon I miss the hell out of that." With

a chuckle, Cochrane said, "My apartment looks like a major disaster area. Hazmat will have to be called in shortly to clean it up. Or maybe the Environmental Protection Agency will have to take over."

Ellen laughed and began opening the files on her desk. Her heart beat a little harder as she saw him consider her softly spoken question.

He glanced over at her as he sat down again. "Why do you ask?"

"Single life isn't all it's cracked up to be. I find myself very lonely in that new apartment of mine."

"Missing marriage, are you?" He sure did. And it was obvious that Ellen did, too. He watched her slender fingers skillfully sort the files. She had such grace. What would it be like to have her fingers grazing his flesh? Groaning to himself, Jim realized he was physically aching for her again.

"I guess I am." Ellen sat back in her chair.

"If we didn't have to work our tails off on this investigation," Cochrane stated as he stuffed several papers into his briefcase, "we might be able to enjoy one another's company more." And then he said in a gritty tone, "I wish things were different, Ellen, but they aren't."

"You're a mind reader."

"We can be miserable together, can't we?"

"Yes, misery loves company," Ellen said. She rested her elbows on the desk. "I keep wondering why Susan put that photo in a book from her childhood, and left it in her office. She could have put it anywhere."

"Reckon if it was for blackmail purposes, I think I'd have burned it a long time ago. Whoever took the photo must have had the negative or others, that's for sure. So, why would she leave it lying around?"

"It wasn't exactly lying around," Ellen reminded him archly.

"I try and look at it from both perspectives," Jim said. "If Susan did do this kind of thing routinely, why shouldn't she keep the photo around? But the curious question is why at the office instead of at her condo?"

"Remember? We looked through her books at home as well as every other place we could find. We never found anything except the marked-up volume of *Don Quixote*. Not so much as a bookmark in any of the others."

"Well, that photo isn't exactly bookmark material." Ellen gave him a frown of disapproval.

"Conversely, if she was forced into the situation and was being blackmailed, she *would* hide it," Jim speculated.

"I know," Ellen whispered unhappily, tapping the side of her head with her index finger. "A child's book, of all things. And at work. I think Susan would be fearful of having it discovered there. She was so careful with her image at Top Gun. Why on *earth* would she put the photo in her office?"

"Well," Jim said, "one thread is consistent."

"What?"

"Susan and her bears. She put the photo in a bear book—"

"Oh, my God! Jim!" Ellen shot to her feet. "That's the other clue!"

Jim raised his head and frowned. "What clue?"

"I've got it!" she shrieked excitedly, turning to him and waving her hands. "That's it! The teddy bear!"

He growled, "You're not making any sense, gal."

Grabbing the evidence sack and setting it on her desk, Ellen said, "Yes, I am! Don't you see? Susan's teddy bear. The one in your dream. This morning, before I drove to the office, I dropped over to La Mesa's police department and talked with Detective Gardella. They had the teddy bear and Susan's mother's photo in their evidence locker. Eventually, at the conclusion of the case, it would've been sent to Robert Kane. I couldn't stand to have him burn or destroy them. We'd promised the teddy bear would go to Tommy after the investigation, so I brought it with me this morning. I was going to send it to him as soon as Susan's case was closed."

"Okay..." Jim said, not understanding her sudden enthusiasm.

"Oh, Jim, the dream! Remember your dream? The bear's just been sitting there waiting for us to ask!"

"It can't talk."

"Not talk, but see! We've got to get the bear's eyes tested for fingerprints." She saw him scowl. "Don't you get it? There could be fingerprints on those plastic eyes!"

Jim threw his hands up and shook his head. "Gal, I

reckon you've lost it. There aren't going to be any fingerprints. It's fake fur."

"Jim, the eyes are large, shiny buttons. Please," Ellen said breathlessly. "I just *know* there are prints on one of them! The bear ties to your dream, too. Susan handed you her bear with *no eyes* in its head. Remember?"

"Hell, woman, leave my stupid dream out of this conversation. It meant nothing—nothing," he muttered irritably, looking around his desk.

"Jim, I know you're tired and sleep deprived, but humor me on this request, please?"

"This is harebrained, Ellen. You're knocking around like a blind hound dog in a meat house."

"Maybe," she said excitedly, "but maybe not. Susan was holding that bear in her arms when she died. It ought to be tested for fingerprints, but for anything else as well—like a human hair or whatever else could be clinging to it."

"Okay, okay," he muttered, "I figure if I humor you, I'll get more work done much sooner. I don't know what the hell all this bear stuff is going to prove."

"Just have the lab dust for fingerprints, for starters. This makes so much sense to me. Don't you see?"

"I'm as tired as a rutting tomcat after an all-night prowl through a neighborhood of female cats in heat. This is bad timing."

Ellen reached out and patted his shoulder. "Thanks for humoring me."

"I just think you're feeling guilty about smudging the fingerprint on that photo," he said defiantly.

Ellen shook her head. "Jim, you stick to being an attorney and I'll stick to being a therapist, okay?"

CHAPTER SIXTEEN

July 13

"COCHRANE SPEAKING...."

"It's Ellen. Listen—"

"I'm asleep...."

"I'm sorry. I know how late it is, but this is important." Ellen heard him slurring other words she couldn't understand. His Missouri twang was most pronounced when he was sleepy, she discovered.

"Geez, it's after midnight. What's this flap-doodle all about?"

Holding the phone more tightly, she said, "Listen to me, will you? I just got a fax from Chief Hazzard from the forensic lab. Remember how we took the bear over to him to be dusted for fingerprints? You'll never guess whose print is on the bear's eye!"

"What? Hold on, I'm not awake, gal. Slow down and speak clearly. You're blitherin' on like a fool..."

"The only fool is at your end of this line!" she yelled into the phone. "Wake up, Jim! This is *important!*"

Lowering her voice, she rasped, "The fingerprint on the bear's eye belongs to Commander Brad Kane!"

Ellen waited for a response. She pulled the phone away from her ear, looked at it, wondered if it was working and then listened again. "Jim? Are you there? Did you fall back asleep on me?"

"What print are you talkin' about?"

"Chief Hazzard found a fingerprint on the bear's right eye. He checked it against the four names you supplied for comparison to the partial print on Susan's photo. Brad Kane was a match to the print taken off the bear's eye."

"Brad Kane?" he repeated thickly.

"Yes," she said triumphantly. "Of all people, I never expected *his* print on it."

"Hold on…."

She heard a bed creaking, then a groan. Ellen assumed Cochrane was finally sitting up. Impatiently, she asked, "Remember Ann said Brad hadn't seen Susan for two years? If so, those prints wouldn't be on there at all. He *had* to be there. How else could you explain her brother's fingerprint on Susan's bear? Something's not right here."

"Slow down, gal. You're worse than a broken down nag who thinks she can win at a county horse race."

"I'll take that as a compliment, Jim. It had better be one."

"Okay, okay. Just creep along, will you? I don't think well the first hour after I get blasted out of bed."

"We didn't think to check if Brad or Tommy Kane were on their carriers around the time Susan took her life. We do know from Susan's attempt to reach him through the Red Cross that Tommy was supposedly aboard his. I'll check tomorrow morning on Brad. What if he was in San Diego at the time of Susan's death?"

"Yeah, right. Those are good questions, gal. Makes me wonder if it really was suicide, after all." He yawned. "Look, I'm whipped. Let me go back to sleep. We'll follow up on these leads come Monday, okay?"

Disappointed, Ellen said, "I think we ought to postpone Lieutenant Commander Hodges's interview until we get this other information, don't you?"

"We can't do that in the middle of the night. Besides, we've already postponed Hodges's interview. Our next one starts at 1030 hours on Monday, and that's with Lieutenant Parker Davis. We'll just check first thing then. We should be able to do that and still make the scheduled interviews, including Hodges's Monday afternoon."

Ellen heard Jim yawn again. "I know it's the weekend," she sighed. "I've got redecorating to do in my new apartment and you have family things lined up."

"There's not much we can accomplish on a weekend, gal. Now, let's get some shut-eye. I'll see you Monday morning bright and early."

Ellen biting back her frustration. "Good night, Jim." She hung up the phone. Well, what did she expect? Cochrane had been up all night.

July 16

COCHRANE ENTERED their office Monday morning at 0730 to find Ellen sitting at her desk. Her orange and yellow outfit nearly blinded him, but the excitement in her eyes lifted his spirits. His heart swelled. He felt like the most blessed man in the world, to come to the office and have such a beautiful woman waiting. He saw the warm welcome in her eyes, too.

"You're gonna hit me with a pile of stuff before I've even had my coffee," he complained, taking off his hat and carefully putting it on the coat hook.

"No, I'm not," Ellen said archly as she stood. "Here, it's a mocha latte, Jim. Drink it. I guarantee it's like getting a jolt of caffeine directly into your bloodstream."

He eyed the paper cup on his desk. "Whipped cream?"

"Are you complaining again, Mr. Cochrane? How often do you get a free latte at 0730?" She gave him a teasing look. "It's basically coffee! Stop eyeing it like it's going to kill you."

"Hmmph," he said, sitting down and taking a sip. "This is too fancy to be called coffee." His heart filled with joy at seeing her again. He had spent his weekend with Merry at his apartment. He always looked forward to time with his little girl. Every moment with his daughter was special. And it was becoming evident that each moment with Ellen was special, too.

"I suppose it is fancy," she said. "You're partial to hill folk coffee."

As he sipped his latte Cochrane riffled through a pile of phone messages. "My ma makes the best coffee in the world. She has a patch of chicory she tends. Plus she goes once a month to buy coffee beans at Hiram's General Store down in Raven Holler."

Ellen smiled. "I've never tasted chicory in coffee."

"Go to New Orleans. That comes closest to my ma's coffee."

"Well, that latte doesn't have vanilla or chicory," she grumped good-naturedly. Seeing him made her feel good. This morning, he looked wide-awake, with no dark circles under his eyes or redness. In fact, he looked damn handsome. She absorbed his silly grin, knowing his high spirits came from spending time with Merry. Ellen was so happy for him and his daughter. Divorce was such a painful thing.

"It don't taste too bad," he said, surprised. He sipped again. "Thanks for the thought, even if you had ulterior motives. I know this is a peace offering for waking this poor hill boy up late Friday night." He chuckled perversely.

Ellen's brows shot up. "It's true I felt bad about waking you out of a dead sleep."

"From the look on your face, you've got some more info on Brad Kane and you wanted me wide awake to listen to your latest discovery."

Ellen touched her reddening cheeks. "You don't miss much, do you?"

His grin widened wickedly as he polished off the rest

of the latte and tossed the cup into his wastebasket. "Not much, gal. Now that I'm sufficiently awake, what do you have on Bad Boy Brad?"

She passed him a printed report. "According to the records on board Brad's carrier, the *John C. Stennis,* he left for unexpected emergency leave *two days* before Susan's death. He arrived back on the carrier just in time to be told to take off again—that his sister had died and he was granted emergency leave to attend her funeral."

"Hmm," Cochrane said, studying the report intently. "The original reason for the original leave is stated simply as 'family emergency.' Susan was that family emergency?"

"Had to be. Why else would Brad have been let go?"

"That's true. Emergency leave isn't just handed out like candy in the military. You had better damn well have an emergency, or else."

"Why didn't Brad tell us about seeing Susan, then?" Ellen wondered.

"Good question. My first hunch is the good ole boy system is at work again. And we didn't ask Brad if he was on board his carrier two days before Susan's death, so he wasn't going to volunteer that information."

"But why?" Ellen demanded in a frustrated tone.

"We'll find out." Jim rubbed his hands together. "The plot thickens, like my ma's vanilla pudding."

"I have a feeling this interview with Hodges this afternoon isn't going to be very appetizing, either."

Cochrane grimaced. "Since we delayed his interview, it might put some serious pressure on him and he'll spill the beans. Maybe…"

Glumly, Ellen nodded. "I didn't get a good feeling about him from his personnel file."

"You and your vibes. They won't stand up in any court of law, Ellen," Cochrane sighed.

"Hodges was mighty unhappy about the Ares Conference interview in the first place, and liked it even less when I rescheduled him once again. He gave me a lot of grief about it."

"Hodges is a sourpuss. Unless we get some miracle information out of this morning's interviews, the bastard will probably skate through without our laying a glove on him."

"I understand through Yeoman Camden that Hodges is bringing along an attorney," Ellen said.

Snorting, Cochrane sat up, elbows on his desk. "Barring some surprise from Hodges, we've got as much chance as a grasshopper in a chicken house full of hungry hens of nailing him."

Ellen giggled. "What did I ever do until you walked into my life, Jim? I never realized hill folk had such a rich subculture. All those sayings and ways of looking at the world…"

"Stick around, gal, and some of it might rub off."

"That's what I'm afraid of. But I'd like to stick around, anyway."

Picking up the phone, Jim saw the smile on her face. "Music to my ears. You know, Hodges is an arrogant jock." He gave her a wolfish grin. "It'll be mighty interesting to see how he sits in this stew pot. This afternoon, we may have to implement my world-famous Plan B. If we play this right, we might get another puzzle piece. Or, Hodges could tuck that puzzle box under his arm and walk away from us," he growled.

July 16

LIEUTENANT COMMANDER Hodges came in at exactly 1300, dressed in his summer white uniform. Cochrane curbed a smile as he surveyed the man. Ribbons representing every medal Hodges owned decorated the left side of his powerful chest. His dark blue eyes were intense, and his thin, weasel-like face was taut with tension. At his side was his expensively attired lawyer, Walter Rapaport, a well-known San Diego military criminal lawyer with whom Jim had sparred on several other cases involving Navy or Marine Corps personnel.

Rapaport was like a fox to Hodges's weasel. The dapper attorney had sharp darting eyes and a quick way of talking. This man could manipulate the truth to serve his client. And in keeping with his background as an ex-JAG attorney, his military bearing was impeccable. Cochrane wasn't sure which man had his shoulders thrown back more, Hodges or Rapaport.

The men shared one other trait: hyperactive, quick movements.

Cochrane respected Rapaport. He didn't respect

Hodges. There were differences between foxes and weasels, and Hodges had an innately sneaky air that seemed to ooze out of him no matter how hard he tried to hide behind his Navy uniform.

"Ya'll have a seat for this little chat, gentlemen," Cochrane drawled in his best Missouri accent. He gestured magnanimously to the two chairs directly in front of him and Ellen. She sat to his left, poised and ready with many reports.

"This is a waste of my valuable time, Mr. Cochrane," Hodges snarled, dropping his expensive cowhide briefcase on the table next to his seat.

"Why, Commander, I think you'd complain if you were hanged with a new rope," Cochrane said, offering him a wolfish grin. Screw Hodges. Jim wasn't taking his crap lying down. Rapaport started to smile, then glanced at his angry client and seemed to reconsider.

As Cochrane introduced Ellen to the unflappable attorney, he watched the expression on her face. She unconsciously sat back in her chair, as if threatened by Rapaport's foxlike smile. Chuckling to himself, Jim rummaged through his notes and questions. This time, he was going to take that proverbial new rope he'd joked about and tighten it around Hodges's neck. Would the officer break? The bastard was up for commander and wasn't about to spoil his chances by having anything too substantial turn up in this investigation. So this time Jim would have to resort to subterfuge—of a sort. The question was would Hodges fall for it, hook, line and sinker? A fish had to be caught before it was landed.

CHAPTER SEVENTEEN

July 16

"I CONSIDER THIS TO BE a form of harassment," Hodges began irritably as he signed the papers agreeing to the investigation process. Glancing at his attorney, he added, "And this kind of game could hurt my chances of making commander. I've done nothing wrong, yet I'm being dragged in here because of Susan Kane. This sucks."

Cochrane put the signed papers aside. Hodges was blowing smoke and they all knew it. Hell, he was so fixed about getting his commander's gold leaves that he'd jump through any hoops he came to.

"I think you understand how the commander feels," Rapaport said soothingly, flashing his foxlike smile at Cochrane.

"Ya'll are caught up in this dance and I do understand." As Jim spread his notes in front of him he noticed an envelope. What was in it? He'd been in such a hurry to get over to Giddings on time that he'd jammed whatever was on his desk into his briefcase. He opened it and pulled out four digital photos. Of course, he didn't allow Hodges or Rapaport to see these teddy bear photos. Because they were irrelevant to this interview, he placed the photos facedown on the table. "I'll try to make this as quick and painless as possible, Commander."

Hodges seemed distracted **by** the photos. "I hope the hell you do, Mr. Cochrane." He dramatically waved his hand. "And why was my appointment for this interview canceled on such short notice the other day? I'm due to go TDY in three hours. I have to fly north for a meeting up in Seattle, and stay overnight. I won't get back to Giddings until 1400 tomorrow. I need time to pack."

"Unfortunate circumstances occurred, Commander. We're pulled in many different directions, as I'm sure you are in your work. My apologies, sir. It was not done to create stress on you. We'll make sure you're out of here in time to go TDY."

Hodges sat there, drumming his fingers. "It's just ridiculous, that's all. I'm an instructor here. I've got flights scheduled. There's enough built-in stress around here to choke a horse. I don't need this on top of it."

Cochrane slowly rearranged his notes, allowing Hodges to discharge his long-held bile. He'd gotten word via Sharkman Hillyer that the lieutenant commander had been loud and harsh in his opinion of the Kane investigation over at the O Club. Out of the corner of his eye, Jim could see Ellen's lips tightening. She didn't like Hodges any more than he did. His pa had a saying for the likes of Hodges: "Son, ya don't dare sleep alongside a' him with yore mouth hangin' open if ya have gold teeth." Hodges was a real pecker head of the first degree.

"The lieutenant commander could have the decency to answer our questions," Ellen said curtly.

"Easy, Agent Tanner," Cochrane said. "I'm sure the commander is very busy, and we will conclude this interview as swiftly as possible."

Ellen's mouth compressed. "I have my own questions, Lieutenant Cochrane. I'll ask them as soon as you're finished with yours."

Hodges scowled at her.

She scowled back.

Cochrane could see that Ellen had just gone from an invisible grain of sand to a major burr under Hodges's saddle. She was now on the officer's radar screen, and an acute protectiveness welled up in Jim. He wanted to keep Ellen out of the line of fire from this aviator, if possible. "I reckon we can accommodate your request, Agent Tanner." Jim returned his attention to Hodges, whose focus was still on Ellen. "Commander, if you'll humor me and tell me what you did at the Ares Conference, I'd appreciate it," he stated.

He sat there listening as Hodges went through his expected diatribe. Occasionally, Jim made notations in the margins of the interview transcript they had created over the last week from other officers' stories. By the time Hodges was done, the man's thin face was taut, his dark blue eyes narrowed.

"You've left out a lot from what I can tell," Cochrane noted.

"Dammit," Hodges snapped, "it's the best I can do! The conference was months ago. Memory fades with time."

"It was a long time," Jim agreed sympathetically, picking up his papers and glancing over at Ellen. "You said you had some questions, Agent Tanner?"

She nodded. "Absolutely, Lieutenant Cochrane." She trained her attention on Hodges, who looked at her with open defiance.

"Commander, did you see Lieutenant Susan Kane at the convention?"

"No."

"That's odd," Cochrane said, pointing to his notes, "we have an eyewitness who stated you were present in the third-floor passageway when the groping of women took place, at approximately 1730 on May 15th."

"What?" Hodges jerked and glanced at Rapaport, then glared at Jim. "That's completely false."

"Not only that," Cochrane stated calmly, "but the witness testified you were in the passageway when Lieutenants Hawkins, Jillson and Kane were assaulted. This witness states you took no steps to assist or report the incident like a senior officer should."

Flushing, Hodges sputtered, "That's a blatant lie!

There was always a massive crowd in the third-floor passageway. I could've passed within two feet of the aforementioned officers and not even seen them, much less witnessed some alleged incident."

"Commander," Ellen said, "two other witnesses place you in the Leopard Radar Corporation suite when a female Navy officer was dragged into the room and then forced to her knees before a dildo by two junior officers. I believe the time was 1700 on May 15th. What can you tell us about that?"

"Not a damn thing! I don't recall the aforementioned incident."

"Were you in that suite at that time?" Cochrane made sure his tone was derisive. The aviator seemed spooked, and Cochrane wanted to panic him now.

Sweat popped out on Hodges's wrinkled brow. "I may have visited that suite at some point during the conference. There were a number of suites and I didn't keep a log of my activities."

"You do remember being at the suite in question when this female Navy officer was dragged in against her will and abused?" Ellen asked.

"I have no recollection of witnessing any such incident."

Ellen continued, "Do you have any idea when you were in the Leopard Radar Corporation suite?" She tinged her tone with disgust, and Hodges's eyes widened at her unexpected attack.

"Listen," the man said. "*Everyone* visited *every* suite

at numerous times during the conference. I just don't recall specific times."

"Why?" Cochrane pressed.

"There was a lot going down."

"Yes, and it appears some suites hired strippers as floor shows," Cochrane said.

"I never said anything about witnessing, much less participating in, these alleged activities. This was a private civilian function, and some defense contractors held private parties in their suites. Haven't you ever been to a private party where some of the people were drinking, and some may have been dancing of their own volition?"

Cochrane smiled. "Of course, Commander. I do understand this was a private function and not an official Navy affair."

There was a knock on the door. Jim put the tape recorder on Pause and asked whoever it was to enter. When the door opened, he recognized one of the petty officers from the secretarial pool, Yeoman Irene Johnson. She was young, in her midtwenties, with a short cap of shining black hair.

"I'm sorry to interrupt you, Mr. Cochrane, but I was ordered to drive over here by Commander Dornier. A message arrived at your office for Agent Tanner, and the commander felt you needed it right now, for your investigation." She handed him a large red envelope. He passed it to Ellen.

"Thank you, Petty Officer Johnson," Cochrane said.

"If you would kindly stand by? Agent Tanner may have a reply."

"Yes, sir," she said, then exited.

Ellen felt all eyes on her as she carefully opened the envelope. It contained a telephone record sheet as well as the official regulations for granting immunity during an investigation. Ellen showed Jim the latter and asked, "Is that what we expected, Lieutenant?"

"Reckon it is," he murmured, glancing at the telephone memo she held.

"I'll have to call him at the time he requested," Ellen said briskly.

"I'm not totally sure where this is going, Agent Tanner." Cochrane looked at his watch, then glanced over at Hodges, who was staring hard at them, as if trying to figure out what the hell was going on.

Ellen quickly gathered up the regulations, tucked them into the bright red envelope marked immunity, and slid the documents beneath her other papers. Folding her hands, she smiled sweetly at Hodges, who appeared completely shaken by the unexpected disruption.

"Go ahead with your questioning, Mr. Cochrane. I apologize for this interruption," she said.

Cochrane knew that Hodges and Rapaport were aware that Commander Dornier was his C.O. at JAG. The attorney seemed coolly interested in their ploy. Hodges's brow was beaded with sweat.

"For the record, Commander Hodges," Cochrane

began, "can you tell me where you were at 2300 on the night of May 15th?"

Hodges scowled. "I—" he raised his eyes to the ceiling, as if thinking "—I believe I was in bed by that time. In my room."

"What floor was your room located on?" Jim already had the information, but wanted to keep Hodges talking and off balance.

"I believe it was the fifteenth floor," Hodges growled.

"Hmm," Cochrane said, studying the screen of his laptop. "That's odd." He tapped his fingers on the tabletop.

"What's odd?" Hodges leaned forward, scowling.

"Are you *sure* you were in bed at 2300 hours on the night of May 15th?"

"I don't care to keep repeating myself. I've answered that question to the best of my knowledge."

"You weren't out near the third-floor patio?" Ellen asked, looking over at the paper Jim had underlined in red.

"I don't recall."

"How about around the elevators?" she asked.

"I don't recall."

Rapaport leaned forward. "Mr. Cochrane, what's all this browbeating about? Could you spare my client and just present the evidence?"

Cochrane lifted his head and pinned Hodges directly with his gaze. "We've got a report from an interviewee who identified at the elevator at 2300 on May 15th, you with Susan Kane in your arms. Care to comment, Commander?"

Hodges's eyes bulged, and then he caught himself, resuming his mask of confidence. He sat rigidly, and sweat ran down the sides of his temples.

"I believe the interviewee is mistaken. I've already stated where I was to the best of my knowledge."

"Come on, Commander," Cochrane cajoled in his drawl, pointing to the red Immunity envelope sticking out from beneath Ellen's papers. "This is a Navy aviator like yourself who saw you."

"I don't believe that makes a difference."

"Are you calling him a liar, then?"

Hodges glared. "He's mistaken!"

"Answer my question, Commander Hodges."

"You have some drunken aviator swearing I was at a location where I wasn't. This is just so much trash, Lieutenant!"

Jim shrugged nonchalantly. "It's a witness statement."

Hodges turned to his lawyer. "This is your area of expertise!"

Rapaport leaned forward. "Really, Mr. Cochrane, you're busting my client's balls for no reason. If you have proof, let's see it. That's the least you can do for us."

A smile appeared at the corners of Cochrane's mouth. "Mr. Rapaport, our proof would have to be presented at a trial. Of course, it would be on your discovery list."

"Oh, for Christ's sake!" Hodges leaped out of his chair. "This is harassment! You're trying to set me up and blame me for something I didn't do! Dammit, Rapaport, speak up! I'm sure as hell paying you enough to defend me!" he said as he resumed his seat.

"Lieutenant Cochrane," Rapaport said smoothly, "had the witness—the one who alleges the commander was present in the elevator at the time stated—been drinking?" He awaited a reply. When none was offered Rapaport continued. "We both know that my question in regard to the witness having been drinking is meant to address the credibility of the witness's powers of observation."

Ellen glanced at her watch and quickly rose to her feet. "I'm afraid I have to make that telephone call right now, Mr. Cochrane. Would you gentlemen excuse me? I'll return as quickly as possible to continue my questions of Commander Hodges."

Cochrane held up his hand. "Agent Tanner, I don't believe this is the best way to resolve this particular item."

She ignored him and went to the door.

"Agent Tanner?" He saw Ellen turn and halt.

"Look, Lieutenant Cochrane, we disagree on procedure. I'll be back as soon as I can." She left with an air of finality.

Shaken, Hodges turned to stare at the closed door.

"Hey! What's all this shuffling around about? Are you two just wasting my time?" He leaped to his feet and stalked toward the door, clearly ready to leave in turn. "This song and dance is just to bust me, isn't it, Lieutenant?"

"Calm down," Rapaport snapped at him. "Come and sit back down, Commander Hodges."

The officer stood his ground. "This is an abuse of power. First I have to give this time-wasting interview, then it's canceled at the last minute. They get this goddamn envelope and then Miss DOD leaves in a rush. I won't stand for this."

Cochrane held up his hands. "Reckon we're sorry for these unexpected intrusions, Commander. They're not of our making, believe me. Let me make amends?" He smiled. "How about a coffee break? We'll get this interview back on track after Agent Tanner returns. Is that fair? Walt, what do you say?"

The lawyer shrugged. "I suppose a short break might be in order. But I would feel better if this could be concluded as quickly as possible."

Cochrane rose. "Let's go down to the coffee station." He opened the door. Yeoman Johnson stood at parade rest at the end of the passageway, and he motioned her over.

"Yes, sir?"

"Kindly remain in our interview room to keep it secure, Yeoman? We'll be stepping out for a moment." Jim could not have their interview room or the evidence compromised.

"Yes, sir." She went into the room and firmly shut the door after they trailed out.

Once in the passageway, Cochrane walked with Hodges and Rapaport past classrooms in session. Halfway down the corridor Hodges slowed his steps. His lips parted and his eyes broadcast surprise. Inside another office stood Agent Tanner with Lieutenant Michelson. She was near the door, handing a bright red file to the man. Michelson took the file, then looked up. His eyes narrowed when he saw Hodges standing at the partly opened door. Hodges hesitated before he strode on ahead of Cochrane and Rapaport. A look of rage and betrayal was written all over his flushed face.

ELLEN SMILED REASSURINGLY at Michelson and gestured for him to follow her. She deliberately didn't look down the hallway where Jim, Hodges and the lawyer had gone. After opening the door to their interview room, Ellen nodded to Yeoman Johnson, who stood at parade rest near their table.

"Thank you, Yeoman," she said, then picked up some papers from the desk. As she did so, the photos were revealed, their white sides up. "Here, will you take these documents back to my other office and set them on my desk, please?"

Johnson snapped to attention and briskly took the proffered papers. "Of course, ma'am."

"Thank you. That will be all, Yeoman."

"Yes, ma'am."

Michelson's eyes narrowed on the photos. "What are those?" he demanded in a tight voice.

Ellen leaned over the desk, searching for another paper he needed to sign. "What?" She lifted her head and followed his pointing finger. "Oh, those. Just evidence." He didn't need to see the photos of Susan's teddy bear Jim had taken earlier at the condo. She quickly found the red Immunity envelope and deliberately placed it on top of them. Looking up, she said, "Here you go, Lieutenant. If you'll just sign this release form saying your interview is concluded and the report finalized for us, you can go. You'll be all done."

Michelson was still staring, like a man who had been gut shot. His eyes were huge. His mouth was open and the look of disbelief on his face surprised her. Why was Michelson coming unglued? Stymied, Ellen waved the paper in front of him. "Lieutenant?"

"What? Oh, yeah." Michelson grabbed her pen and signed the paper with a shaky hand. His handwriting was nearly illegible, and Ellen was tempted to ask if anything was wrong. But she knew better. Not only that, her analytical mind told her that Michelson was intensely paranoid over the content of the photos. The man definitely was hiding something important.

"That's all. Thanks," she said.

Michelson kept his eye on the red Immunity envelope, then looked at Agent Tanner. His scowl deepened as he straightened up and squared his shoulders. Opening his mouth as if to speak, Michelson seemed to think the better of it, spun abruptly on his heel and strode out the door.

AT THE COFFEE STATION, Jim watched as Hodges poured himself a cup with trembling hands. The man kept looking back up the passageway where they'd spotted Michelson and Ellen.

"What's Michelson doing here?" Hodges demanded.

"Reckon I can't answer that," Jim drawled, sipping his coffee. "He contacted Agent Tanner by telephone early this morning. Apparently, Lieutenant Michelson is concerned about his interview."

Hodges wiped his brow. "His Ares interview?"

"I expect so. Lieutenant Michelson specifically asked to speak only to Agent Tanner. It may appear that I'm in charge of this investigation, but Agent Tanner has the links with Washington, D.C., and mine are to the Navy." He gave a wry smile. "Does that tell you who's in charge?"

Hodges's eyes bulged, and his coffee slopped dangerously, nearly spilling across his hand.

"It's a shame that this Ares Conference is turning officer against officer," Jim continued in a low tone. "Since we're able to create a worldwide network of information about the conference, with almost instant reporting, we can access any officer's story and either corroborate it or discover its discrepancies. Yup, one little word typed in, and it goes into the big computer back in D.C. All kinds of valuable information come whipping back to us in no time. For example, we typed in 'a woman in uniform' to track the testimony about the elevator. You should have seen what came back. Impressive."

"I—I thought Michelson was done with his interview?"

"Well, he was," Jim admitted hesitantly. "But he made an appointment with Agent Tanner and she faxed Washington, D.C., for some authorization forms."

"Authorization?"

Jim nodded gravely. "I really shouldn't discuss this any further." None of it was a lie. Michelson had done exactly that, because he wanted a transcript of his interview sent to his lawyer to make sure the *i*'s were dotted and the *t*'s crossed.

Hodges went pale.

"We've been watching the wall break," Cochrane said to Rapaport, ignoring Hodges completely. "You know how the aviation arm has this code of silence, that no brother will snitch on another brother? Well, it's breaking down, Walt. Not only that, but we have amassed nearly one hundred photos from that conference. Imagine that, aviators identifying other aviators. There's a scramble to be granted immunity."

Rapaport frowned. "So a source is protected from prosecution if he'll testify against other pilots?"

"That's it in a nutshell, Walt."

"That type of testimony very rarely holds up under

cross-examination," the lawyer muttered. "The pilot with the immunity can be portrayed as a highly unreliable witness. Any lawyer knows that."

Hodges stared down the passageway. "Michelson is giving more testimony? More than his original interview?"

Cochrane shrugged. "I can't comment on your question, Commander. A person can be cleared at a trial, but the Navy is a closed community. His career might be tarnished just from allegations."

Hodges's mouth was a straight line, hiding his obviously explosive feelings. He set the cup down on the counter with such a bang the contents sloshed out.

Cochrane turned to Rapaport. "I'd like just a moment with your client, Walt."

Before the attorney could say anything, Cochrane gripped Hodges by the elbow and led him about ten feet away from the coffee dispenser. "I thought you should see this." He drew the digital photo of Susan Kane on the hotel bed and turned it over so the officer could see.

Hodges instantly grew white and sucked in a hard breath.

"What do you say, Commander? Can you and I talk, officer to officer—without your attorney present? No outsiders. If you do this, it's off-the-record. You could tell me what really happened—"

"Where'd you get that picture?" Hodges rasped, his eyes widening enormously.

"Isn't it enough that I have it?" Cochrane said.

Hodges snapped another glance down the passageway, his gaze pinned on Michelson, who stood stiffly outside the interview room. "Son of a bitch," he snarled under his breath.

"Mr. Cochrane," Rapaport protested, walking over to them, "you can't talk to my client without—"

"Get lost, Rapaport," Hodges ordered sharply.

Cochrane slipped the photo into his pocket before the attorney could see it.

"I'm talking to Lieutenant Cochrane, officer to officer. Butt out," Hodges said.

"Commander, are you quite sure you want to do this?" Rapaport asked, sounding stunned.

"He said it's off-the-record. It can't be offered as evidence," Hodges said.

"What can't?" Rapaport asked, assessing his client closely.

"Never mind," Hodges muttered. "This is between Mr. Cochrane and me. I don't need your services anymore. Just send me your bill."

Rapaport stood there in shock. "Well…of course." He turned away.

Cochrane looked grimly at Hodges after the attorney had disappeared down the passageway. "Shall we take a stroll back to the interview room, Commander Hodges?"

As they walked along the corridor, Hodges said, "I know where you got that photo. Michelson is snitching on me."

"I'm not at liberty to divulge where this photo came from, Commander."

"Hell, I can see the handwriting on the wall. Why would Michelson be here now? He wants to save his and his admiral daddy's asses."

"A good point," Cochrane said. "Reckon you might be a sacrificial lamb in all of this. He may be trying to save his career. But immunity is a fool's path, by the time it's granted—if it is granted. The guy is considered an unreliable legal witness, and his career in the Navy just turns to crap."

Wiping his brow, Hodges muttered, "Christ, I don't know what I should do."

"You talk and I'll expose Michelson for the weak bastard he is. And I'll be able to keep Kane's photo out of a Washington show trial. Otherwise, I'll just let Agent Tanner run with this. And even though we both know any charges will be thrown out in court, your career will still be down the tubes, Commander."

"Yes. I'll tell you."

Cochrane nodded. "Nowadays, it's hard to know whom to trust." Because Ellen used a red file for Michelson's authorization papers, Hodges thought it was an immunity agreement. It wasn't, of course, but that had been Cochrane's ace-in-the-hole to make the commander break. His conscience was clear since their Plan B ruse had done the job. Hodges was going to talk.

"He's broken the code," Hodges said. "Michelson took immunity, turned over the photo and squealed. I'll be goddamned if I'm going down on this alone. I've worked too damn hard for my rank."

THEY ARRIVED BACK at the interview room and shut the door. Ellen nodded curtly in Hodges's direction.

"Commander Hodges is willing to tell us what really happened, Agent Tanner." Cochrane gave her a significant glance that said in effect, *play along.* "The testimony he gives will be off-the-record." Jim turned on the tape recorder, explaining to Hodges that it was not legally admissible but they had to have a copy of this interview. Hodges agreed.

Ellen barely nodded. "If you think that's best, Lieutenant Cochrane."

Cochrane motioned to the chair. "I do, Agent Tanner." He turned his attention to the aviator. "Commander?"

Hodges slowly sat down and wiped the sweat off his upper lip.

"Tell me about the photo of Susan Kane on that bed. At least, your side of the story," Cochrane said.

"I don't like being framed for what happened," he snarled. "By God, I know there's not enough hard evidence. Whatever Michelson expects to accomplish out of this will not benefit anyone. Especially Kane. She's dead."

"What happened after you and Kane were seen at the elevator? She was in your arms that night, and we have witnesses to prove it. Are you ready to tell us the truth?" Cochrane asked.

Hodges got up and paced. "Hell yes, I am. Kane had it coming. The bitch."

"Had what coming?" Cochrane asked.

"She came to me demanding I report Michelson and Bassett to hotel security for roughing up Hawkins a little in the Leopard Radar suite." He halted and looked angrily at Cochrane. "Any woman who went up on the third floor was fair game and everyone knew it. What did they expect? When they were groped a little, Kane got her nose bent out of joint. She came running to me afterward, telling me Hawkins was in shock. I laughed at her and told her she shoulda had more sense than to go up there in the first place."

"What was her reaction?" Cochrane asked.

"She got pissed off. As usual." Hodges threw up his hands. "It took some fast talking on my part to keep her from going to the Reno police to report the incident. I told her I'd take care of it, and the people involved would be punished. I managed to talk her into having a drink with me at the patio bar to seal the deal. I put Rohypnol in her drink while we sat at the swimming pool bar. She didn't know it and started getting woozy. I hauled her up the elevator. Some guy came into the elevator with us and I told him she was my girlfriend and was drunk. We both had a good laugh over it." Frowning, he muttered, "We took her to my room."

"Who's 'we'?" Cochrane demanded.

"Michelson, Bassett and myself." With a grimace, he said, "I wanted Kane to keep her mouth shut about what happened to Hawkins in the Leopard suite. I wasn't going to do anything I promised her about nailing the guys there. We figured if we stripped her to her waist, put her in my bed, took my web belts, threw them around her wrists and tied them to the bedposts, that would do it. I took five digital photos of her in that position. She was unconscious and didn't remember anything. We forced her lids open so it looked like she was awake."

"Why?" Ellen demanded tightly. She glared at the sweaty aviator.

"To blackmail her." He looked beseechingly at Cochrane. "You understand. If Kane put us up on charges, everyone's career was down the tubes. The photos were meant to force her to keep her mouth shut about what happened to Hawkins. That was all."

Hodges wiped the film of sweat off his brow and cast a look around, first at Ellen, then at Jim. "We bundled her up in a blanket, went down the emergency stairs and took her back to her room to sleep off the drug. No one saw us do it. I've used Rohypnol before. Women don't remember anything the next morning. I know Kane didn't recall anything about it, so we were safe. I kept all five photos with me to show them to her later, once we got back to the station, to ensure she kept her mouth shut about the conference."

"But something went wrong when Kane came back to the station," Cochrane said, trying to keep the venom out of his tone. "What else happened?"

Hodges cast a feral look around the room. He grabbed the glass of water that sat in front of him and took a gulp. His Adam's apple bobbed dramatically. When he was done, he set the glass aside and wiped his mouth. "Everything was smooth when we got back from the conference. Kane didn't report us. She stayed in her office and taught her classes. All seemed to be forgotten."

"She knew you had the photos?" Ellen asked.

"No, not at first. When we got back to Giddings, I made a point of going to her office that first day. I mentioned our little drink to resolve our differences and that everyone had parted amicably. I told her she'd left us at the bar and went over to talk with some other aviators. Given the fact that she woke up the next morning naked, with a hangover, and a pair of men's skivvies in her room, I believe she thought she got drunk and slept with someone."

"Did this affect her job performance?"

"No, it didn't appear to have any impact on her flying or teaching skills."

"So what happened next?" Cochrane asked.

With a grimace, Hodges said, "I was jumpy because I knew I was going to make the commanders list. Michelson and Bassett were worried because they were lieutenants, and both knew the shit would run downhill in this man's Navy if Kane decided to spill the beans. She came to me one day demanding that I turn in the men from the Leopard suite. It was then I realized we'd have to shut her up. If we silenced Kane permanently, we could save our careers."

"Whose idea was it to go to Kane and blackmail her into silence?"

Hodges hesitated, looked up at the ceiling, then down at his clasped hands. "Mine, I guess."

"You guess?" Cochrane pressed.

"Okay, it was my idea, dammit!"

"Tell us how it went down," Cochrane said.

"I told Kane that she had to get out of the Navy, after I showed her the photo. She said it wasn't fair." Snorting violently, Hodges flashed them an angry look. "Fair? Just what the hell is ever fair in life? My mother gave me up for adoption because she didn't want me. You two tell me, what the hell was fair about that? I got passed through a series of foster homes until I was eighteen. I wanted to make something of myself, anyway. I was going to make them all sorry they didn't want me. I chose a career that everyone would envy, where everyone would point to me and say how great and smart and brave I was.

"Not only was I going to be a fighter pilot flying the hottest, fastest planes in the world, I was going to be the *best* damn pilot in the world. Well, here I am—a Top Gun instructor. It doesn't get any better than this. I have the respect of everyone—with the exception of Susan Kane.

"You know," Hodges continued, relaxing slightly, "I finally hunted down my real mother after all those years. I kept bugging the hospital until they gave me her name." He laughed sharply. "Know where I found her? She was an alcoholic married to a coal miner in northeast Ohio. When I met her, I froze. This small, thin woman with a narrow, pinched face staring back at me from the door, looking at me through those drunk, watery blue eyes of hers. She was in her forties, but she looked sixty. Her hair was gray. I'll never forget it. My God, she had a hard face. I stood there staring at her and not believing I came out of the body of that woman.

"And then, her big, potbellied husband came to the door, beer on his breath. He was in a dirty white T-shirt, his jeans had holes in them and they were hitched up under all that flesh with an old leather belt." Hodges sneered and lifted his chin.

"They were both filthy. Their house was a tin shack and they lived in filth. I ran off their rickety front porch, dived into my rental car and took off just as fast as I could. I couldn't believe that was my mother. Once I got on the highway, I swore I'd never end up like her. She was a drunken old bitch. Worthless. She'd have done better putting a gun to her head and blowing out her brains, as far as I was concerned. She had no right to live."

"But why take all that out on Susan?" Ellen's voice was thin with disbelief.

He smiled at her coldly. "Women are good for only one thing, and that's screwing. She marched in here to Top Gun thinking she was Miss Goody Two-shoes. Kane always thought she was better than us—"

"That's not true!" Ellen protested. Her breathing was chaotic. She actually wanted to hit Hodges! The impulse was so real her fingers closed into a fist. Startled by the power of her rage, she quickly relaxed her hand beneath the table.

"The hell it isn't," he barked, and stabbed his finger at her. "Kane was always perfect. Her uniform never had a wrinkle or a crease. Her desk always looked like it was ready for the I.G." Resentment colored his tone. "She had everyone here at Top Gun thinking she was such a model of perfection. She flew like most of us dreamed of flying. She had all the right credentials, went to all the right schools and got 4.0s. She never picked up a drink. And worst of all, she never tried to fit into our world." His mouth flattened. "She made me sick."

"But that wasn't directed at you, Commander. Why did you take everything she did so personally? I don't understand," Ellen choked out in fury.

"Navy brats are something else, Agent Tanner. Raised in luxury and privilege. Well, I came up the hard way," he said hoarsely. "I didn't have any Navy captain father helping me get all the plush assignments."

"You're wrong, Mr. Hodges. It wasn't like that for Susan at all," Ellen protested. "And Susan was *not* like your mother!"

He glared at her. "You keep my mother out of this!"

"Susan earned everything she ever got in life—"

"Well, so the hell did I! I've got dreams I want to fulfill, Agent Tanner. Dreams I've had since I was a kid. And no one's going to stand in the way of them coming true. Once I make my rank, I'm up for assignment to a carrier as a squadron commander. I want that plum. I've earned it. After that I'm off to the war college, and later I'll get placed on the captains list. I've got my life mapped out. I've gotten my ticket punched at all the right stops. And she was the only fly in the ointment. Because of what happened at Ares, Kane could have ruined my plans. She thought she was so smug, marching up to me on that patio and demanding I put two squadron mates on report for a little ass pinching."

"It was more than that and you know it!" Ellen struck the desk with her closed fist. "Why should any woman stand for that kind of humiliation and subjugation? You and your men were *wrong*, Mr. Hodges."

"Get real, will you? It's been going on for years. It isn't my fault Kane walked in blind, deaf and dumb. You play in the men's house, you play by our rules. Those bitches got what they deserved. I commanded Kane to get her stuff in order. I told her she had to resign her commission within the next five days. It wasn't up for discussion."

Ellen's nostrils flared. "You're part of what's rotten within the military system—you know that, Commander Hodges? But you're not only hurting women, you hurt good men, too, by your attitude and manipulation. Thank God not every Navy aviator is like you."

Coldly, Hodges growled, "There's no room in this man's Navy for women. Especially women like Kane, who won't abide by the rules and traditions. She was willing to break the code of silence and ruin my career. We didn't trust her to honor our system. Wake up and smell the coffee, Agent Tanner." He jabbed a finger at the photo. "I warned Kane that if I didn't hear of her resigning within five days, I was going to circulate copies of this photo to everyone I could think of—inside the Navy and to her family. I'll bet her father would have died of shame. I told her that her two brothers' careers would go down the tubes, as well. I reminded her that she would be the cause."

"Tell me, where are the photos now?" Cochrane asked, trying to throttle the fury in his voice.

Hodges wiped his brow yet again. "They're in a desk at my condo."

Cochrane saw the rage and tears in Ellen's eyes. He saw her fighting to keep her temper from exploding directly at Hodges.

"Does anyone else have access to these pictures?" Cochrane demanded.

"Michelson and Bassett know I have them at my home. When we came back from Ares, we drove over there and I showed them where I put the photos. There were no secrets. We were all involved."

"So either of them could have gotten the photos at any time?" He saw Hodges's eyes narrow with fury. Leaning back in his chair, Cochrane studied the sweating pilot. He was going to let Hodges think that Michelson had taken one and squealed on him. That the photo he'd seen earlier had been turned over by the lieutenant. Hodges couldn't drive home to look for them. He had a TDY flight to catch in an hour. No, Hodges would have to wait until he arrived back at the base at noon tomorrow to find out for sure. Even though Hodges would find all four of them, but by that time, it would be too late; he'd already have spilled the beans to them, which was what Cochrane had wanted.

"Yeah, that's right. They could've retrieved the photos...."

"Do you know Lieutenant Commander Brad Kane? Susan's brother?"

Hodges looked at him questioningly.

"It seems to me," Cochrane drawled, picking up a pen, "that you might know him."

Running his hand along the edge of his collar, Hodges croaked, "Yeah, I know him."

"Did you see him at the Ares Conference? At the Barstow?"

"Yes...I did."

"Was he aware of what you did to Susan? Slipping her a drugged drink and then taking those inflammatory photos?"

"Er...no, he wasn't."

Cochrane shifted his gaze to Ellen, who had gone white. Below the edge of the table, her hands were clenching and unclenching in her lap. He wanted desperately to help her, but couldn't. Their eyes met. He saw the anger, the unfairness of it all, in her green gaze. For the good of the investigation, Cochrane shifted his attention back to Hodges. "Reckon I'm curious," he said. "We found one of Brad Kane's fingerprints on the teddy bear that Susan Kane was holding when she died." He drilled Hodges with a dark look. "What do you know about that?"

"Hey!" Hodges said sharply, suddenly standing and shoving in his chair. "I didn't kill her! I know that's what you think, but I didn't do it!"

"How does Brad Kane fit into all of this, then?" Cochrane asked, keeping his voice deceptively soft.

Pacing back and forth, Hodges muttered, "I contacted him on his carrier and told him that Susan was going to turn several of us in for a misunderstanding over a little bumping and kidding that took place at the defense contractor suites at Ares. I told him Susan was blowing our actions out of proportion, that she was using the sexual harassment boondoggle and was likely to squeal on us. We talked and I told him the only solution was for her to resign for the good of the Navy. He was to arrange emergency leave and talk her into resigning her commission."

"So, you lied to him. You made him think Susan was going to break the code of silence?"

Bitterly, Hodges said, "Yes. He's a brother aviator. He's not about to let anyone break the code among us, not even his sister."

"Before talking to Susan, Brad Kane knew nothing of the photos you took of her. Is that correct?"

"That's right."

"Does he know about them now? Since she died?"

Startled, Hodges retorted, "Hell, no! I didn't think she'd tell him. I knew he wasn't aware of them because of our conversations leading up to him going to see her."

"So Brad Kane took emergency leave. When did he arrive in La Mesa to see Susan?"

Rubbing his brow, Hodges said, "He left the carrier on June 20th and he flew back on June 23rd. After he got back on the carrier, he called me to tell me he'd seen her and told her to resign."

"What else?"

Hodges stopped pacing for a moment and clasped his hands behind his back, in the classic at-ease position. "I guess they'd had a fight. He didn't give me any details."

"Was Susan going to resign?"

"Yes, he said she would."

Ellen said tightly, "You set them both up. Brad went in thinking that Susan was going to tell all and ruin three aviators' careers. Susan thought you were going to send those photos throughout the Navy community and to her family."

Hodges frowned. "Look, I didn't know she was going to kill herself, for chrissakes. How was I to know? I wanted to put family pressure on her because I wasn't sure she was going to resign even under the threat of the photos. She comes from a military dynasty. I was relying on the fact she'd do it to protect her family. Okay?"

Ellen glanced at Cochrane, and he could see tears in her eyes. He wanted to shield her from this kind of awful human behavior, but he couldn't.

He shook his head. "What was Commander Kane's mood when he contacted you by phone?"

"He was pretty clipped and uptight sounding."

"Susan hadn't told him you'd taken those photos of her?"

"No, apparently she didn't." Hodges shrugged. "I was sweating that part."

"Why?"

"Because I wasn't sure if Brad Kane would condone what we did. I knew he'd back us to keep the code of silence. But I wasn't sure what he'd do if Susan spilled the beans on us. I knew their relationship was strained, so I hoped the photo wouldn't be discussed. I knew about the bikini photo of Kane and that married pilot she'd had an affair with earlier. She was defensive about it, so I didn't think she'd willingly tell her brother about a second sexual scandal. That was the risk in my plan."

Ellen shook her head and slowly stood up. "What you did is despicable! You make all good Navy officers, men and women, look bad, Hodges." The therapist in her knew her attack was wrong, but dammit, she didn't care. He'd killed Susan by railroading her into a corner. The son of a bitch!

He glared back. "I did what I felt was necessary to

protect us. It's that simple. You don't break the code of silence. No officer rats on another."

Curling her fingers into her palms, Ellen whispered unsteadily, "Yes, and to make sure that happened, you murdered an innocent woman."

"I didn't murder anybody! How the hell did I know this chick would take her life? She seemed stable. In control. I never saw her break down in tears or act like a woman. I didn't plan for her to die. We just wanted her out of our backyard. Out of the Navy."

"When you heard about her death, how did you feel?" Cochrane asked.

Hodges closed his eyes. "I was in shock."

"Maybe a little relieved? After all, Susan wouldn't be around to tell anyone what happened to her. Everyone's career was safe when she took her life."

Hodges opened his eyes. His voice cracked. "Look, I didn't think anything like this would happen. Not in a million years! Hey, our world is a tough business. How could I know there was a flaw in her that would make her take her life?"

"Do you ever think she could be pushed only so far before she went over the edge?"

"No, I didn't."

"So your first interview with us today was filled with half-truths, faulty memory lapses and flat-out stonewalling?" Cochrane asked.

Hodges glared. "Yeah."

"You lied."

"I'm not giving up my brothers, Lieutenant Cochrane."

"Even if you were the catalyst that took Susan's life?"

His mouth flattened. "I told you—it wasn't planned. We just wanted her out of the Navy. She could have gotten a nice cushy job as a commercial airline pilot. That's what I thought she'd do."

"Hodges, this little unofficial session is over as of this moment. Get the hell out of my sight before I kick your sorry ass clear across this station."

Hodges glared, then spun around. He slammed the door shut as he left to catch his TDY flight.

COCHRANE TOOK an unsteady breath as he looked at Ellen. "Reckon we need a break. Shall we?"

She sat there breathing raggedly. "That low-life son of a bitch killed Susan."

"Technically, no." Cochrane said it slowly as he closed his laptop. Absently, he moved a few papers around. "But the evil bastard certainly set the train in motion."

"There's no way we can nail him?"

"No, because Hodges told us this off-the-record. Even with this information there's still no firm proof that we can tie him to the blackmail. We would have to break Michelson and Bassett. Hodges could claim he had nothing to do with the picture taking. Instead he could argue he was the superior officer of the three, trying to resolve a people issue between subordinates. We already know Lieutenant Morgan can't identify the man in the elevator with Susan. On top of that, we have Bassett identifying Susan with an unknown man an hour later."

"This is terrible," Ellen said, her voice choked with anger.

"Hell's bells," Cochrane muttered in frustration. "Hodges could claim he took Susan back to her own room after trying to sober her up at his. Then she went back out to party. And we'd be out of luck—again. Susan isn't here to tell a jury the identities of the guilty parties involved. She's dead. All the media would do or remember is Susan lying naked on that bed."

Running her fingers through her hair, Ellen rasped, "Who is going to speak for Susan? I don't believe he's going to get off scot-free. What kind of justice system do we have in this country? Hodges blackmailed Susan, pure and simple. Then he set up Brad Kane to push her out of the Navy. My God!" Throwing up her hands, she stalked angrily around the desk. "It's so wrong!"

Cochrane sat down. "Hodges would probably end up getting off," he told her.

"Can't you get him on any charge?" Ellen demanded, her voice wobbling with disbelief.

"We need reliable witnesses and an airtight case." Jim felt a wave of frustration and helplessness. "Other than throwing a punch into the bastard's face and breaking his nose and having him file assault charges against me, I reckon I don't know of any way to get valid charges filed."

Ellen leaned down and picked up her knapsack. Tears ran freely down her cheeks and she searched for a tissue. "This is one of those times when I'd be sorely tempted to take the law into my own hands and see that bastard pay. No one can speak for Susan, for the terrible torture and misery that she suffered."

"I don't disagree with you," Jim said softly. "Look, I've got to get a yeoman to type this up. Even though we can't put any of it in the system, because it was off-the-record." He tapped the appointment book. "When's the Kane family coming in tomorrow?"

"At 1100, remember? We're setting up here at Giddings for that interview?"

Grimacing, Jim said, "I reckon that whole thing is going to become a keg of nitroglycerin." The meeting had been arranged at the insistence of Captain Kane, Susan's father, who had heard that the police had closed the case. Dornier had approved the family-update meeting without notifying Cochrane first.

Maybe Commander Dornier wanted to force him to close the Kane case and get rid of it and Navy involvement at the same time. The CNO, Admiral Caruthers, would have his legal answer, but not the reason why, and Jim knew he'd have to supply the "why"—through back channels—or else. Susan Kane had a sponsor. Jim suspected it was the CNO himself. And he'd have to tell the Admiral everything. At that point, it would be up to the higher ranking officer as to whether Susan's photos ever surfaced. Many times, information became compartmentalized or for certain "eyes only" and he knew this was one of them. His job was to give the CNO and Commander Dornier all the info and let the cards fall where they must.

"Maybe the family knows more than they're telling us," Ellen said. "Brad Kane has already lied by not admitting he visited Susan just before her death."

"Why should we assume he doesn't know about the blackmail?"

"Then, he'd be a worse bastard than Hodges," Ellen snapped.

Nodding, Cochrane released a long, painful breath. "That's true. Maybe we can get Brad to roll over on Hodges—if he knows anything."

"That may be a blind alley. But after what's happened to Susan, I'm willing to try." Ellen sighed. "What a terrible loss of an innocent, fine life. All she tried to do was be a good citizen and follow her dream of being a naval aviator. She was a humanitarian. She loved children. What a waste."

"Hodges is totally self-absorbed. He's doing what he thinks best for him and his brother aviators. He's pretty secure behind the code of silence. It's going to allow him to skate right through this thing."

"He shouldn't even be called a human being." Ellen clenched the tissue in her hand, her lower lip trembling. "Oh, I know I'm an analyst and I shouldn't be saying things like this. I see how his upbringing helped turn him into who he is. But dammit, not every foster child becomes a borderline personality like Hodges. He can't distinguish right from wrong. He plays by his own set of laws. It's a matter of choice." Her voice fell. "It's always about choice…."

"At least we've got a better idea of why Susan took her life. But there are still a lot of unanswered questions. What did Brad Kane say to her? Did she spill the truth about that photo to him? If she did, did he even care?"

Releasing a tense breath, Ellen whispered, "I don't know, maybe we'll find out tomorrow." She shook her head. "This is just too bizarre, Jim."

"Well, we're gonna find out soon enough, gal," he said. "I think we should be prepared for a lot of fireworks with the Kane family. We don't know what they do or don't know."

With a shrug, Ellen stated, "Your plan to talk to Hodges off-the-record sure worked." She gave him a look of appreciation. "Breaking up Hodges's interview threw him off balance. And your Plan B, bringing in Michelson to sign those authorization papers, which could have been signed at any time, was nothing short of brilliant. Did you see how those two looked at one another?"

"Yes," Cochrane said. "Betrayal was written across both their faces."

"I love how synchronicity has occurred. Maybe a higher justice is at work," Ellen murmured.

"Did Michelson say anything to you when he laid eyes on Hodges out there in the passageway?"

Ellen smiled tightly at the memory. "He was angry and really came unglued when we stepped into our office here to sign the papers."

"Oh? Why?"

"When Walter Rapaport came in to tell me goodbye and that he was leaving, Michelson about jumped out of his skin. He asked Rapaport why, and the attorney told him that Hodges no longer needed his services. Michelson went positively white. He started throwing questions at Rapaport."

"Like what?"

"Like was Hodges still with you? Was he still giving testimony about the Ares Conference?'"

Cochrane grinned. "That set the hook into Michelson, I'll bet."

"Did it ever. I've never seen anyone so angry, Jim. Michelson didn't say a peep. He just kept signing all those papers and then stalked out. He was already at the door when I called to him and asked him why he was so upset."

Jim chuckled. "That took gumption. Did he respond?"

"He turned to me and said people need to respect the traditions of the Navy. It was kind of a strange reply, I thought."

"I reckon he thinks Hodges broke the code of silence and told us about their Barstow Hotel fiasco with Susan. That Hodges might resign his commission and the Navy be damned."

Frowning, Ellen said, "That's the least that he deserves."

"But even if Michelson or Bassett cracks and comes forth on the record, Hodges will probably walk free. Maybe with what happened today, Michelson is our best chance at getting testimony. I think I'll pay him a visit in a day or two and see if he's willing to come clean. Maybe cut a deal with him."

"I just can't believe this will be allowed to happen, Jim."

He gave her a wry look. "Maybe we've primed the pump enough among that threesome to make Michelson tell the truth under oath. Then we'd have a case that would wobble to court, with no guarantee that these three would be indicted." Cochrane looked heavenward for a moment. "I don't know of any way to officially open this can of worms. I'm hesitant, because I don't want Susan's good name smeared with a weak court case. It's one of those damned if you do and damned if you don't things."

A fresh round of tears came to Ellen's eyes and she wiped them away. "Right now," she said, "I don't care about the three of them. I care about Tommy and Susan. Robert and Brad Kane have a lot on their shoulders, too."

Cochrane couldn't stand her tears. He got up, went to the door and locked it. There were no windows, so no one could see the two of them. Ellen gave him a questioning look at he turned toward her.

"Come here," he urged roughly, sliding his arms around her shoulders. Right now, Ellen needed a little comfort. Hell, so did he. As he pulled her against him, her soft breasts against his chest, her curly hair tickling his jaw, he felt her arms go around his waist. Cochrane tightened his embrace. Then he felt Ellen sob.

"It's okay, gal," he soothed, kissing her hair, her temple. "Go ahead, let it out. You can cry for Susan, too...." He shut his eyes and rested his chin against her hair. The scent of jasmine drifted up into his nostrils. Ellen was small, but what a package of dynamite she was. A wry smile pulled at his mouth as he began to slowly massage her tense shoulders. Making slow circles with his hands, he absorbed her sobs of grief. Frustration and anger welled up, too. Feeling her tremble, Cochrane continued to gently rock her back and forth. "It's okay, gal, it's gonna work out...." Not the way they wanted, though.

Cochrane eased away a little to dab Ellen's damp cheek. Everything about her was so natural, and so totally appealing. He slid his hand into her tangled, soft hair. "It's gonna be okay, gal," he whispered, leaning down and pressing a kiss to her temple. This time, she raised her face, and her eyes were gleaming with need. Reading the desire in them, Cochrane captured her parted lips. As her mouth hungrily fit against his, he groaned and gripped her more tightly. Her lips were salty tasting.

Wet. Slippery. He felt her hands inching up his chest and around his neck. Hungry. She was hungry—for him.

The last hour of the interview had been filled with such pain. Yet it began to evaporate as Cochrane drowned beneath the assertive onslaught of her mouth tangling with his. They needed reassurance from one another that something good was still left in this world. Drowning in the splendor of her tongue sliding across his lower lip and her hips against his, Cochrane felt the ugly little world of Hodges disappear beneath the pulsing heat of Ellen. She was life. Real life. The goodness in life. He seized her lips in return and let her know how much he wanted and needed her.

Breathing unevenly, Ellen slowly broke away from Jim's mouth. Oh, he knew how to kiss. Throughout her body, she felt the sizzle and aching need to have him— have all of him. Searching his stormy gray eyes, she saw his boyish smile. He lifted his hand and ran it gently through the curly strands of her hair. Somehow, he had assuaged her grief and given her love instead. Love? Where had that word come from?

Jim stroked Ellen's hair, feeling the fierceness of his feelings for her. How could it be love? It was too soon. Or was he just plain needy and he was calling lust, love? No. He wasn't built that way. As he gazed down into Ellen's shimmering green eyes, Jim knew the possibility was there. But how could it happen so fast? Without him seeing it coming? He'd courted Jodi for two years before he realized he was in love.

Giving himself an internal shake, Jim realized that maybe life was handing him a second chance…with Ellen. She was completely different in temperament from his ex-wife. Yes, she had a way of working with him that made adjustments and compromise painless, not pointed.

Grazing her hair, he smiled. "Come on, we gotta get moving. Tomorrow is another brutal day for everyone."

Nodding, Ellen stepped away. She didn't want to, but knew they had to. "The Kane family meeting."

"You sound like it's a death sentence, gal."

Ellen walked over and picked up her knapsack and briefcase. "It feels like one—for everyone."

CHAPTER EIGHTEEN

July 17

COCHRANE TRIED TO GIRD himself emotionally for the forthcoming confrontation with the Kane men. Ellen was like a brilliant beam of sunlight in the late afternoon. He was dreading this interview and she looked like life personified in comparison. Her bright yellow dress and wild hair fueled him with an inner happiness. Cochrane applauded her spirit; it was such a contrast to his by-the-book Navy world. Her eyes gave her away, however. She had as much apprehension over today's interview as he did. She sat at the opposite end of the long table, facing him. Earlier, she had placed the teddy bear on a file cabinet at the rear of the room.

Through the door, Cochrane saw Lieutenant Tommy Kane turn the corner and head in their direction, cap in hand. As the man approached, Cochrane could see the smudges beneath his eyes, as if he hadn't slept well since Susan's death. His expression was highly readable to Cochrane: anxious, worried and exhausted.

Tommy entered the room and stopped. "I guess I'm at the right place?"

"You are," Ellen said gently, going over and shaking his hand. Tommy returned her smile.

He placed his cap on the table and headed for the coffee station. As he stood there pouring the steaming liquid into a white cup, he said, "I just got in. My squadron finished a series of night flights just before I left, so I'm dead on my feet."

Cochrane nodded sympathetically as he watched the aviator. Tommy was all about sensitivity. His hands trembled when he poured in cream and sugar. His smile was vulnerable. But the pilot's dark blue gaze turned assessing as he moved back to the table with his coffee.

"Have you been in touch with your brother or father since the funeral?" Ellen asked.

Tommy shook his head uneasily. "No, not really. Carrier duty doesn't leave you much time to talk, think or feel."

Cochrane was about to say something when both Brad and Robert Kane rounded the corner, walking with gestapo-like imperiousness toward the conference room. "Here they come," he said, more in warning to Ellen than to Tommy. Ellen's face lost its openness and he didn't blame her. These two were ballbusters of the first order, hardened warriors who took no prisoners. Jim found himself bristling inwardly, wanting to somehow protect Ellen from the inevitable confrontation.

Robert Kane, dressed impeccably in an expensive suit and tie, entered first. Right behind him, in his summer whites, was Brad. The aviator had a short stub of an unlit cigar jammed into the left side of his mouth.

"Come in, gentlemen," Cochrane invited, as Ellen quietly closed the door. "There's coffee over there if you'd—"

"Let's dispense with formalities, shall we, Lieutenant?" Robert Kane said crisply. He sat down at the table.

Brad Kane sat at his father's shoulder. Both were opposite Tommy, who gave them a genuine smile of welcome. Neither man acknowledged the younger Kane.

Cochrane scowled, pushed the button on the tape recorder and began. "We're reconvening to ask you more questions in regard to Susan's death."

"Her suicide," Robert snapped, lifting his chin and glaring at him.

"Yes," Cochrane said, "her suicide. We thought you'd like to know why she took her life."

"Very well," Robert snarled.

"New evidence has come to light," Cochrane stated.

Brad Kane's frosty blue gaze darted to Cochrane and then across the table to Tommy, who sat listening raptly.

Ellen zeroed in on Brad. "Commander Kane, we know you were at the Ares Conference earlier this year. We thought that it was probable you ran into Susan there. Did you?" she asked, her tone firm and unyielding.

The cigar shifted in Brad's mouth. "I did not see her there."

"All right," Cochrane said, giving the man an equally cold look. "You do know a Lieutenant Commander Hodges?"

"Lieutenant Commander Hodges is a friend of long standing. He's a fine officer and an excellent pilot." Brad moved the cigar to the other side of his mouth. "So what?"

Cochrane cleared his throat. "And you're *very* sure you hadn't seen Susan in person for how long?"

"Two years."

"Did you ever visit her at her La Mesa condo?" Ellen asked softly. She saw his eyes widen and then narrow like a hunter's upon her. Would he lie, when they had his fingerprints showing he'd been at her condo?

Brad snapped out his answer. "No. I never went to her condo."

Ellen got up and walked over to the file cabinet. Gently, she picked up Susan's teddy bear and brought it to the table. "Then, Commander, how do you explain that we lifted your fingerprint off this bear's eye? It's the same teddy bear Susan was holding when she died."

Brad's lips tightened around the cigar. He stared at the bear and then at Ellen.

The silence lengthened.

Cochrane watched the family closely. Tommy's expression was one of confusion as he looked from the stuffed toy to his brother.

Robert's face grew icy.

Brad's furrowed brow broke out in a sheen of sweat.

"Well?" Ellen demanded softly. "Can you tell us how your fingerprint got on this bear's eye if you *never* were at Susan's condo? How could it have gotten there, Commander?"

"Why should I fall for a stupid ruse like this?" Brad snapped, taking the cigar out of his mouth.

"Excuse me?" Ellen said, raising her brows.

"There's no print on that bear's eye. This is a setup, a frame."

Cochrane produced a document and slid it down the table. "Take a look, Commander. It's an official copy of the print the JAG lab recently lifted off the eye of the bear. There's no denying that it's yours."

A fresh layer of sweat formed across Brad's furrowed brow as he picked up the paper. His hands trembled and he cut a glance to his father.

"Why would your fingerprint be on Susan's bear?" Tommy demanded, searching his brother's face. "She's had that bear ever since she was born. No one was ever allowed to touch it. Ever."

Brad sat very still, his hand flattened on the damning document.

"Look," Robert Kane said nastily to Cochrane, "you're out of line, *Lieutenant*."

"I think that your son knows a great deal more than he's telling us. Maybe *you* know all about it, sir."

Tommy sat back. "Captain? Brad? What's going on

here?" He pointed to the bear, which Ellen was still holding. "Brad, why would your print be on her bear if you weren't at her condo? Did you see Susan and not tell me?"

"Shut up!" Robert hissed, jabbing a finger at Tommy. "Family business is family business. You don't go around talking to strangers. Understand?"

"On the contrary," Cochrane said, strengthening his voice, "I reckon this transcends so-called 'family business,' Mr. Kane. Your oldest son's fingerprint is on the eye of that teddy bear found in Susan's arms at the death scene. Now, that infers that he was at Susan's condo." Cochrane shifted his gaze to Brad, who was chewing hard on the end of his cigar while he stared at the document beneath his sprawled hand. "How about it, Commander? Are you going to come clean now? You *were* at Susan's condo, and we know that. Do you want me to tell you when you were there?"

Brad's eyes narrowed to slits. He slowly took the cigar out of his mouth and held it tensely between the fingers of his left hand. "I don't have to answer your goddamn questions."

Tommy lurched out of his chair. "Yes, you do, Brad." He put his hands on his hips, his face flushed a dull red. "Just what the hell is going on here? You told me you hadn't seen Susan—"

"Goddammit!" Robert roared as he launched himself to his feet. "I said shut the hell up! Sit down, Tommy!"

The young aviator trembled as he dropped his hands to his sides. "No, sir, I won't. What's going on here? Do you and Brad know something I don't about Susan dying? Is this another family secret you're keeping from me?"

Shaking with rage, the elder Kane whirled on Cochrane. "You have *no business* doing this! None whatsoever! Susan is dead. Let it be! She's disgraced us enough."

Cochrane eased out of his chair, his fingertips resting on the table, his attention focused on Brad. "Commander, we're waiting. Or do you want *me* to tell everyone what happened? It's your call."

The silence lengthened. Tommy suddenly moved, making his way around the table. In one swift motion, he hauled Brad to his feet. Even though Tommy was several inches shorter than his brother, he grasped the collar of his brother's uniform and jerked him hard. "Okay, Brad, what didn't you tell me?" he breathed savagely. "What did you do? Dammit, you tell me!"

Robert cursed and pulled his sons apart. "Sit down," he ordered. "Right now."

Tommy took a couple of steps away from the other two, staring belligerently at them both.

"Commander?" Cochrane called. "We're waiting."

Brad jerked the chair away from the table and sat down. "Okay, so I saw her."

"When?" Ellen demanded, sitting down in turn. Her self-assurance rose as she met Brad Kane's desperate look. Susan would be vindicated today, and no one would stop it from happening. Not even this severely dysfunctional family.

"Just before she died," Brad said finally.

Tommy gasped. "What? You saw her? Why didn't you tell me? What did you say to her?"

With a curse, Brad shoved his brother away. Breathing hard, he said, "All right. All right, I'll tell you."

Tommy was shaking, his fists clenched. "Tell me *all* of it, Brad. None of this hiding stuff." He gave his father a look of warning. "You two *always* hid things from me when I was growing up. Even at Annapolis, you kept things from me. This time isn't any different, is it?"

"I got a call from Lieutenant Commander Hodges," Brad began tightly. "He told me Susan was making trouble—again. She was always a pain in the ass to him at the Top Gun facility. This wasn't the first time he'd called me about something she'd done to him or one of the other officers there. He asked me to take emergency leave on June 20th and go see her."

"About what?" Tommy demanded.

"Hodges said Susan was going to report him and two other aviators on a minor incident that occurred at the Ares Conference. So I flew in to see her. I got emergency leave and arrived at her condo around 2000, June 22nd. I basically told her that Hodges was a friend of mine and he'd called me. I told her she had to resign. That she *owed* us on this one. If she didn't, she was going to cause us a lot of humiliation. I told her to put it into perspective and let the incident at Ares go. If she didn't resign, she'd sink our careers along with hers. I've worked so hard for so long, and then to hear she was going to squeal on our brother aviators over some stupid high jinks at the conference broke something deep inside me. I walked to the door. She started to cry and I saw her old teddy bear sitting on the couch. I picked it up and gave it to her. I guess to comfort her."

Tommy stared at Brad. "Why didn't you tell me about this?" he asked.

Brad shrugged wearily. "It was messy and I didn't want to drag you into the situation. By not telling you, I was protecting you."

"You told Father, though, didn't you?"

"I had to."

"Are you telling me Susan committed suicide because of what you told her, Brad? My God...my God..." Tommy whispered, his voice flooding with emotion.

"Hold it," Cochrane said firmly. "There's one more piece of information you need to have." He settled his gaze on Brad's crumpling features. "Why didn't you come forward and tell us you were at her condo in the first place?"

"Because I didn't want to tell you why I was there," Brad said. He lifted his head and blinked rapidly, fighting back tears. "I had no sooner gotten back to the carrier when I received word Susan was dead." He touched his brow with a shaking hand. "Christ, I killed her…." Rubbing his face harshly, he confessed to Tommy, "I'm sorry. I've had knots in my guts ever since it happened. I thought Susan would resign. I—I had no idea she'd take her life."

"Just a minute," Cochrane warned. "Before you go taking all the blame yourself for what happened, I want you to look at this photo." He passed to each of them a copy of the photo of Susan lying naked on the hotel bed.

With a cry, Tommy gaped disbelievingly at the picture.

As the elder Kane stared down at the copy, his face bore an expression of disgust.

Brad jerked a glance up at Cochrane. "Just what the hell is *this*?"

"What none of you knew was that Hodges had deliberately devised a plan to drug Susan with Rohypnol, the date-rape drug. He put the drug in her glass of wine at the Ares Conference on the evening of May 16th. He and two other aviators, Lieutenants Michelson and Bassett, then carried Susan upstairs as soon as she lost consciousness, took off her clothes and tied her to Hodges's bed. They took photos of her in the position you see. Hodges and Bassett then carried her, still unconscious, back to her hotel room. From that time until just recently, Susan had been living in terror of being exposed as having done something unacceptable at Ares. She was drugged and didn't remember the photo session or who was with her, but she knew something terrible had happened. Rohypnol robs the person of their memory.

"Later, Hodges told Susan to resign from the Navy or else he would distribute these photos to you, as well as throughout the military."

"Oh, God." Tommy choked out the words, staring down at the photo. "Susan would *never* do something like that of her own free will."

Brad picked up the photo. "Then why did Hodges have me fly in and tell her to resign if he'd done all this beforehand? I don't understand," he said.

"Our guess is that he wanted to make *sure* Susan would resign," Ellen said. "He was afraid that her personal integrity would not allow her to quit the Navy, so he manipulated you to come in and read her the riot act. He wanted extra insurance and an airtight case to protect himself and the other two officers. He used you. He was betting family pressure would get her to leave. Hodges was right, unfortunately."

Brad wavered. "I didn't know…. Jesus, I didn't know…. I had no reason to doubt what Hodges said. I had *no* idea he'd done this to her."

Tommy sniffed and wiped his eyes. He jerked the photo off the table and waved it in Brad's face. "You believed Hodges instead, didn't you? You didn't even give Susan a chance to explain! You were so busy defending yourself—the family, the code of silence—that you wouldn't even let her tell you what Hodges had done to her." The photo fluttered to the deck. Turning, Tommy hid his face in his hands and began to weep.

Cochrane watched the elder Kane's hardened features begin to melt, first with grief and then with fury. The tension and shock in the room was palpable, so much so it made Cochrane reel. He saw Ellen sitting very still, clasping the teddy bear as if her life depended upon it. She was silently crying, the tears tracking down her pale cheeks. Brad Kane leaned forward, both fists planted on the table in front of him, his head hanging as he tried unsuccessfully to battle his own tears. Tommy had sagged against the bulkhead, his back to them, his entire body shaking as he wept.

Robert Kane's features grew taut with grief as he stood up, straightening his suit. "Susan didn't deserve this. She was just too damn independent..." His voice seemed to close off. His eyes filled with tears, though he clearly tried to fight them back.

Tommy whirled around, his eyes red. "Sir, that is pure bullshit!" His voice shook with rage. "You abused Susan all her life! Do you have to keep doing it after her death?"

Robert's face went white.

"Be a man for once, will you, Captain? Quit denying the truth," Tommy said, his voice cracking. "We all know what happened in our happy little alcoholic family."

"Please," Ellen interceded gently, "all of you, try to calm down. Don't do this to yourselves. Don't wound each other even more."

Tommy sneered at his father, as if not even hearing Ellen's soft plea. "That's all you're interested in, isn't it? The Navy mask has to stay in place. It has to be perfect. You'd blame Susan for this rather than the institution or the family. Our family is as responsible for Susan taking her life as the man who drugged her." Jabbing a finger toward his brother, Tommy said raggedly, "You're as responsible for her death as Hodges, who staged this whole thing to get Susan to resign."

Robert stood there, frozen.

Ellen moved toward Tommy, aching for the young aviator. She placed her hand on his tense shoulder. "There's enough blame to go around for everyone involved, but blame isn't the answer, Tommy."

"It may not be, but it's deserved," he rasped, his narrowed gaze never leaving his father's face. "Let's start with the Navy as an institution. Boys will be boys, right, Captain? That's what you drilled into us. Protect the Navy, not our sister. So what if she was being blackmailed? That's okay with you, isn't it, sir?"

"I won't stand here and take this kind of disrespect from you," Robert said unsteadily. "There was never abuse!"

Brad removed his hands from the table, straightened slowly and twisted to look at his father. "Don't tell us about abuse. Susan's suicide began the moment she took her first breath. Do you realize that?" He looked toward Tommy, who nodded tearfully in agreement.

"I don't know what the hell you're talking about," Robert said.

Brad slowly thrust his shoulders back, as if he were

carrying an invisible weight. He got to his feet and stared at his father. "I'll never forget how you blamed Susan for our mother's death. You repeated it often enough that I began to believe it, too. You never let Susan forget her innocent part in that terrible tragedy, even though it wasn't her fault. Susan was made to feel less than worthy, far less, than Tommy and me. God knows, she tried to atone for Mother's death with brilliant achievements in school as well as the Navy. I went along with it because I wanted your approval. What a fool I was."

Tommy sobbed and said, "Susan was a sacrificial lamb on the altar of the military's tradition. We're all part of the reason why she chose to take her life. We're all guilty of her death. She didn't get support she needed from any of us. I know Susan well enough to know that she would've died if those photos had been circulated. No one *ever* protected her. Not ever." He looked at Brad. "I'll bet she thought you knew about the photos, that you were supporting the lie behind those pictures Hodges took of her."

Brad shook his head. "I—I swear to you, I didn't know…."

Tommy looked at Cochrane. "What are you doing about Hodges? He masterminded those photos. Aren't you arresting him? *He's* the one who set her up."

"I can't do anything," Cochrane said in an apologetic tone.

"Nothing? He murdered Susan!" Tommy unceremoniously wiped at the tears in his eyes. "Why can't you hang the son of a bitch?"

Cochrane said wearily, "Because I have no proof, no hard evidence of any kind. He supplied this information unofficially and would deny the picture had anything to do with him if I hauled him up on charges. Technically, all we could do is try him on circumstantial evidence. That photo should not be displayed in a court of law. The only loser would be Susan. She isn't alive to tell us what really happened. And Hodges will not indict himself by volunteering the information in court. It's a catch-22, legally."

Brad took in a deep, ragged breath, his mouth a slash and his eyes blazing. "That bastard is going to pay for this one way or another."

Robert leaped up and gripped his son's shoulder. "Hold on, Brad."

He wrenched away, glaring at his father through tear-filled eyes. "This is one time, sir, that you aren't going to order me around. You're no longer in control. You hear me?"

"Keep your nose clean," Robert snarled. "And Tommy, you stay out of this, too. No revenge. Nothing we can do will bring Susan back! Do you hear me?"

Tommy looked over at Cochrane. "Is it true? Hodges is going to walk on this one?"

"Unfortunately, yes. I don't believe he set out to make Susan commit suicide. He seemed as shaken by her decision to take sleeping pills as you are."

Bitterly, Brad turned to his brother. "Susan had this thing about being perfect. We all know that." He cleared his throat. "Hell, she always presented such a perfect, smiling face to the world. There was so much wrong in our family that she always pretended the outside world was the exact opposite of what we grew up in."

"Now, just a minute," Robert interrupted.

Brad whirled on him. "Sir, being part of our family was sheer, living hell. Frankly, I don't know how Susan survived as a child. I got tired of being beaten with a belt every time you came home from carrier duty, for every transgression we made in your absence. I got tired of having Georgia keep a damn list of all the things we did wrong while you were absent from our lives. I used to count up how many beatings I'd get in a row for the stuff Susan and Tommy had done wrong, not to mention what I had." His nostrils flared. "We didn't get love. All we got was a goddamn belt and a lot of criticism."

"That's not true," Robert snapped. "You were rewarded, too, mister, and don't you ever forget that."

"Oh, yes," Brad said with a snarl as he stalked toward the door. "Let me count the ways. We *might* get a nod from you if we joined the football team or earned a sports letter. You got us into Annapolis. But what did Susan get? You *never* paid any attention to her except to criticize her, Captain."

Tommy pulled a white handkerchief out of his back pocket and wiped his eyes. "What a sad testament to our family," he said. "Susan took her life because no one would listen to her, protect her. Why else would she do it? She knew in her heart that none of us really loved or cared for her enough to listen. To be there for her..."

Cochrane held Ellen's tearful gaze. "I reckon Susan Kane's case is closed," he told them quietly. "These photos will never be entered into the file. As far as the official word goes, it will be ruled suicide due to work related stress. Susan's achievements are safe. It's the least we can do for her. She was a good person caught in a very bad, twisted set of circumstances put in motion by others." He pursed his mouth and then looked at the Kanes for a long moment before continuing. Tapping the top of the table lightly with his large, rawboned knuckles, he said, "I'm going after Hodges. I don't know if I'll get him or not. I know it won't be on Susan's death, because he's covered his tracks pretty well. But if there's a way I can get him, I will. This interview is concluded."

Tommy tried to gather himself. He wiped his eyes one more time and stuffed the handkerchief into his pocket. "I've had it," he muttered, more to himself than to them. He grabbed the naval aviator's wings on his left breast pocket and ripped them off his shirt with disgust. He threw them on the table. The wings bounced twice, slid off the surface of the table and fell to the deck. "I'm resigning right now."

Robert Kane gasped. "You can't do that! Tommy, think, will you? Good God, son, you've got—"

"Screw this outfit and screw our happy little family," Tommy barked, his eyes dark with fury. "I won't be a part of this place anymore. This farce took so much out of me when I was growing up. Now it's taken my sister! I loved her! I hurt so much for her when we were growing up, did you know that? Did you know how many times Susan cried herself to sleep, Captain? No, you wouldn't. You weren't there. You were always gone, months at a time. I don't think you ever cared." He threw up his hands. "I've had it with you. With the Navy. I don't know what the hell I'm going to do, but I won't be part and parcel of this stinking family anymore." Without looking at anyone, he left the room, hat in hand.

Brad turned and looked at his father, disdain and rage in his eyes. Without another word, he, too, spun on his heel and marched out of the room.

Robert Kane looked at Jim and Ellen. His mouth hardened into a thin line. As he walked to the end of the table, Ellen held out the teddy bear to him.

"Do you want this, Mr. Kane?"

He looked at the bear and swallowed hard. "No," he said unsteadily. "Give it to my son Tommy. He'll take better care of it than I ever could." Tears trickled down his cheek as he left.

Cochrane witnessed the man's sorrow, a father exposed. He turned his attention to Ellen. Tears were freely flowing down her own face as she wrapped her arms around the bear, hugging it against her breast. He blinked back tears of his own as he gathered up the papers and shut off the tape recorder. After stuffing everything into his briefcase, he walked slowly to the end of the table.

He put copies of the photo and the tape to be transcribed into his briefcase and snapped it shut.

"Come on, gal," he murmured, as he slung an arm around Ellen's slumped shoulders. "Let's get outta here. We'll get an early dinner at O'Leary's here on the station, and then drive back to JAG to write up a final report on this sorry mess."

"I—I'm not hungry, Jim…." She wiped her tears away with the back of her hand as she held the teddy bear close to her.

"I know. Me neither. But we need to eat something. It will give us the strength to complete the last mile on this case." He gave her a tender look. "Besides, right now I need you, Ellen. I need you near me. I just want to hear your voice. Be with you…" Everyone was gone so Cochrane reached over and grazed her hand with his. Her fingers were icy cold. He squeezed them gently, trying to warm them up. When she returned his touch, he leaned over and pressed a kiss to her curly hair. It was all he dared to, with the door open. Someone might unexpectedly show up, see their fraternization and turn them in. Neither of them needed that right now. He released her hand and stepped away.

Nodding jerkily, Ellen retrieved a tissue from her purse and wiped her eyes and nose. Her scalp tingled where he'd planted the kiss, and her fingers ached to caress him. How badly Ellen wanted to walk into Jim's arms and be held. Seeing the burning look in his gray eyes, she knew that was what he wanted, too. But yet again, it was the wrong place and time. Softly, she whispered, "I feel the same, Jim. When this is done…"

He picked up his briefcase and held her shadowy green eyes. "We'll have some downtime, gal. Time to talk. Maybe hold one another."

Her smile was wobbly, her face filled with hope. For the first time in two years, Cochrane felt that even though the world was falling apart around him, he was going to survive it. And he knew it had to do with Ellen being in his life.

CHAPTER NINETEEN

July 17

ELLEN TRIED TO CONTROL her emotions as Cochrane led her down the block away from Ops. The California sun shined brightly in a clear blue sky. It was nearly 4:00 p.m. After the tissue she used to wipe her eyes began shredding in her hands, he fished out a white handkerchief from his back pocket and handed it to her.

"Here," he said teasingly, "use mine for a while. You've pretty wal mangled that pore ole rag of yores, gal."

Sniffing, Ellen nodded and took the offered gift. "Thanks…" She blew her nose loudly, folded the handkerchief and blotted her eyes. "I just feel so sad for all of them, Jim."

"There were losers all the way around." He looked up as a white gull with black-tipped wings sailed effortlessly overhead.

"Poor Tommy. He's completely devastated by all this. I wonder if he'll ever recover."

"Reckon if I had to guess, he probably won't. I for-

got to tell him that Susan tried to get ahold of him
through the Red Cross. We need to touch base with him
on that point. I think that will help resolve a lot of the
guilt. I'll call and let the family know tomorrow.
Tommy will be glad that Susan reached out to him in
that crisis. It seems like he's the only family member
who really loved her." Cochrane patted Ellen's shoulder, aching to hold her. "You going to be okay?"

"Y-yes. I don't think I'm going to make a very good
investigator, to tell you the truth. Everything upsets me.
That's why I never went into counseling work—people's stories always tore me up. I do better with com-
puters, which spout facts and statistics and don't have
feelings. Oh, poor Tommy. My heart aches for him."

Cochrane placed his hand beneath her elbow and
guided her into a large building. "Hey, yore turnin' into
a fine investigator, so don't gnaw yoreself about it. And
yore always gonna wear yore heart on yore sleeve. Let's
go to O'Leary's, here, for coffee. I doubt that either one
of us can eat right now, but maybe it will help settle our
nerves before we go back to the office."

Cochrane saw Ellen try valiantly to bridle her tears.
As they entered the restaurant, he noticed there weren't
too many patrons yet. The place was bright and cheer-
ful, with Irish music playing softly in the background.
The bar, made of mahogany, was trimmed with a brass
rail, the chairs and round tables made from the same
materials.

"Can we take that booth over there in the corner? I

don't want people staring at me because I've got red eyes, a red nose and face to match."

His smile deepened. "Shore 'nuff." Cochrane lifted his hand in greeting to the tall, lean man behind the bar. Sean O'Leary waved in return, a bright smile of welcome across his Irish face.

"Hey, if it isn't my Ozarks friend once again. How you doin' today, Lieutenant?"

"Fine," Cochrane lied. No sense telling him the truth.

The grin on O'Leary's impish features widened. "Glad to have you back."

After the waitress took their order, Ellen sighed and searched Jim's face. "I guess you've seen it all, haven't you? That's why you're taking this so much better than I am."

With a shrug, he moved the white napkin and the flatware to one side. "I've seen a lot. But everything? No way." He lowered his voice. "All cases affect me, gal. Maybe I just don't show it as soon or obviously as you do, is all. Or in the same way."

"You were the strong one in there earlier." She warmed at the compassionate expression in his gaze. How badly Ellen wanted to hold his hand, feel his fingers lace through hers.

"Someone sure had to be," Jim teased. He picked up the fork and absently played with it. "That was an interesting dynamic, don't you think?"

"The family dynamic among the Kanes?"

"I reckon so. Robert Kane was ready to condemn Susan all over again for the sake of propriety. More than willing to indict her, even without hearing all the facts. And after hearing them, he softened his blame of her to a degree, but he has yet to surrender to his guilt and contribution to her death."

"Tommy and Brad knew their part in this once they pieced together the truth of the situation. And they accepted it."

Jim snorted softly. "It's a good thing. There might be a dysfunctional sickness in the family, but at least the sons are healthy enough not to go along with that same pattern forever."

"Now who sounds like a shrink?" Ellen said.

Cochrane gave her a pained, lopsided smile, then looked up as the waitress set the coffee they'd ordered in front of them. After taking a healthy swig of his, he said, "Nothing like thick black coffee on a bad day."

Ellen tentatively sipped her brew. "It does taste good. My stomach is tied in Gordian-size knots. I know it's almost dinner time. If you want to eat, go ahead. I can't."

"Yore setch a softy, Ellen. But that's one of many things I like about you. You bring a human side to an investigation I didn't have before."

She smiled at him. "With no apologies."

"I know." Cochrane nodded. "So was Susan, you know. She was a big softy underneath that jet jock veneer."

"No doubt."

"I wonder what she could have done with her life if it hadn't been brought to an end so soon. Gone on and become an astronaut? Discovered a new design for a plane? What?"

"What about personal things, like meeting the right guy and having some wonderful kids?"

"We'll never know, will we? What a waste of a good life. She was a special soul. Very special." Cochrane drank some more of the coffee. "What we have are jerks like Hodges, Michelson and Bassett, garbage from pre-Tailhook days. Tell me the world's better off with them here instead of Susan Kane?"

"I can't. Those three have to live with what they did, though."

"Reckon so…" Jim said slowly. "I hope it eats like acid through their craw."

"I don't think it will," Ellen muttered. "They'll wall it off, go into denial about their roles in this, and over time, make it less important in their lives. Susan ensured that her last 'mistake' would go to the grave with her, that it wouldn't be found out. Her brothers' careers would be safe and on track." She sighed. "How unfair."

"Reckon life ain't ever fair, but it does go on," Cochrane said. "Shakespeare has a quote to fit Susan's life."

Ellen lifted her head. "You know Shakespeare?"

He grinned. "I'm a country boy, but we had plenty of what Ma called 'good books,' in our cabin. She had most of Shakespeare's works. She especially loved his sonnets. Ma used to read them to us every night before we went to bed."

"I'll be darned. I'm impressed, Jim. What would Shakespeare say about Susan?"

Placing his hands around the warm mug, Cochrane said, "It's from Julius Caesar. 'The evil that men do lives after them. The good is oft interred with their bones.'" He held her gaze. "So, unfortunately, it will be with Susan Kane."

Sniffing, Ellen produced Jim's handkerchief again and blotted her eyes. "I'm going to send Susan's teddy bear and their mother's picture to Tommy tomorrow."

With a nod, Cochrane said, "I think he'd like that."

"Do you think those photos can be buried so that no one ever finds out about them?"

"I believe so. Hodges sure as hell isn't going to peep about them, and neither is Michelson or Bassett. I'll contact Hodges tomorrow and ask that they all be passed to me. I'm sure he'll hand them over, under the circumstances."

"I just wish there was a way to bring those men to justice, Jim."

"There's one possible way to get those bastards. I didn't say it in front of the Kanes, but there's a back door...."

"Oh?"

"I could tell that captain who works for the CNO the true story of Susan's suicide, off-the-record. The one who approached me twice. Remember?"

"Yes, I do."

"I honestly don't think he'll ask to see the evidence, but if he's the man I think he is, restitution will be brought to bear on Hodges, Bassett and Michelson in another way. You might rail against the Navy system of taking care of its own, but in this case, Ellen, the CNO will be their judge and jury. He'll jettison those three pecker heads out of the Navy like torpedoes launched out of a sub tube."

"What if he won't act without proof?"

Jim forced a smile. "That captain is a first-rate human being. He saw between the lines. With those kinds of people on the CNO's staff, with all the evidence we've gathered, and I'll bet my bottom dollar that he'll act swiftly on this situation." He finished his coffee and set the cup aside. "Well, gal, are you up to getting back in the saddle?"

"What do you mean?"

Cochrane looked at his watch. "We've got three other cases sitting in our in-basket just begging for our attention. Plus we have a five-day forensics seminar over in Oahu, Hawaii, coming up next month that we'll have to attend. That's part of the ongoing education for JAG personnel."

"Hawaii? Hey, I like that," Ellen said, brightening. "That's almost like a minivacation."

Grinning, Cochrane nodded. "Yeah, I'm looking forward to the seminar. I have a lot of good friends over at the Navy station on Ford Island in Pearl Harbor. I intend to drop by and say hello." He also thought it would be an excellent time to explore his relationship with Ellen. Out of sight, out of mind of his JAG office and Commander Dornier. The time over in Hawaii could be healing and hopeful for both of them, he realized.

"Sounds like just what we need."

"Because the Kane case is wrapped up doesn't mean we don't have a pile of work running after us, begging for our attention. Are you up for it? Or do you want to take the rest of the day off and I'll go back to the office?"

"Hey, I may be a softy at heart, but I'm no quitter, okay? I'm going back to the office with you."

"Butterflies always look so fragile." He saw the amusement sparkling in her eyes, some of the pain and shadows dissolving.

"Butterflies? What do I have in common with butterflies?" Ellen liked the idea that Jim saw her like that.

Toying with his cup, he studied her. "Have a late dinner with me tonight and find out?" He watched as surprise filled her eyes.

Ellen sat back. "A real date?" Her heart thudded to underscore her joy over his request.

"Reckon so."

She studied him critically in the silence. "Dinner date as in…?"

"I don't want to spend this evening alone. Just dinner…between us? To discuss our growing relationship?" He wanted more than that, but he'd be grateful for that much.

Ellen averted her gaze. "Dinner," she repeated, more to herself than him.

"How about it? You've always been the wild woman of our team. Here I thought you would like another challenge, Ellen—a real, live, honest-to-goodness dinner with all the trimmings. Or maybe it's bad timing?" Cochrane needed her softness and understanding after this gut-wrenching day.

Her lips curved into a smile. "Wild woman. Butterflies. Who knows what else lurks in that facile mind of yours, Mr. Cochrane?"

He chuckled. "From the first moment I laid eyes on you and that wild red hair of yours, I figured you were a wild hill woman at heart." Her face turned red with a blush. "Are we on for dinner?"

"I'd love to have dinner with you." *And more*. But she didn't say that. Ellen was smart enough and old enough to let the dinner invitation lead to wherever it would go.

Her smile was gossamer, her eyes shining with such—love? Cochrane wasn't sure what he was seeing. Although he was afraid to utter the *L* word—it was much too soon— he decided not to try and figure this one out. "Fair enough, gal. Fair enough."

WHEN THEY RETURNED to their interview room at the Top Gun facility, it was nearly 1645. A cloak of sadness still embraced Cochrane, and he allowed himself to feel badly for Susan and her family.

He was about to speak to Ellen, who had just picked up her briefcase, when a tall and brawny sailor rushed in. His features were tense.

"Lieutenant Cochrane, you'd better come with me. All hell's broken loose over at the O Club."

Instantly, Cochrane was on his feet. "What happened?"

The Shore Patrol petty officer stood in the doorway, his hands on his white web belt. "We just got a call from the manager of the club, sir. An unidentified officer went into the bar and started firing a pistol. We've got three men down."

Ellen gasped and turned to Jim.

"Do you know who?" he demanded, grabbing his cap.

"No, sir, I don't. You're the closest JAG officer we could find. I knew you were over here interviewing personnel. Captain Allison from JAG said to come and get you. It's a bloody mess over there, sir. We've got the shooter."

"I'm going, too!" Ellen said, racing around the table after grabbing her purse.

"No," Cochrane growled, holding up his hand. "Stay here, Ellen."

"Why?" she demanded breathlessly. She wasn't about to be left behind.

"This isn't like a cold crime scene," he warned her in a low voice. "There's blood—"

"Count on it," the petty officer said. Moving into the

passageway, he called urgently, "Let's mount up, sir. You're needed right now."

Ellen dashed around Cochrane and ran after him. "I'm going!"

After Cochrane locked the room behind them, he caught up to Ellen. They raced to the awaiting Shore Patrol vehicle, its light bar flashing.

"Ellen," Cochrane rasped as he leaped into the rear seat, "when we get to the scene, don't come in until I tell you to." He knew she'd reel from seeing fresh blood spilled. Not that he enjoyed it either, but he'd seen enough to protect himself emotionally from such a crime scene. Ellen didn't have the experience, and it wasn't something she needed right now on top of today's stressful events.

"Okay…"

Cochrane pulled her in so that she sat close to him. The door was slammed shut and the vehicle lurched forward, the siren wailing.

Biting down on his lower lip, Cochrane listened intently to the numerous radio calls flooding the vehicle.

Ellen looked anxious. "Seems like life as a legal officer is never dull. First Susan's death and now this."

"Reckon so," he said grimly. "We could all do with a little less excitement in our lives…."

"No kidding." Ellen held on as the vehicle screeched down another street.

"It's just the way the cards have, been dealt." Cochrane shook his head and stared out the window. He was unsure why Ellen insisted upon coming, and rationalized that it was because she wanted to prove herself as part of their team. Cochrane saw four ambulances in front of the Officers Club. Shore Patrol was there in force, directing traffic. A number of officers, both men and women, were standing back while gurneys were hurriedly wheeled into the building.

The instant the vehicle braked to a halt, Cochrane flew out of it, jogging toward the entrance. Ellen hurried after him, dodging and ducking between the tight knots of people staring disbelievingly toward the doors to the O Club.

Gasping, Ellen halted just inside the establishment. She had already decided to go in, but now fear rose in her throat, almost choking off her air. She saw Jim's face go pale as he stepped into the bar area. The deck was littered with debris. Slivers of wood and shattered glass from the mirrors crunched underfoot. Eyes widening, Ellen scanned the place. Bullet holes riddled the mirrors and bulkheads. There were broken bottles everywhere.

The odor of alcohol mingled with a sweetish stench made her stomach lurch threateningly. It was the smell of blood.

A number of paramedics and ambulance attendants worked frantically at one end of the bar. Shouts and orders filled the air. Ellen grabbed hold of Jim's arm as he headed in that direction. The air reeked with the smell of gunfire, adding to the blood and alcohol. Holding her hand across her nose and mouth, Ellen kept up with difficulty. As they grew closer to the knot of paramedics who were working over a victim, she gave a cry.

"Hodges!"

Cochrane halted abruptly. He threw out his hand and stumbled to a stop.

Ellen gave a strangled sound of surprise. Hodges lay on the floor, his summer white uniform splattered with blood, especially across his chest. Ellen turned away, gagging. She pressed her hand to her mouth as she moved drunkenly back toward the entrance. Her senses spun. Shock coursed through her. He had just returned from TDY. Why was Hodges here? Had he stopped in for a bite to eat before going home? Or maybe he'd already been home, checked on the photos and come back to the station? Ellen didn't know. Staggering, she threw out her hand to try and find something to brace herself against.

"Come on," Cochrane said, sliding his arm around her waist and hauling her up against him. "I told you to stay the hell out of here."

Fresh air flowing through the open doors had never smelled so good to Ellen as Jim guided her to a chair just inside the lobby. He forced her to sit down.

"Stay here!" he ordered.

Choking, Ellen nodded. Jim's features were hard and expressionless. She watched him as he quickly left to investigate the crime scene. The lonely wails of sirens mingled with the voices of ambulance staff and frantic paramedics. Bile stung her mouth, and Ellen pressed both hands against her throat as a gurney bearing Hodges's lifeless form was wheeled out of the building. Her mind spun with questions. Who had shot him? Had it been Brad or Tommy Kane?

She pressed her hand to her forehead as she watched a number of waitresses holding back tears of shock. The manager of the club stood beside them, a look of horror on his aging features.

A second and third gurney eventually came out of the club. Ellen diverted her gaze, not wanting to see who else had been shot. She felt weak in the knees and didn't want to move. And yet her attention was riveted by all the activity. Several light gray unmarked cars pulled up, and officers in tan uniforms hurried in, their faces sober and serious.

Eventually, Ellen gathered her strength and forced herself up to her feet once again. She staggered unsteadily down the short passageway off the lobby, hoping to find a ladies' room and splash some cold water on her face. She wrapped her arms around herself, feeling suddenly chilled in the air-conditioned club. Nausea rolled through her. Senses spinning, she halted and leaned against a wall for a moment. Where was the restroom? She had to find one.

Taking a shaky breath, she moved deeper into the club. There was an opening on her left. A young Shore Patrolman stepped into the doorway and held up a hand for Ellen to halt. "I'm sorry, ma'am. You can't go any farther. This area is off-limits except for authorized investigation personnel."

Ellen stopped, glanced past the young man into the room, and gasped. Commander Brad Kane sat on a sofa, his head buried in his hands. He was flanked by a stern-faced Navy Shore Patrol chief who carried a sidearm on his hip. Brad slowly raised his chin and gazed toward where she stood.

Ellen saw the wild look in his eyes. It wasn't the gaze of a brave pilot who faced death from the cockpit of a high-speed death machine, but that of a person who had seen death's ugly face up close and personal. Brad's left trouser leg was stained dark red with congealing blood. Questions tunneled through Ellen's mind. Had Brad killed Hodges? Was that why the chief was standing next to him with a pistol?

Spinning away, Ellen started back down the passageway to look for Jim. The pleading look in Brad's eyes tore at her. She couldn't handle any more trauma. Where was Cochrane? As she wove unsteadily down the carpeted expanse, she saw him appear at the end of the hall. Relief showered through her.

When Cochrane saw her, his masklike features thawed briefly. "Come away from there, gal," he said, placing his hand on her elbow when he reached her.

Ellen leaned against him, grateful to feel his arm go around her shoulders, steadying her. "I saw Brad Kane down there," she said as she buried her face against Jim's shirt. His arm tightened briefly.

"I know," he rasped. "Come on, let's get you out of here."

She forced herself to straighten. "Who shot Commander Hodges? Was it Brad?"

Cochrane wiped the sweat off his brow with his fingers. "Reckon it wasn't."

"What?" Ellen jerked to a halt and stared up at him. "But I saw—"

"It was Lieutenant Michelson." Cochrane settled his cap firmly on his head and then gently coaxed her to begin walking again. "What a hog wallow of a mess."

"But—what about Brad Kane? What's he doing here, Jim? My God, his uniform is splattered with blood. He looks like he just walked through a slaughterhouse."

"I know. It was all of matter of bad timing."

"What do you mean?" Ellen demanded, her voice thin with strain.

"I just talked to an eyewitness that NCIS still has inside the club. He said that Hodges had just come off TDY. He'd gone straight from the flight to the O Club and looked up Bassett, who was having a beer there. Commander Brad Kane had just arrived in the bar area and had jerked Hodges around to face him, when Michelson suddenly appeared out of nowhere and pushed Kane aside.

"Michelson growled something about Hodges being a snitch and that he wasn't going to live to see his gold oak leaves. He accused Hodges of turning in the photo from Ares to us. Michelson pulled out a 9 mm Beretta and started pumping shots into Hodges. He took three shots to the chest and died instantly.

"Bassett tried to get away, and took a slug to the chest as he threw himself across the bar to try and hide. Michelson then calmly placed a fresh magazine in the gun, held the barrel of it in his mouth and…" Cochrane stopped the story, but seeing she was all right, he continued. "Hodges fell dead at Brad Kane's feet. Kane wasn't wounded. He was just splattered with everyone else's blood."

"Oh, God," Ellen gasped.

Cochrane shook his head in disbelief and led her out the door and onto the lawn. "Reckon I can't believe it myself. What photo was he talking about? Hell's bells, the only photo we had of Susan was in our possession at all times. No one saw it. I can't figure this out."

Ellen halted. Tears glimmered in her eyes as she turned and faced him. "Oh, Jim, I think I know what happened. Those teddy bear pictures you'd put out on the table, remember? They were with us in the interview room the day we spoke with Hodges? Michelson about lost it when he saw them. They were facedown so he couldn't see what was on them. He seemed mesmerized by them, so I put a red file over them. I thought he was going to grab them and flip them over, so I hid them."

"I'll be damned," Jim muttered, a scowl forming on his brow. Closing his eyes for a moment, he whispered,

"Michelson must have thought Hodges had brought in the pictures he'd shot of Susan."

Blanching, Ellen reached out, her hand on his slumping shoulder. "Even worse, I told him they were evidence. And I—oh, no—I laid the Immunity envelope over them. I'll bet Michelson thought Hodges was not only turning the photos in, but taking immunity and turning him in to us. Oh no, Jim, what did we do?"

He sighed heavily. "I guess Michelson got nervous about our maneuvering with Hodges yesterday. He thought he was being betrayed by Hodges, and snapped. He couldn't take the shame it would bring on his family. Not to mention torpedo his father's Navy career along with his own. By taking his own life, he left his father's career safe and sound, as well as his family's honor intact."

Cochrane shook his head. "The bartender witnessed the whole thing. Michelson told Hodges that he was going to pay for turning in his fellow officers, that he'd broken the code of silence. According to one of the paramedics who worked on him, Bassett is in critical condition but will probably live. Hodges and Michelson are DOA. I reckon the doctor will officially pronounce them dead at the dispensary."

"How horrible," Ellen choked out. "What about Brad Kane?"

"He's not being charged with anything." Cochrane grimaced. "But the stain on his soul may be deeper than the blood on his uniform." He let out a shaky breath. "Talk about twists and turns." Gazing down at her, Cochrane rested his hands on her shoulders. "How are you doing, gal?"

"Not very good. I'm in shock, Jim. How could all of this have happened? Did I cause it?" Ellen couldn't stand the thought.

Cochrane watched the chaotic activity at the O Club entrance and then devoted his attention to her. "Of course you didn't. Don't even go there. I told Captain Allison that my duties of investigating all four officers involved in the Susan Kane case would prevent me from objectively assisting him in this multiple death investigation. The captain will evaluate the information in regards to this tragedy." Cochrane looked up as several officers gestured for him to come over. "He'll contact Dornier and it will be assigned to another JAG officer, not to us."

Jim squeezed her shoulders gently. "I'll be right back, Ellen. I need to talk with Captain Allison. He's waving in my direction. It may take a while. Do you want to be driven back to Ops or wait here?"

"No. No, I'll wait, Jim."

He allowed his hands to slip from her shoulders, and turned toward the awaiting officers.

THOUGH IT SEEMED LIKE an eternity, it was only twenty minutes later when Jim rejoined her. Ellen had found a chair and sat down near the sidewalk. As he approached, she asked, "How did it go?"

"The captain wanted to know how I handled the investigation with Hodges and Michelson, and I told him what we think happened with those bear photos. We're not in any legal hot water over it." He tried to smile but failed. "The captain said Susan was the only decent person in this whole mess and deserved not to have her name tarnished in any way by Hodges's or Michelson's deaths. We'll be going over to his office tomorrow morning to wrap up the official end of the Kane investigation with NCIS. Their PR spokesperson will put out a final media report that will protect Susan and hide this fiasco from civilian eyes. JAG and the CNO will know the whole truth about our investigation."

"I'm so glad they're going to keep Susan's name out of it," Ellen said.

Cochrane pulled her to her feet. To hell with it; he didn't care who was looking. He smoothed her hair with his hand. "I'm sure Captain Allison will be good at his word."

She closed her eyes for a moment. His touch was unexpected, but so desperately needed. When Ellen looked up, she saw darkness in his gaze. "How are you doing?"

He settled his hands on her upper arms. "This ranks up there with my all-time worst day. This is too much for anyone to bear, and then go back to work. We're no longer needed here. I'm going to call Commander Dornier, explain what happened and tell him we'll make our reports tomorrow morning. I know he'll grant it to us under the circumstances."

"Jim, I—I don't want to be alone just now. C-could you—"

"How about if we go the beach? It's a place that always calms me down."

The tender look in his eyes was Ellen's undoing. His face blurred before her eyes as hot tears scalded her cheeks. "That dinner can wait for another night. I'd like to go to the beach with you, too," she whispered unsteadily.

"Stay here, gal. Don't move."

Sniffing, she rubbed her eyes. "I won't." As Ellen sat there and watched Jim move back toward the crowd of investigators, she felt numb and devastated. Susan's death had been avenged in a way she would never have anticipated. Feeling guilty over their plan to make Hodges come clean with the truth might have had an indirect bearing on what happened. Ellen hoped her feelings of guilt would go away as she got a more rational view of what had just taken place. Right now, she was too emotionally involved to do much of anything except work through the feelings she was experiencing.

Were the chains lifted from Susan's soul? The bear had certainly done its work on her behalf. "You can rest now," Ellen said softly. "Just rest, Susan. We spoke up for you, and everyone knows the truth. You can rest in peace."

Ellen looked up. Overhead, two Super Hornet combat jets flew very low, roaring above Giddings. Their thunderous passing shook and vibrated everything and

everyone. Was this a synchronistic and unofficial protest roaring out against the injustice known as the code
of silence? Ellen wasn't sure, but she had to believe that
it was.

CHAPTER TWENTY

ELLEN SIGHED SOFTLY. The waves came and went from a deserted part of the curving La Jolla coastline. Their movement began to soothe her. Jim had stopped off at both of their apartments to get the proper clothing for their impromptu visit to the beach. He'd placed a faded rainbow-colored quilt his mother had made for him in the car. Near La Jolla, situated north of San Diego, they stopped at a liquor store and bought a bottle of white wine. At a 7-Eleven, Ellen bought some sharp cheddar cheese, pears and crackers. Sooner or later, they'd get a tad hungry, and she didn't want to be starving to death as they lay on their blanket watching the sunset.

Lying on her stomach, Ellen cupped her chin in her hands and watched the white-and-gray gulls skim the dark blue waters beyond the breakers. The sun was setting, the sky a pale, diluted blue above turning to light salmon and then a thin red streak where the last rays had dipped below the mighty Pacific Ocean. The sunset looked like a layer cake composed of breath-stealing colors.

Jim lay inches away from her, eyes closed, his head

resting on his crossed arms. Looking at the line of his mouth, she knew he was still thinking about what had happened earlier today.

The haunting cry of the seagulls made Ellen keenly aware of the sadness she knew they both continued to feel. Turning on her side, she lifted her hand and gently smoothed the short strands of his dark hair against his skull. His lashes fluttered slightly. His mouth relaxed. Ellen continued her ministrations, understanding that right now they needed a little tenderness and care from one another. She noticed how his navy T-shirt outlined his well-shaped chest. Jim wasn't heavily muscled, but built like a sleek long-distance runner. On days when he could, she knew he jogged at least two or three miles, as well as worked out at a fencing *salle* once a week. He practiced épée, using the same type of blade as the Three Musketeers. In some ways, Jim was a throwback to the past, a hero in her eyes. There was a lean, quiet strength emanating from him, carefully hidden but powerful.

The roaring breakers spilled their foaming, bubbling life on the sloping golden sand. The salty breeze whispered across her skin. All these sounds conspired to make Ellen feel a subdued joy despite the heaviness in her heart. Sitting up, she poured the last of the Echo Canyon Vineyard chardonnay into their plastic glasses. Looking at the label of a cowboy silhouetted against the wall of a red sandstone canyon, Ellen smiled wryly. Who would have thought anyone could raise grapes in Arizona?

She was hungry to know more of Jim's world. He'd taught her so much in just a few short weeks. Ellen hoped that some of her knowledge had transferred to him, as well.

"More wine?" she asked, setting the cup near his hands. He opened his eyes, which looked sleepy. He had to be worn-out, down to his soul. So was she. "It's a great chardonnay. I really like it."

Groaning, Cochrane rolled onto his side and took the proffered wine. He smiled up at her, raised the plastic cup and said, "To the purtiest gal in San Diego County...in California...why, in the whole U.S. of A...." He drank.

Ellen smiled at his toast. Running her tongue across her lower lip, she said, "This stuff is really good. How did you come to know wines so well?"

With a lazy look, Cochrane eased upward and crossed his legs, their bare feet barely touching. "My pa always made moonshine, but my ma, well, she liked the grapes. We had a patch of 'em out back. Every year she'd make about a hundred bottles of red and white wines. Everyone in the county came to her door, let me tell you. She never sold it. She gave it away to people she knew who really loved good-tasting wine. I guess I inherited her curiosity about types of grapes, the way a bottle was shaped, wine tasting and things like that."

"You're a man of immense curiosity," she said, finishing the contents of her cup. Ellen put it back into the old, dilapidated picnic basket that Jim had said was given to him by his grandmother when he left for the Navy.

Shrugging, feeling the wind riffling pleasantly through his hair, Cochrane looked overhead. The sky was turning a darker blue. His mouth stretched faintly as he lowered his chin and met Ellen's gaze. "What I'm looking at is incredible. You. I'm curious about you, too. You know so much about things I don't." He lifted his cup for a sip.

"I think we complement one another in an oddball but positive way," Ellen agreed with a soft smile. The breeze blew several curls into her eyes, and she pushed them away. The sun had set, leaving the horizon striated with red and purple.

"That's a fact. You don't have to be a lawyer to know that." Cochrane chuckled dryly over his own joke.

Warming to his teasing, Ellen watched as he finished his wine and placed the cup back in the basket. "I'm so glad we came here. I keep thinking that this was what Susan loved to do—come sit by the ocean and let the cares of the world slide off her shoulders, if only for a minute."

"She needed something to lift that unbearable load she'd carried from the day she was born." Cochrane held out his arms. "Come here, gal. Let me hold you while we watch the sky turn colors."

Nothing had ever felt so right to Ellen. She was no longer afraid. No ripples of anxiety coursed through her. Perhaps because of the intensity of the investigation, the pressure and stress to get it solved, perhaps because of the horrible killings at the O Club, she wanted Jim's nearness. Snuggling into his arms, her spine against his chest, she leaned back on his shoulder and closed her eyes.

"Mmm, this is perfect, Jim. Thanks for suggesting it."

He wrapped his arms around her, and she grasped his forearms. They were thickly haired and she explored them slowly, feeling the leap of muscles wherever she touched. Quiet strength. Yes, that was what Jim Cochrane was all about. He never showed off or bragged about the power of his hands, the knowledge in his head. Ellen like that about him.

"I was just thinking to myself how quiet and strong you are," she said. "I never did like braggarts. Neanderthals like Hodges and Michelson."

Leaning down, Jim pressed a kiss to her curly hair. It tickled his lips and cheek. With a slight chuckle, he rested his chin lightly against her shoulder. "My ma always said I held my cards close to my chest."

"I like your ma a lot. She's a woman with common sense."

"She'd like you." He inhaled Ellen's special fragrance—a sweet, womanly scent that made him yearn to taste her.

"Hill people are unique," Ellen said, snuggling against him. She could feel the sandpapery texture of his cheek. Her heart fluttered with desire, and her pulse bounded erratically as he pressed a series of soft kisses from her cheek to her jawline. Then she felt him pull away and wait.

Understanding that he would do no more unless she gave him the go-ahead, Ellen sighed. "Jim?"

"What is it, gal?"

Lifting her chin, she opened her eyes. He was so close. So male. So sexy. Those dark gray eyes studied her intensely. The crashing waves seemed to muffle all other sounds, and she felt as if they were the only two people in the world.

The rich red, purple and golden hues of sunset filled the sky. The refreshing salt breeze played with her hair. "I want to love you here, now."

There, the words were out. Ellen's heart seemed to stop beating momentarily as she anxiously searched his face. His black pupils became huge in the gray crescents of his irises. And then his look became hooded and intense. She'd felt his arms tighten momentarily. Had she said the wrong thing? Was it too soon? Was this some kind of crazy infatuation caused by her widowhood and grief? Ellen had no answers. She only knew what her heart wanted.

"I want the same thing, gal."

Nodding, she licked her lower lip. Instantly his eyes focused on her mouth. "Jim, this has never happened to me before, this instant attraction to a man. I didn't come to the West Coast to have a serious relationship. It was the furthest thing from my mind. I've finally come to the conclusion that I wasn't aware I was ready to begin living again after Mark's death." Ellen touched her heart. "Grief takes its own time. So many people think it's over in a year, but it never is. It's been two years since Mark left me. Somehow, unconsciously, I've finally laid him and our life together to rest, here in my heart. I'll always remember what we had."

"Rightfully so," Cochrane murmured, listening to her husky voice. "What you had should never be forgotten. Good marriages are hard to come by, and losing the man you love is a terrible deal."

"Yes," Ellen whispered, giving him a sad smile. "I'm so glad you understand. I was ready for the right man to walk into my life, but completely unconscious of the fact. And never in a thousand years did I believe I'd find someone like you, Jim. I thought I'd be a widow the rest of my life, because men like Mark don't grow on trees."

Her body ached for Jim's touch. His mouth...

Cochrane looked beyond her to the sea. The water was darkening now, the colors beginning to fade. After scanning the beach, he was confident they were completely alone. Returning his attention to her, he said, "I know that. Trust me, it wasn't on my priority list to fall for another woman, either. It just sort of...blossomed."

"Yeah," Ellen agreed, running her fingers along his forearms to his strong wrists and then trailing them upward once more. "Are you going to be sorry if I turn around and begin to undress you?"

Chuckling, Cochrane said, "Let's find out...."

She met his bold grin with one of her own. It was so easy to leave his embrace, turn around and kneel between his spread legs. The sunset cast red hues across their universe. The beach was their own. She gave him a mischievous look. "I think we're alone—at last...." In one smooth motion, she stood up. "Come on!"

He gave her a startled look. "What?"

Ellen shimmied out of her shorts and pulled off her white tank top. Dropping them, she grinned down at him. "I'm just dying to jump into the ocean. Come with me? Let's skinny-dip!"

With a pleased chuckle, Cochrane got to his feet. As Ellen pulled off her white silk camisole and panties, he said, "Red-haired women are notorious for their spontaneity."

Giggling, Ellen leaped away as he reached out to grab her. "I'll keep you on your toes, Mr. Cochrane." She watched as he pulled off his T-shirt. Indeed, he was a man who worked out. She liked what she saw.

"Hurry!" she pleaded. He responded by pushing off his shorts and then his briefs. With a wave of her hand, she dashed down the beach. The wind tugged at her hair and caressed her skin as she ran. Oh, how wonderful it felt to be free again!

With a leap, Ellen landed knee-deep in the cooling ocean. The foamy waves flowed and surged around her. Gasping, she quickly plunged forward in a dive, closing her eyes.

The thrill of the cool water gliding across her naked

body made her feel more like a dolphin than a human. Moments later she felt the water on her right surge, and she turned in that direction. Jim was only a few feet away. She laughed and pushed her streaming hair back from her face. Wiping the salt water from her eyes, she stood up in the hip-deep surf, which boiled and eddied around them.

Seeing the wicked smile on Jim's face, Ellen lunged toward him. Opening his arms, he took her full weight. At the same instant, a wave crashed down upon them.

Swallowing water, Ellen felt herself being dragged under. Instantly, Jim released her and pushed her toward the surface. Sand and grit churned around her legs for a moment, and then the tide washed it away.

Bobbing to the surface, Ellen coughed, spat and found her footing. The wave had propelled them a few feet closer to the shore. Standing once more, she ran her fingers through her hair.

The crimson colors of sunset bathed Jim as he stood up and wiped the worst of the saltwater from his eyes. The teasing smile on his face, the predatory look in his gaze made her laugh with the pure joy of living. In that moment, Ellen felt like a child again, free and willful, unafraid to follow her heart.

This time, she boldly walked up to him. As she drew close, he snaked out his arms and slid them around her waist. The sudden warmth and strength of his male body against her feminine form made her sigh. As he lifted her upward, Ellen framed Jim's face with her hands.

Without a word, she closed her eyes, leaned over and captured his mouth with hers. The sounds of the ocean broke around her. She heard the waves crashing as she pressed her mouth wantonly to his. His body was hard and insistent against her belly. Lifting her legs, she wrapped them around his hips. Deepening the kiss, she slid her tongue inside his mouth, and felt him groan.

The salt water mingled with the wetness of their mouths. She felt him shift her, until he brought her down upon him ever so slowly. For a moment, Ellen tensed. It had been so long since she'd made love. And Jim was sensitive enough to understand that.

The cooling water lapped around them, between them. The world was turning a deep purple, chased by the night. As Ellen lifted her lashes and looked deeply into Jim's stormy eyes, she used the power of the next wave to move down upon him and absorb him into her.

The union of water and heated flesh matched that of their throbbing bodies. Another wave lifted them, flowing powerfully, like cooling hands against their skin. She felt Jim anchor his feet and brace himself as the next wave surged.

Smiling against his mouth, Ellen moved her hips in suggestive, rhythmic movements. His groan was like a drumroll crashing through her. Holding him, kissing his mouth, his closed eyes, licking his lower lip all conspired to release her in a way she'd never experienced before. The ocean seemed to breathe with them. The water, cool and invigorating against the enflamed heat of their bodies, urged them to new heights of abandon in the embrace of Nature herself.

Moments later, Ellen cried out. She tensed like a tightly drawn bow against Jim's body. He held her, moved within her, prolonging her climax until she moaned in relief and exhaustion, her brow resting against his. Only then did he groan and hold her tightly—so tightly the air rushed from her lungs. And then yet another wave caught them and they were swept off their feet.

Laughing as she came up for air, Ellen was dragged back into Jim's arms. He laughed with her. Splashing out of the ocean, their arms around one another, they raced up the dark, spongy beach, where the foam looked like a white necklace of lace in the darkening dusk.

"Fantastic!" Ellen cried, grinning as she walked toward the blanket where their clothes were spread.

"More than that," Cochrane said. He squeezed her and smiled.

The breeze was softer now. Ellen felt overheated, her body tingling, the flow of life once more surging through her. She had thought her life was over when Mark had died, but that wasn't true. As she and Jim dashed up the dry sand toward the blanket, she laughed joyously. Gazing at him, she realized how much younger he looked. No longer was there that seriousness and sadness in his eyes. For once she saw only happiness.

As they dressed, Ellen thought of Susan Kane. Perhaps this was the best way to acknowledge her life—by taking risks and daring to live themselves. Susan had been a risk taker in some ways, but in others, she had remained a prisoner. While Ellen pulled on her clothes, she silently said goodbye to the courageous female aviator who had truly been a role model for so many girls with similar dreams.

Ellen knew that those girls would grow up to live their own dreams. That was the best accolade to give Susan Kane. Women who would walk in her footsteps. Aspire to the stars.

"Hey, how about stopping at that hot dog stand at the other end of La Jolla? I could use a mug of hot coffee."

Turning, Ellen looked at Jim, then stepped into his embrace. It felt good to have his arms go around her, hold her and rock her. Running her fingers through his damp hair, she pushed several strands aside.

"I'd love nothing more."

"A cup of coffee, a hot dog and thou…"

"A man who can quote Shakespeare. You gotta love him."